# THE MUSEUM
# OF LOST QUILTS

# THE MUSEUM
# OF LOST QUILTS

*An Elm Creek Quilts Novel*

## JENNIFER
## CHIAVERINI

WILLIAM MORROW
*An Imprint of HarperCollinsPublishers*

HarperCollins books may be purchased for educational, business, or sales promotional use. For information, please email the Special Markets Department at SPsales@harpercollins.com.

FIRST EDITION

*Designed by Nancy Singer*

Library of Congress Cataloging-in-Publication Data

Names: Chiaverini, Jennifer, author.
Title: The museum of Lost Quilts / Jennifer Chiaverini.
Description: First edition. | New York, NY : William Morrow, 2024. | Series: An Elm Creek Quilts novel ; book 22
Identifiers: LCCN 2023016392 | ISBN 9780063080799 (hardcover) | ISBN 9780063080812 (Digital Edition)
Subjects: LCSH: Compson, Sylvia (Fictitious character)—Fiction. | Quilting—Fiction. | Quiltmakers—Fiction. | Women—Fiction. | LCGFT: Novels.
Classification: LCC PS3553.H473 M87 2024 | DDC 813/.54—dc23/eng/20230410
LC record available at https://lccn.loc.gov/2023016392

ISBN 978-0-06-308079-9

24 25 26 27 28 LBC 5 4 3 2 1

*In celebration of the twenty-fifth anniversary of the Elm Creek Quilts series, this novel is dedicated with gratitude and affection to the many loyal readers around the world whose enthusiasm and support for my work through the years have made this happy occasion possible.*

# THE MUSEUM
## OF LOST QUILTS

# 1

The cabdriver chose the scenic bypass from the Elm Creek Valley Regional Airport rather than the more direct route through the downtown past the Waterford College campus, adding a few winding miles through rolling countryside to the trip but saving at least twenty minutes. Summer's rural Pennsylvania hometown barely qualified as a small city, with a seasonal population topping out at about fifty thousand when the college's fifteen thousand undergraduates were in residence. Yet even now, in mid-June, Waterford's main streets would be bustling with students, faculty, and staff strolling and biking between campus and the quaint shops, sports bars, and trendy restaurants in the downtown district, slowing traffic to a leisurely amble—ideal for sightseeing but not for getting anywhere fast.

And now that Summer was so close, she didn't want to delay her homecoming a minute longer than necessary.

She wasn't looking forward to explaining why she had returned to Elm Creek Manor so unexpectedly, but at least she knew everyone there would be delighted to see her. She would be even happier to see them. As soon as her mom folded her in a warm embrace, the heavy burden of worry and self-doubt that had been weighing her down for months would finally begin to lift. When her longtime friends and colleagues gathered around to welcome her with hugs and fond teasing, she might forget her troubles entirely, at least until one of the Elm Creek Quilters asked her what she was doing there when she was supposed to be back at the University of Chicago, getting a head start on her doctoral studies.

Then Summer would admit the truth, and her friends' joy would abruptly vanish, confusion and disappointment clouding their faces. She couldn't bear to imagine it, so she quickly returned her focus to the cabdriver's conversation. Waterford was not such a small town that everyone knew everyone, but degrees of separation invariably ran in the single digits, and they had soon established that Summer had attended middle school with the driver's niece. He updated her on the local news, not that there was much of it, aside from the town council's recent announcement that a generous benefactor had donated fifty acres of wetlands to the Waterford College Arboretum. The driver was so caught up in his story that he didn't slow down as they approached Summer's turnoff, a barely visible curve of brown on the edge of a dense green forest.

Almost too late, she realized he was about to sail past the turn. "It's here," she interrupted, gesturing to the solid oak Elm Creek Quilts sign marking the T intersection—four feet wide atop sturdy support beams, angled to be clearly visible to traffic from both directions, with beautifully carved letters freshly painted every March.

"On it," the driver replied, quickly spinning the wheel.

Summer instinctively clutched her canvas backpack closer to her side as the taxi turned sharply off the highway, swinging wide onto the grassy shoulder before swerving back onto the road. Behind her seat, her suitcase slid across the floor of the trunk and struck the side with a soft, dull thud. Fortunately, the only valuables she carried were made of paper or fabric.

"Sorry 'bout that," the driver said cheerfully, raising his voice to be heard over the rattle of rusty axles on the rough, gravel road that wound through the leafy wood encircling the Bergstrom estate. "I've been taking folks out this way for years—though less often now that they have their own shuttle—but that turnoff always catches me by surprise."

"It's easy to miss the sign," she said diplomatically, although it wasn't really, except at night or in a heavy fog, conditions that were not currently impairing that clear, warm, sunny day.

"If you say so," he replied wryly, grinning at her in the rearview mirror before promptly returning his gaze to the road. That was fortunate for them both. The road was so narrow that if an oncoming car suddenly appeared, one of them would have to swerve off onto the shoulder or into the trees. Occasionally the Elm Creek Quilters debated widening and paving the road during the offseason, when traffic to the manor diminished. Summer's mom always talked the others out of it, citing the expense and inconvenience of construction and concluding with a passionate plea not to sacrifice a single precious tree to the idols of commerce and fossil fuels.

At that moment, the late afternoon sunlight broke through the leafy canopy and illuminated a fork in the road up ahead. "Take the left, please," Summer quickly said as the driver veered right.

"Are you sure?" He slowed the cab to give her time to reconsider. "The left fork takes you around back. Most visitors like to be dropped off at the front entrance."

Summer knew that to be true. For most guests of Elm Creek Manor, the approach was a significant, almost reverential act, filling them with the sense that they had arrived at a unique, separate, sheltered and sheltering place, a haven from the chaos and disappointments of ordinary life. As their cars emerged from the dense forest, the gray stone manor would suddenly appear in the middle distance, steadfast and welcoming, surrounded by a wildflower meadow. Moments later, the visitors would glimpse the tall, white pillars supporting the high roof of the broad verandah that spanned the width of the manor. As they drew closer, they would see the twin arcs of the stone staircases descending from the verandah to the driveway, which encircled a fountain in the shape of a rearing horse, the symbol of the Bergstrom family.

Through the years, Summer had always enjoyed observing their arriving guests as they took in the scene for the first time, awestruck and thrilled that they would be able to spend a week in such a magnificent setting. She too still experienced that same thrill from time to time, even though Elm Creek Manor had become as familiar to her as her childhood home, only a few miles away. Sometimes the manor felt like her true home, the home of her heart.

"I'm sure," Summer assured the driver, smiling. "Please take the back way. I'm not a visitor."

"You mean you're one of the quilt ladies?"

Her smile deepened. "You could say that, although that's not my official job title."

He shrugged, bemused, and drove on. "You don't look old enough to be a quilter."

"Careful," she teased. "Don't judge by appearances. Quilters come in all ages, all genders, all shapes and sizes and colors. You should know that already, if you bring quilt campers here as often as you claim."

"Fair point," he said amiably. "No offense intended."

"None taken."

"So you're a real Elm Creek Quilter." He shook his head, impressed. "And at your age."

"Not only that," she said, "I'm a founding member."

She could understand his surprise. She was still a student at Waterford College in 1997 when the Elm Creek Quilters welcomed their first campers to the renovated and refurbished historic manor for a week of quilting, friendship, and celebration of their beloved traditional art. Elm Creek Quilts had utterly transformed Summer's life—and not only hers, but those of her colleagues and all the quilters they had hosted through the years.

Even now, with Elm Creek Quilt Camp securely established as the most popular and renowned quilter's retreat in the country, Summer marveled to think that if events had not unfolded as serendipitously as they had, Elm Creek Quilts never would have existed.

Summer was ten years old in 1986, when she and her mother moved to the Elm Creek Valley for Gwen's new job as an assistant professor of American Studies at Waterford College. By the time Summer started fifth grade that fall, her friends from her new neighborhood had already told her of the mysterious mansion hidden away in the woods on the outskirts of town, falling into ruins around the reclusive elderly widow who lived there, alone, with no family and few visitors. Some people said Elm Creek Manor had become a station on the Underground Railroad soon after German immigrant Hans Bergstrom built it in 1854. Others said the stately old mansion was haunted by the ghosts of its former occupants, too fond of their beloved ancestral estate ever to leave. Summer believed the first rumor but not the second, though she had little evidence to support her conclusions. She had never seen Elm Creek Manor except in old photographs, and she had glimpsed its sole living occupant, Mrs. Claudia Bergstrom Midden, only a handful of times on her rare visits into town.

One day, Summer and her mother were browsing for fabric at Grandma's Attic, the cozy, charming quilt shop across the street from the campus's main gate, when the tinkle of the bell on the door announced a new arrival. Glancing up at the sound, Summer froze at the sight of the mysterious Mrs. Midden entering, dressed in monochrome grays and whites, support hose, and sturdy black low-heeled pumps. A hush fell over the shop as the silver-haired, stooped figure moved slowly through the aisles leaning heavily on her black cane, the strap of a worn leather purse over her shoulder, a shopping basket dangling from her elbow. Summer was extremely curious but too well brought up to stare, so she merely watched from the corner of her eye as the older woman bent to peer closely at one bolt of fabric and then another through horn-rimmed glasses, the lenses so cloudy and scratched Summer wondered how she could see much of anything.

After thirty minutes of searching, Mrs. Midden bought only a spool of thread and a packet of needles. When she lingered at the cash register to chat with Bonnie, the shop's friendly, fortysomething owner, Summer was struck by the certainty that Mrs. Midden was profoundly lonely.

"Maybe we should invite Mrs. Midden to join the Waterford Quilting Guild," Summer proposed after she and her mother made their own purchases and headed home.

Gwen threw her a bemused glance. "That's very kind of you, kiddo," she said, "but Mrs. Midden has lived in Waterford all her life. If she wanted to join the guild, she likely would have done so by now. Some people prefer their solitude."

"Some people choose solitude because they're afraid they wouldn't be welcome," Summer replied, and Gwen conceded the point, but the discussion ended there. Without her mother's wholehearted approval, Summer felt uncomfortable inviting an elderly woman she didn't even know to join them. She was one of only a handful of teenagers in the guild, restricted to provisional membership for four more years until she turned eighteen. It wasn't her place to recruit members, especially reluctant ones.

Years passed. Mrs. Midden's visits into town became even less frequent, not that Summer kept track. Busy with school and her friends, and later with graduating from high school and starting college, she all but forgot the reclusive woman. She had just begun her junior year at Waterford College while holding down a part-time job at Grandma's Attic when a customer broke the news that Mrs. Midden had passed away.

"That poor, lonely old soul." Bonnie sighed, tucking a strand of dark brown hair behind her ear, her ruddy cheeks creasing in a pensive frown. "I hope she's found some peace at last."

"I wonder who found *her*," mused Diane, another part-time employee, a chemistry professor's wife whose two young sons Summer often babysat. "The gardener? The postman?"

"Diane!" Bonnie exclaimed. "Honestly! Show some respect."

"What?" Diane protested. Tall and slender like Summer herself, she wore her curly blond hair in a short bob, which she frequently tossed back from her face to emphasize a point. "I'm just saying what we're all wondering."

"I heard she passed away in the hospital, not at home," the customer broke in helpfully, handing Summer several bolts of fabric. "One yard of each, please, except two of the blue."

"Coming right up." Summer carried the fabrics to the cutting table, unrolled the first bolt, lined up the long acrylic ruler with the grid marks on the mat, and took a rotary cutter in hand. "What will happen to Elm Creek Manor now?" she wondered aloud as she deftly made the first cut.

No one there knew, but they spent a good twenty minutes speculating.

Several weeks passed before the staff of Grandma's Attic learned that Mrs. Midden, whom everyone assumed was the last of the proud Bergstrom line, had been survived by her younger sister, Sylvia Bergstrom Compson. The sisters had been estranged for fifty years, according to neighbors and customers who had known them both back in the day. Why Sylvia had left Elm Creek Manor so suddenly in 1945 was unknown, but she had lost her husband and her younger brother in the war, and the sisters' relationship had been fraught with rivalry since childhood. Rumor had it Sylvia had despised Claudia's fiancé and she had fled rather than witness their wedding, but Summer and Diane agreed there had to be more to it than that.

"She could've just arranged to be inconveniently out of town that day," said Diane as they unpacked a shipment of pattern books in the stockroom. "It's a bit excessive to leave home forever because you dislike your brother-in-law, especially when home is a gorgeous mansion."

"*Is* it gorgeous?" Summer asked, curious, but Diane merely shrugged. She had never seen it either, but she had heard from an older quilting friend, Agnes, that it had been absolutely splendid in its day.

In late September, Sylvia Bergstrom Compson herself stopped by Grandma's Attic. Summer had heard her mom's friends say that Sylvia was a renowned master quilter. Her work was regularly displayed in the American Quilter's Society museum in Paducah, Kentucky, and one of her masterpieces was in the museum's permanent collection.

"I need a pair of very sharp scissors, a packet of needles, and a few other notions," Sylvia said crisply when Bonnie approached with a friendly smile and asked if she could help her. "I thought I'd packed the essentials, but apparently I forgot a few things back home in Sewickley."

Summer knew Sewickley was near Pittsburgh, about 150 miles to the west on the Ohio River. The town must have been the inspiration for one of Sylvia's most acclaimed quilts, Sewickley Sunrise. Summer had seen a picture of it in an AQS calendar hanging in Bonnie's office.

"Will you be in Waterford long?" Bonnie asked as she led Sylvia to the notions aisle.

"No, not long, I hope."

Summer felt a mild sting at the implied slight against her home-town, but it left her more curious than insulted. After that, she observed Sylvia surreptitiously whenever she returned to Grandma's Attic. She looked to be in her mid-seventies, with only a passing resemblance to her late elder sister. They shared the same clear, blue eyes, but Sylvia was thinner and seemed a few inches taller, unless that was simply her imperious bearing and good posture; Claudia had always hunched her shoulders as if she hoped to evade notice. Sylvia wore her silver-gray hair parted on the right in a blunt cut a few inches below her chin, and the only softness to her face was in the gentle sagging of the skin along her jaw and in the feathery lines etched around her eyes and mouth. Summer had never seen Claudia without her thick horn-rimmed glasses firmly in place, but Sylvia's wire-rimmed glasses usually hung around her neck on a fine silver chain. She slipped them on only when she wanted to inspect some-thing closely, or when it was necessary to prompt an inattentive clerk into action with a pointed look. She was courteous enough whenever

Summer waited on her at the cutting table or cash register—a bit stern and abrupt, maybe, but never rude.

Eventually, after several return visits, Sylvia warmed to friendly, cheerful Bonnie, if none of the other staff or regulars. Bonnie arranged for Sylvia to sell some of her quilts on consignment at Grandma's Attic, and the beautiful displays in the large front window drew many an admirer into the shop. Even so, as the weeks passed and what everyone had assumed was a quick visit to wrap up her sister's affairs turned into an indefinite stay, not even Bonnie dared ask Sylvia what her intentions were for Elm Creek Manor. Potential buyers were said to be circling, while local history buffs fervently hoped Sylvia would open the manor to public tours. But although Sylvia hired a local landscaping firm to tidy up the long-neglected grounds, it was impossible to guess whether she intended to call her ancestral estate home once more, or if she meant to sell it and return to Sewickley, to the home, friends, and life she had left behind and presumably missed.

Everyone's curiosity remained unsatisfied throughout the winter and well into spring, when a newcomer to Waterford finally drew out the answers. Sarah McClure, a newlywed accountant only a few years older than Summer, had recently moved to the Elm Creek Valley so her husband, Matt, could accept a job with the same landscape architecture firm Sylvia had engaged to tame the neglected and vastly overgrown grounds of the Bergstrom estate. Apparently the manor's interior was in equally poor condition, for Sylvia hired Sarah to help her clear it out and clean it up, a position Sarah accepted only after Sylvia agreed to supplement her wages with quilting lessons.

The quest for fabric and supplies brought Sarah into Grandma's Attic, where Summer, Bonnie, Diane, Gwen, and the other members of their small quilting bee soon befriended her. Through Sarah they at last learned about Sylvia's plans to sell the manor, a decision that Summer found disappointing and sad, even though she had expected it and it was certainly Sylvia's right. Sarah confided that one prospective buyer, University Realty, had spoken of turning the manor into an apartment complex for students of Waterford College, and Sylvia was seriously considering his offer.

"She said that in all the months her estate has been on the market, no one else has suggested anything that puts the estate to better use," said Sarah, shrugging ruefully. "She's a retired art teacher, and she likes the idea of students 'enjoying comfortable homes amid the peaceful seclusion of the beautiful Pennsylvania countryside,' as she put it. I see her point, but I was actually hoping she'd decide to stay, now that the manor is becoming so lovely again."

"Elm Creek Manor, a student apartment building?" Summer wrinkled her nose, dubious. "That doesn't make sense. Students like to live close to campus so we can walk or bike anywhere we need to go. I'm pretty sure the manor isn't on a frequent bus route, so unless you have a car, it would be hugely inconvenient."

"Plus, most college students aren't looking for peace, quiet, and seclusion, except when they're studying, and they have the library for that." Sarah shook her head, her expression pensive. "Something's not right with University Realty's business plan."

Summer thought so too. "Let's hope Mrs. Compson reads the fine print before she signs anything."

Fortunately, Sarah had not left that to chance. Suspicious of the real estate agent's intentions, she quietly investigated his company, and was shocked to learn that Gregory Krolich intended to raze Elm Creek Manor, put up a few hundred condos in its place, and turn over the remaining land to commercial and industrial development. The lovely, historic manor would be reduced to rubble, and acres of thriving, lush forest and wildflower meadow would be uprooted and paved over.

Sarah broke the news to Sylvia just in time. Horrified, Sylvia immediately ceased negotiations with University Realty—and found herself right back where she had started, the sole heir to a grand estate much too large for one woman alone, and too rich with legacy and history to bestow lightly upon a stranger. Determined not to be taken in by another unscrupulous profiteer, she asked Sarah to help her find a way to bring joy and purpose back to the manor, to restore it to its former glory.

Sarah's unlikely and ingenious suggestion was to transform Elm Creek Manor into an artist's retreat, a place for quilters to create, learn, find inspiration, and enjoy the camaraderie of other quilters. Sylvia embraced the idea—and how infinitely grateful Summer was that she had, and that Sarah and Sylvia had invited her, her mom, and their friends from Grandma's Attic to become the founding members of the faculty.

So much had happened since Sarah had first proposed Elm Creek Quilts that it seemed impossible only eight years had passed. The women's friendships had thrived as their business had prospered, and they had seen one another past milestones and through some of life's greatest challenges—graduations, marriages, childbirth, one painful and contentious divorce, and countless reunions and partings, daily failures and small triumphs. Some of their founding members had left to pursue new dreams, allowing other teachers and artists to take their places among the circle of quilters. Summer was well aware that her own position was unique. She was a founding Elm Creek Quilter who had left to attend graduate school at the University of Chicago, but unlike the other former faculty members who had left, she had not made a clean break and started fresh elsewhere. She visited Elm Creek Manor often, taught a class or two during breaks between terms, and had absolutely no intention of ever selling her share of the business to a newcomer.

That didn't mean she considered Elm Creek Quilts to be her backup plan in case graduate school didn't work out. Elm Creek Quilts meant too much to her to be reduced to that. Anyway, a backup plan was entirely unnecessary because graduate school was definitely going to work out—even if she couldn't quite see how, at the moment.

Summer closed her eyes and took a deep, steadying breath. She'd figure it out. She had to. Until then, she would find respite in the company of friends in the halls of Elm Creek Manor, as so many other quilters had before her.

The car followed the narrow gravel road through the trees and soon emerged before a sunlit apple orchard. Summer glimpsed several women strolling amid the trees heavy with ripening fruit, some guests chatting happily in pairs or trios, others alone, lost in thought, perhaps pondering a new quilt design or the solution to a difficult assembly problem. Leaving the orchard behind, the cab passed a two-story red banked barn, climbed a low hill, and crossed the bridge over Elm Creek. The road widened on the opposite side, and all at once the manor came into view—three stories of gray stone and dark wood, its unexpected elegance enhanced by the rambling, natural beauty of its surroundings. The shorter of the two wings pointed west, toward the bridge, and the other wing stretched to the south. Where the two wings met there were four stone stairs and a gently sloping ramp leading to a back door. Campers clad in casual summer clothing passed in and out, enjoying some free time before the Welcome Banquet and Candlelight gathering, the official opening ceremonies of each new week of Elm Creek Quilt Camp.

The road led into a parking lot encircling a wide central island where two towering elms grew, spared from the paving contractors at Sylvia's express command. The lot was half full of campers' cars and a few vehicles belonging to staff and faculty, so the cabdriver pulled up behind the Elm Creek Quilts minivan, easily identified by the bright, multicolored logo displayed on both sides, a patchwork elm tree on the bank of a flowing creek. The minivan served as a shuttle to the airport, the train station, and downtown, and until Grandma's Attic had closed nearly two years before, it had carried eager shoppers back and forth twice daily. Bonnie had been heartbroken by the loss of her business, but within the past year she'd rebounded impressively. The previous autumn, she had accepted an old college friend's invitation to help launch the Aloha Quilt Camp on Maui, and it was off to a fantastic start. Like Summer herself, though, Bonnie would always have a place at Elm Creek Quilts.

Summer paid the driver and thanked him, grabbed her backpack and suitcase, and carried both up the stairs to the back door, a broad grin spreading over her face even as her heart pounded with something like apprehension.

The door swung open just as she reached for the handle.

"Well, if it isn't Summer Sullivan!" the petite octogenarian standing in the doorway exclaimed. She wore light cotton capris in a lilac print, a short-sleeved lilac-hued blouse, and a plum-colored cap atop her cloud of fluffy white hair.

"Hi, Vinnie," Summer greeted the camper, surprised. A lively favorite of the faculty, Vinnie attended Elm Creek Quilt Camp every August to celebrate her birthday and to reunite with far-flung quilting friends she had met on previous visits. "You're here early this year."

"Oh, yes. One of the other Cross-Country Quilters couldn't make it during my birthday week, so we adapted." Vinnie shrugged cheerfully. "Are you teaching this week after all? Sarah said you weren't. Is she holding out on me?"

"No, Sarah's right. I don't have any classes scheduled this week." Summer would have, except that in early March, as Sarah was preparing to arrange the faculty and course schedule for the upcoming season, Summer had told her that she wouldn't be available. After finishing her master's in May, she had intended to remain in Chicago for the summer quarter and immediately plunge into her Ph.D. studies.

Things hadn't worked out quite the way she had planned.

"I'm glad you're here all the same," Vinnie declared, beaming. "I've been wanting to tell you that I finally finished the Confluence quilt I started in your color theory seminar two years ago. Last month it took a blue ribbon at the Hamilton County State Fair!"

"That's wonderful," said Summer. "Congratulations!"

"I understand congratulations are in order for you too." Vinnie gave Summer's forearm an approving pat. "Sarah says you earned your master's degree in history last month. Well done, my dear! Your mother must be bursting with pride."

Summer hesitated. "Well, my mom's always been proud of me, but actually—"

"Oh, there's Megan. I have to run. Did you know she married my favorite grandson? That makes her my granddaughter-in-law, and I couldn't be happier." Throwing Summer one last grin and a cheerful wave, Vinnie hurried down the stairs and away.

Summer watched her go, guiltily grateful for the reprieve, knowing it wouldn't last. She inhaled deeply to steady herself before continuing on inside.

Entering the rear foyer, she paused to savor the delicious aromas wafting through the kitchen doorway on the left before she stowed her suitcase in the butler's pantry across the hall. She wanted to see her mother first thing, but Anna's feelings might be hurt if she found out later that Summer had strolled right past the kitchen without saying hello.

Since Elm Creek Quilts had launched, no other room in the manor had been so thoroughly transformed as the kitchen. For their first few years, the faculty managed to feed dozens of quilt campers three healthy meals a day by adapting to what Sylvia euphemistically called the antique kitchen's charming quirks, but it was a struggle. When Anna was hired as their first professional chef, she made a total kitchen remodel a condition for accepting the job. The following September, after camp ended for the season, contractors had gutted the space, knocking out a wall and expanding into an adjacent sitting room. In the far half of the room, they installed state-of-the-art appliances, marble counters, efficient workstations, a central island, spacious cabinets, and a walk-in pantry. In the half closer to the door, eight cozy booths lined the walls. A dark walnut refectory table with two long benches on either side, a well-made, much-loved heirloom from the manor's early days, filled the space between the booths and the cooking area. On the wall above the nearest booth hung a bright, cheerful quilt Sylvia and Anna had sewn from scraps of fabric from Sylvia's great-aunt Lydia's collection of feed-sack aprons, an appliquéd still life of fruits and vegetables framed by blocks evocative of the room in which it was displayed: Broken Dishes, Cut Glass Dish, Honeybee, and Corn and Beans. The kitchen had become an ideal workplace for the creation of nourishing, delicious meals, but it was also a cozy, welcoming gathering place for faculty and campers alike to catch up with friends over a cup of tea and a snack any time of day.

At the moment, it was a buzz of activity as their talented chef and her staff prepared for the evening meal. "Hi, Anna," Summer called to the robust woman with dark, sparkling eyes who stood stirring one of four copper pots on the eight-burner stove. Anna wore her long, dark hair in a French braid beneath her white chef's toque, and although her crisp white apron was spotted tomato red, her sleeves were immaculately clean. "Do I smell your famous corn and leek bisque?"

"Indeed you do, but you'll have to wait until the Welcome Banquet for a taste." Anna glanced up and nearly dropped her spoon, eyes widening with astonishment. "Summer! You're here—and you cut your hair! I love it."

Summer's hand flew to the wavy locks brushing the nape of her neck. Until a few days ago, her thick, auburn hair had been nearly as long as Anna's, but now it barely skimmed her shoulders. "Thanks. I'm not quite used to it yet."

"It suits you. But what are you doing home? No one told me you were coming or I would have made you something special."

"No one knew, and everything you make is special." Inhaling deeply, Summer savored the fragrance of roasting herbs and spices mingled with—was it pastry, and something umami, mushrooms and wild rice? "Have you seen my mom recently? I'd assume she's in the foyer registering campers, except it's a bit late in the day for that."

Anna shook her head. "Registration wrapped up about an hour ago. I think Gretchen might still be out there, though, waiting for a few late arrivals."

"Oh, okay." Summer turned to go, clasping the straps of her backpack to shift its weight. "Maybe Gretchen has seen her pass by. I'll ask."

"If Gretchen doesn't know, try the library," Anna called after her. "This morning Sarah mentioned something about meeting with your mom and Sylvia before the Welcome Banquet."

Summer thanked her and hurried on her way, down the hall to the front foyer, with its gleaming black marble floor and high ceiling open to the third story. To the left, two long marble stairs descended to the tall double doors of the front entrance, while on the far wall, an open doorway led into the ballroom. During camp season, movable partitions divided the large, elegant chamber into classrooms that hummed with activity throughout the day, the sounds of sewing machines, lectures, conversation, and laughter harmonizing into the familiar, charming music of quilt camp. To Summer's right, another pair of doors led into the banquet hall, where campers and faculty savored Anna's magnificent feasts three times a day. The grand oak staircase in the corner climbed gracefully to the second story, which, like the floor above it, was open to the foyer below. Colorful quilts of all patterns and styles hung from the high balustrades, offering an enchanting display of heirlooms from the Bergstrom family collection alongside project quilts the campers could learn to make during that week's classes.

Every Sunday morning of quilt camp season, from late March through the Saturday before Labor Day, the Elm Creek Quilters gathered in the foyer early to prepare for the arrival of their new guests. They would set up long folding tables on the black marble floor, arrange a few chairs on both sides, and organize various stations for the registration process. By midafternoon, nearly all guests would have arrived and would be settling happily into their rooms, wandering the halls to meet their neighbors, or exploring the beautiful estate. As other tasks summoned most of the Elm Creek Quilters away, registration would diminish to a single table, with the few remaining forms and keys and a single faculty member to mind them.

So it was when Summer entered the foyer.

Gretchen Hartley sat alone at a table in the center of the room, perfectly content, smiling as if she expected a camper to rush in at any moment. Though she was the newest member of the faculty, Gretchen was one of their most experienced quilters, having taken her first quilting lessons from none other than Sylvia herself as a high school student in Ambridge, Pennsylvania. She was in her late sixties, with steel-gray hair cut in a pageboy and a thin frame that seemed whittled down by hard times. When Gretchen had first come to Elm Creek Manor for her job interview, Summer had been impressed by her quiet, thoughtful manner and kindness, through which a core of decency and strength were evident. Her knowledge of and love for traditional quilting were equally impressive, but it was her deep understanding of the spirit of Elm Creek Quilts that had won her a place on the faculty.

Gretchen spotted Summer the moment she stepped into the foyer. "Summer," she called out, rising, her smile lighting up with surprise. She came around the table to welcome her with a hug, looking casually professional, as befit the first day of camp, in a tan poplin skirt, white blouse, and a lightweight blue cardigan tied over her shoulders. "What an unexpected pleasure! Your mother didn't mention that you were coming home."

"She doesn't know," Summer said, realizing, too late, that she probably should have called ahead. "Have you seen her around?"

Gretchen gestured toward the staircase. "She hurried by on her way to the library not ten minutes ago. She'll be so pleased to see you."

Summer managed a smile, though she knew her mother wasn't likely to stay pleased once she knew why Summer hadn't stayed at school.

A few campers greeted Summer in passing as she crossed the foyer and ascended the stairs, the carved banister so familiar beneath her hand, worn smooth from the touch of four generations of Bergstroms who had inhabited the manor and the great many friends and guests who had visited since Sylvia's return. At the top of the stairs, Summer turned left and passed two guest suites on her right, and the balcony open to the foyer below on her left. Just past the staircase to the third floor, she paused for a moment where the hall ended at a pair of French doors. Steeling herself, she grasped the handles, eased them open, and stepped cautiously inside, unsure whom she would find there and what important discussion she might interrupt.

All of Elm Creek Quilts' business operations were conducted from the office in the manor's stately library, which spanned the entire width of the manor's south wing. Light spilled in through tall diamond-paned windows on the east and west walls, and between the windows stood tall bookcases, shelves bowing slightly under the weight of hundreds of volumes. Gentle cross breezes cooled the room on that summer afternoon, but in winter, a fire burning in the large stone fireplace on the south wall kept the library warm and snug. On the wall beside the fireplace hung a most unusual Winding Ways quilt, comprised of nine panels, nine blocks each, hung side by side so closely that they appeared to be a single, unified whole—or they would have, except that several sections were absent, with only slender brushed-nickel rods and brackets to indicate where they belonged. Two armchairs and footstools sat invitingly before the fireplace, while more chairs and sofas were arranged in a square in the center of the room, where Elm Creek Quilters often lingered to discuss camp business or to relax during breaks from the busy classrooms downstairs.

Three familiar figures sat there now, so engrossed in conversation that they did not notice Summer as she entered and softly closed the French doors behind her. Summer had expected to find Sarah seated in the tall leather chair behind the large oak desk that had once belonged to Sylvia's father, her long, reddish-brown hair tucked behind her ears as she scrutinized paperwork or entered important information into a spreadsheet. Instead she was in an armchair in the center of the room, facing the French doors, a pen in one hand, a clipboard resting on her lap. Even from behind, Summer immediately recognized the two women seated on the sofa across from her—Sylvia and Gwen.

"Matt anticipates an excellent crop this season, so if we can manage even a small advertising budget to get the word out, we should see a profit this fall," Sarah was saying, as Gwen nodded thoughtfully. "But you've seen the numbers, and we can't ignore the facts. Generating more income from the orchards will help, but we'll have to find other new sources of revenue to sustain us over the long term."

"Why do we need new sources of revenue?" Summer broke in, without thinking. "Is enrollment down? What's going on?"

Startled, Sarah glanced up, and when her eyes met Summer's, they widened in astonishment. "Summer!"

As Gwen and Sylvia started and glanced over their shoulders, Summer drew closer and let her backpack slide to the floor beside the desk. "Hey, everybody," she said, her smile faltering. "Surprise."

"Indeed it is," said Sylvia, turning around in her seat and smiling up at her fondly. "The very best kind. What a becoming hairdo, my dear. Very stylish."

"Thanks, Sylvia." Summer touched her hair self-consciously. "Hi, Mom."

Gwen was already on her feet, her beaded necklaces clicking faintly as she hurried over in a swirl of her long batik skirt and tunic, her gray-streaked auburn hair rippling in thick waves down her back. "Kiddo," she exclaimed in wonder, kissing Summer on both cheeks before pulling her in for a warm, solid hug so strong it almost took Summer's breath away. "What on earth are you doing here?"

"Do I need a reason?" Summer said, her voice muffled against her mother's shoulder.

"Never." Gwen loosened her embrace, but only enough to hold Summer out at arm's length, her hands clasping her daughter's shoulders as she peered intently into her eyes. "What's wrong?"

"You tell me. Is Elm Creek Quilts in financial trouble or something?"

"No, no, of course not," said Sarah, too quickly. "Well, to be perfectly honest, we're breaking even, but our operating expenses rise every year, and the manor could use some repairs. If the alternatives are to raise tuition or cut corners—"

"No and no," said Sylvia firmly. "A week at Elm Creek Quilt Camp must remain within the budget of an average quilter, and we've worked too hard to establish our excellent reputation to lower our standards now."

"Which means," said Sarah wryly, "we need additional sources of revenue. But getting back to the more important question, why have you come home? What's wrong?"

"Why does something have to be wrong? I just got homesick, that's all." Summer tossed off a shrug and forced a smile. "Also, I missed Anna's cooking and playing with the twins."

Gwen's eyes narrowed as they searched her daughter's face for clues. "That much is true, but what else?"

"I needed a change of scene." Summer wriggled from her mother's grasp and knelt beside her backpack. "I'll fill you in soon, but first things first." Drawing back the flap, she withdrew a small, soft bundle wrapped in clean muslin. Unwrapping the protective cloth as she crossed the room to the Winding Ways quilt, she hung her own nine-block panel in its designated spot—second row, first block on the left, just below her mother's and above Diane's, with Gretchen's to the right. Then she stepped back to admire the effect, tranquility settling over her, the reassurance that came from restoring something to its true and proper place.

Sylvia had made the unique Winding Ways quilt two years before, as Judy and Summer prepared to leave Elm Creek Quilts, Judy for her dream job in Philadelphia, Summer for the University of Chicago. The pieced mosaic of overlapping circles and intertwining curves, the careful balance of dark and light hues, and the unexpected harmony of the disparate fabrics and colors evoked the sense of many winding paths meeting, intersecting, parting, creating the illusion that the separate sections formed a single quilt. Sarah would always remember the words Sylvia had spoken that August day as she had presented the panels to the original Elm Creek Quilters. "The Winding Ways quilt will remind us of friends who have left our circle to journey far away," Sylvia had explained. "When one of our circle must leave us, she'll take her section of the quilt with her as a reminder of the loving friends awaiting her return. The empty places on the wall will remind those of us left behind that the beauty of our friendship endures, even if great distances separate us. When the absent friend returns to Elm Creek Manor, she will hang her quilt in its proper space, and the loveliness of the whole will be restored."

As there were eight founding Elm Creek Quilters and nine panels, Sylvia had dedicated the one in the center to all the Elm Creek Quilters yet to come, which now included Gretchen and Maggie. That section would always remain on the library wall, despite the comings and goings of the people it represented. With Summer's panel restored, only two empty places remained: Judy's in the lower left corner, and Bonnie's in the lower right. Summer wondered when all nine panels would once again complete the whole.

Taking a steadying breath, she turned around and smiled brightly, only to find Sylvia studying her over the rims of her glasses. "Does this mean you intend to stay awhile?" she inquired, gesturing to Summer's Winding Ways panel. "That would be lovely indeed."

"Yay! I'll have a room made up for you," said Sarah. "It'll be like old times."

"I'd love that," said Summer, hesitantly, "unless I'd be taking a room that could go to a paying customer?"

Sarah waved that off. "Not at this late date. Don't you remember? Registration closes the Thursday before the camp week begins. Any room that's free now is yours for the taking."

Summer did remember, but now that she was aware Elm Creek Quilts was just breaking even—an unsettling revelation—she'd wanted to make sure.

"You could always come home instead," said Gwen. "Your bedroom is exactly as you left it. Maybe not *exactly*. I've requisitioned your closet for auxiliary fabric storage, and there's a considerable pile of unfinished quilts on the bed, but we can move all of that back into the sewing room easily enough."

"Thanks, but just leave it," said Summer. "I'm not staying long enough to justify the effort. You'd just have to shift everything back at the end of August."

At that moment, Diane burst into the library, her blond curls bouncing. Agnes, the second eldest Elm Creek Quilter and Sylvia's erstwhile sister-in-law, hurried along close behind. "Anna told us Summer is home," said Diane, incredulous, sweeping the room with her gaze until it landed on Summer. "And there she is. Love the hair. What's going on? You never show up unannounced."

"Welcome home, dear," added Agnes, her blue eyes affectionate behind her pink-tinted glasses.

"Since when does Summer have to warn us she's coming home?" Gwen asked Diane, a trifle defensively.

"So you didn't know either. Interesting." Diane turned back to Summer and planted a hand on her hip. "Spill it. What's wrong?"

Summer looked around the room, stalling. "Isn't anyone with the quilt campers right now?"

"Maggie and Gretchen," Diane and Sarah said in unison.

"We don't have any scheduled activities until the Welcome Banquet," Agnes pointed out helpfully. "It would be perfectly fine if indeed we *were* all here to greet you."

"Or as some would have it, to *interrogate* her," said Gwen, folding her arms and frowning.

"Now, Gwen. No one is doing any such thing." Sylvia regarded Summer sympathetically. "Travel can be exhausting. Why don't we let Summer settle into her room and join us later for the banquet? After a good meal and some rest, she can explain why she's delighted us with this wonderful surprise visit. Or not, as she wishes."

"She *has* to explain," Diane protested. She held up a hand and began ticking off points. "She wouldn't let us attend her graduation ceremony even though we were all eager for a road trip. She refused to come home during her summer break even though it's the height of camp season and we need her to teach. Then suddenly she appears, sneaking in the back door—"

"Sneaking?" Summer protested, forcing a laugh. "I always come in the back door. So do you."

"Cool it, Diane," Gwen warned.

Summer's heart plummeted as Diane fired back a retort, her mother responded in kind—and all at once, her other friends were chiming in to admonish one or the other, an overwhelming chorus.

"Ladies, please," said Sylvia, holding up her hands and raising her voice, to no avail. "Let's all calm down and—"

"I didn't graduate."

Silence descended. Everyone turned to Summer as she stood before them, heart pounding, feeling light-headed and faintly queasy.

She swallowed hard and spoke again, softly. "I didn't graduate."

A stunned silence filled the library as she sank into an armchair and buried her face in her hands.

# 2

Summer sat with her eyes closed, wishing there was an "undo" feature for spoken words. Eventually Diane broke the silence. "That's impossible. You're the valedictorian of everything."

Summer heaved a sigh, let her hands fall to her lap, and sat back heavily in the chair. "Not of the master's program in history at the University of Chicago, as it turns out."

"There must be some mistake," said Gwen, brow furrowing.

Summer laughed wanly. "Oh, there are plenty of mistakes involved. All of them mine."

Her friends exchanged glances, their worry and bewilderment evident. She realized then that she would have to tell them everything, before they imagined even worse scenarios than what had actually happened.

And maybe—she thought, a thin whisper of hope—maybe together they would come up with a brilliant solution, one that she had overlooked in her distress. The Elm Creek Quilters were marvelous collaborators, each one wise in her own unique way. Although Summer's roommates had urged her to stay in Chicago, within walking distance of the university's excellent libraries and her adviser's office, her impulse to take sanctuary at Elm Creek Manor suddenly made perfect sense. Where better to find insight, compassion, and creative solutions than here?

"Summer?" her mother prompted gently. "Why didn't you graduate?"

"And why didn't you tell us sooner?" Frowning, Diane dropped into the armchair opposite Summer's, leaned against one armrest, and crossed her legs, every crisp movement an expression of her displeasure. "We should have known something was up when you ordered us not to attend your graduation ceremony. And to think we believed you when you said it was because you didn't want us to cancel a week of camp and spend hours on the road."

"That part was true," said Summer. "I'd never expect you to close everything down in the middle of camp season and disappoint all those quilters just to watch me walk across a stage. I made that decision weeks before everything went wrong."

"'Everything went wrong?'" Sylvia echoed, eyebrows rising. "Summer, dear, would you please tell us precisely what you mean by 'everything'?"

"Maybe not *everything* went wrong," Summer amended. "I passed all my classes—"

"With straight A's, I have no doubt," said Agnes, glancing around for a vacant chair before coming over to sit on the sofa near the armchair Sarah was sitting in.

"Well, yes," Summer admitted. "My classes weren't the problem."

"Because the problem was?" Gwen prompted, turning her wrist as if to unspool the thread of the story.

"I didn't finish my thesis."

Gwen sat back, perplexed, as the others murmured disbelief— perfectly rational responses. The thesis, a graduation requirement for all master's degree students in the history department, was a fifty-page work of original historical scholarship intended to demonstrate a student's expertise, knowledge, and ability to carry on independent research. It often became the foundation of the student's doctoral studies and, eventually, their dissertation. Ideally, the Ph.D. candidate would develop their dissertation into a book manuscript, which would be accepted at a top scholarly press just as they were entering the very competitive job market.

With so much at stake, the master's thesis was a challenging project, but the Elm Creek Quilters knew Summer was more than capable. No wonder they were eyeing her as if they were sure she must be joking.

"But you're such an excellent writer," said Sarah. "And when you first told us about the thesis last summer, you were so enthusiastic about the topic."

"That part hasn't changed," said Summer. "I still believe it's an important subject of academic study."

So had other scholars, for better and for worse.

Her thesis adviser, Dr. Alvarez, had wholeheartedly approved her proposal to investigate the 1913 Woman Suffrage Procession in Washington, D.C., which at the time was the largest civil rights demonstration in the nation's history. Summer had paid particular attention to the work of Ida B. Wells-Barnett, Jane Addams, and other Chicago-area women who had participated in the extraordinary march down Pennsylvania Avenue the day before President-elect Woodrow Wilson's inauguration. For more than a year, Summer had researched and studied and organized her notes, and she'd practically eaten, slept, and breathed every primary source and scholarly article she'd painstakingly uncovered. All along, Dr. Alvarez had praised Summer's diligent research, her deft analysis, and her lucid, graceful, compelling writing, certain that she would produce an excellent thesis and earn her degree with distinction.

It pained Summer now to remember her adviser's encouragement, so sincerely intended, so willingly believed, so tragically misplaced.

"If you still believe your subject is important, why didn't you—or *couldn't* you—finish the paper?" asked Gwen. "When you came home for Anna and Jeremy's wedding, you said you'd made so much progress since winter break that you thought you might finish early. What changed in the past three months?"

Summer hesitated, remembering that cheerful, breezy conversation at the reception all too well, only a few days before everything went disastrously awry.

"Did you lose the file?" Sarah asked, wincing. "I know how devastating that can be, but maybe we can help you reconstruct the document. In my senior year, Matt accidentally deleted my ten-page English Lit paper the day before it was due, but I had printed out some rough drafts, and I had some handwritten notes. It took all night, but with both of us typing furiously—"

"That can't be it," said Gwen, shaking her head. "Summer always backs up her files, and sometimes she backs up the backups."

"I suspect we're dealing with an acute case of writer's block," mused Diane, studying Summer intently. "Summer is too ridiculously competent for the problem to be anything within her own control." Before Summer could speak, Diane held up a hand to cut her off. "Don't deny it. It's true. You're almost annoyingly perfect. I can totally relate."

"Diane, this isn't helping," said Sarah.

"Let me finish. Logically, therefore, the problem must be something entirely *out* of her control. Ipso facto, writer's block."

Gwen rolled her eyes. "There are so many flaws in that syllogism, I hardly know where to begin."

"And yet," Summer said tentatively, "she's not exactly wrong."

Diane flung open her arms in a flourish and threw Gwen a triumphant look. "I called it. 'Not exactly wrong' is mostly right, as far as I'm concerned."

But Gwen's gaze was fixed on her daughter. "Why would you be blocked?" she asked, no less puzzled by the explanation than by the original question. "You say you're still interested in the subject. You have pages and pages of notes and an extensive, detailed outline. You were more than halfway through with the first draft."

"Three-quarters by the time I stopped," Summer said wanly.

"Then what went wrong?" said Sarah, turning to a blank page on her clipboard and uncapping her pen. Was she really going to take notes? "We're here to help, whatever it is, whatever we can do."

As the others chimed in agreement, Summer nodded, inhaled deeply, and traced the thread of the problem back to the tight knot that held it firmly in place. "My mom's right," she said forlornly. "Everything was progressing beautifully until three months ago. And then—"

Her friends drew closer to listen intently as she explained, their faces full of concern and sympathy.

A few days after Anna and Jeremy's wedding at Elm Creek Manor, Summer had set off on another trip, this time traveling to Boston for the annual Conference on American History sponsored by the Organization of American Historians, one of the most important professional societies in her field. Several professors from the University of Chicago Department of History attended, including Dr. Alvarez. They had invited along several of their most promising graduate students, including Summer, her two closest friends in the program, and several doctoral candidates.

The conference began well enough. Summer and her companions attended fascinating lectures and lively panel discussions with some of the world's most prominent historians. They spent hours exploring the exhibit hall, where academic book publishers, professional journals, libraries, and dozens of vendors offered a tantalizing array of products and professional opportunities. Social events allowed them to network with potential collaborators. More important to Summer, she could simply enjoy the company of other scholars who shared her passion for history.

But it was at one of those events where the conference took an unsettling turn. On the second night, at a cocktail reception in the main ballroom, Summer and her friends discovered that the primary topic of conversation among the new Ph.D.s and all-but-dissertation students was the scarcity of tenure-track job offers. In hushed, anxious voices, accomplished young scholars confessed that they were scrambling to secure postdoc research fellowships instead of the assistant professorships they had aspired to, while others gloomily admitted to settling for adjunct teaching positions, and still more had received no offers at all.

Summer and her friends left the reception feeling stunned and anxious.

"Maybe it's just a routine dip in the employment cycle," said Summer as they made their way back to their hotel rooms. "Maybe by the time we graduate, universities will be hiring again."

Her friends agreed that it was possible, but none of them felt very hopeful.

Then, on the third day of the conference, Summer and her friends met up at the main lecture hall for presentations of advanced doctoral students' original research in a session titled "Emerging Scholars on Notable Women of the Twentieth Century." A fascinating lecture about Julia Ward Howe and her women's peace movement was followed by another about Elizabeth Van Lew, a Virginian who had spied for the Union in the Confederate capital of Richmond during the Civil War. All was well until the third presenter was introduced, her topic announced—

Jane Addams, Ida B. Wells-Barnett, and the 1913 Woman Suffrage Procession.

"Summer," the friend on her right murmured uneasily, as her other friend seized her left arm. Summer could only watch in dismay as the speaker—a young woman around her own age, impeccably attired in a navy pantsuit, cream blouse, pearls, and sensible heels, a doctoral candidate from an Ivy League university, confident, articulate, with a subtle sense of humor—delivered an insightful, engrossing lecture on the exact same subject as Summer's master's thesis. Even the basic structure was the same, as were the significant points of analysis, the primary sources, and the most relevant conclusions.

There were, of course, striking differences between their two projects. First, the Ivy League doctoral student had already finished writing her dissertation, and all that remained was to defend it and earn her degree. Second, she was a descendant of Jane Addams's sister, with access to private family papers that had been authenticated but never published, and had remained virtually unknown to scholars for more than sixty years.

Summer could scarcely breathe as she listened to the lecture, fascinated but heartsick. No amount of selfless admiration for the other student's discoveries could disguise the fact that all of her own research, hard work, and painstakingly composed pages had become suddenly and thoroughly redundant. She had nothing new to contribute to the topic that the other student had not already unveiled. She definitely lacked a private family archive overflowing with fascinating documents full of revelations unavailable to other scholars.

And then, the conclusion: Summer muffled a gasp and clutched the armrests of her seat when the doctoral candidate modestly announced that her dissertation would be published by Oxford University Press the following year, by which time she would be working as an assistant professor at Columbia.

Light-headed from shock, Summer belatedly joined in the well-deserved applause. Now her master's thesis would never become the basis of her doctoral studies and her own brilliant book that would secure her a tenure-track position at a prestigious university. Summer's thesis had been thoroughly preempted, and she hadn't even finished it.

Murmuring apologies to her friends and to the people she stumbled past on her way to the aisle, she fled the lecture hall before the next speaker took the stage.

Unable to find a quiet corner in which to compose herself, she left the busy convention center and went for a walk around the large city block. Her only consolation was that she hadn't broken down in pathetic sobs in front of her potential future colleagues and employers.

Eventually she returned to the conference and found her friends, who were very much relieved to see her. As they led her off in search

of dinner, they talked over each other in their determination to assure
her that not all was lost. Maybe the other student would beat her into
print, but Summer was still a brilliant historian.

"Talk to Dr. Alvarez," one friend urged, and the other quickly
echoed her.

Summer nodded glumly. Of course she must talk to her adviser,
and soon. Her thoughts were too scattered for her to gather them up
and find another way forward alone. Dr. Alvarez would guide her.

But the professor was in such demand at the conference that it
wasn't until two days later, as their group waited to board their flight
back to Chicago, that Summer was able to tell her about the doctoral
student's forthcoming book. She struggled to keep her voice steady
as Dr. Alvarez's expression shifted from surprise to concern to weary
resignation.

After Summer's voice trailed off at the end of her sad confession,
Dr. Alvarez paused to think, then rearranged the group's seat assignments so they could sit together. As they boarded, stowed their
carry-ons, and settled in, Summer watched her professor from the
corner of her eye, trying to interpret her furrowed brow and thoughtful frown. It wasn't until the plane took off and reached cruising
altitude that Dr. Alvarez turned to her and offered an encouraging
smile. "It's a disappointment," she acknowledged, "but a scholar of
your ability will be able to overcome this. You may be feeling demor-
alized at the moment, but this is hardly the end of your academic
career. It's barely the beginning."

At last Summer felt a faint glow of relief. "But . . . what do I do
now? Can I still publish my research? I can't, can I?"

Dr. Alvarez shook her head sympathetically. "No, I'm afraid not.
Not unless you intend to refute the other student's arguments."

"I can't. I agree with every point she made."

"In that case, you'd need to come up with an entirely different
angle or new primary sources."

Summer managed a bleak laugh. "You mean like another trove of private family papers no one else has ever studied?"

"That would be perfect, yes." Dr. Alvarez sighed. "So you can't publish this research. That's unfortunate, but you'll have many other opportunities during what I trust will be a long and successful career. Let's focus instead on the real purpose of the master's thesis—to demonstrate your competence in your field and your ability to carry out independent research. Your thesis will still accomplish that."

"But I wanted to continue with this research for my doctorate."

"Many students use their master's thesis as the basis for their doctoral dissertation, but it's certainly not required. Look at this as an opportunity to explore another topic that interests you."

At the moment, Summer was too crushed to think of any. "Sure," she said nonetheless, nodding. "Sure. I'll just . . . do that."

Dr. Alvarez smiled. "You sound skeptical. You needn't be. Just take a deep breath, put your disappointment behind you, and finish the excellent paper you've already begun. When the autumn term begins, you'll enter the Ph.D. program right on schedule, and I'm sure you'll find a new research subject before midterms. We'll figure it out together."

Summer nodded, somewhat reassured. All she had to do was finish her thesis, turn it in, earn her master's degree, and start fresh in the fall. This wasn't the first time in her life she'd changed academic or career plans that had seemed fixed and clear, and everything had worked out for the best.

"So what's the problem?" Diane interrupted. "Just put your hair in a bun, pour yourself a cup of coffee, and pound out a few more pages. It doesn't have to be good. It just has to be finished."

"It couldn't possibly be that simple," said Sylvia, offering Summer a sympathetic look over the rims of her glasses. "Summer would never settle for less than exemplary work."

As the other Elm Creek Quilters chimed in their support and encouragement, Summer couldn't bring herself to confess that she might be willing to make an exception this once and settle for merely adequate work. Unfortunately, that wasn't an option.

"I can't explain it," she said. "I just haven't been able to do it." She heard the strain in her voice and paused to compose herself. "Every time I sit down at the computer, I find myself absolutely frozen, unable to write a single word."

Or so it had been for the past three months as she had toiled away in her apartment in Chicago, avoiding department gatherings, sending halfhearted replies to Dr. Alvarez's increasingly urgent requests for updates on her progress. Her roommates had been at a loss for how to help her, for they had each cleared the master's thesis hurdle easily. They had offered encouragement, brought her cups of coffee when her energy waned, and had taken over her share of the household chores. None of it helped her put words on the page.

All too soon, the deadline for submitting her thesis in time to graduate at the end of the term had come and gone, and still the incomplete document languished on her hard drive.

"Oh, you poor dear," said Agnes, shaking her head. "You've been pushing yourself too hard."

"Why don't you take some time off?" Sarah suggested. "Fine, so you didn't graduate when you planned. So what? Lots of students need more than the standard number of semesters to earn a degree."

"Sarah's right," said Diane. "Take a break, spend a few weeks quilting and relaxing, and get back to your thesis after you've had a chance to clear your head."

"I wish I could, but I can't afford to," Summer said. "I missed the deadline for spring graduation. My adviser convinced the department chair to give me an extension until the end of the summer term in August. If I submit my thesis by then, I'll earn my master's degree and I'll be allowed to enroll in the doctoral program. If not—"

"You lose your fellowship," Gwen finished for her.

"And without my fellowship, I literally can't afford graduate school."

"Oh, kiddo." Sighing, Gwen rose, came around to Summer's side of the coffee table, and bent to hug her. "It's going to be okay. We'll figure it out."

"Perhaps all you need is a change of scene," said Agnes. "Here at Elm Creek Manor you'll surely be newly inspired."

"That's what I was hoping," Summer said, clinging to her mom until she released her and settled on the sofa beside Agnes, still holding her hand. "I think part of the problem was my roommates wanted so badly to help when only I could do the work. They mean well, but they ask me several times a day whether I've made any progress."

The other Elm Creek Quilters exchanged significant looks. "We promise no hovering, no pressure, no nagging," Sarah said for them all. "We'll just bring you coffee and snacks and let you work."

Summer looked around the circle of friends, feeling hopeful, truly hopeful, for the first time since that dreadful conference. "I'm not planning to lock myself away in my room," she assured them. "I'll need time to finish that thesis, but I also want to make myself useful, to earn my keep."

"There's no need to earn what is freely given," said Sylvia. "Elm Creek Manor is your home. There will always be a place here for you—for every Elm Creek Quilter—whenever you need it."

Summer felt a rush of affection for their beloved matriarch, for all of them. "Thank you, Sylvia. I'm grateful. But I'd feel better if I could make myself useful." She turned to Sarah. "I know all the quilt camp classes have already been assigned for the season, but I'd be happy to work as an assistant or a substitute teacher whenever you need me."

"You could take over my Beginning Piecing class on Thursday," Diane interjected before Sarah could reply. "How do you feel about sewing curves by hand? Would you be okay with that, or are you strictly a machine girl now?"

"We'd all welcome your help, Summer," said Sarah, amused, "as Diane has made abundantly clear. But we'll respect your time too. Your thesis must come first."

"Oh, absolutely," said Diane, her eyes wide and innocent. "I wouldn't have it any other way."

"Let us know how much time you can spare," said Sylvia, "and we'll add you to the schedule."

"Or," mused Agnes, studying Summer thoughtfully, "you could do something else entirely."

Summer shook her head, uncomprehending. "What else is there? Anna has the kitchen covered. Matt has a full crew of gardeners."

"A local nonprofit that is about to launch an exciting project, the highlight of a very important capital campaign," said Agnes, her blue eyes hopeful and eager behind her pink-tinted glasses. "The position requires a historian's research skills and a thorough understanding of the art and traditions of quilting. Would you be interested?"

With a tease like that, how could she not be? "Very interested," said Summer, smiling. This was precisely why she had returned to Elm Creek Manor, for the unconditional love, the encouragement, the comfort—and the abundant surprises and possibilities. "Tell me more."

# 3

"Have you heard about Waterford Historical Society's recent work at Union Hall?" Agnes asked.

"A bit," said Summer. "My mom mentioned that a massive restoration effort is finally underway, all thanks to you."

Agnes waved off the praise. "Nonsense. It's been a group effort."

"Maybe the renovations are," said Gwen, "but Union Hall would be a pile of rubble in a landfill right now if you hadn't figured out how to save it."

"I had a lot of help," Agnes insisted. "The other members of the historical society pitched in, as did all of you."

Undoubtedly Agnes had needed all the help she could get. Through the years, whenever Summer had passed by Union Hall, she had wondered why the stately Civil War–era building in the heart of the historic district had been allowed to fall into disrepair. Whatever Union Hall had once been to the community, the long-neglected Greek Revival edifice had become an eyesore, a magnet for vandals, graffiti, and litter. It was common knowledge among generations of local children that it was haunted, a reminiscence that amused her now, older and wiser at twenty-eight.

"My mom told me the city zoning commission had condemned Union Hall," Summer said. "It was going to be razed—"

"Yes," Sarah interrupted, "and you can place the blame on my mortal enemy."

"Gregory Krolich?"

"Who else? The man is a menace. He's never encountered a lovely historic building he didn't yearn to run over with a bulldozer."

"He might have done exactly that to Elm Creek Manor if you hadn't intervened, Sarah," said Sylvia. "I will never trust that man."

"Nor will I," Agnes declared. "I don't believe for a moment that he's abandoned all hope of seizing Union Hall. There's much work to be done before it will be safely out of his clutches—and that's where you come in, Summer dear."

Summer shook her head, puzzled. "I'd like to help, but I don't know the first thing about renovating a building."

"I had something else in mind." Agnes rose and gestured for Summer to do the same. "It would make more sense if I showed you."

"I'll drive," said Gwen, planting both hands on the sofa cushion and pushing herself to her feet.

"What about the Welcome Banquet?" Sarah called after them as Agnes linked her arm through Summer's and steered her toward the French doors. "Summer's probably famished after her long trip."

"We'll be back in plenty of time." In a quick aside to Summer, Agnes added, "You don't mind, do you, dear?"

"Not at all," Summer said as the trio headed down the hallway toward the stairs. "At the moment, I'd rather satisfy my curiosity than my appetite."

Together they made their way down the grand oak staircase, past the kitchen with its tempting aromas, and out the back door to the parking lot where Gwen's car waited in the shade of the two elms. As Gwen took the wheel, Summer climbed into the back, leaving the more comfortable front passenger seat for Agnes.

"Where to begin?" Agnes mused as the car rumbled across the stone bridge over Elm Creek. "At the beginning, of course. More than one hundred and forty years ago, in the bleakest months of the Civil War—"

"No, no, no," protested Gwen, laughing, as she steered the car past the orchard and into the forest. "You've gone back too far."

"I'm merely following chronological order. That's when the Union Quilters—"

"We didn't discover that until later. No spoilers!"

Agnes smiled indulgently. "Where should I begin, then?"

"Last fall, at the beginning of the current crisis."

"Crisis?" Summer echoed.

"It certainly felt like a crisis to us," said Agnes, "and it isn't over yet."

The previous autumn, a few weeks after Summer returned to Chicago for her second year of graduate school, the *Waterford Register* ran a front-page article announcing a proposal to replace the long-vacant and neglected Union Hall with modern, efficient condominiums. Gregory Krolich, CEO of University Realty, had appeared before the town zoning commission and had offered to take the eyesore off the city's hands, but his proposal had encountered a few snarls: The city of Waterford didn't actually own the building and therefore couldn't authorize the sale, and several members of the commission were reluctant to permit a modern, multi-residential high-rise in the middle of the town's historic district. According to the article, Gregory Krolich expected to "iron out the wrinkles" in a closed-door executive session to be held the following week.

Concerned that Krolich would finagle his way into a morally dubious sweetheart deal, the executive board of the Waterford Historical Society demanded to be included in the executive session. They deserved a say in the matter not only because Union Hall merited preservation due to its historical and architectural value to the community, but also because they owned it.

"Demanding a seat at the table was Agnes's idea," Gwen said.

"That seems only fair," said Summer. "Agnes, I didn't realize the historical society owned Union Hall. No offense, but why haven't they taken better care of it?"

Agnes turned around in her seat, her expression rueful. "I'll give you three guesses."

"Money?"

"Very good, dear. You got it in one." Agnes sighed. "It may seem that we were dreadfully negligent, but our budget wouldn't cover any maintenance expenses except for the bare minimum to keep the pipes from bursting and the roof caving in. Even so, the society's long-range plans always included a complete renovation and restoration before reopening Union Hall as our headquarters and a museum of local history."

"Ambitious," Summer remarked approvingly. "So, since the historical society owns Union Hall and didn't want to sell, I assume they sent Krolich away to sulk in his fancy new office."

"Don't even get me started on his 'fancy new office,'" said Gwen sharply. "I can't even bear to glance at that wretched sign."

It pained Summer too, to glimpse that steel gray–and–blue sign hanging above the entrance to University Realty on Main Street. Once, from that same post, the red-and-gold sign for Grandma's Attic had welcomed quilters to Bonnie's quilt shop, and beautiful quilts, books, and bundles of fabric had brightened the front window display where foam board advertisements of properties for sale and rent now stood.

When University Realty had bought the building more than two years before, Gregory Krolich had not only conspired with Bonnie's ex-husband to force her to sell their third-floor condo, but he had also raised the rent on her first-floor shop and his other commercial tenants 75 percent. At the time, Bonnie had wondered why Krolich would impose such an outrageous rate hike, which was all but guaranteed to drive away his tenants. Suspecting that a plot was afoot, Agnes had phoned University Realty in the guise of a prospective tenant only to learn that University Realty planned to relocate their headquarters from the converted Victorian house they had outgrown to Bonnie's building, which was more spacious and more advantageously located.

Summer wished she hadn't dredged up such unhappy memories, but it was nearly impossible to talk about Krolich without remembering all his wrongdoings—at least, the ones the Elm Creek Quilters knew about. "But this time Krolich lost, right?" asked Summer. "So all's well that ends well?"

"Kiddo," Gwen said wearily, "Krolich was just getting started."

Of course he was. "I'm almost afraid to ask what happened next."

"The Waterford Historical Society was denied admission to the executive session," Agnes said. "Afterward we asked to see the minutes, but the zoning commission refused. All we had were dreadful rumors that Mr. Krolich had urged the city to invoke their power of eminent domain. He wanted them to declare Union Hall abandoned, and sell it to University Realty."

"But until there was an official ruling, Agnes decided to proceed as if the historical society still had a chance for a fair hearing," said Gwen. "She immediately organized a volunteer workday to clean up the property, inside and out."

"I'm not naive," said Agnes earnestly. "I know restoring Union Hall to its former glory won't solve its larger, long-term challenges. Even so, I figured that if the property was no longer a blight, the city council couldn't so easily condemn it."

The Elm Creek Quilters had spread the word through their network of former campers and local quilters, and on the appointed day, thirty ambitious volunteers showed up to help. Some worked outside, trimming hedges, raking leaves, and yanking weeds from overgrown flower beds. Those with carpentry skills or construction experience inspected each room and began working their way through a long list of necessary repairs. A third group, which included Elm Creek Quilters Agnes and Gretchen, took inventory of the historical society's collections stored there, sorting, identifying, and cataloging everything from collections of personal documents to shoeboxes stuffed with yellowed newspapers to books and daguerreotypes.

"It was a mess," said Agnes, shaking her head. "For each fascinating historical treasure our volunteers discovered, they found half a dozen more ruined by water, time, or mold. Some papers were so fragile they disintegrated the moment we picked them up. Others were so faded that scarcely any of the words remained legible. But someone, years ago, must have thought they were valuable enough to save."

"The loss is incalculable," said Gwen. "Irreplaceable documents and artifacts, and all the knowledge and insight they had preserved for so many years, gone."

Summer felt a memory kindle. "But weren't most of the historical society's research archives moved to the Waterford College Library decades ago? Their research archives are kept in a local history room in the Rare Books and Special Collections Department. I used them myself when I was an undergrad."

"Yes, that's right." Agnes clutched her armrest as the car emerged from the forest and Gwen turned off the gravel road and onto the paved highway. "Fortunately too, it turned out that only about a third of the materials stored in Union Hall were damaged beyond salvaging. As our tidying-up continued, we discovered a treasure trove of well-preserved documents, and something else." She turned around to catch Summer's eye. "A trunk containing two absolutely exquisite nineteenth-century quilts."

"Aside from their historical significance, they're absolutely stunning," said Gwen. "One is a sampler quilt with one hundred and twenty-one unique pieced blocks, with a floral appliqué border. The other is a sixteen-block appliqué sampler made in the Baltimore Album style."

"That's amazing," said Summer, astonished. "By historical significance, do you mean their age?"

"Oh, so much more than that," said Agnes. "We uncovered the secrets of these heirloom quilts with barely a moment to spare. But that's all I'm going to say for now. It's better to show you."

"You can't leave me in suspense like that," Summer protested, but when Agnes only laughed and refused to say another word, Summer heaved a comical sigh and settled back to enjoy what remained of the ride.

They had reached Waterford proper by then, and Summer found herself rendered unexpectedly nostalgic by the familiar street scenes. Here were her favorite shops and restaurants, her undergrad apartment building, and the Waterford Public Library, where she had spent so many childhood hours engrossed in spellbinding books. Students toting backpacks and cups of coffee filled the sidewalks on their way to and from apartments and classes at Waterford College, but Gwen turned onto Church Street toward the historic district before they reached campus.

Summer glimpsed Union Hall through the windshield as they approached, and she gasped aloud, marveling at the changes Agnes's volunteers had brought about in just a few short months. "I wouldn't have recognized the place," she said as Gwen parallel parked across the street in front of the original city hall, an even older building that had been renovated and converted into shops and apartments within its original, meticulously preserved Neoclassical exterior.

All of the buildings in the historic district sat fairly close to the street, but Union Hall boasted a small front lawn, lush green and freshly mowed, enclosed within a formerly rusty wrought iron fence that had been painted a striking obsidian black. Every trace of graffiti had been scrubbed from the building's white stone walls, the broken windows had been replaced, the hedges were neatly trimmed, and the front gate swung open smoothly and silently when Agnes unlatched it. She led Summer and Gwen down the cobblestone walk and up the limestone stairs to the shaded porch, each stair slightly concave in the middle, worn from the footsteps of more than 140 years' worth of visitors. They passed between tall, freshly whitewashed columns supporting the two-story pediment and entered Union Hall through a pair of tall double doors. Once inside the foyer, Summer turned around in place, taking in the scene, astonished, as Agnes watched her expectantly, smiling at her reaction.

No one would mistake Union Hall for an abandoned building now.

The foyer was smaller than the one that welcomed guests to Elm Creek Manor, but it was equally splendid, with a gleaming gray-blue marble floor, marred only by a few scattered drifts of sawdust and a faint path of scuff marks, two parallel lines suggesting a careless person had once dragged something heavy across it. To the right, a curved staircase climbed gracefully to the second floor. High above, elegant crown molding echoed the Greek key patterns of the ceiling medallion, which encircled a tiered candle-style chandelier with tapered bulbs. Dozens of polished, engraved copper plaques affixed to the walls flanking the front doors gleamed softly in the light. Directly across the foyer from the front entrance, a wide doorway led into a large, dark room—a theater, Summer realized, glimpsing a bare stage at the far end, although a few metal folding chairs rather than fixed rows of plush seats were scattered throughout the house. Somewhere unseen, hammers banged, power tools buzzed, and voices called out questions and commands.

Agnes gestured for Summer and Gwen to accompany her across the foyer to a door on the left, which she gave two quick knocks. "Anyone home?" she called, and when no one replied, she turned the knob and led her friends into a small office with a single window that looked out upon the side yard. There was barely enough room for a desk, two armchairs, a cluttered bookcase, and several tall filing cabinets. Five small cacti in terra-cotta pots sat on the windowsill, and an ancient computer blinked a luminous green cursor at them from the desktop between an overflowing wire basket labeled "In" and an identical, though empty basket labeled "Out."

"Is this your office, Agnes?" Summer asked, dubious, for her friend was famously tidy and organized.

"Oh, goodness no." Agnes chuckled as she made her way around the desk to a steamer trunk tucked into a narrow space between the armchairs and the back wall. "It belongs to Patricia Escher, president of the Waterford Historical Society. Gwen, dear, this latch is a bit tricky. Could you give me a hand?"

After a bit of tugging and fiddling, Gwen loosened the stiff hinge and lifted the lid. Summer's anticipation grew as her mom and Agnes withdrew a soft, folded bundle wrapped in clean muslin. As they carefully unfurled it and held it open between their outstretched arms, Summer quickly came forward to help. As she gingerly took hold of one edge so it would not touch the ground, she wished she could slip on a clean pair of white cotton docent's gloves rather than allow the oils of her skin to touch the aged fabric.

Then she slowly drew in a breath, awestruck.

She had expected an antique sampler, of course, but not one so lovely or so well preserved. This evidently was the first of the two quilts her mom had mentioned, but Gwen's glowing description had not done it justice. The fabrics evoked mid- to late-nineteenth-century tastes and fashions, a glorious bouquet of Turkey red, Prussian blue, dark green, navy, brown, and light tan, faded but not worn. A quick count of eleven rows and eleven columns told Summer there were 121 blocks, each apparently unique, separated by striped sashing and quilted with tiny stitches in an intricate pattern of scrolls, feathered plumes, and flowers. A border of elegant floral swags fashioned in appliqué twined around the sampler block grid, with the phrase "Union Forever" embroidered along the top edge and "Water's Ford, Pa." along the bottom.

"How wonderful," Summer breathed, enchanted. "I recognize many of these blocks—there's Pinwheel Star, Lincoln, Broken Window—but some I've never seen before. I wonder if they're original to this quilt."

"If you look closely," said Gwen, "you'll see subtle variations in technique and quality of piecing that suggest this is not the work of a single quilter."

"We have other, more conclusive evidence of that," Agnes remarked. "Gwen, if you would?"

Summer released her edge of the quilt as her mother and Agnes carefully turned the quilt over. "Look for the embroidery in the bottom right corner," said Agnes. "The color of the thread has faded so much over time that the stitches are barely distinguishable from the backing, but your sharp young eyes shouldn't have any trouble making them out."

Summer bent closer to examine the corner, and she soon discerned the small, delicate letters, the script as elegantly formed as if the quiltmaker had written with pen and ink. "'The Loyal Union Sampler, made by the Ladies of the Elm Creek Valley in Wartime,'" Summer read aloud. "'Completed July 4th, 1862. Union Hall, Water's Ford, Penna.'" Below those lines, the thread became slightly darker, the embroidered letters noticeably larger and rounder, suggesting they had been added later by a different person. "'Presented to the Waterford Historical Society in loving memory of Faith Cunningham Morlan, 1813–1882.'" Summer glanced up to her companions, puzzled. "This quilt was completed here, in 1862? I thought Union Hall wasn't built until 1863."

"The building wasn't *finished* until 1863," Agnes corrected. "It was begun the previous year."

"The 'Ladies of the Elm Creek Valley' apparently had a quilting bee here, while the building was still under construction all around them," said Gwen. "As it happens, Union Hall never would have existed if not for this quilt."

"What do you mean?" Summer asked.

Together, as Gwen and Agnes gently refolded the quilt on the bias, wrapped it in muslin, and set it aside on one of the armchairs, they explained what their research had uncovered.

In 1862, in the bleakest months of the Civil War, the women of the Elm Creek Valley were dismayed when their loved ones who had marched off to war wrote home describing the shocking conditions they endured, including inadequate clothing and shelter, poor rations, and scarce medical supplies. Led by Dorothea Nelson and Anneke

Bergstrom, Sylvia's great-grandmother, a group of friends took it upon themselves to provide for the men's needs. Fundraising was necessary, so the women created an elaborate sampler of 121 unique blocks contributed by quilters from throughout the Elm Creek Valley. When the quilt was complete, the women raffled it off to raise money to build Union Hall. When the building opened the following year, the Union Quilters hosted many successful fundraisers in the hall's theater, garden, and galleries, with the proceeds benefiting local soldiers—the 49th Pennsylvania Infantry Regiment, the 6th United States Colored Infantry Regiment, and the Veterans' Relief Fund, which provided for the wounded soldiers of the Elm Creek Valley and their families.

"I had no idea that Union Hall played such an important role in Waterford's Civil War history," Summer marveled. "And just think—it was the women of the town who made it happen. How awesome is that?"

"Very awesome indeed," said Agnes, "but it wasn't enough to convince the zoning commission to spare Union Hall."

"While Agnes's volunteers were renovating the building, Krolich was relentlessly lobbying the city council to exercise their power of eminent domain and sell the property to him," said Gwen. "He wanted Union Hall, and he wasn't about to let a bunch of quilters and history buffs stand in his way."

"Sprucing up Union Hall was never going to be enough to protect it," said Agnes. "We needed evidence that it had unique historical significance. If we could prove that it did, Union Hall could be added to the National Register of Historic Places. That designation would bring us tremendous benefits—we'd get protection from the wrecking ball, and some tax breaks, so we could afford to maintain the building properly. We could also apply for grants, so we could finally open our local history museum."

"And did you find the evidence?" Summer could tell from Agnes's shining eyes that she had. "How? What was it?"

Agnes beckoned Gwen to assist her once more. Reaching into the steamer trunk, they withdrew a second muslin-wrapped bundle and carefully unfolded it.

This too was a sampler quilt, smaller than the first and fashioned in a markedly different style. Instead of many small blocks, almost all of them pieced, the second quilt boasted sixteen large appliqué blocks that looked to be fourteen inches square, more than twice the size of those in the Loyal Union Sampler. The intricate designs reminded Summer of quilts made in the Baltimore Album tradition, with appliquéd pieces creating still life portraits in fabric—a basket of garden vegetables, a red banked barn like the one on the Bergstrom estate, a farmhouse, a school, a ring of maple leaves and seeds, a wooden bucket half encircled by flowers, branches of elm leaves framing four lines of embroidered words, a book, and other tableaux. The most unusual block depicted what looked to be a large black kettle hanging above an open fire from a pole suspended between two bare-limbed trees. But whereas most Baltimore Albums offered flat, stylized images of elegant subjects, this quilt depicted more ordinary, homey things, and for the buildings, especially, perspective had been used to create more realistic portraits of daily life in the Elm Creek Valley. The quality of the work was flawless, the calico flowers, leaves, and figures sewn meticulously by hand to the soft muslin backgrounds. The sixteen blocks were arranged in four rows of four and separated by light tan sashing with Turkey red cornerstones, and an appliqué border of elegant swags gathered by roses framed the blocks beautifully.

"This is extraordinary," said Summer, drawing closer to read the words embroidered on one of the blocks. "'Creek's Crossing Album. Appliquéd by Miss Dorothea Granger, 1849. Quilted by Mrs. Abel Wright, 1850. Presented to Mrs. Wright by Miss Granger in celebration of her marriage, 1847, on the occasion of her arrival to her new home in 1849.'" She glanced up at Gwen and Agnes, amused. "Miss Granger was a little late with her wedding gift."

"Name a quilter who hasn't missed an important gift deadline at least once," said Gwen. "I've done it."

"I confess I have too," said Agnes.

Studying the exquisite quilt, Summer felt a faint tug of memory, which became more insistent until suddenly it came to the fore. "I've seen those names before, in Gerda Bergstrom's memoir about the early years of Elm Creek Farm, back when Waterford was still called Creek's Crossing. Gerda mentioned the Granger, Wright, and Nelson families often." She paused, searching her memory. "Granger was Dorothea Nelson's maiden name. Mrs. Abel Wright was Gerda and Dorothea's friend Constance Wright. Abel had been born into freedom in Pennsylvania, but Constance had been born in the South. They married while she was still enslaved, but eventually Abel was able to buy her freedom and bring her north."

"You likely recall from Gerda's memoir that Abel Wright was a local dairy farmer, carpenter, and Underground Railroad conductor," said Agnes. "What you probably don't know is that he later became a Civil War veteran and an acclaimed author, with six books to his credit. He wrote three of them here in the Elm Creek Valley, and three after he and his family moved to Colorado."

"Finding the quilts led us to Abel Wright," said Gwen. "The Loyal Union Sampler and the Creek's Crossing Album prove a connection between Dorothea Granger and Constance Wright, and between both women and the founding of Union Hall. Constance and Abel were connected by marriage. What we lacked was evidence of a direct connection between Abel Wright and Union Hall."

"Yes, of course," said Summer, nodding. "Proof of his involvement would give Union Hall indisputable historical significance, enough to earn it a spot on the National Register of Historic Places."

"We thought his books would offer more insight," said Gwen, "but time wasn't on our side. Krolich was relentless."

"Waterford College Library kept copies of Abel Wright's books in the Rare Books Room," said Agnes. "I went there to read them—or rather, I tried to. You'll never guess what I found when I arrived."

Summer shook her head, shrugging. "Krolich bending over one of Abel Wright's books, slicing out relevant pages with a razor blade?"

"Close, but not quite. There was an empty gap on the shelves where Abel Wright's books had been."

"But books in the Rare Books Room don't circulate."

"Exactly."

"Abel Wright's books had been stolen?" asked Summer, aghast.

"Right again," said Agnes. "In case they had simply been mis-placed, the head archivist, two student workers, and I spent hours shelf-reading, but there was no sign of the books. Later, the archivist— a very dear friend of mine—discovered their security tags in the trash, still attached to their torn-out pages."

"We suspected Krolich," said Gwen, rolling her eyes, "because really, who else would have done it? But once again, we had no proof."

"What we *did* have," Agnes said, "was our very own expert on the life and works of Abel Wright, a graduate student in history—"

"Your ex, Jeremy," Gwen broke in.

"Don't call him that," Summer protested, chagrined. "Honestly, Mom. We dated for a few months years ago. He's Anna's husband now. Don't make things awkward."

"Sorry, kiddo," her mother replied, clearly not sorry at all.

"Jeremy knew Abel Wright's books by heart, or nearly so," said Agnes. "Imagine our excitement when Jeremy told us that Abel Wright was the architect and the construction foreman of Union Hall!"

"Seriously?" Summer gasped. "Hold on. Did you have irrefutable proof? I can totally imagine Krolich arguing that Abel Wright exag-gerated, or that he wrote fiction, not memoir."

"We have proof," Agnes declared. "Let's tuck these treasures away for safekeeping and we'll show you."

Reverentially, Agnes and Gwen folded the Creek's Crossing Album, wrapped it in muslin, and returned it to the steamer trunk. Taking up the Loyal Union Sampler, Agnes gave it an affectionate pat and set it on top with great care. "I hope we won't have to keep them in storage much longer," said Agnes, closing the lid and latching it. "Now, Summer, I suppose you're impatient to see our evidence."

Summer stepped aside to allow Agnes room to pass as she strode toward the door. Agnes led her and Gwen back into the foyer, where she gestured dramatically to the largest of the copper plaques affixed to the wall near the entrance.

Raising her eyebrows at her mother, and receiving a cryptic smile in reply, Summer crossed the foyer to the plaque and read the commemorative phrases. "It's all right here," she murmured in wonder as she read the names of the Union Quilters who had conceived and executed the project, including Dorothea Nelson, Gerda Bergstrom, Anneke Bergstrom, Constance Wright, and several other women whom she recalled from Gerda's memoir. Last of all appeared the name of the architect and foreman of construction—Abel Wright.

She turned back to Agnes. "I don't understand. If the evidence you needed was here all along, in plain sight—"

"But it wasn't in plain sight," said Gwen. "It had been hidden behind an enormous curio cabinet."

With a sweep of her arm, Agnes indicated the faint scuff marks on the otherwise well-preserved marble. "You can see the damage Gregory Krolich and his hired thugs left behind when they moved it from the theater."

"Hired thugs?" Summer echoed.

"Well, he must have had help—the cabinet is simply too large for one person to manage alone—and I picture them as burly hired thugs."

"And you know Krolich was behind it?"

Agnes hesitated. "Well, we don't have an eyewitness account or security camera footage, but we *know*. Mr. Krolich alone had motive and opportunity."

"So you *strongly suspect*," said Summer carefully, "but you don't actually *know*."

Agnes's smile faltered. "Well, yes. That's more accurate. If we'd had actual proof, we could have gone to the police."

"What we *did* have, finally, was the evidence the historical society needed," said Gwen. "When Agnes and Patricia told the city council about the plaque, the majority voted to reject Krolich's bid to purchase the property. Naturally, Krolich claimed not to know anything about the plaque or how that curio cabinet wound up in front of it."

"Naturally," said Summer. "I guess it was too much to hope he'd be overcome with remorse, confess, and mend his ways."

"He didn't confess," said Agnes, "but Abel Wright's missing books did mysteriously turn up in the Waterford College Library return bin a week later."

"Only because Krolich didn't need them anymore," Gwen countered. "He didn't want to risk being caught with stolen goods. Then there's University Realty's large contribution to the arboretum—"

"My cabdriver said a generous benefactor had donated fifty acres of wetlands to the arboretum," said Summer, incredulous. "That was Krolich?"

"He must have been tormented by a guilty conscience," said Agnes.

"Doubt it," said Gwen, shaking her head so emphatically that her beaded necklaces clicked. "More likely, he was trying to bolster his public image so the press wouldn't examine his shady dealings too closely. He managed to tie up those loose ends before the spring election, when his best pals got voted out of the city council."

"So Union Hall is finally safe from Krolich," said Summer. When her mother and Agnes exchanged a wary glance, she added, "Right? Union Hall is safe?"

"It's safe from condemnation," said Agnes, "but the work of restoring and renovating Union Hall will be very expensive, almost prohibitively so. Also, when we open our museum, there will be operational costs, salaries—" Her sweet expression turned uncharacteristically anxious. "If the Waterford Historical Society can't afford to maintain the property, we'll have to sell—and I've no doubt that University Realty will be first in line to purchase it."

"You haven't fought this hard to lose Union Hall now," said Gwen, putting an arm around her older friend's shoulders. "You have many friends and supporters, and we won't let you down."

"You can count me among them," said Summer. "You said you needed my skills, as a quilter and historian. How can I help?"

Agnes immediately brightened. "Follow me upstairs to the east gallery, and I'll show you."

She led the way up the curved staircase. Several stairs and balustrades evidently had been replaced recently and still awaited staining, while the banister had been polished to a soft gloss, the rich cherrywood fairly glowing in the light of the chandelier. On the second-floor landing, Agnes turned to the right, smiling at Summer over her shoulder as she beckoned her and Gwen to follow her down the hall. "It's not quite finished," she said as she halted at a pair of double doors, turned the knobs, and eased them open, "but it's already our pride and joy."

Following Agnes inside, Summer found herself in a lovely gallery, about twice as long as it was wide, with gleaming hardwood floors and pristine, ivory-colored walls still smelling of fresh paint. The white baseboards and crown molding, smaller in scale but echoing the pattern from the foyer, added another note of elegance to the room. Three partitions were spaced equidistantly along the length of the room, offering additional display surfaces. A bank of windows on the longest wall, opposite the door, were ingeniously shaded to diffuse the natural light, and to supplement this, two electricians were installing track lighting around the room.

"The society's treasurer owns a home improvement store," said Agnes as Summer took in the splendid gallery. "He not only donated all the lighting and other contraptions we need, but he didn't charge us anything for installation."

Summer was already certain what Agnes intended to display there.

"We've already begun applying for grants and loans, but in the meantime, we urgently need to raise funds to cover repairs already underway," Agnes said. "I propose opening the east gallery to the public as a quilt exhibit."

"This would be the ideal place for one," said Gwen, casting an appraising look around the room.

"We'll display the Loyal Union Sampler and the Creek's Crossing Album, of course," Agnes continued, "but I believe that additional quilts with intriguing ties to local history would draw even more visitors and help spread the word about the important work we do here. Admission fees and donations could provide revenue we very badly need, and we could hold a grand opening gala to get our capital campaign off to an excellent start. And you, Summer, as a longtime resident of Waterford, accomplished quilter, and trained historian, would be the ideal curator."

"A curator?" Summer echoed, intrigued. "What would you need me to do?"

"I haven't entirely worked that bit out yet," Agnes confessed. "I never expected the perfect candidate to show up so soon. I suppose your duties would include tracking down suitable quilts, arranging to borrow them from their current owners, verifying the quilts' provenances, writing up object labels, organizing the exhibit, and caretaking the collection. We can make the rest up as we go along."

"Sounds like the perfect job for you, kiddo," Gwen remarked.

Summer thought so too.

"You'll be providing a valuable service to the community, and you'll still have plenty of time to finish your thesis." Agnes regarded Summer expectantly through her pink-tinted glasses. "What do you say, dear? Do you want to think it over while we enjoy a delicious banquet back at Elm Creek Manor?"

"I don't need to think it over," Summer assured her, smiling. "It's yes to the banquet, and yes to the job. When do I begin?"

# 4

S hall I give you a tour of the rest of Union Hall?" Agnes asked as they left the gallery.

Although Summer was eager to see the ongoing renovations, she shook her head. "Another time, please. I'd like to freshen up and change before the Welcome Banquet."

Agnes cheerfully agreed to postpone the tour a day or two, and soon they were in the car, Gwen at the wheel, on their way back to Elm Creek Manor. They sighed with anticipation when they entered the rear foyer and were immediately enveloped in the delectable aromas wafting from the kitchen. "I'll see if Anna needs my help," said Agnes, excusing herself and bustling off.

"As for me," said Summer, "I need to find Sarah and get a room key."

"She's probably in the library, sorting out some last-minute changes to the campers' schedules." Gwen cupped her daughter's cheek in her hand affectionately. "My offer to restore your old bedroom to its former condition still stands."

"Thanks, Mom, but really, it's fine. If I were staying longer, sure, but—"

"But for the next few weeks, you'd prefer a lovely resort in the countryside, and that's Elm Creek Manor."

"Exactly."

Together they went to the butler's pantry so Summer could collect her suitcase and backpack. From there they could see into the elegant banquet hall, where Anna's staff were busily preparing for the most formal meal of the camp week. The season was so close to midsummer that the floor-to-ceiling windows on the western wall let in generous sunlight despite the hour. A pair of double doors on the wall opposite the windows, closed at the moment, led into the front foyer, while another pair on the far adjacent wall stood open, offering glimpses of the ballroom, dark and quiet now, with no classes in progress. Tomorrow, though, it would be bustling.

Summer had just slipped her backpack over her shoulders and picked up her suitcase when a familiar voice called out her name. She and Gwen turned to find Sarah entering through the ballroom doorway, her toddler daughter straddling her hip. Sarah was making only slow progress thanks to Caroline, who was amusing herself by swinging her feet and giggling every step of the way. "Wait up, Summer," Sarah called as they approached. "I have your key."

"Stay put. We'll come to you," said Gwen, and she and Summer hurried across the room to meet her.

A bit breathless, Sarah shifted a squealing Caroline to her other hip, and tried, and failed, to reach into her back pocket with her free hand. Sighing, she turned her back to them. "Summer, do you mind?"

"Not at all," said Summer, making a goofy face for Caroline, who burst into giggles and hid her face against Sarah's shoulder. Glimpsing the key fob poking out of Sarah's right back pocket, Summer deftly plucked it free and noted the room number. "Thanks for finding me a bed on such short notice."

"It's not your usual room," said Sarah. "It's the smallest, sorry, but it was the only one vacant."

"No worries. I like it. It's not small. It's cozy."

"Can we catch up soon?" Sarah struggled to keep hold of her wriggling daughter, who appeared to be attempting back dives from her mother's arms, certain that Sarah would not let her fall. "I've hardly seen you since you arrived, but I've got to change for the banquet. I couldn't find the candleholder, and Caroline begged to be allowed to help me look—"

"I've got this, Sarah. Come to Auntie Gwen, little one." Gwen reached for Caroline, who promptly stopped squirming, released her mother, and fairly pitched herself at her honorary aunt. "I'll mind this rambunctious little creature. Which reminds me—where's James?"

"With Andrew," said Sarah, already looking less harried as she caught her breath and worked a knot of tension out of her neck. "He dotes on the twins like they're his own grandchildren. Thanks, Gwen. I owe you one. And Summer—"

"We'll catch up tomorrow," Summer affirmed, waving her on. "It's okay, I know you have to run. I'll see you at the banquet."

"See you then," Sarah said, already backing away, before turning and breaking into a trot. "It's good to have you home."

"She needs to learn to slow down and take it easy," Gwen remarked to Summer, although her gaze and singsong voice were all for Caroline.

Summer laughed. They both knew that Sarah relished the hectic pace of Elm Creek Quilts at the height of camp season and wouldn't dream of taking a step back. "With toddler twins and a business to run? I don't see that happening anytime soon."

"You should take a night off too," advised Gwen, her expression revealing that she didn't expect her daughter to heed that advice.

"I will, tonight, more or less. I'm coming to the banquet and to Candlelight."

"Promise you won't stay up too late staring at your computer afterward?"

"Promise." Summer gave her mom a kiss on the cheek, sparing another for Caroline. "See you in a bit."

Nodding, Gwen set Caroline down and held her hand as she scampered toward the ballroom after Sarah.

Summer watched them for a moment before she left the banquet hall through the double doors to the foyer and headed upstairs. Despite its small size, the third-floor room was actually one of Summer's favorites, nestled in the west wing, with a distant view of the gazebo in the north gardens and, if she craned her neck just right, glimpses of the cornerstone patio below. An Evening Primrose quilt in shades of sage, lavender, pink, and cream was spread upon the twin bed, and eyelet lace curtains stirred in the cool evening breeze that drifted through the window, fragrant with the faint scent of magnolia and evergreen, and perhaps a lingering trace of lilac. A small nightstand stood next to the bed, a closet door hung slightly ajar on the right, and a desk with a chair and a lamp awaited her beneath the window.

Closing the door behind her, Summer opened her suitcase on the floor and withdrew one of her favorite summer dresses—soft, sage-green jersey knit cotton with a jewel neckline, cap sleeves, and pockets. Draping it on the bed, she hurried off to the bathroom to wash up and to run a brush through her hair. Slipping on the dress, pulling on her favorite sandals, she hurried downstairs to the foyer, where Gwen and Sylvia were directing their guests into the banquet hall. As Summer descended the stairs, a few surprised and delighted campers who recognized her from previous visits called out greetings, which she returned with a smile and a wave.

As she crossed the foyer, so many friendly campers wanted her to stop and chat that it was a few minutes before she could join her mom. "Did Sarah find the candleholder?" Summer asked in a murmur.

"Yes, and just in time. It wouldn't be much of a Candlelight ceremony without it. I suppose in a pinch we could stick a birthday candle in an empty spool—"

When Gwen broke off abruptly and her gaze shifted, Summer glanced over her shoulder and spotted an eager camper hurrying toward them. "We heard a rumor you'd come back," the camper exclaimed, beaming. "Will you be leading a Sunrise Yoga class tomorrow morning, like you did last year?"

It hadn't occurred to her, but why not? "Absolutely."

"Wonderful!" The camper clasped her hands together and gave a little bounce. "I'll spread the word!"

"See you on the verandah," Summer called after her as she darted off to share the good news.

"You're much loved around here, and much missed while you're away," Gwen remarked, giving Summer a playful nudge. "I hope you realize that."

"I do," said Summer. She sometimes forgot while she was caught up in her studies, but coming home always reminded her anew.

Eventually Summer, her mom, and Sylvia ushered the last of the quilt campers into the banquet hall and followed them inside. Sylvia closed the doors behind them. By custom the Elm Creek Quilters did not all sit together at the same table at mealtimes, but dispersed among their guests, the better to create a friendlier, more welcoming, more inclusive atmosphere. "Dining with different campers through-out the week provides us with an excellent opportunity to draw out our shier guests and introduce them to new friends," Sylvia had said years before. "Informal conversation is also an ideal way to learn how the camp session is going—what the campers are particularly enjoy-ing this week, and what problems might need a remedy."

Sylvia's arrangement had proved as beneficial as she had pre-dicted. Summer had made many new friends over delicious meals in the banquet hall, and on several occasions she had been able to sort out misunderstandings or offer guidance to an overwhelmed new-comer. Sylvia was the heart and soul of Elm Creek Quilts, and her wisdom was a resource Summer cherished. The beloved matriarch seemed to believe that her greatest contribution to their business was the estate and the manor, but the other Elm Creek Quilters knew better.

Since there were more Elm Creek Quilters than dining tables, typically two faculty members sat together, with campers completing the set. With only moments to spare before the banquet was to begin, nearly all their guests had already seated themselves. Summer and

Gwen found two chairs at a table where no faculty had yet claimed places, while Sylvia joined Diane at a nearly full table nearby.

The banquet hall had been transformed from its more casual lunchtime atmosphere by white tablecloths, centerpieces of flower petals sprinkled amid candles, and Sylvia's fine heirloom china, nearly translucent, with the Bergstrom rearing stallion in the center. Voices were hushed yet full of anticipation. Summer had barely seated herself when Anna's servers emerged from the entrance near the butler's pantry, neatly attired in black slacks, white shirts, black ties, and white aprons. With practiced grace, they placed steaming bowls of corn and leek bisque before the campers and their hosts, and Summer knew even before she took her spoon in hand that the soup was going to be flavorful, not too rich, and with a hint of sweetness, just as she remembered from the summer before. The organic baby green salad with balsamic vinaigrette that followed was crisp and delicious, and the vegetarian main course of mushroom Wellington in port reduction with wild rice was utter perfection. Judging by the murmurs of delight and satisfaction Summer heard all around her, she knew she was not the only one to think so.

She could only manage two small bites of the lemon meringue tart served for dessert—not because it wasn't delicious, but because she honestly couldn't manage another morsel.

"You probably get tired of eating like this every day," one of her dinner companions said enviously, savoring her own last sweet, tart mouthful from her spoon.

"Never," Gwen declared.

"I haven't been eating like this every day," Summer said, comically woeful. "I've been off at graduate school dining on beans and rice and ramen, dreaming about Anna's fabulous cooking and waking up with my tummy growling."

As the others at their table smiled and laughed, the first camper regarded Summer with utter bewilderment. "If I had the chance to be an Elm Creek Quilter, and live here at the manor and do quilty things all day long for my actual job, I'd sign up for life. How could you bear to leave all this?"

As a murmur of curious assent rose around the table, Summer hesitated, searching for the proper, diplomatic response. "That's an excellent question," said Gwen, buying her time to think. "It helps to know that my daughter is absolutely brilliant, and she'd excel at any career she might choose."

"She takes after you, then," another quilter piped up, and everyone laughed.

"Obviously," said Gwen, and laughter rose again.

"To be honest, it really is as difficult to leave Elm Creek Manor as you imagine," said Summer, glancing up and smiling to thank the server as he poured her coffee. "I didn't manage it the first time."

"The first time?" another quilter echoed, surprised.

"That's right." Summer offered a wry smile as she stirred a hint of cream into her coffee. "My first attempt came during my senior year as a philosophy major at Waterford College. I was accepted into the graduate program at Penn."

"Accepted with a fellowship guaranteed for six years," said Gwen, wistful. "A full ride at an Ivy League university. If I'd been given an opportunity like that when I was her age—"

"Please excuse my mom. She's still in mourning," said Summer. "And she did have an opportunity like mine, a full ride at Cornell. Anyway, Elm Creek Quilts was new and growing, and I was working part-time here and at our local quilt shop while taking classes and finishing my degree. By spring semester, a few months before graduation, I realized that I didn't want to leave Elm Creek Quilts. It was so exciting to be part of founding a successful new business, and I wanted to be here to nurture it." She had also planned to continue working at Grandma's Attic, in hopes of taking over the shop when Bonnie eventually retired. That dream had been quashed soon thereafter, collateral damage of Gregory Krolich's greed. "So I declined Penn's offer, breaking my mother's heart—"

"Not so," Gwen countered. "All I ever wanted was for you to follow your dreams and to be happy."

"That's what she says now," said Summer, tossing her mother a teasing smile, "but she took it hard."

"Well, who could blame her?" another camper said, offering Gwen a commiserating look. "A full ride to Penn is nothing to discard lightly."

"Maybe not, but Elm Creek Manor is very difficult to leave," the first camper replied, catching Summer's eye, her expression now full of understanding.

"Difficult, but not impossible," said Summer. "Almost two years ago, I entered the master's program at the University of Chicago—a different major, a different school, but with the same goal, to earn my doctorate."

"Just like your mother," said the same camper who had teased Gwen about the source of Summer's brilliance.

"Not *just* like my mother," said Summer. "She's in American Studies; I'm in history. And that's not why I—"

She would have explained herself, but a sudden hush in the room distracted her.

Evening had fallen, and the floor-to-ceiling windows on the western wall offered breathtaking views of a violet and deep pink sky in the distance beyond Elm Creek. On the opposite side of the room, Sylvia stood near the entrance to the foyer, the doors now wide open. "I hope you all enjoyed the banquet," she said in a clear voice that carried the length of the banquet hall. "Now, if you would all please follow me, we'll continue our welcome festivities outside on the cornerstone patio."

It was time for one of the most cherished moments of quilt camp, the Candlelight ceremony.

With the other Elm Creek Quilters bringing up the rear, Sylvia led the campers from the banquet hall, across the foyer, and into the west wing, but instead of turning left toward the kitchen and the back door, she proceeded straight head, past the accessible guest suites. The short hallway ended at another door, which Sylvia held open for her guests as she gestured for them to precede her outside. Murmuring to one another, their curiosity growing, the campers stepped out onto a square patio surrounded by evergreens and lilac bushes several weeks past peak bloom, and paved in the same gray stone that made up the manor itself. As Summer passed through the doorway, she caught Sylvia's eye and smiled. Sylvia smiled back as she too came outside and closed the door behind them.

Summer knew that the cornerstone patio was very dear to Sylvia, for it had been her mother's favorite place on the estate, quiet and secluded, yet bursting with color and fragrance in springtime when the lilacs bloomed, and full of birdsong and the hum of honeybees from spring through autumn. Long ago, the doorway through which they had just passed had been the front entrance to the manor, and if one looked closely through the lowest tree branches where the patio met the northeast corner, one could read the engraving upon the large stone at the base: Bergstrom 1858. Sylvia's great-grandfather, Hans Bergstrom, had placed that cornerstone with the help of his wife, Anneke, and sister Gerda, and had built the original residence, now the west wing of the manor, upon it.

Summer knew the cornerstone patio had become even more special to Sylvia in recent years, because of all the memories that had been made, confidences shared, and friendships kindled there.

When the campers' voices rose above a murmur, Sylvia smiled and gestured for silence, adding to the aura of mystery. Earlier, Sarah's husband, Matt, and Sylvia's husband, Andrew, had arranged chairs in one large circle on the patio. Sarah beckoned the campers to sit. Whispering to one another, the campers took their places, and occasionally a nervous laugh broke the stillness. The campers fell silent as Sylvia lit a candle, placed it in the crystal votive holder, and took her place in the center of the circle. As the dancing flame in Sylvia's hands cast light and shadow on her features, Summer sensed a familiar frisson sweeping through the gathering.

Slowly Sylvia turned in place, gazing into the faces of her guests. "One of our traditions is to conclude the first evening of quilt camp with a ceremony we call Candlelight," she told them. "It began as a way for our guests to introduce themselves to us and to one another. Since we're going to be living and working together closely this week, we should feel as if we are among friends. Yet our ceremony also has another, equally important purpose. It encourages you to focus on your goals and wishes, and helps prepare you for the challenges of the future and the unexpected paths you might set forth upon."

Sylvia allowed the expectant silence to swell before she explained the ceremony. The campers would pass the candle around the circle, and as each woman took her turn to hold the flickering light, she would explain why she had come to Elm Creek Quilt Camp and what she hoped to gain that week. There was a pause after Sylvia asked for a volunteer to speak first.

"Not me," someone whispered so timorously that a ripple of laughter rose from the circle.

"I'll go," Vinnie sang out merrily, reaching for the candleholder. "I've done this so many times that I don't get even a smidgeon of stage fright anymore." Her closest friends smiled and shook their heads fondly, as did some of the teachers, for it was impossible to imagine Vinnie ever being too nervous to speak her mind. "My name's Lavinia Burkholder, but everyone calls me Vinnie—except for my grandchildren, who call me Nana. I return to quilt camp every summer to reunite with my quilting buddies and to celebrate my birthday, but we came early this year so I guess we'll have to skip my annual surprise birthday party."

As her companions smiled and a few campers laughed quietly, Summer overheard another guest murmur to a friend, "How can it be a surprise if it's annual?" Whatever her friend whispered in reply, it apparently satisfied her, for she nodded and pressed a hand to her mouth to stifle laughter.

"I attended Elm Creek Quilt Camp during its very first year," Vinnie continued, "so I proudly claim the distinction of being one of

Elm Creek Quilt Camp's first and most frequent campers. As for my goals and wishes, they're the same—to celebrate quilting and friendship to my one hundredth birthday and beyond." She rose and bowed comically to a round of applause, then handed the candle to the woman on her left.

The second quilter cupped the crystal votive in her palms, silent for a moment while all around them, crickets chirped in the gradually deepening darkness. "My name is Molly Earnshaw," she said. "I'm a high school principal from Traverse City, Michigan. I've been quilting for about five years. I prefer strip piecing projects and working with kits. I came to camp to learn additional skills because our school is going to lose one of our most dedicated and inspiring teachers next year. To retirement," she quickly added as a murmur of apprehension and dismay went up from the circle. "Honestly, it's hard to imagine our school without Mr. Jankowski. He's made such a difference in the lives of so many young people, especially those students who have participated in the school theater program through the decades."

"Tell us how that inspired you to come to quilt camp, dear," Sylvia prompted kindly. "We're here to listen."

As those around her quietly added their encouragement to Sylvia's, Molly nodded, her eyes on the candle. "As you can imagine, the theater kids are dreading his departure. They're all very creative and expressive young people, but they've struggled to process the loss—because it *is* a loss, even though they wish him well. They'll miss him terribly, and they want to give him a proper send-off next June."

"I assume they'll put on a spectacular show," one quilter mused aloud, "with music, dancing, maybe even fireworks?"

Again soft laughter broke out, and Molly smiled. "No fireworks, but certainly there will be music, dancing, and maudlin speeches with quotes from pop songs and Shakespeare. The students also want to present him with a special gift. This is where quilting comes in, Sylvia. For every drama club production, it's a tradition for the cast and crew to receive a show shirt, a T-shirt with artwork from the play on the front, and the student's role printed on the back." Molly smiled wistfully. "Mr. Jankowski's shirts always say 'Director,' and he wears them as proudly as his students do. I thought the theater students could gather as many as they can from their own closets and alumni donations, cut out the emblems, and piece them into a quilt. It would be a wonderful keepsake for Mr. Jankowski, and the creative process would help the students to reflect upon the wonderful memories they've shared through the years."

"I've made many T-shirt quilts through the years," said Donna, one of Vinnie's friends. "We should talk. I have lots of tips to share."

Molly thanked her, and with that, she passed the candle on to the next woman in the circle, who accepted it with trepidation. "I'm embarrassed to follow a story of so much generosity and thoughtfulness," she said abashedly. "I only came to quilt camp because I've been a huge fan of Maggie Flynn ever since her pattern book came out years ago, and I wanted to take her sampler class. My hope for this week is to get my book signed and to learn how to make that tricky State Fair block without having to rip out every other seam and do it over."

A ripple of laughter rose from the circle, and Summer felt the lingering shyness lift with it.

Around the circle the candle went, passed from hand to hand as the violet sky deepened and the stars came out. Women who could barely thread a needle had come for their first lessons; accomplished quilters had come for the opportunity to learn new skills or to work uninterrupted on long-neglected masterpieces. They had come to sew quilts for brides and for new grandchildren, to cover beds and to display on walls, for comfort, for beauty, for joy. Through the years Summer had heard similar tales from other women, and yet each story was unique. One common thread joined all the quilters who came to Elm Creek Manor: Those who had given so much of themselves and their lives caring for others—children, spouses, aging parents—were now taking time to care for themselves, to nourish their own creativity, to discover the artist within themselves and let her speak.

It was little wonder, Summer reflected, that their campers were surprised that she had decided to leave Elm Creek Manor. It was, for the brief time they resided within its gray stone walls, the world as it should be: women of all ages, from widely varied backgrounds, coming together in harmony to create objects of beauty and comfort. Differences were not merely tolerated, but accepted and even admired. For one week, the stress and monotony of daily routines could be forgotten, and they could quilt—or read, or wander through the garden, or stay up all night laughing with friends—as their own hearts desired. Patient mentors stood by willing to pass on their knowledge; friends offered companionship and encouragement. Confidences were shared at mealtimes and in late-night chats in cozy suites or on the moonlit verandah. Resolutions were made, promises kept. Quilters took artistic and emotional risks because they knew they were safe, unconditionally accepted.

If only the same could be said of the world they would return to when the idyll was broken.

As the night darkened around them, the cornerstone patio was silent but for the murmuring of quiet voices and the song of crickets, the only illumination the flickering candle and the light of stars glowing high above them as their voices rose into the sky.

After the last quilter had held the candle and spoken, Sylvia thanked everyone for their trust and their honesty, and she bade them good night. Summer lingered to help tidy up, and then she saw her mom to the parking lot and waved goodbye from the back steps. Returning inside, she chatted a bit with some happy but yawning campers on the second-floor landing before making her way upstairs to her own snug room.

Once there, she procrastinated a bit more by unpacking her suitcase, but eventually she ran out of excuses. Retrieving her laptop from her backpack, she set it on the desk, powered it up, and paced a bit before settling into her chair.

Obviously it would have been irresponsible not to check her email in case there were urgent messages from Dr. Alvarez or her roommates, so she did that first. Julianne had written to ask how her trip had gone and to wish her well; Maricela had said much the same but had added a photo of a box of delectable pastries from Medici on 57th and the note, "Wish you were here to enjoy these with us." Summer sent off one breezy, cheerful reply to them both, but she hesitated before deciding not to tell them about her new project at Union Hall, which they would probably consider an alarming distraction from her thesis. She would tell them about it later, after the exhibit and the last pages of her thesis were both well underway.

Glancing at the nightstand clock, she heaved a sigh, braced herself, and opened the document. She read the last few pages she had written to remind herself where she had left off, correcting a word here or there. Then she flexed her fingers and rested them on the keyboard.

She slowly, painstakingly wrote a sentence.

She struggled to write another.

When more words wouldn't come, she read the first sentence again. She decided it was insipid and awkward, and so she deleted it.

She stared bleakly at the screen for another fifteen minutes, hands clenched in her lap, before saving the document and closing the laptop. Her mom was right to encourage her to take the night off after such a long and exhausting day. It was impossible to wring coherent prose out of a tired brain.

She got ready for bed, and as she turned off the lamp, climbed beneath the soft quilt, and plumped the pillow, she told herself that tomorrow would be better. It had to be.

## 5

Summer woke the next morning to the subtle creaks and distant footfalls that composed the familiar music of daybreak at Elm Creek Manor. As gentle sunlight, a soft breeze, and birdsong sifted through the curtains, she felt hope kindle that her previous night's wish for a better day might actually come true. She was home, and she had every reason to believe that a good day awaited her.

She rose and stretched, pulled on some workout clothes, and went downstairs to the rear foyer to retrieve her old yoga mat from the top shelf of the closet, where it lay buried beneath haphazard strata of winter hats, mittens, and scarves. A few minutes later she was stepping out onto the broad front verandah, inhaling deeply the cool country air, admiring the forest, backlit by the rising sun, and dew sparkling on the wildflower meadow that swept downhill toward it. She missed this view so much whenever she was away, the sublime contentment nature's beauty inspired, and the restful calm that descended upon her in the absence of the general cacophony of the city.

Soon eight other campers joined her on the verandah, some eager to begin a new day, others still blinking sleepily. After a gentle warmup, she led the class through a dynamic vinyasa flow, one of her favorites, the movements comfortingly familiar. Thirty minutes later, they were all perspiring and panting, yet vitally awake, relaxed, and happy, ready for whatever the morning might bring.

For Summer, that meant a refreshing shower, a change of clothes, and a delicious breakfast in the banquet hall, where she was again welcomed joyfully by campers and resident faculty alike. In addition to the usual buffet of fresh fruit, baked goods, and an assortment of cereal and yogurt, Anna was serving made-to-order omelets, which in Summer's case was stuffed with fresh spinach, feta cheese, and other flavorful vegetables harvested from the manor's gardens. She wouldn't tell her roommates, but as much as she loved pastries from Medici on 57th, they could not compare to Anna's culinary marvels.

About twenty minutes before the first class of the day, as the quilt campers hurried off to collect their supplies and report to their class-rooms, Gwen strolled in, laden with tote bags stuffed with demon-stration samples and instruction sheets for her students. She headed for the beverage table to refill her travel mug with tea, but she scanned the room eagerly as she crossed it, and when her gaze found Summer, her face lit up with happiness.

"Morning, Mom," Summer said, meeting her at the table and kissing her cheek, careful to avoid the steaming mug.

"Good morning, kiddo," Gwen said fondly. "Did you sleep well?"

"Very well." It was the most restful night's sleep she'd had since—well, since March, when she had returned to Elm Creek Manor for Anna and Jeremy's wedding. "May I borrow your car?" she asked, smiling to Agnes and Sylvia as they approached. "I want to measure the two samplers at Union Hall so I can order the right hanging rods and hardware."

"Oh, we have all that already," Agnes assured her. "Everything you need is in the theater, on the floor in front of the stage. Shall I call and ask some of the workers to move them to the gallery for you?"

"Thanks, but I'm sure I can manage," said Summer. "I thought I'd hang the first two quilts today, unless you'd like to approve the arrangement first. Maybe you'd like me to wait until I have enough quilts for a complete collection instead of hanging them as we acquire them?"

"That's entirely up to you, dear," said Agnes, her blue eyes amused behind her pink-tinted glasses. "I trust your judgment."

"The sooner you hang some quilts," Sylvia noted, "the sooner you can welcome visitors to the exhibit."

"Which means the Waterford Historical Society could begin charging admission and raising money." Gwen retrieved her car keys from the smallest of her tote bags and placed them in Summer's hand. "Have fun, kiddo. Wish I could help, but the classroom beckons."

"May I tag along, Summer?" asked Sylvia. "I'm not teaching today. I haven't toured the east gallery since before the renovations began. I'm eager to see the improvements."

"Of course," Summer said. "I'd enjoy the company."

"Let me fetch my purse and tell Andrew, and I'll meet you out back."

"Summer dear, you'll find the file of information about the Loyal Union Sampler in Patricia's office," said Agnes, as Sylvia hurried away. "I'm afraid the file about the Creek's Crossing Album is much thinner."

"I don't mind," Summer assured her, smiling. "I wouldn't want this project to be *too* easy."

Before long she and Sylvia were driving through the leafy wood, Summer listening, captivated, as Sylvia entertained her with stories of highlights and mishaps from the first months of the quilt camp season. Summer wished she had some amusing anecdotes of her own to share, but aside from spending time with her roommates cooking dinner together, grabbing student rush tickets for Chicago's theaters and concert halls, or getting happily lost in the Rare Books Collection at the Regenstein Library, she couldn't really say she had *enjoyed* much of the previous semester. She respected and admired her professors, and she had made a few good friends among her fellow students, but classroom discussions often resembled verbal sparring matches, crafted to expose a rival's weaknesses and impress their professors. After years of enjoying more collaborative, supportive communities, Summer found the highly competitive environment jarring. Her fellow graduate students seemed to be thriving, so obviously the problem was with her, not the program. She told herself she just needed to develop a thicker skin and get used to it, but the effort was exhausting.

Summer didn't want to burden Sylvia with her complaints, but fortunately, they reached Union Hall before Sylvia ran out of stories and Summer was obliged to offer any of her own. In the foyer, they took a moment to admire the renovations already completed and to watch the carpenters staining the replacement treads on the staircase before knocking on the door to the historical society president's office.

"Come in," a voice sang out. Just as Summer reached for the knob, the door swung open, revealing a woman in her mid-fifties, a bit short and stout, with more silvery gray than black in her wiry curls. "Sylvia, how lovely to see you again. And you must be Summer," she said, shaking Summer's hand. "I'm Patricia Escher, president of the Waterford Historical Society, but please call me Pat. We're all delighted that you're taking on this project."

"I'm delighted to be involved," Summer said, smiling.

"Let me get you those files." Pat scurried around behind her desk, stooped to pull open a drawer, and retrieved two manila folders, one about a half-inch thick, the other alarmingly flat. "We have old newspaper articles and other documentation about both quilts, but far more for the Loyal Union Sampler than the Creek's Crossing Album. My favorite is an article from the November 1863 issue of *Harper's Magazine*. 'Pennsylvania Ladies Wield Their Needles for the Union.' That was quite a find."

"I can't wait to read it," said Summer, quickly leafing through the more ample folder. "The Loyal Union Sampler placard might write itself, thanks to the work you've already done."

Pat's expression turned pensive. "What will you do for the Creek's

Crossing Album, though? We haven't turned up anything else in our archives."

"I thought I'd begin by consulting our own local expert on Abel Wright, Jeremy Bernstein." Summer had emailed him earlier that morning, and he had agreed to meet with her downtown the following day. "After that, I'm planning to read Abel Wright's books, and I'll ask the head archivist at the Waterford College Library's Rare Books Room for help finding additional resources. She and Agnes are good friends."

"Oh, excellent." Pat breathed a sigh of relief. "I've been concerned since we have so little to go on, but at least you have a plan."

Summer smiled and nodded, reluctant to dash Pat's newfound hope by warning her that this was only the beginning. Hanging and writing object cards for quilts already in their possession would be simple. Finding and acquiring additional quilts for the exhibit would likely be far more difficult.

As Summer tucked the files into her backpack, Pat unlatched the steamer trunk and removed the two precious quilts. Summer took one bundle and Pat the other, and as the carpenters paused in their work to let them pass, Sylvia led the way up the curved staircase to the east gallery, noting and admiring one perfectly refurbished feature after another.

Evidently Agnes had called ahead as promised, for a broad folding table draped with a clean white cloth had been set up at the near end of the room, the hardware for hanging the first two quilts arranged neatly on the floor beside it. Together the three women unfolded each quilt, taking measurements and closely examining the blocks. They were impressed, but not at all surprised, to discover how superbly Agnes had managed the necessary cleaning and repairs.

With Sylvia chiming in suggestions, Summer chose the ideal place to display the two quilts, side by side, visible from the entrance, so a visitor's first glimpse of the exhibit would be of the two masterpieces that had inspired it. Space remained on the wall for another quilt of similar size, as well as the three object cards Summer would write to tell museum visitors all about them.

She couldn't wait to share the quilts' fascinating stories—and to acquire more fabric treasures for the exhibit, to build a collection that would offer new insight into the history of their community, stories written with fabric and thread.

Later, on the way back to the manor, Sylvia remarked, "We're having a quilter's scavenger hunt for our evening program tonight, so perhaps you should place a Do Not Disturb sign on your door so your work isn't interrupted."

"Maybe I should." Their quilt campers didn't typically make a habit of knocking on faculty members' doors after hours, but in the frenzy of the hunt, the usual unspoken but commonly understood boundaries became a bit lax. "I'd like to finish a rough draft of the first object card before I tackle my thesis, but that might be too ambitious for one night."

"I don't know about that. I imagine you could do anything you put your mind to."

Summer could feel Sylvia studying her, but she kept her gaze on the road ahead.

"You know, Summer," Sylvia said eventually, breaking the silence, "sometimes I have creative blocks with my quilting, which I imagine is very much like your writer's block."

"You do? Really? An experienced quilter like you?"

"I think every creative person suffers from this peculiar affliction from time to time. What I've found is that it does no good to force the ideas to come. I believe it's a mistake to think of your creative source as a well that has run dry. You can't just drill down deeper until you reach the depths where the ideas are hiding."

For a moment Summer found herself dumbfounded, wondering if Sylvia could read her mind. She actually had been thinking about her problem, and its solution, in exactly that way. "But people use that metaphor all the time—'the well has run dry.'"

"I prefer to imagine creativity as an underground spring," said Sylvia. "Ordinarily the ideas, or the words, or the quilt designs, bubble up to the surface, cool, fresh, and clear, continuous and plentiful. But sometimes the source runs dry—until it is replenished by rainfall."

"Replenish an underground spring," Summer mused. She liked the image Sylvia's words evoked.

"Yes, dear. If your well is empty, you let it fill up—with fresh, new, inspiring experiences, ideas, and conversations."

"Or music and art. Or a change of scene. Or interesting new acquaintances."

"Exactly."

They approached the sign for the Elm Creek Quilts turnoff. Summer slowed the car and turned onto the gravel road that wound through the forest to the manor. "Thanks, Sylvia," she said after taking a long moment. "That might actually work. I'll try it."

Perhaps she already was replenishing her wellspring, just by coming home.

After a delicious lunch with the faculty and campers, Summer took her computer to the library, easily one of her top three favorite places at Elm Creek Manor. In Sarah's absence, Summer could have taken the desk, but instead she settled down on the sofa and spread out the notes from the Loyal Union Sampler file on the table in front of her. Before long, much to her surprise and satisfaction, she had completed an outline for the quilt's object placard. Deciding that she had earned a break, she went downstairs to the kitchen for a cup of tea and a chat with Anna while her assistants took care of dinner prep. Afterward, hoping that a change of scene would keep her imagination engaged, she returned to the library for her computer, found an old, tattered quilt in the back closet, and wandered outside until she found a secluded, grassy spot between the creek and the orchard. There she wrote and wrote and revised, undisturbed, scarcely noticing the hours passing until her computer popped up a warning that its battery was down to 1 percent. Only then did she get up, stretch, and make her way back to the manor.

Upstairs in the library, she found Sarah seated at the oak desk with James on her lap while Caroline dozed in the playpen nearby. Sarah and Matt had arranged a play area in the corner farthest from the fireplace, with a block table, two small chairs sized for little legs, a shelf of board books, an easel with a pad of paper on one side and a chalkboard on the other, and a bin full of toys and stuffed animals, everything their toddler twins might need to amuse themselves whenever Sarah had to get some work done and no one else was free to whisk them off to the third-floor nursery or outside to play.

"Need help?" asked Summer, watching Sarah struggle to type with one hand.

"Yes, please," Sarah said, brushing hair out of her eyes with the back of her hand. "Fifteen minutes to focus on these camper registrations is all I need, twenty at the most."

Summer set her computer on the nearest armchair and hurried forward to sweep James into her arms. He crowed with delight, spread his arms, and begged her to fly him around like an airplane. She swung him around—carefully—making airplane vrooming noises—quietly—while Sarah's hands flew over the keyboard. Eventually Sarah sat back with a sigh, finished, but just as Summer handed James over, Caroline woke up and begged for a turn to play airplane. Summer complied, and so she and Sarah passed the afternoon, each holding a twin. They caught up on their news, including Sarah's adventures in parenthood, Matt's ambitious plans for the estate's orchards, and Summer's new project with the Waterford Historical Society. The hours flew by as they talked and laughed and commiserated, just like old times.

Suddenly Sarah gasped and checked her watch. "Dinner began an hour ago," she exclaimed, bolting to her feet and settling Caroline on her hip. "Why didn't Matt come for the twins?"

"Maybe he lost track of time too."

"Or maybe he wanted to enjoy just one meal in peace, without the stress and distraction of child wrangling. I don't blame him. It's been ages." Sighing, Sarah inclined her head toward the French doors with her chin. "Do you mind carrying James?"

"At the moment there's nothing I'd rather do," said Summer, pretending to tickle the boy's tummy as he giggled and pushed her hand away.

They left the library and headed down the hall, but they paused at the top of the staircase at the sight of Matt coming their way, taking the stairs two at a time. He stood about a head taller than his wife, with sun-streaked, curly blond hair, a ready grin, a muscular build, and a perpetually sunburned nose from spending nearly all his time working outdoors.

"Sorry I'm late," he said, taking James from Summer's arms. "I thought I'd grab a quick dinner while I waited for you to bring the twins down. When you didn't show, I realized I was probably supposed to meet you in the library."

"That was the plan," said Sarah wryly as they headed downstairs. "Fortunately, Auntie Summer was here to help."

"Now *you* can feed and entertain the twins while Sarah relaxes," Summer teased.

Matt shrugged, grinning. "That's only fair."

The banquet hall was less formally decorated than the previous evening, but as before, eight chairs were arranged at each table, and nearly every one of them was occupied, as campers and teachers enjoyed excellent food, conversation, and laughter. The air was deliciously fragrant and the atmosphere relaxed and happy after a busy day of classes, demonstrations, and workshops. Two long buffet tables had been placed end to end along the west wall, laden with gleaming stainless-steel warming trays, platters, and baskets, all filled with the enticing bounty of Anna's kitchen.

The queue barely qualified as a line by the time Summer, Sarah,

Matt, and the twins joined it. A few latecomers like themselves were filling their plates for the first time, while several other guests were indulging in second helpings of dessert. Summer took a plate and began serving herself some polenta with chickpeas and tomatoes, balsamic grilled asparagus, and panzanella, glancing over her shoulder now and then as she considered where to sit. Two servers hurried forward to assist the McClures, filling their plates so Sarah and Matt only had to worry about holding on to their squirming twins. From there the family seated themselves at a vacant table farthest from the buffet, an exception to the usual mingling rule made out of consideration for their guests who had come to quilt camp to take a break from the small, impulsive humans in their own lives.

"I realize that my children may not be as adorable to the rest of the world as they are to me," Sarah had admitted to the other Elm Creek Quilters one afternoon the previous August, after a lunch in which the twins had been in particularly rare form, obliging Sarah and Matt to whisk them off to the kitchen so their guests could eat in peace. "Hopefully the older they get, the less disruptive they'll be."

"James and Caroline will always have a place in this kitchen," Anna had assured her, smiling. "I don't care how much food they fling. In my last job, I saw far worse behavior from fully grown adults."

But today the twins were in a delightful mood, perhaps due to all the make-believe airplane rides, so it seemed that the McClures would manage perfectly well at their small table in the corner.

As for Summer, she took the last empty chair at Maggie Flynn's table, where Vinnie and her friends were lingering over their coffee and dessert, chatting merrily about the day's adventures and their anticipation of that evening's entertainment. Vinnie and her four companions—Megan Wagner, Grace Daniels, Donna Jorgenson, and Julia Merchaud—had met at quilt camp several seasons earlier, all of them strangers except for Megan and Donna, who had become friends on an online quilting group years before they finally met in person. Since the five friends hailed from different parts of the nation, they called themselves the Cross-Country Quilters in honor of the distances they traveled to reunite at Elm Creek Manor for one fabulous week every summer. Grace visited Elm Creek Manor even more frequently, for she was a longtime friend of Sylvia's, an expert on African American quilts and a curator at the de Young Museum in San Francisco.

"I might need to seek your professional advice in the weeks ahead, Grace," said Summer, going on to describe her new project.

"I'd be happy to answer any questions you have about curating an exhibit," said Grace. She had luminous brown skin, strong cheekbones, a knowing smile, and she wore her natural, black-and-gray hair in a crown of spiral curls. "I'm familiar with Abel Wright's work as well. I'd very much like to see his wife's quilt."

"I'd very much like to see that Loyal Union Sampler," said Donna. She was in her early fifties, with a strong Upper Midwest accent and long, straight blond hair swept back into a loose bun and held in place by a blue plastic claw clip. "I love Civil War reproduction fabrics. I can't imagine anything better than a glorious assortment of *authentic* vintage prints all pieced together in an exquisite quilt."

"Nothing better? Not even Anna's chocolate espresso cannoli?" asked Vinnie, admiring what remained of a decadent pastry on her dessert plate. With a happy sigh, she took another morsel and savored it, gazing heavenward as if she believed the chef must have been divinely inspired.

Donna hesitated, glancing from Vinnie's plate to the buffet table as if contemplating whether she ought to go back for a second helping. "The cannoli is a close second, but antique quilts come first for me. Don't tell Anna."

Everyone smiled and promised they wouldn't breathe a word.

"Maybe you can stop by Union Hall to see the quilts before you head home on Saturday afternoon," Summer suggested, evoking a chorus of lamentation from her dinner companions. "What's the matter? It wouldn't be that far out of your way. I can give you directions."

"That's not the problem," said Julia Merchaud—and she was indeed *that* Julia Merchaud, winner of five Emmys and a Golden Globe, best known for her roles as Grandma Wilson in the acclaimed television drama *Family Tree* and Mrs. Dormouse in the classic, beloved children's film *The Meadows of Middlebury.* Currently she was starring as Sadie Henderson in the PBS historical drama *A Patchwork Life,* soon to embark on its fifth season. Summer remembered how aloof and out of her comfort zone Julia had been when she had first arrived at Elm Creek Manor, taking her meals in her room, skipping Candlelight. She had come to quilt camp somewhat reluctantly to learn quilting skills for a role in a different sweeping historical drama, but although she had mastered the techniques, the part had ultimately gone to a much younger actress. Fortunately, the sting of that indignity had faded long ago, and Julia adamantly insisted that she had come out ahead in the end. She had made wonderful new friends, had learned to quilt at the studio's expense, and had not had to work with "that dreadful hack of an ageist director," as she put it.

Donna nodded earnestly. "We don't talk about leaving quilt camp until the moment of our departure."

"Until then, we prefer to live in denial," said Megan. A mechanical engineer, she usually preferred a fact-based reality, but she was far from the only guest who pretended, however briefly, that quilt camp would go on forever.

"Sorry," said Summer. "I didn't mean to remind you of—that sad event we won't mention again. The exhibit is scheduled to begin at the end of August. Maybe you could come back for the grand opening?"

The Cross-Country Quilters exchanged glances, some hopeful, others uncertain.

"I do love a premiere," Julia mused.

"I might have trouble getting off work," said Megan, glum. "And Robby's old enough to get along fine without me for a week, but Lily is still so young. It's hard enough leaving her once a year—"

"Bring her along," said Vinnie. "I'd love to show off my great-granddaughter, and she can play with Sarah's twins."

"I have an exhibit opening at the de Young at that time," said Grace, "but maybe the dates won't overlap. Or I could move some things around, find someone to cover for me."

"Well, I'm in," Vinnie declared. "Reuniting with my best quilting buddies at Elm Creek Manor is the highlight of my summer, so why not do it twice?"

"I so want to join you," said Donna mournfully, "but that's when we'll be taking Becca back to college."

The friends traded rueful glances around the table.

"Well, if it doesn't work out for August, we can see the exhibit when we return to Elm Creek Quilt Camp next year," said Vinnie brightly, finishing off her cannoli. "It'll still be up next summer, won't it?"

"I'm sure it will be," Summer replied, although if everything went as she hoped, a new curator would be in charge of it by then. She herself would be in Chicago, happily engrossed in some fantastic, amazing new historical research—assuming she finished her thesis by the end of the summer.

Her thesis, still twenty pages short of completion. She felt a catch in her throat as she considered the daunting task she was putting off at her own peril. One paragraph at a time, she told herself, deliberately steering her attention back to the delicious food and pleasant company.

The Cross-Country Quilters finished their desserts and excused themselves to prepare for the scavenger hunt. Maggie too had finished eating, but she lingered at the table after the others departed. "An exhibit of local antique quilts at Union Hall is a marvelous idea," she said, her long, elegant fingers interlaced around her water glass, where only a few small ice cubes remained. Maggie looked younger than her forty years, with long waves of light brown hair held back by a tortoiseshell barrette, hazel eyes set into a gentle, oval face, and a sprinkling of freckles across her nose and cheeks. "Sarah filled me in about your struggles with your thesis. I'm sorry it's not going well at the moment, but I know you, and I know you'll get through it."

"Thanks, Maggie," said Summer. "I appreciate the vote of confidence. Ordinarily I enjoy writing, but under these circumstances—" She sat back in her chair, shrugged, and heaved a sigh, leaving the sentence unfinished—just like her thesis. Was this going to be her thing from now on? Had writer's block infiltrated even her ordinary conversation?

"I understand how you feel, at least a little," said Maggie. "It's not the same situation, but for years, my publisher has been asking me when I'm going to submit a proposal for a new pattern book."

"You can hardly blame them," said Summer. "*My Journey with Harriet* has sold more than a million copies so far, and that's not counting the translations. Do you even want to write another book, though?"

"I'd love to, but that depends upon another extraordinary stroke of good luck like the one that led me to finding Harriet Findley Birch's sampler at that garage sale." She sighed, but her comically rueful smile couldn't conceal her genuine worry. "I tell my publisher I'll write another book when I find another quilt like Harriet's."

"Have you taken to prowling Waterford's garage sales?" Summer teased.

"I've been tempted," Maggie admitted.

"Maybe you won't need to," said Summer, inspired. "What about the Loyal Union Sampler?"

Maggie's eyes widened. "Of course. That's a brilliant idea. It would be perfect—if the Waterford Historical Society would give me access to it. I'd need to take photos, measurements, to make sketches—"

"I'm sure they'd be delighted. Didn't they rely on your expertise when they first discovered the two samplers?"

"Mine and Agnes's," said Maggie modestly, sharing the credit. "Thank you so much, Summer. Isn't it wonderful how a simple conversation with a friend can help you discover possibilities you hadn't considered?"

"Yes, it really is," said Summer, remembering her chat with Sylvia earlier that day.

"I'll email Pat Escher tonight, right after the evening program. We'll have much to discuss, but I really think we could make this happen."

Summer felt a nervous flutter in her stomach as she remembered her own evening program. "I hate to miss the scavenger hunt," she said, rising, as two teenagers from Anna's part-time kitchen staff came by to bus their table. "Unfortunately, after I finish some writing for the exhibit, I have a date with an incomplete thesis."

"I'm due to help set up for the show," said Maggie, rising as well. "Are you sure you can't take one night off to relax and enjoy yourself? The campers would love to spend more time with you. So would the rest of us, especially your mom."

"Another time," said Summer, smiling to soften her words. Taking one night off, and then another, would become a habit if she wasn't careful, and it would be September before she knew it. "I need to get some writing done and get to bed at a reasonable hour. I'm leading Sunrise Yoga tomorrow morning again."

"Just like old times," said Maggie, smiling. "Good night, then."

Summer wished her good night in return and headed upstairs to her room. In many ways, it did feel like old times, but she couldn't remember ever dreading the passage of the days as she did now. Once, not long ago, every morning seemed to promise a new adventure, and she couldn't wait to see what the day would bring. Now she desperately wanted the days to slow down, not only so she would have more time to complete her thesis, but to delay her departure from this wonderful place.

She supposed this was how their campers felt, year after year.

Alone, Summer returned to her bedroom to revise the object placard for the Loyal Union Sampler until every word felt just right. As the evening waned, she heard campers passing in the hallway, chatting softly among themselves as they retired for the night. At last the object placard was as perfect as she could make it. She saved the file, stretched and yawned, and sat back in her chair, satisfied with a job well done. She hoped in the morning when she showed it to Agnes, she would be too.

She considered, for a moment, staying up late to work on her thesis, but the day had gone so well she dreaded ruining it with abject failure.

Her thesis could wait one more day. A peaceful night's rest could not.

**Loyal Union Sampler.** 98" x 98". Cotton top and backing with wool batting. Pieced, appliquéd, and quilted by the Union Quilters and the Ladies of the Elm Creek Valley, Creek's Crossing, PA, 1862. Presented to the Waterford Historical Society in memory of Faith Cunningham Morlan (1813–1882).

This distinctive sampler is an excellent example of an "opportunity quilt," a collaborative project raffled off to raise funds for a worthy cause. In 1862, in response to soldiers' letters from the front describing the hardships they endured, including inadequate clothing and shelter, poor rations, and scarce medical supplies, prominent Creek's Crossing abolitionists and suffragists Anneke Bergstrom and Dorothea Nelson led the effort to provide for the soldiers' needs. In order to raise money to build a venue where they could host more lucrative fundraisers, the Union Quilters, as the organizers and their friends called themselves, embarked upon an ambitious plan to create the *Loyal Union Sampler*. From 121 six-inch patchwork blocks contributed by quilters from throughout the Elm Creek Valley, the Union Quilters created this exquisite sampler and offered it up in a raffle, as well as the valuable patterns and templates for its blocks, earning an impressive sum that allowed them to begin construction on Union Hall.

The architect and foreman was Abel Wright, a freeborn Black dairy farmer, carpenter, and Underground Railroad conductor. When Black men were permitted to join the Union Army, he enlisted in the 6th United States Colored Infantry Regiment at Camp William Penn in Philadelphia in July 1863. He served honorably until he lost an arm fighting in the trenches at Petersburg about a year later. After the war, his memoir of his military service, *On the March with the Sixth USCT*, became the first of his six acclaimed books.

After Union Hall opened in 1863, the Union Quilters hosted many successful fundraisers in the hall's theater, garden, and galleries, with the proceeds benefiting local soldiers from the

49th Pennsylvania Infantry Regiment and the 6th United States Colored Infantry Regiment. The Union Quilters also contributed to the Veterans' Relief Fund, which provided for the wounded soldiers of the Elm Creek Valley and their families.

The Union Quilters' remarkable achievements garnered them national attention. "Pennsylvania Ladies Wield Their Needles for the Union," praised *Harper's Magazine* in November 1863, noting that not only had they organized an impressive fundraiser and construction effort, but the Union Quilters had also "formed a body corporate, meaning they themselves owned and operated Union Hall, a remarkable accomplishment for the fairer sex, which they would not have been obliged to undertake if not for the absence of their brave husbands, sons, and fathers serving in the war. The story of the Union Quilters offers yet another example of how patriotic women of the North proudly used their feminine talents to serve their country."

# 6

Summer woke to birdsong and sunshine, feeling well rested and perfectly content. It took her a moment to realize how unusual this sensation was, and then, as the weight of her unfinished thesis settled upon her again, she remembered why.

She sighed and threw back the covers as if she were flinging away the thesis itself.

Finishing the Loyal Union Sampler placard had left her with a welcome sense of accomplishment, she reflected as she brushed her teeth, threw on her workout clothes, and grabbed her yoga mat. Hurrying downstairs, greeting a few other early risers in passing, she stepped out onto the verandah to find two campers already warming up for Sunrise Yoga. When they welcomed her with bright smiles and cheerful good mornings, she didn't regret a single minute of extra sleep the night before, even though it had come at the expense of progress on her thesis. She was replenishing herself, just as Sylvia had counseled, and when her deep wellspring was restored, she had to believe the words would come.

In the meantime, she was happy to immerse herself in Agnes's project.

After another delicious breakfast amid the warm camaraderie of quilt camp faculty and students, Summer borrowed her mom's car and drove into downtown Waterford. She parked near the town square and walked a block to the Daily Grind, her longtime favorite coffee shop, to meet Jeremy. She was the first to arrive, so she joined the queue behind a dark-haired man about her own age, so intent on a well-worn paperback that he was always a few beats late to move up when customers ahead of him collected their orders and left. Summer discreetly tried to read the title to see what so enthralled him, but could only make out that it was a Gabriel García Márquez novel in the original Spanish.

When the man finally reached the counter and ordered an Americano and a blueberry scone, she couldn't help offering him a quick, approving smile when he happened to glance her way. The Daily Grind was famous for their scones and the blueberry was her favorite, although Anna's were even more delicious.

"I'd like an Italian roast with steamed almond milk," she said when the barista turned her attention to Summer. "And a blueberry scone."

The barista's face fell. "I'm so sorry," she said, her glance darting to the man ahead of Summer, who had just picked up his cup and plate and was turning to go. "We just sold the last one. Could I get you something else?"

"No, thanks, just the coffee."

The dark-haired man paused and turned around. "Here," he said, extending his plate to Summer. "You can have mine."

Summer was so surprised, she laughed. "Oh, no, thank you," she said. He had warm, dark brown eyes, and was strikingly handsome. "It's fine. First come, first served."

"Are you sure? You're welcome to it."

Summer shook her head, smiling. "I'll get one next time."

"Why wait when we could share this one?" He looked from Summer to the barista, eyebrows rising in inquiry. "Could you cut this in half, please, and get us another plate?"

The barista quickly complied, smiling indulgently, and before Summer could think of a way to decline without seeming rude, she was presented with her Italian roast and half a scone. "Thank you," Summer said to the man as she dug in her backpack for her wallet. "Let me pay you for half."

"You can get the next one," he said, flashing a quick grin and hurrying off before she could insist.

Shaking her head, amused, Summer paid for her order, gathered her things, and claimed a table near the sunny front window. She retrieved her notebook and pen from her backpack and was reviewing her notes when Jeremy arrived, pausing to hold the door for an elderly couple on their way out. She watched as he joined the queue, placed his order, and glanced around for her while the barista prepared his drink. A familiar grin lit up his face when he spotted her, and she raised her mug in a mock salute.

He joined her at the table a few minutes later, carrying a large cappuccino with nutmeg sprinkled on the foam and a massive double dark chocolate chip muffin. "Sorry I'm late," he said, setting his cup and plate on the table, taking a seat, and leaving his backpack on the floor beside his chair. "A curriculum meeting ran long."

"No worries. From what Anna says, you've been insanely busy. I'm glad you had time to meet at all."

"I'm always happy to discuss Abel Wright." Jeremy offered a wry grin. "It might surprise you to know that not everyone is as fascinated by the minutiae of his life as we are."

"I think you meant to say as *you* are," Summer teased. "I'm actually more interested in his wife, Constance, the quilter. I'm hoping that historical documentation of *his* life will shed light on *hers*."

"Then you'll be happy to know that he mentions his wife and their two sons quite frequently in his memoirs." Shaking his head, Jeremy added, "Not the first one so much."

"The memoir of his wartime service with the Sixth USCT?"

"Exactly. For most of that time, he was separated from his family, so they only appear at the beginning before he enlisted, and in the last chapter, after he recovered enough from his battlefield injuries to return home."

"I think Sarah said that his second and third books were memoirs also."

"Yes, that's right. His second book is an account of his work with the Underground Railroad in the years leading up to the Civil War. In one chapter, he describes how he brought his wife out of slavery in Virginia to freedom in Pennsylvania. He mentions a visit from the Granger family and a quilt that nineteen-year-old Dorothea Granger gave to Constance to welcome her to her new home." He shrugged. "Obviously I'm no quilt expert, but certain details in the description convinced Sarah and Maggie that the quilt absolutely had to be the Creek's Crossing Album. The passages verify the embroidered details on the back of the quilt."

"I assume that's how they were able to confirm that the quilt was unquestionably connected to Abel and Constance Wright." Summer quickly jotted down the most important details, a sketch to fill out later when she read the memoir. "What about his third book?"

"That volume focuses on his experiences during the postwar years and Reconstruction. It was the last book he wrote in Pennsylvania before the Wrights moved to Colorado. He mentions his wife and family, but I don't recall anything about Constance's quilts. As for his final three books, they're collections of essays and treatises on a variety of social and political subjects, with little information about his personal life."

"And nothing about quilts."

"I'm afraid not." Jeremy took a thick stack of papers bound by two crisscrossed rubber bands from his backpack and set it on the table between them. "This is probably more information than you need, but for what it's worth, here's the most recent draft of my dissertation. It's still a work in progress, but the notes and bibliography might be useful."

"Thank you, Jeremy." She thumbed the nearest corner of the stack, which was easily two hundred double-spaced pages. Her master's thesis seemed rather small and simple in comparison—really quite manageable, definitely something she could finish by the end of August. "There's something I've been wondering, and maybe your thesis covers this, but since I have you here—"

"Ask away."

"It sounds like Abel Wright wrote extensively about his life in Creek's Crossing in the antebellum era and in the immediate aftermath of the war. He also wrote an entire book about his wartime experiences, which I assume takes place in Pennsylvania and wherever the Sixth was deployed. And as you said, he wrote his last three books after his family moved to Colorado."

Jeremy nodded. "Yes, that's right."

"So we know *where* and *when,* but *why* did Abel Wright move from Pennsylvania to Colorado? He ran a thriving farm and a carpentry business, and he was involved in community affairs. Constance had many close friends and was active in local suffrage and civil rights organizations. One of their sons was training as a physician with Dr. Jonathan Granger, Dorothea Nelson's brother. The Wrights had extended family elsewhere in Pennsylvania. When they apparently had every reason to stay, why did they leave it all behind and start over in Colorado? The usual impetuses for western migration don't seem to apply."

Jeremy paused. "In his fourth book, Abel mentioned that his siblings and their families also settled in Colorado."

"Okay." Summer nodded, thinking. "So, did his siblings head out west first, and Abel and Constance missed them too much to stay behind? I can totally understand giving up everything and moving to a new state to reunite the family."

Jeremy shook his head slowly. "I'm fairly certain the families traveled west together and settled in the same area."

"But why?" Summer persisted, leaning forward to rest her arms on the table. "It was a dangerous, difficult journey, with no guarantee of prosperity at their destination."

Jeremy shrugged, brow furrowing. "Maybe Abel's siblings weren't as successful in Pennsylvania as he was, so he migrated for their sake. To be honest, I don't recall anything from his books that would confirm this one way or the other."

"He never offered an explanation for the move?"

"Not explicitly, not that I recall."

Summer sat back in her chair, puzzled. "That seems odd to me. I'd think that would be a rather important detail for a memoirist to include."

"Yeah." Jeremy rubbed the back of his neck, wincing. "And it seems like a rather significant omission from my dissertation."

"Sorry, I guess?"

"Are you kidding? Don't apologize. I'd rather learn that from you today at the Daily Grind than a few months from now standing before my doctoral committee with my degree on the line." He heaved a sigh and sat back in his chair, frowning thoughtfully. "This merits another close reading of his books."

"I was planning to start reading them today, after my appointment with Agnes's librarian friend," said Summer. "I can let you know what I find."

"Would you? Thanks," said Jeremy, relieved. "I owe you one."

"Only if I find something."

"If it's there, you'll find it. If it isn't there—"

"The search continues elsewhere."

As they finished their coffee, the conversation shifted to Jeremy's dissertation and his preparation for his doctoral defense, and then, inevitably, to her thesis. "I'm sorry about your writer's block," he said, lowering his voice, as if those around them, fearing contagion, would recoil in horror if they overheard. "You're a brilliant historian and you're perfectly capable of finishing your thesis. If there's anything I can do to help, please let me know."

"I'd welcome a proofreading before I turn it in."

"You got it. Just say when."

"Probably not until August." She wished it could be sooner, but that was unlikely, considering how little progress she'd made since March. "Jeremy, do you ever—" She paused and tried again. "How do you stay motivated? I know graduate school isn't supposed to be fun, and I keep telling myself that the struggle will be worth it when I have my doctorate in hand. But how do you push yourself when you don't really enjoy the work?"

He regarded her quizzically for a moment, and in his eyes she recognized the kindness and sympathy she had always found so endearing when they were together. "Is that how you feel?"

"Most days," she admitted. "Not when I first started."

"Is it just the thesis?"

"Maybe. I don't know."

He sat back and ran a hand through his unruly curls. "I wish I had some motivational secrets to share, Summer, but to be honest, I *do* really enjoy the work. Not everything and not every day, but almost always."

"Me too," she said quickly. "I'm just, you know, a bit stressed at the moment. It'll pass."

"Sure," he said, nodding, but he didn't look entirely convinced.

Soon thereafter, they parted outside the coffee shop, Jeremy to return to his cubicle in the warren of graduate student offices in the college's liberal arts building, Summer to pass through the main gates of campus and head up the hill toward the library. As an undergrad, she had comically lamented to her friends that she spent at least a third of her life in the Waterford College Library. The truth was, she had exaggerated the amount of time and greatly understated how much she enjoyed it. She always felt at home in a library, in the same way she felt entirely at ease at Elm Creek Manor and once had at Grandma's Attic. Not even her mom knew that she had chosen the University of Chicago not for the generous fellowship—other schools had offered similar incentives—but for the Regenstein Library.

At the library's main entrance, Summer swiped her alumni association card to activate the turnstile, and a familiar security guard nodded politely as she passed through to the lobby. On her right was a set of glass double doors leading into a long, spacious gallery Summer knew well, for it was the site of the Waterford Quilting Guild's annual summer quilt festival. The Rare Books Room was in the original wing of the library rather than this modern addition, so Summer headed up the central stairs to a remote section where the Waterford Historical Society had transferred its archives years before. Although nearly everyone on campus referred to it as the Rare Books Room, singular, it was actually comprised of several distinct rooms, each with varying degrees of security and restrictions, but all virtually silent except for the whisper of turning pages, the occasional muffled clearing of a throat, and the rare, intriguing gasp of discovery. One room contained map cabinets, shelves of books, and computer terminals with access to local and national databases, while a larger room across the hall offered more overflowing bookcases, as well as reading tables and study carrels, all arranged around a central U-shaped reference desk. There the librarian on duty and a student employee or two could usually be found, awaiting requests to retrieve materials from Special Collections or to recommend obscure sources where answers to all sorts of perplexing questions might be found.

The third and smallest room had undergone significant changes since Summer had last visited. As before, it was reserved for patrons who wished to examine the library's most precious volumes, fragile or exceptionally rare items that were stored in climate-controlled vaults and retrieved only upon special request, usually by professors or independent scholars who had acquired the proper clearance. But now a security guard kept watch outside its glass double doors, and, according to the sign, patrons who sought admittance had to leave their IDs at the desk and pass through an electromagnetic detection gate before entering. Through the glass, Summer glimpsed a gray-haired man engrossed in a large volume resting on a special stand that prevented the spine from fully opening. Beyond him, high on the far wall, she spotted two unobtrusive cameras. Agnes had mentioned that tighter security measures had been implemented after Abel Wright's books had disappeared, and although they just as mysteriously had been returned, the library staff was clearly taking no chances. Summer reckoned that the surest form of security would be to put Gregory Krolich under constant surveillance, but that would probably be legally and financially prohibitive.

She entered the largest room, where she found a single librarian working behind the reference desk. Summer had seen her, like the security guard at the main entrance, many times before, and had occasionally approached her with research queries, without ever exchanging names or discovering they had a dear friend in common. She looked to be in her mid-sixties, with steel-gray hair cut into a smooth, modern bob, slightly longer in the front than in the back. Her silver-rimmed cat's-eye glasses dangled around her neck on a beaded chain, different in style yet reminiscent of Sylvia's, and she wore a peach silk tunic blouse over wide-legged black trousers. She held a book open on the desk before her, and she frowned slightly as she compared a line on the page to something on her computer monitor.

Summer hung back, reluctant to interrupt, but when the librarian looked up inquiringly, Summer smiled and drew closer. "Hello," she said softly, not wishing to disturb either of the patrons reading at nearby tables. "Are you Audrey Pfenning? I'm Summer Sullivan, Agnes Emberly's friend."

The librarian's face lit up with recognition. "Oh, yes, of course, Summer Sullivan." She extended her hand for Summer to shake. "One of our most frequent patrons. Lovely to meet you officially, at long last."

"I'm glad to meet you too. Is this still a good time to chat?"

"As good as any." The librarian pressed the back of her hand to her forehead and sighed in comic exhaustion. "The summer term is always less hectic than the rest of the year, but it's been quite a day nonetheless. Tragic, even."

"I'm sorry to hear that." Summer shifted her backpack on her shoulders, concerned. "I hope no other books have gone missing."

"No, thank goodness. Not that. Our new security measures seem to be working." Audrey offered an apologetic smile. "Please excuse my lamentations. My assistant archivist gave his two-week notice this morning."

Summer recalled the tall, broad-chested blond man she had occasionally seen behind the reference desk, although he would have looked equally at home in the athletic director's office. "Oh, that's too bad."

"For me and my department, indeed it is, but for Bradley, it's wonderful news. His partner, an associate professor here, was just hired away by the University of Delaware, and they offered Bradley an excellent position in their main library to sweeten the deal." She folded her hands on the desktop. "I'm trying my absolute best to be thrilled for them both instead of selfishly dismayed for myself. But you didn't come here to console me while I mope. Agnes says you're interested in learning more about our renowned local author Abel Wright?"

"Yes, although I'm really most interested in his wife, Constance," said Summer. "I'd like to begin by reading Abel's memoirs, but if you can recommend any other resources that might mention her, I'd be grateful."

"I'm less familiar with Constance, but I do recall that she was active in one of the Elm Creek Valley's first suffrage groups. Perhaps that connection will help us turn up more information. But first, let me fetch those memoirs so you can start reading." Audrey gestured to the numerous unoccupied tables. "Please sit anywhere. I'll bring them to you."

Summer thanked her and found a seat at a table near the back, switched on the brass desk lamp, and took out her notebook and pen. She had barely settled in when Audrey returned with the three volumes. Summer began with the Civil War memoir, delighting in the familiar names she discovered in the early chapters set in Creek's Crossing. She was well past the midpoint when hunger compelled her to leave the library for a quick bite of lunch at Chuck's Diner, right across the street from the main gates to campus. Returning to the library to pick up where she had left off, she read through the afternoon, finishing the last page with moments to spare and returning to Elm Creek Manor in time for dinner.

The next morning, again after a refreshing good night's sleep, yoga, and a scrumptious breakfast, she returned to the Rare Books Room and spent the day reading Abel Wright's second memoir. She took copious notes, broke for lunch, finished the book, and stayed until closing in order to get a head start on the third volume. It was long past twilight when she finally returned to Elm Creek Manor, and as she entered the rear foyer, the distant sounds of music and laughter told her that the evening program was well underway. Stomach rumbling, she made haste for the kitchen, where Anna had stowed labeled containers of leftovers in the stainless-steel commercial refrigerator, enough for a modest feast. Fixing herself a plate, she heated it up in the microwave while the kettle warmed, then settled into one of the booths to read Jeremy's dissertation while she ate.

A few hours and two cups of tea later, her mom stopped by to pick up the car keys and bid her good night. "Any breakthroughs?" she asked, taking a seat in the booth opposite Summer.

"I've learned a lot about the Wright family," said Summer, setting Jeremy's dissertation aside and rubbing her eyes, unable to suppress a yawn. "I have nearly everything I need to write the object placard, but I still have questions."

"Such as?"

"I haven't stumbled over a single sentence that explains why the family left Pennsylvania for Colorado, or, more curiously yet, why Constance would have left such a lovely quilt behind."

Gwen nodded, thoughtful. "I've been wondering about that too.

It's in excellent condition. Someone evidently valued it enough to care for it properly before it wound up in a trunk in Union Hall."

"Yes, but *who* cared for it? It couldn't have been Constance. She was in Colorado."

"My guess is someone who cared about Constance, or someone who cared about quilts, or both." Rising from the booth, Gwen squeezed Summer's shoulder affectionately and kissed the top of her head. "If anyone can figure it out, you will."

Summer hoped so, but by the time she finished reading Jeremy's dissertation and went upstairs to bed, she had pages of notes, several theories, but no conclusions.

"Not only was the Creek's Crossing Album an exquisite quilt, but it surely had great sentimental value," Summer mused aloud the next morning at breakfast, with Gretchen and the six campers seated at their table forming a rapt audience. "It had been given to her in honor of her marriage by the woman who became her best friend in Creek's Crossing. That's not something you simply forget to pack."

"Maybe she gave it back to Dorothea before she left?" one of the campers ventured. The general consensus around the table, expressed in the shaking of heads and murmurs of doubt, was that the return of such a lovely wedding gift would have been a very strange thing between friends. Wouldn't the quilt have become even more precious to Constance through the years, a memento of the beloved friend she might never see again?

Later that morning, Summer arrived at the Rare Book Room only minutes after the library opened and settled down with Abel Wright's third memoir. She finished it by noon without finding the answers she had sought. When she returned the book to the reference desk, Audrey studied her expression and said, "No answers within these pages, I presume?"

"Many answers, but not every answer I need." Summer paused to fasten her backpack while the librarian checked in the book. "Maybe I'm searching in the wrong place. We know that the Wright family was still in Pennsylvania in early 1882, and they had settled in Denver by 1884. If I could use census records to narrow down when they left—"

"I'm afraid that might be impossible," said Audrey. "Pennsylvania never had a state census, and most federal census records for 1890 were destroyed by fire in 1921." She hesitated, frowning thoughtfully. "Several years ago, I helped compile research for a professor studying the African diaspora in central Pennsylvania. I recall that 1882 was a particularly dreadful year for Black families in the Elm Creek Valley. Several moved from Creek's Crossing to Grangerville, where there was a larger, thriving Black community, while others left the county altogether."

"Really? Why?" Several notable events of that year quickly came to mind—a recession had begun, the Chinese Exclusion Act had passed, lynchings continued to be a terrible scourge in the South, but Summer didn't recall anything specific to their county that would have affected Black citizens more than their white neighbors.

Audrey sighed. "It's hardly our proudest moment. I'm not surprised schools don't include it in the sixth-grade local history curriculum."

"Maybe they do now, but for me, sixth grade was a long time ago." Intrigued, Summer leaned forward, resting her arms on the tall desk between them. "What happened here in 1882?"

"The Ku Klux Klan happened."

"What?" Summer exclaimed, startling the other scholars. After offering them apologetic looks, she turned back to Audrey, lowered her voice, and said, "The Klan, here?"

"Unfortunately, yes."

Summer shook her head, astounded. "If we were talking about the 1920s, I wouldn't be so surprised. The Klan was exploiting anti-Catholic and anti-immigrant sentiment just about everywhere in the twenties. But you're saying they were already in Pennsylvania in the 1880s?"

"They were making incursions," Audrey clarified. "They were firmly established in the South and wanted to gain a foothold in Northern states as well. Klansmen would travel here from Southern states to hold rallies and promote themselves as a fraternal organization, a lodge system like the Masons or the Elks. During those excursions, they would harass and threaten our Black citizens."

"Of course they did." Summer inhaled deeply, tamping down her anger. "Dare I hope local authorities and the press condemned them?"

"Many did so," Audrey assured her, but then she frowned. "However, eventually enough local men joined the Klan so that it was no longer necessary to send recruiters from the South."

"I wish I could say I'm surprised." Could the rising threat of the Klan, in a place Abel Wright had once assumed was safely beyond their reach, have convinced him to move his family out west? "I'd like to see what I can find in the *Creek's Crossing Informer* from 1882. Wait, that's not right—by then the town had changed its name. I need to see the microfilm for the *Water's Ford Register,* please."

Audrey smiled approvingly and sent her lone student employee to retrieve the microfilm.

Summer was very familiar with the library's microfilm readers, and with the layout of the *Register* itself, thanks to her past research for Sylvia. She spent the rest of the day scrolling through the grainy, gray-scale images of the old newspaper pages, taking occasional breaks to stretch her legs and rest her eyes, pacing in the hallway outside the room and mulling over what she knew and all she hoped to find. Although she had discovered several advertisements for Bergstrom Thoroughbreds, which she printed out for Sylvia, and many interesting articles she wished she had time to explore further, she found nothing on the subject of her search.

When the usual announcement came over the PA system that the library would be closing in fifteen minutes, Summer reluctantly shut down the reader and returned the boxes of microfilm to the student working the late shift at the reference desk. "These you can put away," she said, smiling tiredly as she handed over the boxes from January through July. "I'll need these others back first thing tomorrow morning."

"I'll keep them here at the desk with a sticky note so no one else can request them," the student said with a conspiratorial grin.

Summer thanked her and made her weary way home.

Over a cup of chamomile tea in the manor's kitchen—where she found a bleary-eyed Sarah sipping coffee as she studied various spreadsheets and ledgers—she began drafting the Creek's Crossing Album object label. After several days of intense study, she had gathered enough material to write a good description of the quilt, but without a clear explanation of why the Wrights had left the Elm Creek Valley and why Constance had left her beautiful quilt behind, the label felt unsatisfyingly incomplete. In the absence of irrefutable proof, Summer would have settled for a plausible theory, but she lacked even that.

Tomorrow, revived by sleep, yoga, and breakfast, she would try again.

Muffling a yawn, she rose, took her teacup to the dishwasher, and returned to her booth to load her notebooks and papers and pens into her backpack. "You should go to bed," she advised Sarah, slipping one strap over her shoulder and heading for the door.

"*You* should go to bed," Sarah retorted comically, pulling a face. "I'm used to sleepless nights. You're not."

Summer smiled and bade her friend good night.

The next morning, after Sunrise Yoga and a quick shower, instead of a leisurely breakfast in the banquet hall, Summer downed a cup of coffee and a delicious blueberry muffin in the kitchen and hurried off for the Waterford College Library as soon as her mom arrived and she could nab the car keys. Mere moments after the Rare Books Room opened, she reclaimed her microfilm from the reference desk, spooled up the next roll, and resumed her search.

It took hours, but eventually she found the answers she sought, or enough for that plausible theory.

On the second page of the August 10 morning edition of the *Register,* a single paragraph announced a rally of the Knights of the Ku

Klux Klan to be held on the town square two days later. The next day, a letter to the editor appeared on the front page just beneath the fold, written by Cyrus Pearson, a former resident of Creek's Crossing who was returning to town to lead the meeting. He offered a wildly idealized description of his "fraternal order," as he called it, and encouraged interested gentlemen to attend the rally to learn more. He concluded by sternly condemning the "ungracious, prejudiced, political Ladies" who had refused to let the Klan reserve Union Hall for their event.

Summer knew which ladies he meant, and she knew Cyrus Pearson too. According to Gerda Bergstrom's memoir, she had thoroughly despised him, even before he led slave catchers to Elm Creek Farm to recapture the fugitive woman sheltering there. Afterward, disgraced and notorious, Cyrus Pearson and his mother had left Creek's Crossing for the "friendlier climes" of the South, and Gerda wrote no more of him. Summer was astounded that he had dared show his face in the Elm Creek Valley after the Civil War. Perhaps cruelty, spite, and his confidence in the strength of his mob's numbers had emboldened him.

Two days after the letter had appeared, the *Register* had published an article with a stark headline that took Summer's breath away: "Local Colored Family's Farmhouse Ransacked & Set Ablaze."

Heart pounding, she read the article and printed copies to add to her steadily accumulating pile. She read on through November, when references to the Wright family slowed and then ceased. Then she returned the microfilm to the reference desk and swiftly left the library, calling Jeremy from her cell phone the moment she stepped outside.

They met at the Daily Grind, arriving at nearly the same time. "I'll get drinks, you grab a table and catch your breath," Jeremy said as he pulled the door open. She nodded, gulping air; she had come twice as far and run all the way.

By the time he joined her at the table, carrying an Italian roast with steamed almond milk for her and cappuccino for himself, she had arranged the articles in chronological order on the table between them. "It's all here," she declared, gesturing. "A group of KKK thugs led by Cyrus Pearson held a rally in the town square in August 1882. Abel, Constance, and their sons were among the local citizens who gathered to protest. While the Wrights were away from their farm— which Cyrus Pearson surely had anticipated—someone, probably several men, broke into their house and stable and set them on fire. The Wrights arrived home to find the barn nearly engulfed, but they managed to extinguish the blaze in time to save most of the house. They reported 'numerous household goods and valuables' and two horses were missing." Summer tapped a paragraph in the printout. "I'm sure the Creek's Crossing Album was among the stolen items."

Jeremy studied the article, resting his chin in his hand as he read. "If the quilt never left Creek's Crossing," he said, eyes fixed on the page, "that would suggest that the thief, and therefore at least one of the arsonists, wasn't some interloper from the South but a local man."

"I had the same thought," said Summer. "I couldn't say who it was, but I'm sure they were acting on Cyrus Pearson's orders. He hated the Wrights and their friends, including the Bergstroms. I can't believe it was mere coincidence that the Wrights were the victims of this hate crime."

"They might have been targeted simply because of their remote location. Fewer witnesses, better opportunity." Jeremy sighed and ran a hand through his unruly curls, his gaze sweeping over the articles. "Still, it's reasonable to conclude that this attack convinced the Wrights to move to a more hospitable region."

"Advertisements for the sale of the Wright farm begin appearing in the *Register* in mid-September," said Summer, indicating the relevant pages. "By late November, the ads have ceased."

"We can assume the farm had sold by then. It would have been difficult to move to Colorado with winter approaching. They could have done it, or maybe they stayed with family for a few months and moved in the spring." He glanced up from the papers and grinned, shaking his head in admiration. "I can't thank you enough, Summer. It's not irrefutable evidence, like a handwritten letter to Hans Bergstrom explaining why he was leaving town—"

"For all we know, a letter like that is lying around Elm Creek Manor somewhere, tucked into a book in the library or lying at the bottom of a trunk in the attic, awaiting discovery."

"—but it does give us a plausible theory," Jeremy finished, amused. "This is exactly what my dissertation needs, and I didn't even know such a crucial piece was missing until you asked the right questions."

Summer shrugged. "If I can't write my own thesis, I'm happy to help you with your dissertation."

"You *can* write yours," Jeremy said emphatically. "You can and you will. Just take it one paragraph at a time."

She considered. "How about one *sentence* at a time?"

"That'll get you there too."

"You're not wrong," she replied, but it was so much easier said than done.

They examined her notes and the newspaper articles as they finished their coffee, then Jeremy returned to his office and Summer drove back to the manor. Invigorated by her successful historical detective work, she took her computer to the library, settled down on the sofa, and, referring to both her extensive notes and Gerda's memoir, completed the first draft of the Creek's Crossing Album object label just in time for supper. Afterward, she gave in to the Cross-Country Quilters' entreaties and stuck around for the evening program, a concert by a jazz quintet from the Waterford College Music Department. Julia Merchaud surprised campers and faculty alike by joining the ensemble as a vocalist for "When Sunny Gets Blue" and "The 'In' Crowd," in the style of Ramsey Lewis, earning fond, enthusiastic applause.

After the concert, Sylvia took the stage and announced that the last breakfast of the week would be served on the cornerstone patio, where they had held the Candlelight ceremony. "We'll have one more good chat before you leave," she said. "Bring something you made this week for show-and-tell."

Then she bade them good night.

As the campers drifted off to go to bed, or perhaps to stay up all night chatting with friends, Summer stayed behind to help the other Elm Creek Quilters tidy up. Then, still buoyed from the day's success, she withdrew to her own room, softly closed the door, and frowned thoughtfully at her computer, plugged in and charging on the desk where she had left it before dinner.

Inhaling deeply, steeling herself, she opened her thesis, scrolled down to the end, and read the last few paragraphs. An hour passed as she painstakingly wrote two more paragraphs, one sentence at a time.

It wasn't much progress, but it was something. The attempt itself mattered. The *work* mattered. Injustices from the past still resonated in the present, and she had uncovered a story worth sharing.

One sentence at a time, she would tell it.

**Creek's Crossing Album.** 98" x 98". Cotton top and backing with cotton batting. Appliquéd by Dorothea Granger, quilted by Constance Wright, Creek's Crossing, PA, 1850.

This exquisite sampler quilt is reminiscent of the distinctive variety of appliqué sampler that originated in the Baltimore, Maryland, region in the early nineteenth century and was especially popular from approximately 1840–1860. Baltimore Album quilts presented highly stylized images drawn from botanical, patriotic, nautical, and other themes, often signed by the maker and embellished with embroidery, ink drawings, and other fine needlework. Baltimore Album blocks are typically rendered in a flat, two-dimensional style, but the *Creek's Crossing Album* employs perspective to create more realistic scenes of daily life in the Elm Creek Valley. This intriguing variance suggests that the artist did not learn of this new, fashionable style from more experienced Baltimore Album quiltmakers or by observing finished Baltimore Album quilts, but through secondhand descriptions or sketches. It is also possible that the quiltmaker was well aware of the norms, but deliberately departed from them to suit her own artistic vision.

According to the inscription embroidered on the back of the quilt, *Creek's Crossing Album* was a collaboration between Dorothea Granger, who completed the top in 1849, and Constance Wright, who quilted and finished the sampler in 1850. The inscription also notes that the quilt was a gift from Dorothea Granger in honor of Constance Wright's 1847 marriage, and that the quilt was presented to her two years later. A memoir written by Underground Railroad conductor and Civil War veteran Abel Wright, Constance's husband, confirms that Constance was enslaved in Virginia until he bought her freedom and brought her home to his farm, which was on the outskirts of Creek's Crossing at the time, but would now fall within the Waterford city limits.

Constance Wright and Dorothea Granger (who took the name Dorothea Nelson upon her marriage) were active abolitionists, suffragists, and members of the Union Quilters, a group of Elm Creek Valley women who organized the funding and construction of Union Hall. The Nelson family remained in the area for generations afterward, but in late 1882 or early 1883, the Wright family sold their farm and moved to Colorado, where they settled in the Denver area alongside members of Abel's extended family. Although neither Abel nor Constance left behind a written record of their reasons for leaving Creek's Crossing, on August 11, 1882, their farmstead came under attack while the family was away at the town square, protesting at a KKK rally. In their absence, an unidentified person or group ransacked their property and set fire to the buildings, destroying the barn and seriously damaging the residence. Two horses and numerous valuables and household items were reported stolen; it is possible that the *Creek's Crossing Album* was one of these stolen objects. The quilt's location during the interim between the Wright family's departure and its discovery in Union Hall in 2003 has not been determined, but one possibility is that it remained in the thief's possession for many years, perhaps even changing hands several times between unwitting buyers or heirs until it was donated to the Waterford Historical Society.

In time, additional research into the remarkable lives of Dorothea Granger Nelson and Constance Wright may illuminate the mysterious provenance of their extraordinary quilt.

# 7

Although the next morning dawned humid and overcast with a distant rumble of thunder in the west, Summer's heart was sunny, the clouds that had shadowed her finally breaking. She had finished another object label for Agnes, and she had, at long last, resumed work on her thesis. She wasn't sprinting to the finish line—more like crawling—but any forward progress would bring her closer to her goal.

She might actually finish her thesis in time to begin her doctoral program on schedule after all.

Pulling on her workout clothes, she snatched up her yoga mat and headed downstairs, humming a tune from the previous night's jazz concert as she crossed the marble foyer. Outside on the verandah, she found her two most dedicated students warming up, conversing quietly, and they glanced up and smiled when Summer greeted them. Four other campers soon joined them, but although they seemed to enjoy the flow as much as they had the previous day, Summer detected wistfulness in her students' smiles, eyes that shone with something other than merriment. She understood perfectly. The last day of the camp week was difficult for everyone, even those who had already resolved to return the following summer.

After yoga, Summer showered and slipped into a blue, yellow, and white madras sundress, then hurried downstairs to the kitchen to help Anna and her staff set up for the Farewell Breakfast. "Are we still on the patio?" she asked, tying on an apron. "I thought I heard thunder."

"The forecast calls for scattered thunderstorms, but not until one o'clock," said Anna, peering through an oven window to check on the deliciously fragrant herbed red potatoes roasting inside. "Farewell Breakfast on the cornerstone patio is such an important tradition that we've decided to go for it. Jeremy promised to keep an eye on the weather radar and call my cell if anything changes."

"I'll be ready to grab some serving dishes and sprint inside if the rain arrives ahead of schedule," Summer promised. Anna thanked her with a smile before turning away to issue instructions to her sous chef.

Donning a pair of oven mitts, Summer carried a tray of miniature spinach and feta omelets from the kitchen, down the hallway through the west wing, and out to the cornerstone patio. There Matt, Andrew, and Joe had arranged chairs and tables, which Sylvia and Gretchen were draping in cheerful blue-and-white-checkered tablecloths. They all bustled through their well-practiced preparations as quickly and efficiently as they could. The campers weren't supposed to arrive for another twenty minutes, but a few invariably appeared earlier, unable to contain their curiosity. Although their guests were encouraged to explore most of the estate, by Sylvia's personal decree, gatherings on the cornerstone patio were limited to the Candlelight ceremony and the Farewell Breakfast. The aura of mystery made the patio all the more tantalizing, but the Elm Creek Quilters had learned to graciously deflect their guests' appeals to hold classes or evening programs there. Sylvia's friends understood that she wanted to reserve her mother's favorite place on the estate for special occasions and for her own private reflection. Considering how generously Sylvia had contributed to the quilting community, Summer thought it perfectly reasonable for her to keep one special place mostly for herself, without being obliged to apologize or explain.

Summer hurried back and forth from the patio to the kitchen carrying baskets of croissants fresh from the oven, bowls of fruit salad, and carafes of hot coffee and tea. Campers greeted her in passing, some cheerfully, most already wistful. Summer offered bright smiles to everyone, promising them a delicious breakfast and fun with friends very soon.

At last, Summer left her apron behind in the kitchen and joined the other Elm Creek Quilters on the cornerstone patio, mere moments ahead of the first campers, whom they welcomed and encouraged to help themselves at Anna's marvelous buffet. Delicious aromas wafted and, more distantly, insects droned in the warm, heavy air that promised a stormy day to come. Their guests, soon to depart, would miss the worst of it, but Summer suspected many would be willing to endure less than ideal weather for one more day of quilt camp.

Before long, everyone had gathered on the patio, the mood subdued and nostalgic. Summer could read their guests' mixed emotions in their smiles and glances; they missed their families back home, but Elm Creek Quilt Camp had fulfilled their fondest wishes and exceeded every expectation, and they couldn't bear to see the week draw to a close. Summer hoped they knew that they could return next year, and every year, to find inspiration and friendship within the strong, gray stone walls of Elm Creek Manor.

Anna's cooking was as sublimely delicious as ever, and the campers seemed especially reluctant for the meal to end, savoring every morsel and lingering over their coffee. But eventually, after the servers quietly swept in to clear the dishes and move the tables aside, Sylvia invited their guests to arrange their chairs in a circle in the center of the patio.

It was time for show-and-tell, one of the most poignant, gratifying moments of quilt camp for the faculty; for the campers, it offered a last opportunity for reflection and sharing. Sylvia began by explaining for the newcomers how show-and-tell would unfold. Each quilter would display something she had made that week and share her favorite memory of Elm Creek Manor, often referring to the hopes she had expressed at the Candlelight welcoming ceremony and how they had been fulfilled—or not, which often made for the most interesting and amusing stories. Through the years, Summer had observed that even the novice quilters could proudly display their simple pieced blocks or partially assembled tops, for which they received ample praise and encouragement. Yet it was the stories quilters shared of the moments they would cherish when the summer sunshine was only a memory that sent the campers into gales of laughter and sometimes made them blink away tears. As each camper spoke in turn, Elm Creek Quilters would look on from outside the circle, proud and honored to know that they had contributed to each quilter's journey, both within the classroom and outside it. Yet it seemed to Summer that the campers learned as much from one another as they did from the faculty, lessons that might have little to do with quilting, but would resonate with them long after they returned home.

Sylvia glanced around the circle, eyebrows raised in inquiry. "Would anyone care to—"

"I'll go first!" Vinnie declared, raising her hand so quickly she almost knocked off her baseball cap, blue today, to match her striped blouse.

A ripple of laughter went up from the group. Amused, and not at all surprised, Sylvia gestured graciously to indicate that Vinnie should proceed.

Beaming, Vinnie held up a flawless New York Beauty block, stitched from a whimsical selection of bright, multicolor plaids and vivid Amish solids. "I'm especially delighted with this block, which I hope will be the first of enough for a new lap quilt for my screen porch," she declared, holding up the twelve-inch block for all to admire, a complex design of arcs, wedges, and triangular shapes with curved bases. "Why is it so special to me, and why don't you remember seeing a New York Beauty class on the schedule? Well, to answer the second question first, there wasn't one. I learned how to paper piece the triangle arches in Gwen's Foundation Paper Piecing class, and I improved my curved sewing skills in Gretchen's Ahead of the Curve workshop. Just for fun, I threw both skills together and came up with this." Holding the block higher, she shifted in her seat so everyone around the circle could take a proper look. "To answer the first question last, this block is special to me because on a whim, just to satisfy my curiosity, I put together two things that wouldn't seem to fit, and I discovered that they actually work together beautifully. Making this block taught me that I shouldn't ever let my assumptions and habits prevent me from seeing new possibilities." With an emphatic nod, she set her block down in her lap and turned to the quilter on her right, smiling brightly. "Your turn, Megan dear."

"Not quite yet," said Sylvia, raising a finger. "Tell us, Vinnie, what was your favorite memory from this week?"

"Oh, goodness. I usually say my surprise birthday party was my favorite part, and I forgot to come up with something else." Vinnie paused briefly to think. "My favorite memory is enjoying Anna's chocolate espresso cannoli for dessert on Monday night. They were absolutely heavenly." When the others burst out laughing, Vinnie joined in, protesting, "They were! Anna should have her own cooking show on television."

"No, thank you," Anna called out emphatically from her place near the recently cleared buffet table, provoking more laughter.

When the merriment subsided, Megan glanced around the circle and held up two six-inch blocks pieced in soft, neutral tone-on-tone prints, patterns Summer recalled from Maggie's *Harriet's Journey* quilts. "Like Vinnie, I decided to try something new this week. I usually prefer one-patch quilts, sometimes scrappy, other times with a modern twist, but my friend Donna persuaded me to get out of my rut—"

"I didn't say you were in a rut," Donna broke in, blushing. "I'm sure I said 'branch out' or 'stretch your creative wings,' or something less insulting like that."

"Maybe I misquoted you," Megan acknowledged, with a teasing grin. Turning back to the group, she added, "However Donna put it, I took her advice to heart, and so we signed up for Maggie's sampler class together. It really challenged me, and I learned so much that I plan to make the remaining ninety-eight blocks in the months ahead."

"And I look forward to seeing your completed quilt," said Maggie. "Perhaps next summer?"

"Maybe not quite that soon," said Megan, "but eventually. As for my favorite memory of quilt camp, it's the same as last year—the wonderful, joyful, annual reunion with my best quilting friends. Every year, these long-enduring friendships become more precious to me, and I'm so thankful we decided years ago to meet in person every summer and renew them."

"Oh, I should have said that," lamented Vinnie, clasping her hands together in her lap. "I feel the same way. Can I change my answer?"

"I'm sorry, no," said Sylvia, clearly trying not to laugh. "We have to move on. Why not save that answer for your next visit?"

Vinnie nodded, satisfied, so Sylvia beckoned the next quilter to share.

One by one, each camper proudly showed off a new creation, from the first row of a T-shirt quilt Molly had begun, to the very nicely stitched State Fair block Maggie's longtime fan had pieced, to the simplest blocks the novice quilters had made. As for favorite memories, the Candlelight on their first evening together was mentioned fondly, as were the late-night chats in their cozy suites and the private moments spent strolling through the beautiful grounds.

Donna seemed to sum up the consensus of the group when she said, "As many times as I've visited Elm Creek Manor, and as much as I've tried to describe for my family and friends back home how magical this place is, they never quite understand." She paused to look around the circle, taking in the murmurs and nods of affirmation. "They wouldn't understand how restful and nurturing it is to be among people who understand our passion for quilting, who realize that the bonds that unite us are so much stronger than the dozens of petty differences that divide us."

"Well said," another quilter murmured.

"Words to live by," another chimed in.

"The whole world should go to quilt camp," Vinnie declared, and soft laughter rose into the warm summer air.

A hush fell over the cornerstone patio then, and someone sighed. Every quilter had taken her turn to share her handiwork and her memories. The week of camp had drawn to a close, and it was time to depart, to return to the families and homes they loved and missed. Summer trusted that each of their guests would carry the spirit of Elm Creek Quilts with them in their hearts.

The quiet was broken by a low, ominous rumble of thunder.

Everyone gave a start, and Sylvia clapped her hands together twice for attention. "Friends, I believe that's our cue to head indoors. If you have any questions about checkout procedures, Sarah will meet you in the foyer."

Chattering excitedly, glancing warily up at the sky, the campers hurried inside while Sylvia held the door open for them, and the other Elm Creek Quilters swiftly put away chairs and tables, finishing just as the first heavy raindrops began to strike the gray stones beneath their feet. Summer returned to the kitchen, where an extra pair of hands never went amiss, while her colleagues dispersed to other duties. She knew that meanwhile, the campers were returning to their suites to finish packing and to bid their newfound friends sad goodbyes. They carried suitcases and tote bags downstairs, Sarah collected room keys, and Matt loaded luggage into the Elm Creek Quilts minivan for the first shuttle ride to the bus station and airport.

Gradually the upstairs halls fell silent, and the back parking lot emptied.

Alone again, the Elm Creek Quilters went from room to room in pairs, collecting linens, emptying trash, discovering forgotten items under beds or in drawers. When the professional cleaning crew arrived to do the manor's weekly deep cleaning and thorough scrubbing, the friends washed the dust and sweat from their hands and faces and broke for a simple lunch of salads and sandwiches, which they enjoyed in the shelter of the verandah's high roof. As rain pattered overhead and on the circular drive, empty now, they reminisced about the week past, sharing amusing stories about their favorite campers and unexpected classroom mishaps. Afterward, they regrouped in the library to discuss the next week's agenda—changes to the course schedule, registration numbers, plans for evening programs, campers with particular needs they should all be aware of, and so on. An hour passed before Sylvia and Sarah declared that they had covered everything, and the meeting was adjourned. Except for the usual chores that they saved for Sunday mornings, they were ready to welcome a new group of guests the following day, when a new week of camp would begin.

Diane let out a weary cheer at the news, and the other Elm Creek Quilters chimed in with laughter. Congratulating one another on another successful week, they made their way downstairs to the kitchen to refresh themselves with lemonade and iced tea, except for Sarah, who bade her friends goodbye and hurried off in search of Matt and the twins. Soon thereafter, when Jeremy arrived to pick up Anna, she too departed with a cheerful promise to see them all bright and early the next day. Gwen gave Summer a warm hug and ordered her not to stay up too late working, and then she too headed home. Moments later Agnes set off with Diane, who always gave her a ride, leaving the permanent residents of Elm Creek Manor plus Summer behind.

Saturday was Anna's night off, so by long-standing tradition, they would fend for themselves for dinner, enjoying leftovers that would suffice for fine gourmet dining anywhere else. Dinner was hours away yet, though, so as the sky darkened and thunder pealed, and flashes of lightning illuminated the steady rainfall, Maggie excused herself, smiling shyly as she explained that her long-distance boyfriend, Russell, was eagerly awaiting a phone call. Gretchen set out to join her husband in his workshop, pulling on galoshes, retrieving the sturdiest umbrella from the back closet, and braving the storm to make her way to the red barn on the other side of the bridge over Elm Creek.

"Well, it looks like it's just us," Sylvia remarked to Summer from the far end of the other side of the refectory table. "How do you plan to spend the rest of the afternoon? Toiling away at your thesis, I presume?"

She probably should, but she'd rather not. "Maybe later. For now, if you don't already have plans with Andrew, I could really use your help with the Union Hall project."

"I'd be delighted. How can I help?"

"You're a longtime resident of the Elm Creek Valley and a master quilter, so I hoped you could recommend some quilts I ought to include in the exhibit, and where I might search for them." A bit tentatively, Summer added, "I was also hoping you might be willing to contribute a quilt or two from the Bergstrom family collection."

Sylvia regarded her appraisingly over the rims of her glasses. "I might be persuaded to lend you a quilt or two, with the understanding that they would be well cared for and would be returned to me if and when the exhibit closes."

"Of course. I'm sure Agnes would personally guarantee it."

"Did you have a particular Bergstrom quilt in mind?"

"Given the theme of the exhibit, something that played an important role in local history would be ideal," said Summer. "I know it's a big ask, but would you be willing to lend us the quilts you found in Anneke's hope chest?"

"A big ask, you say." Sylvia's eyebrows rose. "That's an understatement indeed."

"You can't blame me for trying. Even one of those quilts would elevate the educational and cultural value of the exhibit tremendously. If it's too much, you can decline. Really. No hard feelings."

"Summer, my dear," said Sylvia, her gaze turning mirthful. "You're going to have to work on your pitch if you hope to persuade *strangers* to lend you their quilts. You're almost talking *me* out of it, and I'm a friend."

"Sales and marketing was never my thing," Summer reminded her. "That's Sarah's department. But I appreciate the critique. I promise to write up a very convincing pitch and rehearse it before I meet with the next potential donor."

"An excellent idea." Sylvia cupped her chin in her hand, thinking. "I'm afraid I'd have to decline to lend you the Underground Railroad and the Birds in the Air. They're simply too fragile for public display."

"Of course." Summer quickly smiled to hide her disappointment. "I understand."

"Gerda's Log Cabin, on the other hand . . ." Sylvia fell silent, mulling it over. "It's in excellent condition, given its age. I don't believe it was ever used on a bed."

"That's my impression too. Gerda suggested as much in her journal."

Sylvia planted her hands on the tabletop and rose. "Shall we go have a look at it?"

"Absolutely." Quickly Summer bounded to her feet. "Lead the way."

Together they made their way to the ballroom, the west wing hallway and the foyer seeming strangely hushed, the only sound the rain falling outside and the echo of their footsteps. "I always forget how quiet it can be around here without the campers bustling about," Sylvia remarked as Summer opened one of the double doors of the ballroom entrance for her. "It makes me want to romp around with the twins in the nursery for a bit. They certainly know how to liven up a room."

"That they do," said Summer. "No doubt that's why Sarah so rarely allows them in this one. Too much potential for mischief with all the rotary cutters, needles, and other shiny, sharp objects lying around."

Sylvia beckoned Summer to follow her across the room, the largest in the manor, spanning the width of the south wing like the library above it. Rectangular windows topped by semicircular curves, narrow in proportion to their height, lined the south, east, and west walls. A carpeted border roughly twenty feet wide encircled a broad parquet dance floor, which during the camp season was covered with padded, removable carpeting, not only to protect the wood beneath but to pamper the feet and knees of quilters who might be standing at various workplaces throughout the day. The room was subdivided into classrooms by movable partitions, each small space filled with an assortment of sewing machines, overhead projectors, felt design boards, ironing stations, cutting tables, and all other imaginable accoutrements of the quilting arts, depending upon what the particular instructor required. High above, a chandelier hung from a ceiling embellished with a meandering vine pattern fashioned from molded plaster. At the far end of the room was a raised dais that served as a stage for their evening programs and, occasionally, for special daytime lectures the entire camp attended together. In the southeast corner stood a rectangular quilting frame, large enough for three quilters to sit comfortably, and four to sit more snugly, on each of the longer sides. A few yards away, a longarm quilting machine, currently unplugged and silent, awaited students eager to practice their stitches on the unfinished Northumberland Star quilt on the rollers. Longarm Quilting was one of their most popular workshops, and successive groups of quilters managed to complete two or three quilts each season.

The longarm quilting machine was a recent addition to the room, and Sylvia was leading Summer to another—a superb cedar quilt cabinet that Joe, a master woodworker, had expertly crafted for storing the manor's most precious quilts. Broad and solid, sanded to a satin-smooth finish inside and out to avoid snagging fragile fabrics, lined with acid-free material to protect the quilts within, the cabinet offered spaces for small quilts folded on the bias as well as larger pieces stored on rolls.

"Would you assist me, dear?" Sylvia asked, opening a deep drawer, the third from the bottom. Summer quickly came forward and helped her remove a muslin-covered bundle wound around a long rod, which they carried to a clean table near the classrooms. Carefully they unrolled the quilt, removed the protective muslin, spread it upon the table, and stepped back to admire it.

Gerda's Log Cabin was both familiar and unfailingly breathtaking.

Summer's gaze took in an extraordinary miscellany of shirting flannels and chintzes, calicoes and velvets—the scraps left over from household sewing or cut from the salvageable parts of worn clothing. The pieces had been cut into rectangles of various sizes and sewn in an interlocking fashion around a central square, light fabrics placed on one side of a diagonal, dark fabrics on the other, creating blocks seven inches square. The blocks were arranged in a Barn Raising setting, fourteen rows of ten blocks each, so that the overall pattern was one of concentric diamonds, alternately light and dark.

According to tradition, the central square in a Log Cabin quilt should be red, to symbolize the hearth, or yellow, to represent a light in the window. According to folklore—though refuted by modern historians—in the antebellum United States, a Log Cabin quilt with a black center square was a signal to slaves escaping north along the Underground Railroad, a sign indicating sanctuary.

"As a young girl," Sylvia said, "I hung on every word of my great-aunt Lucinda's story of how Great-Grandmother Anneke Bergstrom's Log Cabin quilt with the black center squares had welcomed fugitive slaves into the safe haven of Elm Creek Manor. When I discovered this quilt in the attic, I was certain it provided the evidence I needed to document this important part of Bergstrom family history."

"But Gerda's memoir offered a different explanation."

"Indeed it did, one I found far more fascinating than the legend. The Birds in the Air and the Underground Railroad quilts were the real signal quilts, displayed outside the home when it was safe for a fugitive to seek refuge here. The Log Cabin was made for an entirely different reason." Sylvia sighed, shaking her head and offering a faint smile. "When I unfolded the Birds in the Air quilt for the first time and Gerda's small book tumbled out, I had no idea how many family stories it would call into question—including my own heritage."

"An adopted child is as much a part of a family as one born into it," Summer reminded her. "You've said so yourself. Heritage is so much more than genetics."

Sylvia nodded, acknowledging the point. "Two boys were born at Elm Creek Farm in the spring of 1859, one to Anneke Bergstrom, the other to Joanna, the brave runaway they were protecting. Not even Joanna knew she was pregnant by her white enslaver when she fled the plantation. When Cyrus Pearson's slave-catcher cronies captured Joanna, her son was left behind."

Summer remembered Gerda's revelations well. "According to Gerda's memoir, Joanna was very light skinned. The Bergstroms passed the boys off as twins. The family's closest friends insisted it was true, and Dr. Granger signed the birth records confirming it."

"Why, yes, of course he did. Dorothea's brother was an abolitionist too. He didn't want to see the poor child enslaved, as would have been legal under the horrid laws of the time. It was dreadful enough that the baby had been separated from his mother, though he never knew it. Anneke and Hans doted upon both boys as if they were both their own."

"And Gerda never gave up searching for Joanna."

"But she never found her." Sylvia ran a hand lightly over a corner of the quilt, her gaze faraway. "They never divulged the truth to anyone, not even their own descendants, which is why even today I don't know which of the two boys—my grandfather or his ostensible twin—is Anneke's son and which is Joanna's."

"DNA science has come a long way," said Summer carefully. "You could be tested, and your second cousin Elizabeth's descendants in California could be tested, and then—"

"And then I would know the facts, but not the truth." Sylvia sighed again, but she managed a smile. "If you truly believe Gerda's quilt belongs in an exhibit celebrating local history—"

"I do, definitely."

"Then you have my permission to include it, and to share the story behind it."

Summer thanked her, and after a brief discussion, they decided that it would be best to return the precious quilt to its cabinet for safekeeping for now. When Summer next visited Union Hall, she could hang it in the gallery, safe from the dust and debris of the remodeling effort elsewhere in the building. In the meantime, she could write the object placard, using Gerda's memoir as a reference.

After the quilt was safely wrapped and put away, they went to the library to retrieve Gerda's memoir, which had been given pride of place on a bookshelf devoted to Bergstrom family history. "Do you know of any other quilts with ties to local history I ought to look for?" Summer asked Sylvia as they climbed the grand oak staircase.

Sylvia pondered the question as they walked along. "This is going back decades," she said as Summer opened the French doors to the library, "but I used to visit the Waterford Public Library frequently as a girl, and I recall seeing a signature quilt displayed behind the circulation desk."

"A signature quilt?" echoed Summer as she followed Sylvia to the Bergstrom shelf, on the wall behind the oak desk between two tall windows. "I don't remember it."

"You wouldn't, dear. This was before your time. I'm referring to the original library building, which was torn down sometime in the 1950s. You would have visited the new library on Second Street."

"Yes, that's right." Summer wished she had her notebook and pen handy. "Do you remember any details about the quilt—what it looked like, when it was made, who made it?"

"It used the traditional Album block, and it must have been made before the library was built, because it was raffled off to raise money for the construction. Each block contained a piece of muslin autographed by a famous author or other dignitary, which was what made the quilt so valuable as a prize."

"Famous authors? Like who?"

"Oh, let's see. Walt Whitman, Elizabeth Barrett Browning, Frederick Douglass—"

"Really?"

"Oh, yes, and at least a few dozen more. That's what gave the quilt its name, Authors' Album. As to who made it—" Sylvia shrugged. "I regret I don't know. Local women who loved books, I imagine."

"Including some Bergstroms?"

"Perhaps," said Sylvia, intrigued. "I wish I would have asked one of the librarians back in the day, or one of my great-aunts, but it never occurred to me."

"There might be a record of it somewhere." Turning to the desk, Summer opened drawers until she found one full of printer paper, then took a pen from the holder next to the computer keyboard and began jotting down Sylvia's reminiscences. "Do you have any idea what became of the quilt?"

"I don't, but you could inquire with the Friends of the Library."

"That's a good place to start." Summer tapped her pen against the page, thinking. "I wonder why they didn't move the quilt to the new library along with the books?"

"Perhaps it was regarded as too old-fashioned for such a modern building," Sylvia said archly. "Perhaps it clashed with the décor."

"Unless it *is* at the new library, but it's displayed out of public view, in an office or the staff break room or something."

"That's possible too, I suppose. Better that than lost in the move or unintentionally discarded."

Summer shuddered, feigning horror. "Perish the thought."

"Group quilts are just the thing for your exhibit, wouldn't you agree?" Sylvia mused as she plucked Gerda's memoir from the shelf, gazed at it fondly for a moment, and handed it to Summer. "I believe a group quilt truly reveals the spirit of a community. Cooperation, collaboration, often in support of a worthy cause—"

"Like the Loyal Union Sampler."

"Precisely." Sylvia paused to think. "A few months after I returned to Elm Creek Manor following my sister's passing, Sarah and I were sorting through cartons of slides, photographs, and things, when she came across an old newspaper clipping I had saved about a quilt the Waterford Quilting Guild made to raise money to support the war effort. World War Two," she added, just to clarify.

"Do you still have the clipping?"

"Yes, of course. We discarded many worthless things Claudia had accumulated during my absence, but not my quilting souvenirs. The slides are in boxes in my closet, the photos are in the album on the bottom shelf over there, and the newspaper clippings—oh, yes. The scrapbook. Sarah put all of my newspaper clippings in a scrapbook." Turning back to the shelf of Bergstrom history, Sylvia retrieved a thick, squarish book bound in dark green leather and opened it on the desk. Summer came around to her side and peered over her shoulder, resisting the impulse to implore Sylvia to slow down, as she was turning the pages too fast for Summer to get more than an enticing glimpse of each. Summer decided to return and savor the entire collection on her own later.

"Ah! Here it is," said Sylvia triumphantly, holding the book open to a faded, yellowing newspaper clipping and sliding it toward Summer.

"'Waterford Quilting Guild to Raffle Victory Quilt,'" Summer read aloud. The headline appeared above a photo of several women, their hair in rolls, pin curls, or twisted chignons, holding up a large Grandmother's Flower Garden quilt. "Are you in this photo?"

"I'm holding up one of the corners." Sylvia indicated which one. "That determined-looking young woman staring down the photographer is me."

Summer smiled, studying the young woman in the photo, glimpsing signs of the matriarch she would become. "Why do you look so fierce? Do you remember?"

"Oh, it was such a foolish, petty thing given the crisis of the times. The photographer ordered us to smile, but I thought our fundraiser was very serious business and I wasn't inclined to obey. He called me out—'You, on the end, with the scowl'—and told me I'd be prettier if

I smiled, which would sell more raffle tickets. I might have managed a grin except my sister—that's her, two girls to my right, with the big, cheerful grin—well, she had to put her two cents in. 'Oh, Sylvia, just smile,' she ordered. 'You owe it to the boys at war.' Naturally, I wasn't inclined to smile at all after that."

"I totally get it. I don't like being ordered to smile either."

"But you have a lovely smile. You smile all the time."

"But never on demand."

"Ah, yes. An important distinction."

Summer returned her gaze to the photo. "I've heard of victory gardens. What's a victory quilt?"

"It's not a particular pattern if that's what you mean. Any quilt made to raise money for the war effort could be called a victory quilt. We chose the Grandmother's Flower Garden because the small pieces were well suited to using up scraps, and with the war on, it was important to be frugal." Sylvia bent closer, adjusting her glasses on the bridge of her nose. "One wouldn't know it from this black-and-white photo, but inner rings of six hexagons each are various red fabrics, while the hexagons surrounding the separate 'blooms' are blue."

"Red, white, and blue. Appropriately patriotic."

"Red, unbleached muslin, and blue, rather," said Sylvia. "Another detail that isn't quite visible in this photo is actually the most important. Each of the light-colored hexagons in the centers was embroidered with the name of a local young man in the service. We stitched a gold star near his name if he had given up his life for his country." She sighed and straightened, shaking her head. "We embroidered so many gold stars that summer."

"Do you remember who won the quilt in the raffle?"

Sylvia thought for a moment. "I'm afraid I don't. I doubt it was anyone I knew well. I'd surely remember if one of my friends had won."

"Do you recall when this was?" Summer asked. "This clipping doesn't include the date."

"That's my fault. I trimmed it close when I cut it from the news-paper, probably because someone else wanted to read an article on the other side." Sylvia studied the photo again, frowning slightly. "It was the summer of 1943, when I was guild president. This was months before my husband and brother enlisted, so their names weren't in-cluded in this quilt."

Then Summer realized something else. "Agnes isn't in this photo."

"No, she wouldn't have been. She was still living in Philadelphia with her family. She and my brother didn't marry until April of 1944, right before he went off to war."

"I wonder if the newspaper announced the winner of the raffle. If so, that could lead me to the current owner."

"They may have done. I hope so. I'd be delighted to see that quilt again, after so many years."

"Just imagine how the families of the men whose names were embroidered on that quilt would feel if they could see this tribute to their lost soldiers proudly displayed on a gallery wall," said Summer. "I bet most of them have no idea this quilt ever existed."

"Let's hope it still does, and that you can acquire it, as well as the long-lost quilt from the old library." Sylvia gave Summer's arm an affectionate pat. "You've helped me solve historical mysteries more perplexing than this. If anyone can find these missing quilts, you can."

Summer managed a faint smile in reply, wishing she shared her friend's confidence. She hoped Sylvia's trust, and Agnes's, would not prove to be misplaced.

**Gerda's Log Cabin.** 70" x 98". Cotton and wool top (assorted weaves) and cotton backing with cotton batting. Pieced and quilted by Gerda Bergstrom, Creek's Crossing, PA, c. 1865–1880.

In January 1859, a young woman named Joanna escaped from the Wentworth County, Virginia, plantation where she had been held in slavery. Driven from her intended route along the Underground Railroad by a blinding snowstorm, she sought refuge at Elm Creek Farm, the home of husband and wife Hans and Anneke Bergstrom and Hans's sister, Gerda Bergstrom. The Bergstroms, recent immigrants from Germany, concealed Joanna from the slave catchers pursuing her. When they discovered that Joanna was pregnant, the Bergstroms offered to shelter her until she delivered her child and she and the baby could safely continue their journey to Canada.

Awakened to the plight of enslaved persons in their new homeland, the Bergstroms made Elm Creek Farm a station on the Underground Railroad, guided by their friends Thomas and Dorothea (Granger) Nelson and Abel and Constance Wright. For several months, and in defiance of the law, the Bergstroms welcomed dozens of fugitives into their home, providing them with food, clothing, shelter, and guidance or transportation to the next station on the route north.

In June 1859, the Bergstroms, Nelsons, and Wrights were betrayed to the authorities by Cyrus Pearson, a local businessman and stepson of the mayor. Although many cities in the North refused to obey the federal Fugitive Slave Acts, which authorized local governments to capture and return fugitives to their purported owners and imposed strict penalties on anyone who aided their escape, Creek's Crossing law enforcement nonetheless arrested the families, including the Wrights' two young sons. A posse of Southern slave catchers seized Joanna, presumably to return her to Virginia.

As news of the shocking events spread throughout the North, outraged citizens demanded justice for the Creek's Crossing Eight and freedom for Joanna. Eventually the Bergstroms, Nelsons, and Wrights were released and all charges against them were dropped, but Joanna had disappeared. "After Joanna's capture, finding her became my obsession," Gerda Bergstrom wrote in her memoir, but "my efforts were repeatedly thwarted by one obstacle or another." After the Civil War, she so "feverishly believed" that Joanna would eventually return that she began making her a quilt "in anticipation of her arrival." As Gerda wrote:

> I chose a pattern that would be easy to sew . . . but one that had special significance: the Log Cabin, named for the interlocking design of its rectangular pieces. The design was invented, or so Dorothea once said, to honor Mr. Abraham Lincoln, and since he had granted Joanna her freedom, I thought it an appropriate choice for her quilt. The square in the center of the block was supposed to be yellow, to signify a light in the cabin window, or red, to signify the hearth, but I cut my central squares from black fabric, to symbolize that an escaped slave had once found sanctuary within our own log cabin.
>
> Time passed, and as my Log Cabin quilt neared completion, the black center squares took on another meaning. Black was also the color of mourning, and as my relentless searches proved fruitless over and over again, I began to mourn my lost friend, whom I feared would never see the quilt I had made for her.

The Creek's Crossing Eight scandal proved so damaging to the town's reputation, and thereby to the local economy, that years later, civic leaders ruled to change the town's name to Water's Ford, which eventually evolved into Waterford. The fate of the woman known to the Bergstroms only as Joanna remains unknown.

*Gerda's Log Cabin* appears in this exhibit on loan from the private collection of Sylvia Bergstrom Compson, great-grandniece of Gerda Bergstrom.

# 8

On Sunday morning, after a solitary yoga session on the verandah, Summer enjoyed breakfast in the kitchen with several of the manor's permanent residents, who came and went as their schedules required. Her mom arrived to refill her travel mug just as Summer was finishing her yogurt, fresh blueberries, and coffee, so Summer lingered in her booth as her mom scooted into the opposite side, glad for a chance to catch up.

"I've made some progress on my thesis," Summer told her as Gwen stirred sugar and cream into her coffee. "But don't plan a surprise graduation party just yet."

"Some progress is better than none," said Gwen cheerfully. "If I could get through graduate school, you can do it."

"So you've often told me. And you did it as a single mother."

"Yes, after some significant detours and risky choices I hope you'll never emulate." Gwen shuddered with feigned horror. "But I didn't do it alone. I had a lot of support and encouragement from my parents and mentors, as well as the most perfect daughter in the world."

Summer smiled and sipped her coffee to disguise a pang of dismay. She knew her mother was mostly exaggerating for comic effect, but sometimes her reputation as the perfect daughter was difficult to live up to.

Soon thereafter, the other Elm Creek Quilters and several Elm Creek Husbands, as they were fondly called, met in the foyer to prepare for camper registration. Gretchen collated maps of the estate with class schedules and descriptions of the evening programs, Agnes and Diane arranged fresh flowers from the cutting garden in each suite, and Gwen carefully matched room keys with quilters' names. Matt, Andrew, and Joe prepared to valet park cars and assist arriving guests with their luggage. Summer helped Diane arrange tables and chairs in their usual places in the front foyer before helping Sarah and Maggie inspect the classrooms, replenishing supplies and testing the sewing machines, lights, and audiovisual equipment to be sure everything was in perfect order. But as everyone kept reminding her, Summer wasn't on the payroll that season, and she had already done enough to earn her room and board. "Are you trying to get rid of me?" Summer teased.

"Never," Gwen declared.

"Sort of," Sarah admitted. "We know you have other important things to do. We've got this, so you're dismissed. For now. I'm sure we'll be begging you for help later, if something unforeseen comes up."

"Something always does," Agnes remarked cheerfully.

Laughing, Summer wished them all good luck and returned to her room for her computer, notes, and Gerda's memoir. By the time the first guests arrived—a moment she noted by the sound of the Elm Creek Quilts minivan pulling into the circular drive and halting in front of the manor, followed almost immediately by a taxi—she was comfortably settled behind the oak desk in the library, revising the object label for Gerda's Log Cabin, which she resolved to finish before the Welcome Banquet that evening. The writing challenged her in a very different manner than her master's thesis did, requiring her to balance emotion with objectivity. The antique quilt's scraps and stitches chronicled a story of painful loss and stubborn hope that never failed to move her deeply, regardless of how well she knew it and how long ago the heartbreaking events had unfolded.

When she finished the first draft, she carefully read it over, altering a phrase here, adding a detail there, all while pondering what seemed to be a very obvious omission. She mentioned that Joanna was pregnant, and that she had been captured, but not that Joanna's baby had remained behind. Wouldn't anyone reading the story of the Log Cabin quilt wonder what had become of the child? Should Summer explain about Anneke's son, born within weeks of Joanna's, and the Bergstrom family's long-enduring deception? Summer was reluctant to leave a curious viewer's questions unanswered, but as much as she appreciated historical accuracy, she valued Sylvia's privacy more.

In the end, Summer decided that the mystery of Sylvia's heritage was Sylvia's story to tell and hers alone.

She finished the second draft shortly before noon. After a quick, solitary lunch in the kitchen, she returned to the library to polish the text until she was completely satisfied, then rewarded herself with a walk around the estate to stretch her legs and clear her mind. Although she took the long way around and paused often to chat with strolling campers, she nonetheless returned to her room with two hours to spare before she needed to dress for the banquet.

"No more procrastinating," she murmured, taking a few deep, cleansing breaths and settling down at the desk. Steeling herself, she scanned her notes and picked up her thesis where she had left off two days before. Line by line the document grew, though sometimes getting the words out felt like pushing rocks through a sieve. Occasionally she needed to pause to study her outline or page through one of her research sources, but she didn't let such small interruptions completely derail her, as she too easily had back in Chicago. Whenever she was tempted to give up, she reminded herself that she didn't have to finish the entire thesis today, but only to put one sentence down, and then another, and eventually she would reach the end.

The Welcome Banquet that evening felt like a well-earned reward, but Summer skipped the Candlelight in order to review her notes from her intriguing conversation with Sylvia the previous day.

The newspaper article about the victory quilt was such a tantalizing lead that she decided to pursue it first. That meant a trip to the Rare Books Room, and while she was there, it wouldn't hurt to ask Audrey Pfenning if she knew anything about the Authors' Album. Even if she had never heard of it, she might be able to put Summer in touch with someone at the public library who could answer her questions.

The next day, a warm, hazy morning that presaged the need for cooling glasses of iced tea on the verandah later, Summer arrived at the Waterford College Library shortly after it opened and hurried upstairs to the Rare Books Room. When she approached the reference desk, she found Audrey working alone, a trifle harried but still good-humored, sorting books and other items that apparently had been abandoned overnight on a wheeled cart instead of being properly shelved. "Special Collections must have been exceptionally busy last night," the librarian said, excusing her coworkers as she completed the evening shift's duties.

"That's unusual for a Sunday, isn't it?"

Audrey shrugged as she swiftly arranged books in Library of Congress order on the rolling cart. "Yes, but it's not unheard-of. Ever since Bradley gave notice, he's been preoccupied with tying up loose ends in the back office. Since he has less time to spend at the reference desk, the burden falls upon our student staff. After he leaves, I'm afraid their workload will only get heavier."

"Theirs and yours," said Summer, sympathetic. "Do you think you'll find a replacement soon?"

"Soon, no. Eventually, I certainly hope so."

"I would've thought you'd have stacks of applications to choose from. Doesn't Waterford College have its own Master's of Library Science program?"

"We do, although we call it the Master's of Library and Information Science now. Unfortunately, none of our recent graduates or current candidates in the Archivist concentration was interested in the position or I would've offered them the job on the spot." A trifle dryly, she added, "It might surprise you, but not everyone wants to launch their professional career in a small college town in rural Pennsylvania. Some people actually prefer large, exciting cities with boundless opportunities for entertainment and adventure."

"That *is* surprising," said Summer, matching Audrey's ironic tone, though she felt a pang of chagrin, remembering how thrilled she had been to leave Waterford for Chicago two years before. "I'll ask around. Some of my friends who left town after graduation have said they're hoping to return. If any of them are qualified for the job, I'll send them your way."

"Thank you, Summer. No pressure, but time is of the essence."

"Right." Summer hesitated. "In the meantime, I hate to make extra work for you—"

"Oh, no worries on that account." Audrey waved a hand, dismissing her concern. "Nothing makes me happier than helping researchers track down the resources they need."

"Good, because I need more microfilm." Summer took a photocopy of Sylvia's scrapbook article from her backpack and placed it on the counter. "I'm trying to track down this article and any others that may have mentioned the victory quilt, especially the results of the raffle."

Audrey slipped on her glasses and studied the page closely. "Given the subject, it's almost certainly from the *Waterford Register*, although we couldn't rule out the *Centre Daily Times*."

"Wasn't there a Grangerville newspaper back then?" Summer asked.

"You're thinking of the *Grangerville Herald*. It ceased publication during the Great Depression."

"Oh, too bad. Let's start with the *Waterford Register*, then. This is Sylvia Bergstrom Compson." Summer indicated her friend in the photo. "She recalls that they made the quilt in the summer of 1943. The raffle would have been in late summer or fall."

"That narrows it down considerably. I was half afraid you'd need to search every issue for all of World War Two. Would you like to begin with June?"

When Summer agreed, Audrey retrieved the rolls for June through October 1943, to start. Summer set up the first roll at her usual microfilm reader and settled in for a long morning of scrolling and scanning. The work soon proved to be swifter and less conducive to eye strain than searching for references to the Wright family had been, since the image quality of the more recent newspaper was much better, and she needed only to skim for a familiar photograph rather than examine line after line of small text.

Even so, her eyes were weary and her neck stiff two hours later when, finally, with a jolt of recognition, she spotted the photo on the screen. A quick zoom to enlarge the masthead revealed that the article had been published on July 26, 1943. Sylvia would have been twenty-three years old, Summer reflected, five years younger than herself—happily married, working for Bergstrom Thoroughbreds, and volunteering for the war effort on the home front, entirely un-aware that in nine months the men she loved would be enlisting in the army. Less than a year after that, she would be a widow.

Shaking off the grim thought, Summer printed the page, informed the student worker at the reference desk that she would return soon, and went for a walk around the picturesque campus, all redbrick and stone colonial architecture set amid green lawns shaded by leafy elms and towering oaks. The sleepy, interterm hush was broken only by bird-song, the quiet conversations of passersby, and the distant, unobtrusive sound of an occasional passing car. Even at its busiest, the Waterford College campus was more serene than the quadrangles of the University of Chicago, which offered a very different aesthetic: acres of bustling, designated botanical gardens and green space surrounded by towering Gothic structures of gray limestone. As fond as Summer was of her undergraduate alma mater, she felt a sudden pang of longing for the U of C and her friends, and she had to laugh. Wherever she was, she always found herself missing the other. If only they weren't so far apart.

Summer paused for a quick bite to eat at the student union before returning to the library and resuming her search. It was not until midafternoon, and in mid-August of the *Register*, that she spied a small announcement that raffle tickets for the Waterford Quilting Guild's victory quilt were available for purchase at the Waterford Public Library or from any guild member. The winning ticket would be drawn at noon on Saturday, October 16 at Union Hall.

Exultant, Summer restrained a cheer, but she couldn't resist pumping a fist in the air.

She was tempted to skip ahead to October 17, but rather than risk missing out on something unexpected and important, she continued as meticulously as before. Her prudence was rewarded in the September 20 edition, where she found a brief announcement in the Grangerville News column noting that anyone who wished to add a name or contribute a Home Sweet Home block to the victory quilt should submit them to the Bethel A.M.E. Church on Philadelphia Street by November 30.

Summer sat back in her chair, puzzled.

Was this a new victory quilt, or had the reporter made a mistake? As Sylvia had mentioned, any quilt made to raise money for the war effort could be called a victory quilt, regardless of block pattern or design. Summer studied the paragraph closely, intrigued. Based upon the few specific details provided, she could infer that the Grangerville Quilt Guild had made their own victory quilt, one that included names—perhaps the names of soldiers, like the Waterford Quilting Guild's project, but not necessarily. In any case, her chances of finding a single victory quilt to add to the exhibit had just increased significantly. If she could track down *both* quilts, how wonderful it would be to display them side by side, so viewers could compare and contrast two important artifacts of local World War Two history.

Summer scrolled on through the microfilm, only to become increasingly puzzled when she found nothing else about the Grangerville Quilt Guild's project. Eventually she reached the October 17 edition, where she learned the name of the Waterford Quilting Guild's raffle winner, Mrs. Doris Stover of Sixteenth Street. Also provided was an alphabetical list of the soldiers whose names were embroidered on the quilt, along with their hometowns. Nearly all of the men were from Waterford, but several were from Grangerville, and a few others hailed from small, unincorporated areas, most of which had been annexed by larger communities in the sixty years that had passed since the quilt had been made.

It was a wonderful find, and Summer could have walked away feeling proud of a job well done—but it bothered her that although she scanned the microfilm carefully, page after page as the hours passed, she learned nothing more about the second victory quilt. She returned the microfilm to the reference desk, checked out several more rolls, and searched on through March 1944. Curiously absent was a single photograph of a Home Sweet Home victory quilt or any details about where to purchase tickets, when the drawing would be held, or who had ultimately won.

Had the Grangerville project been abandoned after the initial announcement? Had the editors decided that victory quilts were no longer newsworthy? It was all very puzzling, but Summer was too tired and bleary-eyed to search any more that day.

Audrey had already left by the time Summer packed up her backpack and returned to Elm Creek Manor, too late for dinner in the banquet hall, but right on time for another meal of excellent leftovers in the kitchen. Her mom found her there after the evening program, just as Summer was loading her dishes into the washer. "Mom, what do you know about the Grangerville Quilt Guild?" Summer asked as she dug the car keys out of her back pocket and handed them over. "Do you recall if the Waterford Quilting Guild and the Grangerville guild ever collaborated? Was there any overlap in membership? You'd think that with two quilt guilds in a place the size of the Elm Creek Valley, there would be opportunities for cooperation—unless it was more of a competitive relationship?"

Gwen frowned, thinking. "I don't remember any competition or ill will between the groups when we were members, but I wouldn't have been in the loop. I always had enough to do without wasting time engaging in silly feuds."

Just then, Sylvia and Agnes entered, cheerfully arguing about the best needles for hand appliqué. "Just the quilters I wanted to see," Summer greeted them, smiling. "Do either of you remember a local woman named Doris Stover? In the 1940s, she lived on Sixteenth Street."

"My sister had a friend named Doris Stover, but I don't recall what street she lived on," said Sylvia. "She was Doris Preiss before her marriage."

"I knew her too," said Agnes. "We met a few years after the war, when I joined the quilt guild."

Summer nodded eagerly, relieved to learn that she was on the right track. "It turns out Doris won the raffle for your victory quilt, Sylvia."

"Did she indeed?" said Sylvia, visibly moved. "I'm sure she treasured it. Her late husband's name was on that quilt, with a gold star beside it."

"Are either of you still in touch with Doris?" asked Summer. "If so, could you introduce me? If she still has the quilt, I'd love to acquire it for the exhibit, even if it's only for a brief loan."

Sylvia shook her head. "I'm sorry, dear, but I lost touch with everyone when I left Waterford."

"As for me, I didn't know Doris well," said Agnes apologetically. "I do recall that she remarried and moved away, but that was more than forty years ago. I remember because I took over for her as guild secretary when she stepped down. I haven't heard from her since."

Summer's heart sank. "Do you know if she has any relatives in the area?"

Agnes shook her head. "I don't believe so, dear."

"If I recall correctly," mused Sylvia, "her best friend at the time was Edith Merkle. Edith might know how to reach her."

"Mrs. Merkle, the nurse?" Summer turned to her mother. "From down the street?"

"Must be," said Gwen, shrugging. "Our Mrs. Merkle's first name is Edith. I could stop by on my way in tomorrow and ask her for Doris's number."

"That would be great, Mom. Thank you so much." Summer turned back to Sylvia. "Did you know that the Grangerville Quilt Guild made a victory quilt around the same time the Waterford Quilting Guild made theirs?"

"I didn't, but I'm not surprised," said Sylvia. "Back then we were all determined to do our part for the war effort—scrap drives, war bonds, and so on."

"They apparently included names on their blocks too." Summer glanced around, directing her question to all three women. "Do you suppose one guild got the idea from the other?"

"Not necessarily," said her mom. "Names have been included in quilts, especially community quilts, for as long as quilters have quilted. Often the names were autographs."

"On other occasions they were written or embroidered by a single quiltmaker, to record other people's names for a particular purpose," said Sylvia. "Such was the case for our victory quilt."

"In other words, no one was a copycat," said Agnes. "The style was so popular, it belonged to everyone."

"So even though they were only a few miles apart, the two guilds in the Elm Creek Valley didn't necessarily influence each other," Summer noted. "Is it fair to say that quilters typically kept to the guild in their own town, without much mingling or collaboration?"

"That sounds about right," said Agnes. "Then, as now, it's simply more convenient to participate locally. And it's nice to gather with one's own friends and neighbors."

"That's not what I was hoping to hear," said Summer, sighing comically. "I needed one of you to tell me you have a friend in the Grangerville guild, someone I could contact to ask about their victory quilt."

"You could check our mailing list," said Gwen. "Maybe some of their members have attended Elm Creek Quilt Camp."

"Maybe you've even had them in class, Summer," said Agnes brightly.

"Maybe so," said Summer. "I'll check the spreadsheet. Thank you all so much. I thought I'd hit a dead end until you came through for me."

"No trouble at all," said Gwen. "We can't help it. We're a veritable font of knowledge."

The next day, after Sunrise Yoga and a delicious, leisurely breakfast in the banquet hall with the campers and faculty, Summer went upstairs to the library, browsed the shelves while Sarah finished up a report, then took over her friend's place at the computer. Within ten minutes of opening the master address file, she had compiled a list of more than twenty former campers with Grangerville addresses, half of whom had taken one of her classes.

Summer waited until ten o'clock to start calling rather than interrupt anyone's busy early morning routine. The first student did not answer, so Summer left a message. The second quilter was delighted to hear from her, but unfortunately, she wasn't a member of the Grangerville guild and didn't know whom Summer might contact about guild history.

The third quilter had attended camp in early May, and her only regret about the week was that the schedule had not included Summer's Sunrise Yoga or Modern Quilting classes. "I've been a member of the Grangerville Quilt Guild for six years," she said proudly. "I've never heard of a victory quilt, ours or anyone else's, but our guild historian, Denisha Williams, maintains all of our records going back decades. I'm sure she'd be happy to help you."

Summer had her pen and notebook ready and quickly wrote down the number as her student read it aloud from her guild directory. "Tell Denisha I told you to call her," she advised, and when Summer thanked her, she teased, "You can thank me by returning my two favorite classes to the schedule next year."

She hung up before Summer could explain that she wasn't planning to teach next season either, because she intended to be in Chicago pursuing her doctorate. She'd have to find another way to express her gratitude.

After taking a moment to close the spreadsheet and clear her papers away before Sarah reclaimed the desk, Summer called Denisha's number. When a busy signal buzzed, she hung up, pocketed her phone, paced to the far window and back, then tried again. This time a woman with a rich alto voice promptly responded, "Hello?"

"Hi, this is Summer Sullivan from Elm Creek Quilts." She wasn't calling on behalf of the company, but she was an Elm Creek Quilter, and she needed all the credibility that title conveyed. "May I speak with Denisha Williams, please?"

"This is she. Hello, Summer. A friend from my guild said you might be calling."

That explained the busy signal. "Yes, she kindly gave me your number. I understand that you're the Grangerville Quilt Guild historian?"

"I am, for two years and counting. I hear you're interested in a raffle quilt our guild made back in 1943?"

"Yes, that's right, a victory quilt made from Home Sweet Home blocks. Does it sound familiar?"

"Only vaguely, but I can pull our files from that year and see what's there. Why don't I call you back after I take a look?"

"That would be wonderful, thanks," said Summer. She gave Denisha her number and they hung up.

It occurred to her that she could probably write another paragraph or two of her thesis while she waited for Denisha to call, but she wandered downstairs instead, reaching the ballroom entrance just as the break between classes began. Amid the bustle of campers, she found her mother in one of the classrooms, chatting with lingering students as she tidied up after one class and prepared for the next. Gwen's face brightened when she saw Summer approaching. "Good morning, kiddo," she sang, placing a hand on Summer's shoulder and kissing her on the cheek before resuming her work. "I'm afraid I have bad news."

"Bad news?" Summer echoed, laughing. "With that big grin?"

"The grin is because I'm happy to see you," her mother retorted, tapping a stack of handouts on the tabletop to even out the edges. "I spoke with Mrs. Merkle this morning. Doris Stover passed away eight years ago. She had at least two children, but Mrs. Merkle never met them and doesn't know how to get in touch."

Summer's heart sank. "I assume Mrs. Merkle doesn't know what became of the victory quilt either."

Her mother shook her head. "I'm sorry, kiddo. One of her children may have inherited it, but unless you can find a way to reach them—"

"We'll never know." Summer sighed. "Well, at least I have a good lead on the Grangerville victory quilt. I spoke to a former student, and—" Her phone buzzed in her pocket, and when she checked, the caller ID announced Denisha's number. "Sorry, Mom. I have to take this." As Gwen waved her on, Summer hurried from the ballroom, leaving the din behind as she raised the phone to her ear. "Hello?" she said, crossing the foyer and stepping outside onto the verandah. "Denisha?"

"Hi, Summer. I have some good news for you."

"Really? What did you find?"

"Only an entire folder devoted to the Home Sweet Home quilt—flyers with the participation guidelines, a list of contributors, graph paper sketches of the quilt, photos, and more."

"That's fantastic! And so fast! You must be the best guild historian ever."

Denisha laughed. "I don't know about that, but I enjoy the work and I'm happy to serve the guild. Would you like to see the file?"

"I'd love to. When can we meet?"

"I have some time this afternoon if you'd like to come over. The guild doesn't keep a separate office, so the archives are all here at my home. Would two o'clock work for you?"

Summer would have made *any* time work, day or night, but she gladly confirmed for two o'clock.

And she knew how she had to fill the intervening hours—no excuses.

As the manor hummed and rang with the sounds of quilters working and learning and laughing together, Summer withdrew to the relative quiet of her third-floor room. She opened her laptop and scrolled through the thesis, changing a word here and there, her thoughts returning again and again to the lost victory quilts. Doris Stover had at least two children. If Summer could get her last known address from Mrs. Merkle, she could search for an obituary in the microfilm of Doris's local newspaper. An obituary would surely include her children's names, perhaps even their hometowns, maybe an address where condolences could be sent.

Or rather, could have been sent, eight years ago. The passing of time did not work in Summer's favor. But surely not every detail in an eight-year-old obituary would be outdated. It very well could yield one or two promising leads she could pursue.

With no new paragraphs to show for her time in front of her laptop, it was a relief to put it to sleep, claim the car keys from her mom, and set out for Grangerville, the previous day's microfilm printouts in her backpack. About a half hour later, she pulled into the driveway of a redbrick colonial in a neighborhood with narrow driveways, one-car detached garages tucked behind the residences, and lovely mature trees bathing sidewalks and perennial beds in cooling shade. After climbing the steep stairs to Denisha's front porch, Summer rang the bell and stepped back, smiling at a glimpse through a window of a blue and white quilt casually draped over the back of a sofa.

The door opened, and a dark-skinned woman slightly shorter than herself and about twenty years older gave her a swift, appraising glance. "Summer Sullivan?" she inquired, a deep dimple appearing in her right cheek. She wore a white scoop-neck knit top over a striking yellow, black, and white batik skirt, and her dozens of long, glossy braids were gathered at the nape of her neck in a silk scarf in the same shade of yellow. "Come on in."

"Thank you for seeing me on such short notice," said Summer, following her inside.

"From the sound of your voice, it seemed urgent," Denisha replied, her expression amused as she led Summer into the living room and gestured to the sofa. "I understand urgent quilt business quite well, and our mutual friend speaks highly of you."

"And of you." Slipping off her backpack, Summer took a seat as Denisha sat down in an adjacent armchair on the other side of a coffee table. Summer's gaze immediately went to the slim manila folder on the table, but rather than greedily snatch it up, she retrieved a folder from her backpack and took out a single page. "I found this brief mention of the Grangerville Quilt Guild's victory quilt in the *Waterford Register*," she said, handing the printout to Denisha. "This piece ran on September 20, 1943. I searched the microfilm through March 1944, but I didn't find any other references to the Home Sweet Home victory quilt."

She went on to explain why she was searching for the two victory quilts and other quilts relevant to Elm Creek Valley history, and what she envisioned for the Union Hall exhibit.

Denisha studied the page while Summer explained. "I haven't seen this article before," she said when Summer finished. "May I keep it for our files?"

"Of course. I have another copy."

"Then I imagine you'd be interested in making copies of these." Denisha opened the folder on the table and gestured for Summer to take a look. Everything was there, just as Denisha had said on the phone— sketches of the Home Sweet Home victory quilt, a yellowed flyer with sewing instructions and deadlines, a typewritten list of names—

Summer bent closer for a better look, reluctant to touch the aging paper. "Local soldiers?" she asked, noting the ranks and hometowns appearing after each surname.

"Yes, divided according to the branch of the service, then alpha-betized. As you can see from this photo"—Denisha carefully moved other papers aside and brought a black-and-white photograph to the front—"the names are barely visible in the center of each block except as a faint line. I wish the photographer had taken a few detail photos, but I assume the intention was to include the entire quilt, as well as the women who made it."

Summer's gaze went to the women holding the quilt up by its edges all around. Some were smiling, others were solemn, and all were Black. Summer paused, taken aback by a sudden realization. All of the women in the Waterford Quilting Guild photo were white.

She glanced up to find Denisha studying her, still smiling, her brow slightly furrowed. Returning her gaze to the documents, Summer pulled out the list of soldiers honored in the Home Sweet Home vic-tory quilt. According to the "Hometown" column, several were from Waterford. She didn't recognize a single duplicate name between the two victory quilts.

For a long moment she pondered the unsettling strangeness of it. "Denisha," she said, "may I ask you an awkward question?"

Denisha's eyebrows rose. "Sure. Go ahead."

"Do you know if the Waterford Quilting Guild was segregated?"

Denisha's shoulders relaxed, and her smile returned, but fainter, and a trifle weary. "Oh, I don't believe so. Not officially."

"Not officially?"

"Faint praise, I know. But excluding people of color was never part of the guild's bylaws. I've read several versions while conducting my own research, and I'm certain that's true."

"Maybe it wasn't official policy," Summer said, dubious, indicat-ing the photo of the women holding the quilt, "but it sure looks like there was one guild for white women and one for women of color—and, apparently, one victory quilt for white soldiers and one for Black. That would explain why there are some soldiers from each town in what was essentially the other town's quilt."

"Yet white women *have* been members of the Grangerville Quilt Guild through the years, even in the 1940s. This photo doesn't indicate that, but other photos in our archives do." Denisha offered a rueful shrug. "That said, our records and stories from our elder members agree that some Black women from Waterford traveled here to participate in our guild, while some white women from Grangerville went to Waterford to be in theirs."

"That's . . ." Summer struggled for the words. "That's very troubling. I really don't like what that implies about our community."

"Both guilds are more diverse now," Denisha assured her, "just as both towns are. But we're talking about a different era, before your time and before mine. Things have changed."

"Not as much as they need to."

"No, but every step forward is progress." Denisha smiled, her dimple reappearing. "Maybe you should raise some of these issues in your exhibit."

"I think I have to, or I'd be leaving out an essential part of our history." Summer inhaled deeply, shook her head, and returned to sorting through the papers and photos. "This is a wonderful resource, and I'm so grateful to you for letting me see it."

"I'll even let you borrow the entire file, so you can make your own copies." Denisha held up a finger. "As long as you bring back everything in perfect condition."

"You have my solemn promise," Summer assured her. "As for the quilt itself, do you have any idea where it might be?"

Denisha shook her head. "I wish I did. We have the winner's name"—she indicated one of the typewritten sheets—"but she's long since passed and her children moved away decades ago."

"The Waterford quilt vanished in much the same way. They could be anywhere."

"Or they could have been worn out and discarded long ago." Denisha paused, considering. "Personally, I think that's unlikely. These were the sort of quilts a family would appreciate for their historical and artistic value and save for best. They wouldn't undergo the wear and tear of daily use."

"Yes, but quilts can be lost in other ways, and their stories lost with them."

"That's why your project is so important," said Denisha. "We're reconstructing and passing on the stories of these lost quilts right now."

Later, back at Elm Creek Manor, Summer asked Sylvia, Agnes, and Sarah to join her in the library after dinner while the other Elm Creek Quilters prepared for the evening program. As she described what she had learned over the past few days, their eager smiles faded. Sylvia and Agnes, especially, looked pained and mortified.

"It never occurred to me that the Waterford Quilting Guild might have been segregated, intentionally or otherwise," said Sylvia. "My sister and I never would have joined if Black women had not been permitted."

"I wouldn't have joined either," said Agnes. "But there were always Black ladies in the guild when I was a member. It never occurred to me it had ever been otherwise."

"Quilters join the guild where they feel most welcome," Sarah pointed out. "Apparently, some felt they had to travel to the next town over to find a place where they belonged."

A solemn hush settled over the library. From the ballroom below, Summer heard the muffled sounds of voices and movement as their friends and campers prepared for the evening program.

Eventually Summer broke the silence. "I haven't found either victory quilt," she said, "but the stories they tell are too important to leave out of this exhibit. I thought I would frame some of the documents and photos and display those instead."

"An inspired idea," said Agnes.

Summer turned to Sylvia. "If you'd like me to omit the more disturbing details from the object placards—"

"Absolutely not," Sylvia declared. "I'll have nothing do with any such whitewashing of history."

"I just wanted to offer you that option, as a friend," said Summer. "I'm very glad you didn't accept."

"My dear, you're a historian," Sylvia reminded her. "You must tell the whole truth as best you can piece it together. Acknowledging past wrongdoing is the first step toward making things right."

**Victory Quilt.** 72" x 58" (estimated). Cotton top and backing with cotton batting. Pieced and quilted by the Waterford Quilting Guild, Waterford, PA, 1943.

**Victory Quilt.** 56" x 72". Cotton top and backing with cotton batting. Pieced and quilted by the Grangerville Quilt Guild, Grangerville, PA, 1944.

During World War Two, quilt guilds and other community groups throughout the United States made victory quilts, opportunity quilts sewn and raffled off to raise money for the war effort. While any block pattern was acceptable, victory quilts often incorporated patriotic themes and colors. Another popular practice was to include the names of local servicemen, usually applied to solid muslin or white patches within a pieced block using ink or embroidery.

The Waterford *Victory Quilt* is a Grandmother's Flower Garden, a popular one-patch design often made using the English paper piecing technique. According to Sylvia Bergstrom Compson, a contributor to the quilt and a former guild president, this design was chosen because "the small pieces were well suited to using up scraps, and with the war on, it was important to be frugal." Each of the fifty-three light hexagons encircled by six red hexagons was embroidered with the name of a local serviceman. Evoking the tradition of the Gold Star Service Banner, the quilters embroidered a gold star beside a soldier's name if he had died while serving his country. The Waterford Quilting Guild's raffle took place at Union Hall on Saturday, October 16, 1943. The winner, Doris Preiss Stover, later left the Elm Creek Valley, and the whereabouts of this victory quilt are not known.

The Grangerville *Victory Quilt* is comprised of forty-eight eight-inch Home Sweet Home blocks arranged in a straight setting with a four-inch-wide outer border. The center squares of all but two of the blocks, which are placed in opposite corners, have been embroidered with the names of local soldiers or sailors serving in the war. Grangerville Quilt Guild historian Denisha Williams notes that the Home Sweet Home block was selected to express the quiltmakers' heartfelt prayers that the young men honored in the quilt would return safely home to the Elm Creek Valley. The drawing took place at the bandshell at Riverview Park on Saturday, April 15, 1944. The winner, Martha Woods, was an acclaimed quilter in her own right and beloved public schoolteacher who served several terms on the Board of Education. The current location of this victory quilt is also unknown, but it is likely that one of Martha Woods's four children inherited it upon her death in 1988.

In lieu of the lost quilts, artifacts such as photos, sketches, newspaper clippings, and other documents are displayed here. A close reading of the lists of soldiers' names reveals that twelve Waterford residents were included in the Grangerville Quilt Guild's *Victory Quilt,* while nine soldiers from Grangerville appear in the quilt made in Waterford. Names were acquired for both quilts independently, submitted either by the men's family members or by quiltmakers who were acquainted with them. The evidence suggests that in some cases, ties of family or friendship with particular quiltmakers, more than town of residence, influenced which quilt would include a particular soldier's name. Although proximity was the primary factor influencing guild membership, the Waterford guild was almost exclusively white, while the Grangerville guild was predominantly Black. Census and enlistment records indicate that inclusion in the two *Victory Quilts* broke down along similar racial lines. Racial segregation was enshrined in law in the South, but it was lived in the North too, and this may be one example. Although neither guild supported an official policy of segregation, the demographics of membership raise challenging questions about racial segregation in the Elm Creek Valley.

# 9

Over the next few days, Summer photocopied Denisha Williams's documents, returned the originals, drafted a single object placard for the two lost victory quilts, and spent hours in the Rare Books Room searching for obituaries for the two raffle winners. Her microfilm skills and historical detective instincts were evidently improving with practice, for she located the names of three descendants of Doris Stover and four of Martha Woods.

The next step would be to match current addresses to the seven names, which meant searching the Waterford College Library's collection of telephone directories.

Returning to the library, Summer passed the atrium on the right and headed for the Rare Books Room out of habit, but halfway up the stairs, she remembered that collections of current microfilm were kept in the main library reference section. Smiling at her mistake, she turned and made her way to the proper section of the library, which she knew well from her undergraduate days. There she submitted her request to the very good-looking library assistant working the reference desk—

And stopped short from surprise, exactly at the same moment he did.

"Daily Grind," he said, eyes widening. "Blueberry scone."

"That's me," she said, nodding. "Well, I mean, I'm not actually a blueberry scone—" She caught herself. "I'm just a fan."

He grinned. "Me too."

Momentarily flustered, Summer glanced to the staff ID on the lanyard he wore around his neck. The glimpse she caught before he left to retrieve the microfilm told her that he was a graduate student, but she couldn't quite make out his name.

"Eventually, all of this information will be available on the World Wide Web," he told her when he returned from retrieving the microfilm. He scanned her alumni association card, and then, in a surprising but considerate bit of customer service, he carried the boxed spools to a nearby reader for her. "Everything's going to be digitized someday."

"Everything?" Summer echoed, slipping off her backpack and taking her seat. "Do you really think so? Even books and newspapers?"

"Especially books and newspapers," he said emphatically. His thick, wavy hair was dark brown with hints of bronze, and his brown eyes were as warm as she remembered. "Imagine—no more scrolling through microfilm and squinting at tiny, low-res print. Just type a keyword into the search engine and follow the links."

"That sounds pretty great." With a system like that, Summer could have saved herself hours of work over the past two weeks. "I'm guessing a lot of scanners with OCR are involved?"

"Plus librarians and techs to run them, and to clear out the bugs from the data collected," he said. "It's an exciting time to be in the MLIS program, don't you think? So many technological advances on the horizon, so many new ways to access information and make it available to patrons." He caught himself. "Not that other specializations aren't equally important. You're in the Archivist concentration, right?"

For a moment Summer could only blink at him. "Sorry?"

His eyebrows drew together in puzzlement. "Aren't you in MLIS?"

"No," said Summer, shaking her head, amused. "Wow. Do I really spend that much time in the library?"

"Ah, sorry about that," he said, wincing. "It's just that I see you here all the time. You're usually upstairs talking to Audrey Pfenning or studying something super intently. I thought you worked here, that you were another graduate assistant."

"I do *work* here, quite a lot, especially recently. I'm just not *employed* here."

"Yeah, I get that now." He shook his head, abashed but smiling. He had a great smile. "I'll let you get to work. If you have any questions, just ask."

As he returned to the reference desk, she opened her notebook to the relevant page, set it beside the keyboard, and loaded the first roll of film for Pennsylvania, a tiny bit crushed that he had not lingered to make sure she knew how. Of course he knew that she knew; hadn't he said he'd seen her in the library many times before? Obviously he had other things to do, other people to help. She could even imagine patrons *inventing* questions for an excuse to chat with him.

She closed her eyes and gave her head a small, impatient shake. She had too much work to do and couldn't afford any distractions, however attractive and charming they might be.

Resisting the temptation to glance over her shoulder to see if he was looking her way, Summer fixed her gaze on the screen and scrolled through the film, searching alphabetically for the cities where the possible descendants lived, then alphabetically again by last name. She located a possible mailing address for Doris Stover's eldest daughter within five minutes, but she needed an hour and three roll changes to track down two options for the youngest. She switched reels twice more, but found nothing for Martha Woods's descendants, which might mean that they had unlisted numbers, had changed their names, or had moved after the obituary had been published—or that they too had passed on.

As she worked, Summer checked her watch occasionally, as she had promised her mom she'd join her for dinner at the manor and she didn't want to be late. Finally, with minutes to spare, her diligence was rewarded with two promising leads for Martha Woods's youngest son and daughter. Quickly she jotted down the addresses, gathered up her rolls of microfilm, and returned them to the reference desk, her backpack dangling precariously by one strap from her shoulder.

She was secretly delighted that the same library assistant was still on duty. "Thanks for your help," she told him as he scanned her ID again to check in the microfilm.

"No problem." He glanced at her card. "'Alumni association,'" he read aloud, offering a self-deprecating smile as he returned her card. "If I had read more carefully, Summer, I wouldn't have mistaken you for an MLIS student."

She couldn't help smiling back. "It's not fair that you know my name but I don't know yours."

He held out his name badge. "Enrique," he said even as she read it for herself. "So, did you find what you were looking for?"

"Almost, but not everything."

His smile deepened. "I guess you'll have to come back and try again."

For a moment she considered explaining that she had found everything she could in the directories, and it wasn't likely she'd be back anytime soon, but that sounded too final. "Maybe I will," she said instead, adjusting her backpack. Almost without meaning to, she gave him one last smile over her shoulder as she turned to go.

The next morning, armed with her list of names and addresses, she wrote to the potential descendants of Martha Woods and Doris Stover to inquire about the victory quilt any of them, or none of them, might have inherited. She knew it was entirely possible that her letters might be on their way to unrelated people who just happened to share the same names as the raffle winners' children. Still, with any luck, at least one recipient would reply with good news, either the location of a quilt or other leads she could pursue.

In the meantime, convinced that the Union Hall display would be incomplete without something about the two victory quilts, she selected a few artifacts for each, bought matching frames from an art supply shop downtown, and matted and framed the documents and photos using archival-quality materials. On Saturday afternoon, after the week's campers had departed and the usual tidying up was done, Summer worked on the last few items in the kitchen, where the refectory table provided ample space to spread everything out within easy reach. She was nearly finished when Gretchen's husband, Joe, entered to refill his empty coffee mug. As a younger man, the seventy-year-old Pittsburgh native had been a machinist in a steel mill until a workplace accident left him with a broken back. Although his doctors warned the Hartleys that he would never walk again, Joe had worked tirelessly to regain his mobility. In the years that had followed, he had built a second career as a skilled carpenter and expert restorer of antique furniture, a successful business he had relocated to a new woodworking shop in the estate's red barn when Gretchen joined Elm Creek Quilts.

"Is all this for the museum?" Joe asked, eyeing the material spread out on the refectory table as he headed for the coffeepot.

"Sure is," said Summer, dusting off the front of one frame with a soft cloth. "I'd rather display the actual quilts, but these items will make excellent placeholders. They contribute so much to the story of our community, I might leave them up even after I acquire the quilts."

"That's the spirit. Not if, but when." Joe set his mug on the table and picked up the photo of Sylvia and the other Waterford quilters, although he seemed more interested in the wooden frame than the image enclosed. "Not bad for mass-produced work," he said, examining the finish and the miters. "If I had known you needed frames, I would have made you a bunch for your birthday."

"Wait, what?" Summer rested the hand holding the cloth on her hip, and regarded him with a look that would have done Sylvia proud. "How do you know my birthday's coming up?"

"I don't recall, exactly." Joe shrugged, chagrined. "I must have heard your mom mention it."

"Joe," she said, drawing out the word, "are the Elm Creek Quilters planning a surprise party for me since they won't get the chance to throw one for Vinnie this season?"

"No," he said emphatically, glancing toward the doorway. When he saw no eavesdroppers there, he lowered his voice and added, "I mean, that's not the reason. They're doing it because they love you and they're happy you're home."

Summer muffled a sigh. "Fair enough. What's the plan?"

"Oh, no. I've said too much already." He gestured toward the framed documents with one hand and seized his coffee cup with the other. "Get back to work. Forget I was ever here."

"I promise I won't tell on you," she called after him, as he rushed from the kitchen. It was just as well he had warned her. Otherwise she might have stayed late at Union Hall, spoiling her friends' plans.

On Monday morning, so many campers wished Summer a happy birthday that she would have known something was up even if Joe hadn't given it away. Her mom arrived early to join her for breakfast, greeting her with an especially warm hug and regaling the campers seated at their table with the story of Summer's unconventional childhood, delighting some campers and shocking others. "Gwen was a flower child," Diane called from the next table over, as either an explanation or an excuse. The campers nodded as if all had been made clear.

Afterward, Summer again borrowed her mom's car and drove off to Union Hall with Gerda's Log Cabin, the artifacts for the two victory quilts, and a manila folder holding printouts of the object labels stowed in the back seat. She needed two trips to carry everything from the car upstairs to the gallery, and when she returned one last time for her backpack, she ran into Pat in the lobby. "I'm so glad you came in today," the historical society president said, placing a hand on her shoulder to guide her into the office. "Our answering machine and our general email inbox are full of messages for you."

"Messages for me, here?"

"For the curator of the new exhibit. Word is spreading, and we haven't even sent out our monthly newsletter yet." Beaming, Pat cleared a stack of papers from the chair behind the desk and gestured for Summer to sit. "We've even had a few visitors tour the gallery."

"But we've hung only two quilts."

"True, but they're extraordinary quilts, and judging by the response, seeing them was well worth the visit. All of the visitors made donations!"

"That's fantastic—but surprising. Very. I wasn't expecting visitors quite so soon."

"Neither were we. To protect the quilts, we keep the gallery doors locked even during regular hours, so someone from the office has to let visitors in and keep watch until they depart. It's no trouble, but we've moved up our timetable for organizing security and docents."

When Pat gestured again to the desk chair, Summer sat down, bemused. "What are the emails about?"

"People have heard that you're seeking quilts important to local history, and they have quilts they consider worthy of inclusion," said Pat. "Fair warning: experience has taught me that sometimes well-meaning donors—or would-be sellers—tend to overvalue their items out of sentiment or simple misunderstanding."

"I'll be tactful," Summer promised. "Who knows? We might discover a few treasures."

"And a few new contributors to our capital campaign." Pat gestured to the answering machine, where a tiny red light blinked eagerly for their attention. "When you've gone through the emails, you can listen to the voice messages. Feel free to delete them afterward." She glanced at her watch. "I'm late for a board meeting. What am I forgetting?"

"Your purse?" Summer suggested, nodding to the brown leather cross-body bag on the edge of the desk.

With a gasp, Pat snatched it up, thanked her, and hurried off.

After Pat's warning, Summer had expected to find dozens if not hundreds of messages, but there turned out to be only fourteen emails and eight voice messages. Even so, it took her the better part of an hour to read and reply to the emails, and to listen to the messages and call back, mostly leaving messages of her own. In the end she had made a list of six quilts that sounded very promising, four probably not suitable but worth a look, and four that could be ruled out immediately. This included one quilt that the emailer herself had made the previous year but would be willing to part with if the price was right; Summer diplomatically explained that the quilt sounded lovely, but was too new to have influenced Waterford's history in a significant way. A caller offering another quilt acknowledged she had bought it at Target, but she didn't need it anymore and she wanted it to go to a worthy cause; Summer recommended donating the quilt to a local charity. As for the other, more promising leads, Summer replied with requests to schedule a time when the owners could bring their quilts to Union Hall to be evaluated. Hoping to spare Pat additional work, she gave out her own contact information so they could reach her directly.

She had just hung up after her last phone call when the computer pinged, signaling a new email. The subject line, "Inquiry about Quilt Exhibit Donation," assured her that she was the intended recipient, so she had no qualms about reading it. Yet even as she double-clicked to open the note, a jolt of recognition struck her when she glimpsed the sender's name—Kathleen Barrett.

Summer knew her. They were only acquaintances, but their meetings, though few in number, had been strikingly memorable. Kathleen was the daughter of Rosemary Cullen and the great-great-granddaughter of Dorothea Granger Nelson. Three years before, Summer had tracked down Rosemary and Kathleen while researching Gerda Bergstrom's memoir. Rosemary's family stories had raised as many questions as they had answered, and had led Summer's inquiries in new directions.

Rosemary had inherited several priceless heirlooms from her great-grandparents, including a trove of letters Thomas Nelson had written home to Dorothea while he was serving in the Civil War. Another invaluable treasure was a Dove in the Window quilt Dorothea had made for him, and which he had carried in his bedroll when he marched off to war three years later. Although the quilt had been a favorite, Thomas had given it away to a young, wounded Confederate soldier desperately in need of warmth and comfort—but eventually, astonishingly, the lost quilt had been returned to the Nelson homestead, Two Bears Farm.

Though she had seen it only briefly, Summer remembered the Nelson family's cherished heirloom well. The block pattern, a seven patch, was a popular Dove in the Window variation, with a one-inch square in the center and, in each of the corners, an irregular pentagon framed by two half-square triangle units on adjacent sides and another square at the tip. Dorothea had painstakingly arranged triangles, rectangles, and squares of Turkey red, Prussian blue, and sun-bleached muslin into eighteen blocks, each slightly larger than twelve inches square. Next she had set the blocks on point and added pieced setting triangles to the ends of the rows to create a balanced, unbroken design, which she had framed with mitered borders of a floral print of small blue flowers scattered on a Turkey red background. Considering the many hazardous miles the quilt had traveled within the span of seven years, it was in remarkably sound condition, with some faded fabrics and worn binding, but otherwise whole.

Summer remembered a good-natured argument between Rosemary and her eldest daughter when Summer had brought Sylvia to meet them at their home. Rosemary planned to leave Thomas's letters and the quilt to Kathleen, but Kathleen had other ideas. "I want to pass these treasures on to future generations, and I know Kathleen will be a faithful steward," Rosemary had told Sylvia and Summer, with a pointed, sidelong look at her daughter. "Kathleen thinks I should leave them to a museum. Can you believe it? The very idea. Giving our family heirlooms to strangers."

"A museum would know how to properly care for them," Kathleen had replied, affectionately scolding, as if this was an old argument she knew she'd never win. "Part of good stewardship is ensuring that something lasts so that it may be passed down. Those papers are getting more fragile every day, Mother, and the quilt is too."

Ever the diplomat, Sylvia had stayed out of it, but Summer had been unable to resist offering an opinion. "I'll bet Waterford College would love to have them."

"That's exactly what I suggested." To her mother, Kathleen added, "Think of what the students could learn from Thomas's letters. And think of your great-grandparents' contribution to history and to the cause of freedom. Shouldn't the memory of their deeds be preserved for future generations?"

Rosemary's reply had made it clear that she was uncomfortable with the subject, so Sylvia had deftly turned the conversation to the Bergstroms' and the Nelsons' daring work for the Underground Railroad. They said nothing more about the bequest of the quilt and the letters that day.

After all this time, had Kathleen persuaded her mother to change her mind?

Though tempted to skip ahead to the end, Summer deliberately read the email through carefully so she wouldn't overlook important questions or caveats. As she had guessed, Kathleen was indeed writing to inquire about donating the Dove in the Window quilt to the historical society—but Summer's excitement was quickly tempered by a pang of regret.

Kathleen had referred to the quilt not as her mother's quilt, but as one she had inherited from her mother. Rosemary had passed away. The news would grieve Sylvia, if she wasn't already aware. She and Rosemary had hit it off at their first meeting, delighted by the knowledge that their great-grandmothers had been best friends.

With a sigh, Summer read on.

Kathleen briefly explained the quilt's significance to local history and offered to bring it by Union Hall for evaluation. She emphasized that before she could decide whether to entrust the priceless heirloom to the Waterford Historical Society, she wished to see the gallery where Dorothea's quilt would be displayed and to ask the curator some pertinent questions.

Summer responded immediately. After expressing her condolences for Kathleen's loss, she thanked her for her inquiry and identified herself as the exhibit's curator. "I remember the quilt your mother showed me and Sylvia, and how much she cherished it, very well," Summer wrote. "Dorothea's Dove in the Window would be a wonderful addition to the exhibit, for both its artistic merit and the fascinating story it tells of life in the Elm Creek Valley during the Civil War era. I'm sure you're eager to know more about the measures we're taking to ensure the security and preservation of the artifacts in this collection. I'd be happy to answer any questions you may have and to take you on a tour of the beautiful new gallery at your convenience." She concluded with her direct contact information and her hopes that they would be able to meet soon.

After she sent the email on its way, she took the folder holding the object labels from her backpack and set it front and center on Pat's desk, marked with a bright blue sticky note asking for suggestions and corrections. Then she hurried upstairs to the gallery, unlocking the doors with the key Pat had entrusted to her. She opened the doors wide and set the doorstops in place, offering an enticing glimpse of the gallery should any curious quilt aficionados wander by. As she did, she noticed a woven wicker basket set against the wall, a small, neatly handwritten note affixed to the front rim: "Donations Welcome."

Inside sat a check for twenty-five dollars and a handful of loose change.

Summer gathered up the coins and the check and tucked them into her backpack for safekeeping. She welcomed the donations, but there had to be a better way to collect them. From a short distance away, the cylindrical basket resembled an upscale trash can a bit too much. What if a well-meaning staff member, tidying up, unwittingly emptied the basket into the garbage?

Summer resolved to come up with something else as soon as possible. But first, other tasks required her attention.

She began by hanging Gerda's Log Cabin on one of the shorter end walls, so a visitor's gaze would flow to it naturally after the Loyal Union Sampler. She took measurements, made small pencil markings, attached the hardware to the wall, and, at last, slipped the rod through the hanging sleeve and hung it on the brackets. Stepping back to admire it, she moved the quilt slightly to the left and scrutinized it once more. Perfect, she decided, immeasurably grateful to Sylvia for lending her precious heirloom to the exhibit. Summer could well imagine how marvelous it would be to hang Dorothea's Dove in the Window nearby, the artwork of two dear friends and brave comrades from the Elm Creek Valley's storied past, long lost and miraculously reunited in Union Hall.

Next, on a center partition wall, Summer arranged the framed artifacts from the two victory quilts. While she worked, two ladies who looked to be in their fifties wandered in and paused to admire the Loyal Union Sampler and the Creek's Crossing Album. Summer greeted them with a smile, then left them to explore on their own, pleased by the murmured praise she overheard as they moved on to Gerda's Log Cabin. She ought to post the object labels soon, she reflected, making a mental note to move that task to the top of her to-do list. The quilts were admirable in their own right as artistic works, but a viewer's experience of them would be enriched tremendously if they knew the backstories.

The two visitors eventually made their way to Summer's end of the room and lingered to watch as she hung the last framed item, the photo of the Grangerville Quilt Guild members holding up their quilt. "May I ask what you're doing?" one of the ladies asked, bemused. "I thought this was a quilt exhibit."

"It is." Summer straightened the photo and explained why she had included the framed artifacts. The two visitors nodded as they listened, intrigued, and when she finished, the second quilter asked if Summer could tell them about the other three quilts. Summer readily agreed. Afterward, the women were so pleased with her docent services, impromptu though they were, that each left a crisp twenty in the basket on their way out.

Summer waited for them to depart before adding the bills to the donations she had already collected. Then she put away her tools, locked up the gallery, and went downstairs to the office, where she found Pat working at her computer. "More contributions," she said, taking the lot from her backpack and handing it over. "Every little bit helps."

"Indeed it does. This is a promising sign of better things to come after we officially open." Pat placed her hand on the folder Summer had left on her desk earlier. "Your object labels are excellent. I wouldn't change a word."

"Really? Not one single word?"

"Not one word, not one punctuation mark."

Summer smiled. "Then I suppose my next step is to figure out how to display them."

When she returned to Elm Creek Manor, she hurried upstairs to her room, emailed Grace Daniels at the de Young Museum for advice, and dressed for dinner. She entered the banquet hall with minutes to spare, only to find everyone already seated, the overhead lights dimmed, the tables adorned with arrangements of candles and Peace roses, the delicious aroma of Indian spices enticing her from the doorway.

"She's here!" she heard someone call, and then everyone together— her friends, the campers, everyone—shouted, "Happy birthday, Summer!"

She was so surprised she pressed a hand to her heart and laughed aloud. Until that moment, she had entirely forgotten Joe's accidental reveal in the kitchen. As applause and laughter filled the hall, her mother hurried over to hug her, and then Sarah did too, little James balanced on her hip. Gwen led her to her seat, a beribboned chair between her own and Sylvia's, where Gwen wrapped her in a white feather boa and Sylvia playfully slipped a rhinestone tiara on her head. Soon thereafter, Anna personally escorted her to the head of the buffet, where Summer discovered all of her favorite vegetarian Indian dishes—dal, chana masala, malai kofta, aloo gobi, jeera rice, mango and tomato chutneys, and three varieties of naan. Everything was wonderfully delicious, and everyone was in such good spirits that Summer couldn't resist their humorous demands that she attend the evening program, even though she knew she ought to put in at least an hour on her thesis. Everyone deserved a bit of fun on their birthday, she reminded herself as they swept her off to the ballroom for the campers' talent show.

She would make up the time later, she told herself as the lights dimmed and the curtains parted, resolving not to spare another thought for her thesis for the rest of the day.

Later, after the final bows and wild applause from a delighted audience, Summer helped tidy up, bade her mother and her friends good night, and headed upstairs to check her email. She had dozens of cheerful, affectionate birthday greetings from friends awaiting her, including one from Julianne with a photo of her and Maricela blowing kisses. "We could never forget your birthday, Summer Solstice Sullivan!" Julianne wrote. "Hope you're having a fabulous day. We'll celebrate in style when you (finally) come home. Miss you much!!!"

"I *am* home," Summer murmured, with a pang of surprise or guilt or a combination of the two. Elm Creek Manor was home; Chicago was where she went to school. She adored her roommates, and she loved Chicago, but Elm Creek Manor always would be home.

Maybe Julianne had meant to say when Summer came *back*. Summer decided to assume as much. She wrote a cheerful reply thanking her friends for their birthday wishes and assuring them that she'd see them in August, or maybe early September, but definitely before the fall term began.

She read a few more birthday greetings before she came to a reply from Kathleen Barrett. "I'm so glad to hear that you're in charge of the exhibit," she wrote. "Knowing that an Elm Creek Quilter is involved with the project eases my worries considerably. Could I come by Friday afternoon, preferably around 1 P.M.? I promise not to take up too much of your time."

As far as Summer was concerned, Kathleen could take up all the time she wanted if it meant adding the Dove in the Window quilt to the exhibit. She quickly replied to confirm the meeting. When she climbed into bed, she was smiling, lighthearted and full of anticipation for whatever the next day might bring.

Just before she drifted off to sleep, she realized that she had felt that way nearly every night since she had returned to Elm Creek Manor. Gone was the persistent dread that kept her awake, thoughts racing, until exhaustion overcame her. She no longer woke with a knot of worry in the pit of her stomach.

Over the next few days, after Sunrise Yoga and breakfast in the banquet hall, Summer fielded emails and phone calls about the Union Hall exhibit, resulting in leads on several promising artworks. She also pitched in around quilt camp as needed, though her friends asked for her help only when they truly couldn't manage without her. Summer still found herself with several uninterrupted hours every day to work on her thesis, sometimes alone in her room, sometimes on a blanket spread on the grass near the orchard, and when the weather didn't cooperate or she wanted company, in the library. She would sit on the sofa with her legs stretched out in front of her, typing on her laptop or brooding over her outline and notes, while Sarah toiled away at the oak desk nearby. By Friday noon, when Summer set her computer aside to prepare for her meeting with Kathleen, she had added two pages to her thesis—not terribly impressive considering how much time she had invested in it, but at least she was gaining momentum.

At a quarter to one, Summer inspected the gallery to be sure everything was in perfect order, then quickly returned to the foyer so she would be waiting to greet Kathleen when she arrived—which

THE MUSEUM OF LOST QUILTS

she did, five minutes early, dressed for the office in a gray pinstripe pantsuit, pink blouse, and gray flats. She was empty-handed except for a black leather purse and a thick manila envelope tucked under one arm, but Summer hadn't expected her to bring the quilt to the meeting, so she didn't take that as an ominous sign.

"Welcome to Union Hall," Summer greeted her, smiling. "Have you seen the building since the remodel began?"

"Only from the outside." Kathleen cast an appraising look around the foyer. "I've been impressed by the improvements to the exterior—long overdue, in my opinion. From the look of things, it won't be long until the interior is restored to its former glory as well."

"We *hope* it won't be long, but there's a lot of work yet to do," Summer acknowledged. "The Waterford Historical Society has ambitious—but entirely feasible—plans for making Union Hall a treasure of the historic district, which is why we're counting on the quilt exhibit to help raise funds."

"And that's where I come in."

"You and other generous donors, I hope." Summer gestured to the staircase. "Would you like to see the gallery?"

When Kathleen accepted, Summer led her upstairs and showed her around the gallery, pausing before each of the artworks so Kathleen could see that the Dove in the Window quilt would be in excellent company. As they moved along, Summer described the important climate control and security features the gallery offered—or soon would, after the installation was complete—to keep Dorothea's quilt safe. Kathleen nodded approvingly as she listened, and Summer responded to her questions as best she could. Whenever she didn't know the answer, she jotted down a note and promised to email her with a reply as soon as possible.

"May I ask you a question?" Summer asked when they had finished the tour and were heading downstairs.

"Of course. It's only fair. I've asked you so many."

"My understanding was that your mother was reluctant to donate

Dorothea's quilt and letters to a museum or Waterford College rather than keeping them in the family. Did she change her mind, or—"

"Or am I proceeding against her wishes?" Kathleen finished for her. "I understand why you'd wonder. My mother changed her mind. It was Sylvia who planted the seed, when she remarked that she and my mother were fortunate to have these fragile mementos of our ancestors. Quilts, letters, and a handwritten memoir aren't nearly as durable as other monuments to the past."

"No, they aren't, unfortunately."

"My mother took it to heart when Sylvia said that they shared a tremendous responsibility to make sure that their family heirlooms endured for future generations. Eventually my mother decided that if I truly believed our family's legacy would be best served by entrusting Dorothea's heirlooms to a museum, she gave me her blessing."

"Even so, I'm sure it isn't easy to decide where to place them," said Summer. "We would be honored if you would entrust Dorothea's quilt to us. If you need any additional information from me or from the historical society so you can make an informed choice, please let me know."

"I've seen all I need to see, for now," said Kathleen. "I'm willing to lend you the quilt for a period of, let's say, six months. If I'm satisfied with the historical society's stewardship after that, I'll consider extending the loan, or making a permanent donation."

"Thank you very much, Kathleen," Summer replied, holding back an unprofessional cheer, but unable to restrain an enormous grin. "I'm confident we'll prove ourselves worthy of your trust."

"I'm sure you will, which is why I'd like your help finding another long-lost quilt."

"Another quilt? One of Dorothea's?"

Kathleen nodded. "In a few letters she wrote later in life, Dorothea mentioned a Delectable Mountains variation she had pieced for her uncle Jacob Kuehner before the Civil War. He wasn't a quilter himself, but he designed one, quirks and all, and he insisted she reproduce it precisely as he demanded."

"Kuehner?" Summer echoed. "As in Kuehner Road, and Kuehner Hall on campus?"

"Yes, that's right. Jacob Kuehner was Dorothea's mother's brother. After Dorothea's parents lost their home to a flood, Jacob took them in—somewhat grudgingly, or so the story goes. He was something of a curmudgeon, but he was also a very successful farmer and maple sugar producer. According to family folklore, he kept the Delectable Mountains quilt at his sugar camp because it offered clues to fugitives making their way north along the Underground Railroad."

"Another stationmaster? It seems to be the family business."

"Indeed, and one I can be proud of." Kathleen handed Summer the thick manila envelope. "These are photocopies of some of the Granger-Nelson family papers. There's also a large file box of original documents that my cousin borrowed for a genealogy project. I'll collect it from her and drop it off at Elm Creek Manor late next week. I hope that you, with your quilting expertise and historian's training, might find some clues in these family papers that might help us to learn, first, if this quilt ever existed, and second, what might have become of it."

The envelope was heavier than Summer had expected, overstuffed and straining. "I'll certainly do my best, but to be honest, it doesn't sound like you have a lot to go on."

"That's precisely why I'd like to turn over the project to you. I've hit too many dead ends. It's time for someone with a fresh pair of eyes to take a look." Kathleen smiled. "As an incentive, if you do find the quilt, you may include it in your exhibit for as long as you like, unconditionally."

"In that case, I'm all in." After a moment, Summer added, "As for the original documents, may I make a suggestion?"

"Certainly."

"If you're looking for an excellent steward for Dorothea's letters, as well as the rest of the Nelson-Granger family papers, I highly recommend the Rare Books and Special Collections Department at the Waterford College Library. The head librarian, Audrey Pfenning, has devoted her entire career to looking after local history collections. I'd be happy to introduce you if you're interested in learning more."

"I might be," said Kathleen, nodding thoughtfully. "For quite a long while, I've wanted these papers to be available for students and local historians. This might be the perfect way to do so. I'll need to think it over and discuss it with my cousins. While I own most of the collection, several boxes belong to other members of the family, and I'd like to have some consensus."

"I understand," said Summer, hopeful despite the caveat. "Whenever you decide you'd like to meet Audrey, please let me know."

How wonderful to think that the Waterford College Library might also benefit from Kathleen's generosity—and all because Summer had asked the question.

**Dove in the Window.** 68" x 85". Cotton top and backing with wool batting. Pieced and hand quilted by Dorothea Granger Nelson, Creek's Crossing, PA, 1858.

This mid-nineteenth-century quilt is comprised of eighteen blocks of a well-known Dove in the Window variation and ten setting triangles of an original, complementary design. The Turkey red fabrics, known as "red-ground prints," were especially popular in the U.S. in the 1840s, even though they were more expensive than other cottons. The dyes were colorfast—a welcome innovation—but the fabrics in this quilt must have been imported from Europe, for mills in the United States did not adopt this printing technology until after the Civil War. Prussian blue, a mineral dye, was an excellent choice for printed cotton fabrics both as a ground color and for printed figures, and were most popular in the U.S. from 1840–1865.

A Turkey red and Prussian blue palette can be quite useful for dating nineteenth-century quilts, but the maker of *Dove in the Window* simplified the historian's task by providing an embroidered note on the back: "Made by Dorothea Granger Nelson for her beloved husband, Thomas Nelson, in our sixth year of marriage, 1858. Two Bears Farm, Creek's Crossing, Pennsylvania."

Three years after Dorothea completed the quilt, Thomas carried it in his bedroll when he marched off to war with the 49th Pennsylvania Regiment. In a letter home to Dorothea dated May 5, 1862, Thomas wrote, "I wish to tell you that you were right to insist that I bring along the Dove in the Window quilt. It has brought me immeasurable comfort in these harrowing months, not only for its warmth and softness, but also for the fond remembrances it evokes of its beloved maker."

More than a year later, on July 7, 1863, Thomas again mentioned the quilt in a letter home:

*My beloved wife,*

*We have made camp for the night and I improve a miserable day greatly by taking pen in hand and writing to you.*

*By now you have surely heard about the tremendous campaign that concluded in Gettysburg a few days ago. Although the VI Corps did not reach the battlefield until the afternoon of July 2, the First Division was promptly deployed and was soon engaged in the fight. I hope you will forgive me, my love, but in the aftermath of the day's fighting, I parted with the beautiful quilt you made for me. If you had seen the poor wounded soldier to whom I gave it, you would have agreed that his need was greater than mine. Perhaps in your compassion for the suffering you would have taken the quilt from my bedroll yourself and draped it over the young man with your own gentle hands.*

Although Thomas did not mention his heroism in this letter, other sources confirm that he carried the wounded Confederate soldier through an active battlefield to the Union field hospital on Seminary Ridge where Dorothea's brother, Dr. Jonathan Granger, a regimental surgeon, saved the young soldier's life. Tragically, the brothers-in-law did not meet that day, nor was Thomas ever reunited with his beloved wife and young daughter, Abigail. Thomas Nelson was killed in the Battle of Spotsylvania Court House in May 1864.

Several years after the war, Jonathan Granger unexpectedly received a parcel from Dallas County, Alabama. The long-lost *Dove in the Window* was enclosed, along with a letter, dated February 10, 1868, from Malinda Jane Holmes Wilson, writing "on behalf of [her] husband, Private Satterwhite Wilson," whose wartime injuries had rendered him blind.

*He has never forgotten your kindness and credits you with the saving of his life as well as the man married to your*

*sister who carried him several miles off the hill they now
call Little Round Top. Your brother in law gave my suffering
husband the gift of his quilt . . . Now that there is peace
between North and South my husband thought it proper
to return it to Mr. Nelson who is to us a hero and a true
Christian . . . [Satterwhite] asks that you would do him
one more kindness and return this quilt which was a great
comfort to him in his hour of need to its rightful owner
along with his sincere thanks . . . [W]ithout you both he
surely would have perished in the war. I add my thanks to
you good men for your kindliness to my husband though he
was Confederate and you Yankee.*

Dove in the Window appears in this exhibit on loan from the
private collection of Kathleen Barrett, great-great-granddaughter
of Thomas and Dorothea Nelson.

# 10

On Sunday morning, Sylvia called a breakfast meeting to remind the Elm Creek Quilters that the upcoming session of quilt camp would be a bit unusual. "All of our guests belong to a single quilt guild," she said. "They've chosen Elm Creek Manor for their annual guild retreat, and they've asked us to accommodate some of their own programs and traditions."

"I said this in March and I'll say it again," declared Diane, pausing to sip her latte. "I don't like it."

"I have misgivings too," said Gretchen. "One of the greatest rewards of quilt camp is coming together as strangers and parting as friends, sharing new ideas and perspectives all the days in between."

A murmur of agreement went around the room, but since Summer wasn't teaching, she merely observed without offering an opinion.

"Well, I understand why a guild might want to enjoy a bonding experience just among themselves," Agnes ventured. "Don't many of our campers attend in groups of friends—the Flying Saucer Sisters, for example—or reunite here annually, like the Cross-Country Quilters?"

"Those are small groups," Diane countered. "This will be the entire population of camp. I vote no."

"Seconded," said Maggie, raising a hand, "for the reasons Gretchen stated."

"How inconvenient for you both that it isn't up for a vote," said Sylvia dryly.

"Sylvia's right," said Sarah, sliding a plate of pastries out of James's reach as he strained for them from his seat on her lap. "Although no guild has ever requested an exclusive week before, we have no official policy against it. The guild president didn't tell us ahead of time that this was their intention, but she booked every spot for the week the moment reservations went live last December."

"Yes, and she must have gotten up very early in the morning to do so." Sylvia turned a firm look upon them all over the rims of her glasses. "The Dogwood Quilters are coming, as one group, and we are going to make them feel most welcome."

"Of course we will," said Agnes, her blue eyes astonished at the very suggestion that they might not. "We welcome everyone."

"Excellent. That said . . ." Sylvia took a sheet of paper from her pocket and unfolded it, sighing. "I received an email last night suggesting—or rather, stipulating—some additional changes to the way we ordinarily do things."

"Here we go," muttered Diane, leaning back in her booth and folding her arms.

"First, they plan to do a block swap in lieu of the Candlelight ceremony," Sylvia said, frowning slightly as she read.

"But the Candlelight ceremony sets the tone for the entire week," protested Gretchen.

"I explained as much, but the guild president replied that they already know one another, so introductions are unnecessary," said Sylvia. "As to sharing their hopes for the week ahead, that is, and I quote, 'each quilter's own business.'"

"Goodness," said Agnes, startled. "I'm sure we never meant to pry."

"Do they still want the Welcome Banquet?" asked Anna warily. "I've already started the prep work."

"Oh, yes, they want everything about meal service to go on as planned." Sylvia paused, studying the page. "Except for Saturday morning, when they would like breakfast packed to go, so they can load up the bus and get an early start."

"So, no Farewell Breakfast," said Anna. "Not a problem. I can adapt."

"Is that everything?" asked Gwen, as if she were bracing herself. "They don't want any changes to our classes, I hope."

"No changes to our curriculum, but—with the exception of the jazz quintet scheduled for Thursday—they want to lead their own evening programs." Sylvia folded the paper and returned it to her pocket. "I suppose that means we'll have most of our nights off, except for tidying up afterward."

"Great," said Diane flatly.

"Try to keep an open mind," implored Sarah over the murmurs of discontent. "Let's not interpret their requests as criticism of what we usually do." She shifted a fidgeting James on her lap and pushed the pastries even farther away as he attempted to climb onto the table. "Change can be good. There may be things about this arrangement we actually enjoy."

"Doubt it," said Diane, tossing her blond curls for emphasis.

Nonetheless, the meeting ended with most of the Elm Creek Quilters promising to adopt Sarah's optimistic attitude. Then they all hurried off to prepare for the Dogwood Quilters' arrival. To Summer's relief, when the guild's enormous bus finally pulled into the circular drive in front of the manor, two hours later than expected, the quilters who disembarked seemed as friendly and as happy to be there as any other campers.

The week passed nearly as pleasantly as any other, with fewer interactions with their guests, and perhaps a few more complaints when not every detail was precisely as their guild president had described. Still, after the Dogwood Quilters departed on Saturday, the Elm Creek Quilters admitted to being pleasantly surprised at how well the week had passed.

"As an experiment, it was a success," said Sarah, with a significant look for Sylvia. "Maybe next year we could consider extending our season into the fall, offering the manor as a retreat for one guild at a time."

Sylvia pursed her lips and shook her head. "We wouldn't have the staff for that. After Labor Day, half of our teachers have other commitments."

"We wouldn't need teachers," said Sarah, "not if the guild is responsible for their own programming, as the Dogwood Quilters were."

"I'd be happy to continue as chef into the fall," said Anna. "During the offseason I take on some catering gigs when I can get them, but I'd much rather have another month of steady paychecks working here."

As the other Elm Creek Quilters chimed in with comments and questions, Sylvia raised her hands for quiet. "This is a discussion for another time," she said. "Thank you all for another successful week, and I'll see you tomorrow."

Summer understood that they were dismissed, but as she bade her friends goodbye until the morning, she felt a pang of worry when she recalled the conversation she had interrupted the day she had returned to the manor. Sarah had mentioned something about needing additional sources of revenue. Was her new suggestion about extending the camp season prompted by that? Why did Sylvia seem so reluctant to discuss it? Should Summer give up her room in the manor to a paying customer?

But when she caught Sarah alone and offered to move out, Sarah assured her it wasn't necessary. "You earn your keep," she said, smiling, "and the income from one room wouldn't make much of a difference."

Sarah hurried off to join Matt and the twins before Summer could ask what *would* make a difference, if there was something more Summer should be doing to support Elm Creek Quilts.

Whether the experiment was ever repeated, one thing Summer had learned from it was that the Dogwood Quilters' independence had unexpectedly granted her extra time in the evenings to work on her thesis. As a new camp week began and the days passed, she needed every spare hour she could find as she toiled away, sentence by laborious sentence. The process was tedious, her once-ardent enthusiasm had entirely evaporated, and there were at least a dozen other things she'd rather be doing, but whenever she was tempted to quit, she reminded herself how relieved and happy she would be to finish. Sometimes a troubling thought crept in, a nagging concern that the academic career she sought wouldn't be much different from this, *if* she were able to earn her degree, if she were able to grab one of the increasingly rare tenure-track positions out there. But dwelling upon such unsettling possibilities was a sure way to bring her writing to a grinding halt, so she shoved the thoughts aside.

Summer much preferred her research for the Union Hall exhibit. In recent days, several of her email and phone queries had resulted in the loan or donation of several wonderful antique quilts, which she carefully cleaned, restored, and mended as needed, under Agnes's expert supervision. Together, and sometimes with Pat looking on and offering suggestions, they found a place for each item in the steadily filling gallery. Sometimes only a newspaper photograph, or a description in a diary, or a sketch in a scrapbook remained of a missing masterpiece. Unwilling to dismiss the artworks as lost forever, Summer displayed the artifacts instead, to honor the quilts' existence and—she hoped—perhaps to prompt a memory from an exhibit visitor, someone who might remember seeing the quilt in a grandmother's parlor or on an antique shop's shelf. Any clue, however irrelevant it seemed, might eventually lead to a lost quilt's discovery.

For each item, whether quilt or substitute, Summer composed a thoughtful, detailed description sharing what she had learned about the quiltmaker and the quilt's place in local history. After all her struggles with her thesis, writing the object labels was relatively easy. Figuring out the ideal way to display them was another matter. Summer didn't want to use the same frames she used for the artifacts, to avoid confusing the two, but the options Grace Daniels recommended far exceeded the Waterford Historical Society's budget. She needed something both attractive and subtle, something that would direct the viewer's eye to the information they needed without distracting from the artistry of the quilts. Until she found the perfect solution, she settled for printing the object labels on heavy, ivory-colored card stock and affixing them to the gallery walls using quilter's removable glue dots.

In the meantime, she continued to search the Nelson-Granger family papers for details about the Delectable Mountains quilt Dorothea had made for her uncle Jacob Kuehner. In an undated letter from Dorothea to her daughter, Abigail, Dorothea reminisced about the aftermath of her uncle's untimely death, when the family discovered that curmudgeonly Uncle Jacob had been a stationmaster on the Underground Railroad and had sheltered fugitives at his sugar camp. In order to continue his work, it was necessary to contact the family running the next station on the route north, so Dorothea had followed the curious patchwork clues she had unwittingly sewn into his quilt. It had not been easy to decipher the symbols, Dorothea had admitted in the letter, but she had done it. A design in the center of the medallion-style quilt resembled a compass rose pointing to the northwest. The traditional Delectable Mountains blocks in the upper left corner of the outermost border had been altered to resemble the peaks of the Four Brothers Mountains to the north of the Elm Creek Valley. Those were the only landmarks Dorothea mentioned in that particular letter, but Summer knew there must have been others along the route, and from the context, Dorothea had previously described them to Abigail. Summer longed to find the letter providing the first part of that conversation, if such a letter had ever existed.

One July afternoon, Summer was curled up in an armchair in the manor's library as rain fell steadily outside the diamond-paned windows, deeply engrossed in a fragment of an adolescent Abigail's diary, when Sarah entered carrying the day's mail. "It's so good to see you enjoying your thesis for a change," she said, taking a seat at the oak desk. "Usually when you're toiling over it, your eyebrows draw together and you thrust out your lower lip like you've never been more miserable in your life."

Summer laughed. "Is that so?"

"Absolutely." Sarah caught herself. "But you're not doing that at the moment, which means you're *not* working on your thesis."

"Exactly."

"That should've been my first guess," said Sarah, suddenly impassioned, "but I was just so relieved to see you happy in your work. The way you used to be when you were on the quilt camp faculty full-time. The way you are when you're working on the Union Hall exhibit."

Summer rested the aged diary on her lap, carefully marking her place with a strip of fabric. "I *am* happy in my graduate school work—not with my thesis, of course, but—"

"Are you, though? *Are* you happy? When you first started the program, your emails were so enthusiastic. You raved about the campus, your classes, the papers you were writing, the library, your roommates, your professors. Lately, though—well, you still seem to love your roommates and the library, and some of your professors, but you don't actually seem to enjoy what you're doing."

Summer shifted uncomfortably in the armchair. "I don't know what you want me to say. Graduate school is demanding. I don't know any graduate student who's completely happy all of the time."

Sarah leaned forward to rest her elbows on the desk, her brown eyes concerned. "Of course not, but are you happy in grad school, ever?"

Summer drew in a deep, steadying breath. "Maybe not, but I'm going to see this through. Things will be different when I have my doctorate and I'm working as a professor."

"Won't the nature of the work be essentially the same?"

"Yes, but I still love historical research, and when I have my doctorate the pressure will be off—" Summer caught her mistake and quickly amended, "Once I have a job and have tenure, the pressure—"

"Listen to yourself," Sarah pleaded, with an incredulous laugh. "You intend to pursue your doctorate even though you only enjoy doing historical research, in hopes that years from now, you *may* have a job that *might* be better?"

Summer regarded her friend for a long moment without speaking, struggling to contain her rising distress. "Are you trying to tell me to quit graduate school? Because I can't."

"I wouldn't ever flat-out *tell* you that, but why couldn't you?"

"Because I already threw away one fantastic opportunity when I didn't go to Penn, and I can't do that again with Chicago." She paused to steady the tremor in her voice. "I can't fail twice at this. Once, okay. Everyone's entitled to one massive mistake, one do-over. But twice?"

"You haven't failed twice," Sarah protested. "You haven't even failed *once*. You decided not to go to Penn so you could help launch an amazing new business, which is now thriving. I'm pretty sure that's the exact opposite of failure."

"Okay." Summer heaved a sigh and slumped back in her chair. "Fair point. But I have to finish my thesis. I've worked too hard for two years to walk away without a degree."

Sarah nodded. "Absolutely. I'm not suggesting otherwise. You're too close to the finish line to quit now. But Summer, you don't have to continue with the doctoral program if it's not what you really want. Leaving a prestigious university with a master's degree is a success by any measure."

"Even if that wasn't the plan? Even if it means falling short of my goal?"

"Even so. Plans change. Goals do too. When I first moved to Waterford, I interviewed for every accounting job listed in the Help Wanted section and sent my résumé to dozens of other companies too, just in case. When Sylvia offered me a job helping her clean up Elm Creek Manor, I felt so overqualified that I was almost too humiliated to accept. But Matt and I needed the money—"

"And you convinced Sylvia to throw quilting lessons into the package."

"An excellent perk, but still, the job was hardly the sturdy rung on a corporate ladder I'd been looking for. And yet." Sarah spread her arms and looked around the library. "None of this was in the plan, but if I had stuck relentlessly to the plan for its own sake instead of considering what truly made me happy, Elm Creek Quilts never would have happened. It wouldn't have happened without you either."

"Thanks."

"I mean it. You know it's true."

Another fair point, but that didn't help Summer see another way forward. If she didn't return to graduate school, what then? Since childhood she had been preparing to become a college professor like her mom, and she couldn't do that without a doctorate. What else was there for her?

A frisson of alarm went through her. Her mom.

"Sarah," she said warily, straightening in her chair, "I hope I don't need to say this, but please don't tell my mom about this—my meltdown, my indecision, any of it."

"You *don't* need to say it, but—seriously? Is that what this is all about? Are you worried about disappointing your mom?"

Summer lifted her hands and let them fall to her lap. "Surely you remember how upset she was when I declined Penn's offer."

"I remember she was bewildered, but when she realized that you had thought it through carefully and you'd made the best decision for your future happiness, she gave you her blessing, wholeheartedly. She'd do the same if you decided not to get a doctorate."

Summer wasn't so sure. She couldn't even count how many times through the years her mom had said, "If I could do it, you can do it." How could Summer *not* interpret that to mean her mom expected her to follow in her footsteps? Of course Gwen would be disappointed if Summer gave up now.

"She might give me her blessing," Summer said, deflated, "but she would be disappointed. I know her. She wouldn't say it, but she would be."

"Maybe you're right," Sarah acknowledged. "But maybe the question you need to ask yourself is if you should plan your future according to someone else's potential disappointment, or your own happiness."

Summer hesitated, but she was spared from a reply when the French doors swung open and Gretchen entered. "Hello, girls," she said cheerfully, but her smile faded as she sensed tension in the room. "Have I interrupted an important meeting?"

"We're finished," Summer said, at precisely the same moment Sarah said, "We're nearly done."

Gretchen looked from one to the other, bemused. "Should I come back in ten? Twenty?"

Sarah nodded, but Summer rose and set the tattered diary aside with the rest of the Granger-Nelson papers. "No, you're fine. We're good. Did you need something?"

"Some*one*, actually. You." Gretchen's eyes lit up with some delightful secret. "Could you spare a moment for a quick trip to the barn? Joe has something in his workshop he'd like to show you."

Summer quickly agreed, in part to escape Sarah's inquisition, but also out of curiosity. She had been to the barn many times, to fetch gardening tools or to find one of her colleagues, but she had never seen Joe's workshop, a more recent addition to the estate. Throwing Sarah a guilty glance over her shoulder, for they both knew she was making a hasty escape, she followed Gretchen from the library. "What does Joe want to show me?" she asked as they descended the stairs.

Gretchen smiled enigmatically. "You'll find out when you get there."

They paused in the back foyer to pull on galoshes and raincoats, but fortunately the rain had diminished to a light drizzle. As they stepped outside, a few sunbeams broke through the clouds, illuminating the path across the bridge, sending intermittent shafts of golden light upon the hill and the orchard beyond it.

They made their way carefully down the dirt road, avoiding the mud and larger puddles. When they reached the barn, they found the two large doors slid open partway, enough to let in fresh air but not gusts of wind-driven rain. Joe was waiting just inside. "Come on in," he called, gesturing.

Curiosity rising, Summer outpaced her friend and hurried inside, where Joe beckoned her to his half of the barn. It was a remarkably tidy woodshop, well organized, with ample lighting and a floor swept clean of sawdust and scraps. Summer took in walls lined with all manner of drills, saws, lathes, racks of hand tools, and workstations for tasks she could only guess at. In the center was a large, scarred wood-and-iron table she supposed Joe had made himself. Several thin, flat objects lay upon it, covered with a cloth, while a waist-high pillar of an object stood on the floor beside it, also draped.

"Show her, Joe," urged Gretchen breathlessly, catching up. "I can't keep this secret another minute."

"Show me what?" asked Summer. "What have you been up to?"

"A belated birthday present," said Joe. "Gretchen told me you've been having some trouble coming up with a nice way to display those description pages for the quilt exhibit, and you've been collecting donations for the capital campaign in a basket. I trust folks, in general, but as I told my wife, you can't just leave money sitting around in an open basket with no one watching it—"

"Unless it's the church collection basket," Gretchen chimed in.

Joe shrugged. "Maybe not even then. So I got to work, and, well, I hope you like what I've done."

With that, he drew back the cloth covering the table, and then the one covering the object on the floor. Summer drew in a breath, utterly amazed. Arranged in neat rows on the table were at least a dozen beautiful wooden frames with glass fronts, satin smooth with a lovely, subtle grain. A two-color LeMoyne Star was inlaid in the center at the top of each frame. The item on the floor was a collection box on a sturdy pedestal of the same wood as the frames, the pedestal embellished with trim reminiscent of the crown molding in the Union Hall gallery, the box generously sized and closed securely with a small but sturdy lock.

"Joe," Summer exclaimed when she could speak. "This is marvelous! It's absolutely perfect!"

"The frames are made of elm from the estate, from that tree that went down in the storm last summer. Except for the inlaid stars. They're made from oak and pine. Now, see this here." Joe picked up a frame and showed her one of its edges. "It's open on the top so you can insert your card stock and swap it out for something new anytime you like. You don't have to remove the entire back, like you would for an ordinary frame, or even take it off the wall." He frowned, thinking. "I should've brought a page out here to demonstrate."

"No need," Summer assured him, admiring the design. "I can see how it'll work. Thank you so much. I can't wait to show Pat."

"You're welcome, but no hard feelings if it doesn't suit."

"Joe," Gretchen chided gently, "she already said they're marvelous and perfect."

"And they are," Summer declared. "I honestly can't thank you enough."

"Glad to help," said Joe, looking proud and a trifle embarrassed. "If you need any more frames, I've still got more of that elm, so just say the word."

Grateful, Summer promised to take him up on the offer.

The next day, since Gwen's car wasn't big enough for the pedestal, Matt drove Summer to Union Hall in the Elm Creek Quilts minivan and helped her carry Joe's generous gifts upstairs to the gallery. Together Summer and Matt set the new collection box in place, moving the basket behind the door out of sight, until a better use could be found for it. Matt kindly stayed to help her attach Joe's beautiful frames to the walls beside the quilts and artifacts already displayed, and while Summer placed the object labels in the appropriate frames, he wandered the gallery admiring the exhibit. While they worked, Summer counted at least ten visitors passing through, and from the corner of her eye, she glimpsed a few slipping checks or cash into the new donation box.

She had just placed the last object label into its frame and was walking the exhibit floor, noting the many empty spaces yet to fill, when a tall, eighty-something woman with shoulder-length silver hair approached her, a tote bag from the Waterford Farmers Market on her shoulder. "Excuse me," she said tentatively, "are you the curator?"

"Yes, I'm Summer Sullivan. May I help you?"

"I hope so." The woman glanced around the gallery through her bifocals, her gaze lingering on the display of artifacts for the two victory quilts. "I understand that you help people who've lost quilts?"

"Not exactly," said Summer. "We do pay homage to some lost quilts here, and I hope that as more people tour the exhibit, more information about these quilts will come to light, but we're not really in the business of finding missing quilts. Our purpose is to showcase quilts that have played an important role in local history."

"My lost quilt does belong here, then," said the woman, sighing. "And it's not missing. I know exactly where my lost quilt is."

Summer regarded her, puzzled. "If you know where your quilt is—"

"Oh, honey, there's lost, and then there's *lost*. Lost as in missing, whereabouts unknown, and lost as in *lost to you*, as in you know exactly where it is but you can't have it."

"Right," said Summer, studying the woman, who seemed nearly bursting with a story she wanted to tell. "Should we find a place where we can sit and chat?"

The woman agreed, and as Summer led her outside to the hallway, to a bench farther from the stairs but with a good vantage of the gallery doors, she introduced herself as Linda McLoughlin from Summit Pass, which Summer knew as a charming village of restored historic buildings in the low mountains that formed the southern boundary of the Elm Creek Valley. "But I was born in Woodfall, about ten miles north of here," Linda explained, setting the tote bag on the bench between them. "I married right out of college, and my then-husband and I moved to Waterford."

"So you're a lifelong resident of the Elm Creek Valley?"

"Oh, yes, unless you count when I was at Swarthmore. That's where I met the ex." Linda frowned, only briefly, but enough to tell Summer that the divorce had not been amicable. "I worked at the First Bank of Waterford on Hill Street until I left when my first child was born. We had two more after that, but when our youngest started kindergarten, I went back to work." She brightened, reminiscing. "It wasn't easy to be a working mother, especially back then, but oh, how I loved my job. Always so many interesting tasks to do, always someone walking through the door who needed my help—friends, neighbors, strangers. It's so important to enjoy your work, don't you agree?"

"I do," said Summer, thinking of Sarah's impassioned plea. "Not everyone is so fortunate."

"Oh, I realized even then that I was lucky. My job gave me independence, an income of my own, a place where I could be myself after the kids left the nest and things weren't very pleasant at home." She dug into her tote and took out a brown envelope stamped with the recycled paper emblem. "But all good things must come to an end. My then-husband pressured me to retire early, and fool that I was, I listened to him. He never really liked me working, although he never complained about the money I brought in. Even so, he said it was time I focused on him for a change, and I hoped that if I did, it would save the marriage."

"He sounds like a real catch."

"I wish I'd thrown him back when I first reeled him in. So I retired, and my colleagues were as sorry to see me leave as I was to go." Linda moved her tote to the floor, lifted the flap of the envelope, and carefully removed four eight-by-ten photographs. "These are reprints, so you're welcome to keep them."

She placed the photos on the bench, and as Summer glimpsed an intricate rust, green, gold, and scarlet quilt, she gasped in admiration.

She recognized the quilt's repeated block immediately—its diagonal symmetry, its many concave and convex curves and sharp points, a stylized elegance that she considered evocative of Art Deco design, and appropriately so, since the pattern was first published in the 1930s.

"It's beautiful, isn't it?" said Linda. "There were several exceptional quilters in my circle of friends, and they made me this masterpiece as a retirement gift."

"It's exquisite." Summer drew closer and moved one of the photos slightly so it did not cover the one beneath. "It's a variation of the Cleopatra's Fan pattern. I love the way the alternate blocks are rotated ninety degrees so that the secondary pattern emerges. It gives the block an entirely different look than if they were arranged in a simple straight setting or on point."

"Cleopatra's Fan?" Linda echoed, eyebrows rising. "Do you mean this is an official quilt pattern? I had no idea, but then again, I've never made a quilt in my life. I know this design as a reproduction of the tile mosaic in the lobby of First Bank."

"Is it really?" Summer wondered why she had never heard this before, from any number of local quilters. Block patterns found in architecture was a popular subject of conversation among quilt aficionados. Come to think of it, she couldn't remember seeing a First Bank of Waterford on Hill Street, either. The only branch she recalled was in a modern building closer to campus.

"Yes, and it's a very accurate reproduction too, except for the colors," said Linda. "The tile mosaic was made in more somber tones of light blue, black, and white, but I love vivid autumn colors. Every year when the leaves changed, I kept an arrangement of autumn leaves in a vase on my desk. If my friends found an especially beautiful leaf, they would bring it to the office for me." She smiled wistfully at the memory.

"I can see how much you cherish this quilt," said Summer. "May I ask how it was lost?"

Linda looked up from the photos, her smile fading. "I want to emphasize that it was *my quilt*," she said. "It was given to me, not to my husband, not to us as a couple."

"Yes, it was a retirement gift," said Summer, nodding, increasingly curious. "I understand."

"I hadn't been retired two years when my husband realized that more attention from me wasn't what our marriage lacked." Linda's voice turned brittle, and she clenched her hands together in her lap. "It turns out he wanted far less of it. He filed for divorce so he could live out his sunset years with the so-called true love of his life, who he had been seeing, off and on, for the past decade."

"Oh, no!"

"Oh, yes. She was already married too, but she wouldn't divorce her husband. Divorce was against her religion. Adultery was too, not that it mattered. When her husband passed away from a heart attack, she found herself suddenly, unexpectedly available." Linda shrugged, feigning indifference, but her chin quivered. "Wayne decided that he needed to get available quickly too or he'd lose her."

"That's awful. I'm so sorry."

"They deserve each other. That's what my daughter says." Linda allowed a small smile. "My daughter also tells me that they're making each other thoroughly miserable."

"I'm sure that's not much consolation after what he put you through. Maybe it's a bit of justice, though?"

"Justice." Linda sniffed. "Funny you should choose that word, right when we get to the part about the divorce proceedings. Our lawyers hashed things out fairly reasonably. I got the house, Wayne got his car and his boat, our other assets were divided. There was some haggling over certain items we both wanted, but eventually we managed to agree on nearly everything."

"And this is where the Cleopatra's Fan quilt comes in?"

Linda nodded. "Wayne claimed that the quilt had been a wedding anniversary gift to us both, and he wanted it. My kids told me that it was really his girlfriend who wanted it, but I had guessed that already. Wayne had never given the quilt a second glance until then. I begged him to let me keep it. I offered him more money in the settlement. I pointed out the tag on the back, the one that read, 'In honor of our beloved colleague Linda McLoughlin on the occasion of her retirement.'"

"The quilt had a tag saying *that*? And he still claimed it was his?"

"Half his, anyway." Linda shrugged, her expression a shifting cloud of anger and loss. "It was the last, unresolved issue in our divorce agreement. Neither of us would budge. It dragged on for months. To be honest, I didn't care how long it took to make the divorce official. Wayne had already left the house, and I had found a new job with a bank in Summit Pass. *He* was the one who needed to wrap things up so he could marry his girlfriend. So he made me one final offer: He would take the quilt, and in exchange, he wouldn't challenge me for custody of our two dogs."

For a moment Summer had no words. "Seriously? Are you kidding me?"

"I wish I were. They were *my* rescue dogs, Biscotti and Macaron. I was the one who took care of them, fed them, walked them, cleaned up after them, managed their vet appointments, everything." Linda shook her head and inhaled deeply, remembering. "Wayne knew how much I loved my pups, that I would never give them up. As much as I cherished that quilt, how could I choose it over my two loyal friends and companions whose comfort I so badly needed, especially when I couldn't trust Wayne to properly care for them?"

"I'm so sorry your ex put you through that."

"Yeah, me too." Linda shrugged, her gaze falling upon the photos again. "Who knows? Maybe I'll get my quilt back someday. Maybe he'll leave it to my kids, and they'll return it to me. But in the meantime it's lost, and so it's perfect for your exhibit."

"It's an exquisite quilt, and the story behind it is compelling to say the least," said Summer carefully. "As I said before, though, this isn't an exhibit for lost quilts, but for quilts that have a significant connection to local history."

"Oh, but this quilt *does*," Linda assured her. "Like I said, its design is based upon the tile pattern at First Bank—the original building, not the new branch."

Summer shook her head, uncomprehending. "I confess I've never seen it."

"Well, you might not be old enough. It isn't there anymore. You know that fancy condo building on Hill Street, the one that doesn't fit in the neighborhood?"

"Yes, I know exactly the one you mean. It's hard to miss."

"A lot of other people thought so too. The original First Bank of Waterford building was one of the oldest in Waterford. Not as old as Union Hall, but pretty close. After it was torn down by College Realty—"

"Wait. Hold on. Do you mean *University* Realty?"

"Same company, but they went by College Realty back in the day. So, after they had that gorgeous old building torn down and started putting up those condos in its place, there was a massive back-lash." Linda spread her hands to indicate something immeasurably vast. "The protests, the outrage—I'd never seen anything like it in Waterford before. Lawsuits were threatened, city council members resigned in disgrace—it was the scandal of the decade. That's what the papers said."

"I can well imagine." And yet Gregory Krolich's predecessors had learned nothing from the experience, except, perhaps, to become more devious.

"Soon, all of that public protest grew into a historic preservation movement, which led to the establishment of an official Waterford historic district so that other important buildings would be protected. Without that, the original city hall across the street and this very building might have been torn down decades ago."

"That's amazing," said Summer. "Really. I hadn't expected your story to take that turn."

"Like I said, this quilt is historically significant." Linda managed a smile. "Did you really think I'd take up so much of your time just to whine about my divorce?"

"I wouldn't have minded." Summer paused to think. "Today the First Bank building would be protected by the ordinances governing the historic district, but those ordinances only exist because it was torn down. I think it's fair to say that the building was important to local history. Your quilt is an important symbol of that building, so—"

"It's in?" Linda interrupted, hopeful.

"I think it deserves a place in this exhibit, yes." Summer gestured to the photos. "With your permission, I'll frame and hang these photos—"

"Permission granted."

Summer stifled a laugh, amused by her eagerness. "I'll also track down a photo of the original First Bank, and some articles about the demolition, the protests, and the establishment of the historic district. I think this could be a very interesting and relevant addition to the exhibit."

"I'm so glad you think so," Linda exclaimed, reaching out to give Summer's forearm a quick, enthusiastic squeeze. "The ladies who made the quilt will be thrilled when I tell them."

"Please invite them to come see for themselves, and to bring their friends." Summer gestured to the gallery doors, in the general direction of the donation box. "We welcome contributions of any size. Every bit will help keep Union Hall open."

"Consider it done." Linda bounded to her feet and reached out to shake Summer's hand. "Thank you so much for your time."

As she hurried off, Summer lingered to gather up the photos. She was pleased to see Linda enter the gallery again, and remain just long enough to leave a check in the donation box.

When she finished for the day, Summer locked up the gallery and took the photos back to Elm Creek Manor to mat and frame as she had the other substitute artifacts. She was working at the refectory table in the kitchen when Gwen, Sylvia, Agnes, and Diane passed through during a break between classes. As they admired the photos, Summer shared Linda's story with them. "When I write the object label, I think I'll omit the gory details about the divorce and just focus on the protest and the establishment of the historic district," she said. "I'm not sure Linda meant for that part of the quilt's history to go public."

"And yet you told us," her mom remarked.

"You're not the public," Summer countered. "You're family. All of you."

Agnes smiled, pleased to be considered family, but Diane's frown suggested she was mulling over something else entirely. "Do you suppose," she said, "theoretically, is there any way we could still get that quilt away from her ex?"

"Short of breaking and entering?" queried Gwen. "I don't see how. He seemed determined to keep it. He might notice if it suddenly disappeared."

"He doesn't deserve to keep that quilt," Diane argued. "It wasn't made for him, and he couldn't possibly appreciate it properly."

"Nevertheless, it's his," said Sylvia. "We can only hope that word of the exhibit will get back to him somehow. It may evoke some pangs of conscience that will inspire him to return the quilt to Linda."

"And perhaps she'll lend it to the historical society," Agnes chimed in, glancing around the circle of friends, hopeful.

"Doubt it," said Diane. "He'll never give it up. It's not fair. Think of what a fabulous addition to the exhibit that gorgeous quilt would be, so much better than framed papers."

"I *am* thinking of it," said Summer. "To be honest, I'm concerned that I may have too many artifacts on display already. If I don't acquire more actual quilts for the exhibit, I'm going to have to call it 'the Museum of Lost Quilts.'"

"You'll find more quilts," Agnes assured her. "I know you will. You've already found so many."

"In the meantime," said Gwen, "the photos and documents are fascinating in their own right."

"I rather like the name the Museum of Lost Quilts," Sylvia remarked, thoughtful. "Although I suppose it is something of a misnomer, since some of those formerly lost quilts, such as Gerda's Log Cabin, were eventually found."

And if Summer had her way, more would be. The quilts she sought were too important, too beloved, to be given up for lost forever.

**In Honor of Linda's Retirement.** Approximately 72" x 72". Cotton top and backing with polyester batting. Pieced and quilted by employees of First Bank of Waterford, 1974. Presumed to be in the private collection of Wayne McLoughlin.

This exquisite Cleopatra's Fan quilt was presented to Linda Schuster McLoughlin in honor of her retirement from First Bank in 1974. Over the span of her twenty-five-year career with the bank, Ms. McLoughlin advanced from teller to senior accounts manager, earning the Employee of the Month Award thirty-one times and Employee of the Year twice.

The distinctive arrangement of the sixty-four identical Cleopatra's Fan blocks reproduce in fabric the intricate tile mosaic from the lobby floor of the First Bank building, which once stood at 358 Hill Street in downtown Waterford. Designed by acclaimed architect J. Ralph Dekker, an apprentice of the renowned John Mead Howells, the First Bank building was the first significant Art Deco structure in a district of predominantly Neoclassical and Italianate structures when it was completed in 1920. In a review after the building's grand opening, the *Waterford Register* praised it as "an outstanding work of American architecture" and "an encouraging example of Modernism that has not gone berserk." The tile mosaic was one of several features noted for its beauty, described as "so exquisitely wrought one feels reluctant to tread upon it." Variations of the lobby tile pattern appear in several of Dekker's later buildings, including Federle Hall in Cincinnati, OH, and the Drayton Opera House in Harrisburg, PA.

In 1976, the First Bank of Waterford building was razed to make way for the construction of a College Realty apartment building, Hill Street Commons, a controversial project from the moment the plans were revealed to the public. The Waterford Historical Society called for a moratorium on the demolition until experts could present evidence about the historic value of the building before the city council. Such requests for public hearings were routinely granted, but the Waterford Historical Society's petition was promptly and inexplicably denied. Demolition was briefly delayed when protestors, including residents of the Elm Creek Valley, Waterford College students, and faculty from the Penn State Department of Architecture, chained themselves to the bank's front doors. After two days, and amid rising national media attention, the police cut the chains, arrested the protestors, and allowed demolition to commence the next day.

Several weeks later, a whistleblower reported to the editor of the *Waterford Register* that College Realty had made "unusual and substantial" campaign donations to the four city council members who had voted against the Waterford Historical Society's petition for a hearing. In the ensuing investigation, the police found insufficient evidence to level criminal charges, but the four city council members nevertheless resigned in disgrace. As construction of Hill Street Commons continued, protestors called for a boycott, which apparently met with some success. According to a March 14, 1982, report in the *Waterford Register*, occupancy rates for the new apartment building remained below 30 percent in its first five years, a below-market average that a company representative interviewed for the article attributed directly to the boycott.

Perhaps the most enduring consequence of the razing of the First Bank building was that the groundswell of public protest gave rise to a historic preservation movement in the city. Soon thereafter, a coalition of historical and architectural preservation groups promoted legislation to establish an official historic district in downtown Waterford. The new ordinances stipulated that a building in the designated area could not be subjected to significant architectural alteration except "what was required to maintain structural integrity." A building could not be condemned or razed unless the city zoning commission determined that it was "neglected, abandoned, and/or a blight" or that "it had been deemed hazardous or unsafe for occupancy" and the owner was "unwilling or unable" to make necessary repairs.

In the decades that have followed the demolition of the First Bank building, the ordinances governing the Waterford historic district have helped preserve the history and unique character of the city's oldest neighborhoods. Through its depiction of the building's tile mosaic, *In Honor of Linda's Retirement* reminds us of the unique architectural features that were lost before the historic district was established, and celebrates all those that will now be saved.

# 11

In the days that followed, Summer framed and hung several vintage photos of the First Bank of Waterford building in the gallery alongside two photos of Linda McLoughlin's quilt—one with Linda smiling rapturously, the quilt draped over her shoulders like a cloak, and another in which she and her colleagues held up the quilt for the camera. Even in a thirty-year-old photo, the love and admiration worked into every stitch was evident. Summer could well understand why Linda had not gotten over losing her cherished quilt to her selfish, spiteful ex.

On the same morning Summer added a reprint of a *Waterford Register* article about the establishment of the town's historic district to the display, she received an email from Dr. Alvarez that made her heart dip. "I trust you're making excellent progress on your thesis," her adviser had written. "I look forward to reading it soon. NB: You won't be able to register for fall quarter classes until all of your master's degree requirements are completed and your matriculation into the doctoral program is confirmed with the registrar. Time is of the essence."

The candid reminder jolted Summer into setting aside her exhibit research for the rest of the week so she could focus exclusively on her thesis. She steadily churned out another two pages, but with every sentence her sense of urgency eased, and her thoughts wandered, time and again, to Dorothea and her lost quilts. Eventually, sustained by caffeine and yoga, she reached an important milestone that had seemed impossibly distant a few months before. Heaving a sigh of relief, she sent a long overdue reply to her adviser: "I'm making progress, slowly but surely. All that remains are the conclusion, notes, and bibliography. I expect to send you a final, revised version by mid-August."

She knew she would be cutting it close, and she might be setting herself up for a mad scramble to secure her funding and register for classes before the fall quarter began. Common sense decreed that she focus on her thesis and see it through to the end, but it was impossible to resist the lure of the Granger-Nelson family papers, so full of enticing secrets. A respite—a *brief* respite—of more enjoyable research might help her clear her head and find a second wind, she told herself as she saved her thesis and closed the laptop.

As Summer searched the Granger-Nelson papers for details about Dorothea's quilts, the portrait of Dorothea Granger Nelson that emerged from the letters, journals, and documents increasingly fascinated her. As a child, Dorothea had lived with her parents and younger brother on Thrift Farm, a utopian community consisting of a few rough-hewn cabins alongside rocky fields of wheat and corn carved into the thick woodlands of the northern Elm Creek Valley. As best as Summer could infer, the adults had been inexperienced farmers but enlightened ethicists and philosophers who advocated for abolition, universal suffrage, humane treatment of animals, and thoughtful stewardship of the land. They also believed that children should be allowed to follow their own hearts' desires without adult interference. Guided by that principle, as a young girl Dorothea had hoped to pursue a college education someday, just as her younger brother planned to attend medical school.

Dorothea was fourteen years old in 1844 when her dream was lost, swept away in a torrential rainstorm that had pounded the Elm

Creek Valley for three harrowing days and nights. Flash floods had poured down from the Four Brothers Mountains and reshaped the landscape, shifting the banks of Elm Creek, destroying the cabins and outbuildings of Thrift Farm, drowning the fields of crops. No one from the commune had perished in the deluge, but even after the floodwaters receded elsewhere in the valley, Thrift Farm had remained underwater.

Summer came across a few letters that mentioned tentative plans to move out west and start anew, but apparently the community had been unable to raise money for the journey or to agree upon a destination. Eventually they had disbanded and dispersed, but the Granger family had not gone far. Having lost everything but their lives, they had been obliged to move in with Dorothea's cantankerous uncle Jacob, whose wife and two sons had perished in a scarlet fever epidemic only a few years before. He was willing to accept his sister's family's help around his farm even though he didn't particularly want their company.

As Summer caught glimpses of Thrift Farm in a sentence here, a brief passage there, the details scattered throughout many pages, the images seemed so curiously familiar that at first she wondered if Gerda had described the commune in her memoir. But Summer quickly dismissed this theory; Thrift Farm had been lost to the flood-waters years before Gerda had immigrated to the Elm Creek Valley in 1856. Then, unexpectedly, in a quiet moment at the manor while she was folding laundry, realization struck: Summer wasn't remember-ing scenes from Gerda's memoir, but from Creek's Crossing Album. Dorothea must have been inspired by places and experiences from her own life when she had made the quilt, capturing her memories of Thrift Farm and the Elm Creek Valley in intricate appliqué. If so, Creek's Crossing Album would have been especially full of deeply personal remembrances and meaning—and yet Dorothea had given the quilt away. Stranger still, she hadn't bestowed it upon a sister or a lifelong friend, someone who would implicitly understand the

symbolism of each painstakingly sewn appliqué, but to Constance
Wright, a newcomer to the Elm Creek Valley. Later Constance would
become a cherished friend, but at the time, she had been practically
a stranger.

"Maybe Dorothea didn't like that quilt very much and was glad to
get rid of it," Diane suggested one morning at breakfast in the banquet
hall, after Summer had given in to her companions' playful badgering
for new revelations from her research.

"That's impossible," said Leah, a camper from Lock Haven who
had stopped at Union Hall to tour the gallery on her way to Elm
Creek Manor. She had read about the exhibit in her local paper, a
fact that astonished Summer and delighted Pat. Word was evidently
spreading, well ahead of their official opening. "That quilt is absolutely gorgeous. You can see the love and care Dorothea put into every
stitch. You don't part with something like that easily."

Diane shrugged. "Maybe she gave it under duress."

"Or she really, really wanted Constance to feel welcome to the
Elm Creek Valley," suggested another camper. "That settles it. I have
to see this exhibit for myself." She looked expectantly from Summer
to Diane and back. "What do you say? Is there any chance we can fit
a field trip into the camp schedule?"

"I'm sure the Waterford Historical Society would welcome you,"
said Summer, "but Sarah's in charge of the schedule. I'm not really
on the faculty this season, so—"

"So you keep insisting," said Diane, rolling her eyes. "And yet
here you are, leading yoga every morning and assisting in classes every
day." To the campers, she added, "We probably couldn't wedge a field
trip into the official schedule since it's already packed. However, if
you want to drive downtown during your afternoon free time, you
could certainly do that, and still be back in time to catch the end of
dinner service."

"I don't have a car here," another quilter piped up worriedly. "Is
there a bus? A cab?"

"The Elm Creek Quilts minivan?" another camper chimed in, hopeful.

Summer and Diane exchanged a look. If Matt or Andrew would be willing to play chauffeur, why not?

"I'm sure something could be arranged," said Diane. "Let me work on transportation, and Summer can arrange things at Union Hall."

Delighted, the campers peppered Summer, and Leah too, with questions about the other quilts they could look forward to seeing at the gallery. As soon as breakfast ended, Diane and Summer hastened to catch Sarah before she hurried off to work. Intrigued, Sarah agreed to check with Matt to see if he could fit chauffeuring duties around his work in the gardens and, especially, in the orchards, where the first harvest of Paula Red and Zestar was quickly approaching.

As Diane dashed off to the ballroom for her first class of the day, Sarah gave Summer an appraising look. "So . . . how's your thesis coming along?"

Summer shrugged. "Fine. At this point I just want to finish."

"And your work for the exhibit?"

"About a million times better than the thesis. You should come by the gallery soon. Pat and Agnes are planning a grand opening gala for late August, but you don't need to wait until then."

"I'd love to. Maybe Saturday, after cleanup." Sarah hesitated. "So, you're still super busy, is what you're saying?"

Summer laughed. "Yes, but don't let that stop you. What do you need?"

"Is there any chance you could squeeze some teaching into your schedule?" Sarah held up her hands to fend off a refusal. "Only one class a week, promise, and we'll schedule it for whatever time of day you prefer. We've had so many requests for your Modern Quilting class, but no one but you, your mom, and Russell have taught it. Your mom is fully booked and Russell—"

"Isn't here," Summer finished for her. Maggie's long-distance boyfriend, an accomplished quilter specializing in abstract designs, occasionally worked as a visiting instructor at Elm Creek Quilt Camp. His visits were far less frequent and inevitably shorter in duration than either Maggie or Russell would prefer. "Of course I'd be happy to teach. Could you schedule my class for first period? I could get my teaching in early and spend the rest of the day working on everything else."

"First period sounds perfect. Could you start next week?"

"Absolutely. Take me off the bench and add me to the active roster."

"Hurrah!" Sarah gave her a quick hug. "Welcome back, Summer."

"Welcome back?" Summer echoed, smiling. "I've been here for weeks."

"You know what I mean," her friend replied. Sarah hurried off smiling, no doubt to rearrange the classroom assignments and add Modern Quilting to their online registration page.

By the end of the day, Matt had agreed to run the quilt exhibit shuttle and Sarah had posted a sign-up sheet in the ballroom. A quick phone call to Pat was all it took to confirm that guests of Elm Creek Quilt Camp were welcome to tour the gallery in small groups any afternoon from Monday through Friday. "Our volunteer docents are eager to begin," Pat told Summer, "so no worries if you can't be there, or if you're too busy working on a display to lead a tour."

The special tours began the next day and continued the following week, when Summer began teaching. It was a thrill to be in front of the classroom again, and she was pleased to see that nearly every spot was filled, even though the course was a last-minute addition to the schedule. She began the class as she always did, by establishing a definition of modern quilting. This not only clarified the general principles for newbies, but also served as a warm-up exercise to spark the imagination and creativity of novices and veterans alike.

"Some quilters and quilt aficionados will say that they can't explain what modern quilting is, but they know it when they see it," Summer said, sharing a smile with her students, enjoying the quiet laughs and sage nods her words evoked. "Nevertheless, let's try to do better than that, and to come up with a definition of our own."

For the next few minutes, the students volunteered answers, guided by an occasional encouraging prompt from Summer. In the end, they agreed that modern quilts were often understood solely in contrast to traditional quilts, which typically were based upon a grid system and were characterized by symmetry; repeated designs; piecing, appliqué, or a combination of the two that could be quite complex; and quilting that ranged from simple, barely visible in-the-ditch stitches to elaborate feathered plumes and arcs and whorls. Modern quilts, in contrast, often departed from a grid layout, employing asymmetry, bold colors, improvisation, minimalist piecing design, and negative space filled with elaborate quilting.

"Always remember, these are lists of characteristics, not rules," Summer said when they ran out of ideas to add to the whiteboard. "You might prefer modern traditionalism, which is a fancy way of saying that you take your favorite elements from traditional quilting, mix in the aspects of modern quilting you most admire, and create something entirely your own."

A student raised her hand tentatively. "Is that allowed?"

"Of course it's allowed. Who's to say it isn't? Quilting is about joy, about expressing yourself creatively, about creating objects of warmth and beauty, however you define that. Quilt to please yourself, not some anonymous, sour-faced, judgmental, so-called quilt expert."

"You sound exactly like your mother," a student exclaimed.

Summer had to laugh. "I'm not surprised. Who do you think taught me my quilting philosophy?" She rubbed her palms together, interlaced her fingers, and flexed her hands. "Enough talk. Let's quilt."

She was not entirely done talking, of course. She laid out some principles for modern quilt design, showed numerous examples, and only then set her students to work on their own designs. For some, this would be their first attempt to create an original modern quilt rather than reproducing a professional designer's pattern. A good number of her students had never made a modern quilt of any kind, and while some eagerly threw off the constraints of the traditional block-and-grid paradigm, others hardly knew where to begin. Summer circulated through the classroom, observing and offering guidance wherever it was needed and wanted. By the end of the hour, the quilters seemed pleased with their first steps and eager to continue the next day.

After class, Summer tidied up the classroom, hurried upstairs for her backpack, and headed off to Union Hall to work on the exhibit, an enjoyable pattern she would follow the rest of that week and into the next. She committed to writing at least a paragraph of her thesis every night, even if that meant skipping the evening program, even when that meant gritting her teeth and forcing the sentences out and ignoring the increasing, and increasingly troubling, sense that she was struggling for something she no longer wanted.

One morning between Sunrise Yoga and breakfast, Summer received an email from Pat with an urgent request: Gregory Krolich from University Realty and Courtney Langdon from the Waterford Public Library wanted to meet with them at Union Hall at one o'clock that afternoon. "Gregory wasn't entirely forthcoming," Pat wrote, "but my hope is that University Realty intends to make a substantial donation to our capital campaign."

"After scheming to demolish Union Hall, he suddenly wants to help save it?" Summer murmured, deeply skeptical. Still, Krolich must have said *something* to give Pat that impression. Maybe he needed the tax write-off.

"Courtney was cc'd on the email but didn't chime in," Pat had continued, "so I'm not sure why she's involved. Perhaps she wants the library and the historical society to collaborate on a project. I do hope so—that would be wonderful for all of us."

Summer thought so too. She quickly replied to assure Pat that she'd be there for the meeting, ready to lead a tour of the gallery or to help however else she was needed.

She hurried off to breakfast, and then on to her classroom, where she led an especially lively design workshop that fairly burst with creativity, sending her spirits soaring until she wondered why she had ever wanted any other career. As soon as class ended, though, she remembered how much she loved delving into historical research, and she really couldn't imagine a career path that didn't include happily exploring one archive or another. She also couldn't ignore her mom's hopes for her future.

Yet none of that changed the simple truth that Elm Creek Quilts would always be very dear to her. Sarah's shrewd questions about why she still intended to pursue her doctorate when she wasn't actually happy had applied a steady pressure of doubt to the fine cracks in her resolve. If she didn't know better, she might suspect that her friend had cajoled her back into the classroom specifically to remind her how much she loved it. But wasn't it possible she'd find that same satisfaction teaching history at a university?

Summer spent the rest of the morning on the shaded verandah studying a ledger from the Granger farm, but although it offered a fascinating glimpse into the family's finances, she learned nothing new about Dorothea's quilts. At noon, she had a quick bite to eat in the kitchen and headed off to Union Hall so she and Pat could confer before the meeting. She found the historical society president already in the gallery, chatting quietly with one of several visitors contemplatively exploring the exhibit under the watchful gaze of a docent. Together Summer and Pat walked through the gallery, inspecting every quilt, artifact, and object label with a critical gaze, imagining the perspective of potential donors who needed to be persuaded that their money wouldn't go to waste. They agreed that everything was about as perfect as could be, but they needed more quilts to fill the still-empty spaces on the walls.

"Preferably quilts rather than artifacts," Summer noted, "or we may need to make the name the Museum of Lost Quilts official."

By one o'clock Summer and Pat were awaiting their special guests in the foyer, debating whether they ought to ask the contractors to halt work for an hour while they toured Union Hall. They decided to let the din continue, since the clatter and shriek and banging of tools and equipment emphasized the important restoration work already underway, a not-so-subtle reminder that donations were very much welcome.

At a quarter past, the front doors opened and in strode a man in his fifties accompanied by a woman in her sixties, both dressed in professional attire, he in a dark, formal pinstripe suit, she in a light-weight lavender pantsuit with gray trim, more in keeping with the season. Summer immediately recognized Gregory Krolich, though he looked thinner than she remembered, his hair grayer at the temples and sparser, combed back into stiff furrows and shiny with prod-uct. He was speaking to the woman in a confidential undertone as they entered, and when he smiled at her, his teeth seemed too bright against his tanned skin. The strap of a large, black duffel bag was slung over his shoulder, the designer logo prominently visible—an odd briefcase, Summer thought, wondering what he carried in it. His companion looked vaguely familiar, enough so that Summer guessed that she had seen her occasionally at the Waterford Public Library or elsewhere around downtown. Courtney Langdon was of medium height and slender, and strikingly beautiful, her mostly white hair interlaced with dark brown and cut in a short, wavy bob. Her dark green eyes seemed both knowing and kind, although the smile she offered Krolich in response to his was small and merely polite.

After introductions were made, Krolich shifted the duffel bag's weight and turned an appraising look around the foyer. "I love what you've done with the place," he remarked.

"Thank you," said Pat, smiling. "We've come a long way, but much work remains."

"Yes, I can see that," he said. "Still, if you ever have to sell the property, you'll be able to ask for much more than you would have a year ago."

Pat blinked at him, taken aback, but she quickly recovered. "The Waterford Historical Society has no plans to sell Union Hall."

"Plans change," he said, admiring the freshly painted crown molding. "If you ever want to sell, or if circumstances force you to sell, I hope you'll be in touch."

Pat's smile had become a thin, hard line. "Thank you, but I can't imagine any circumstances that would prompt us to change our minds."

Krolich acknowledged her words with a nod and a casual shrug. Summer noticed that for the barest of moments, his gaze lingered on the largest of the engraved copper plaques affixed to the walls flanking the front doors, the very one he had concealed behind a curio cabinet when he still hoped to purchase and raze Union Hall before anyone fully understood the building's historic significance.

Suddenly his gaze shifted to Summer, and she managed a polite, professional smile, although honestly, she couldn't stand him. Time and again he had pulled one despicable stunt after another, sometimes purposefully inflicting harm on her friends through actions of questionable legality. Yet here he stood, passing himself off as a decent, dignified, civic-minded businessman, as if he valued community over profit. Summer knew better, and she marveled at his audacity.

But for the moment, she was willing to give him the benefit of the doubt and hear what he had to say.

"Shall we go upstairs to the gallery?" Pat suggested, gesturing to the staircase.

"Yes, please," said Courtney. "I've heard so many good things about your exhibit. I'm eager to see it for myself."

Pat led and Summer followed along behind as they escorted their visitors to the second floor. Along the way, Pat drew their attention to various restored architectural features and repairs in progress, but when they reached the doorway to the gallery, she gestured for them to precede her into the beautifully renovated room, letting their first impressions speak for themselves. Summer counted eight visitors already inside, admiring the quilts and studying the object labels. Their tour paused near the entrance so Pat could describe the room's lighting, security measures, climate control, and other essential features.

"I'd be happy to show you around the exhibit," Summer offered when Pat had finished.

"I'd like nothing better, but first . . ." Courtney turned to Krolich, her eyebrows rising in inquiry. "Well, Gregory? I'm entirely satisfied, and I assume you are as well."

"Absolutely." Krolich slipped the strap over his head, set the duffel bag on the floor, and bent on one knee to unzip it. As Summer watched, curiosity gave way to astonishment as he withdrew a black plastic garbage bag wrapped around a folded bundle, which she knew from its size and shape must be a quilt.

"We've had this in our vault for decades," Krolich said as Courtney stepped forward to help him remove the plastic bag. Instinctively Summer reached out and carefully took hold of an edge as they began to unfold the quilt, with Pat following her lead a moment later.

Summer's gaze took in a lovely antique quilt fashioned from green, Prussian blue, and Turkey red calicoes, sixty-one traditional Album blocks, each eight inches square, set on point and surrounded by a Stacked Bricks border. She drew in a quick breath, astonished, when she realized that the muslin center rectangle of each block was inscribed with a name. The names and penmanship were unique to each block, strong evidence that these were autographs and not a record compiled by a third party, as in the two victory quilts. The ink had faded away long ago and, in some places, had deteriorated the muslin fabric, but the black embroidery over each signature remained. Summer felt nearly light-headed with wonder as she read the names—Washington Irving, James Fenimore Cooper, Elizabeth Barrett Browning, Walt Whitman, Frederick Douglass, Zachary Taylor, Henry David Thoreau, Elizabeth Cady Stanton, fifty-three others—the most renowned authors, artists, and politicians of the mid-nineteenth century.

"This is Authors' Album!" Summer exclaimed, hardly daring to believe it.

"You know this quilt?" asked Courtney. "You've seen it before?"

"I've never seen it, but I read about it in the Granger-Nelson family papers. My friend and fellow Elm Creek Quilter Sylvia Bergstrom Compson mentioned this very quilt to me earlier this summer. As a child, she admired Authors' Album whenever she visited the Waterford Public Library, where it was displayed behind the circulation desk." Summer couldn't tear her gaze away from the quilt, so marvelous, so unexpected a find. She spotted Ralph Waldo Emerson's signature next to Margaret Fuller's, two blocks away from the painter Thomas Cole's.

"Its historical significance is evident," said Pat, eyes shining with wonder. "Lucretia Mott, William Lloyd Garrison—my goodness, what an extraordinary collection of signatures!"

"Yes, but the autographs are only one aspect of the quilt's importance to local history," said Summer. "In 1850, Dorothea Granger led an effort to build a library in Creek's Crossing. Until then, the town's library had consisted of two dozen books on a shelf in the post office. Every so often, a proposal to build a public library would come before the town council, but nothing ever got off the ground. Dorothea was an avid reader as well as a schoolteacher, and I suppose she got tired of waiting."

"Is this the same Dorothea who came up with the Loyal Union Sampler fundraiser?" asked Pat.

Summer nodded. "Yes, although she had married by then and had changed her name to Dorothea Nelson. Perhaps it was her success with Authors' Album that inspired her to make another opportunity quilt a decade later to fund the construction of Union Hall."

"So the signatures of all of these dignitaries are genuine, not merely decorative?" asked Courtney. "That's astonishing. If it were true, this quilt would be—" She shook her head, astounded. "Absolutely priceless."

"You'd need a professional appraiser to determine the quilt's financial value," said Summer, "and I honestly don't know what an expert autograph collector would make of the embroidery over the ink. I suspect the alterations to the originals would reduce the value of the autographs."

"Not to me," Courtney declared, while Pat nodded emphatically beside her.

"I'd need to double-check for specifics, but I definitely recall a few letters in the Granger-Nelson family papers that mentioned this quilt while it was still a work in progress," said Summer. "Dorothea and the other quilters on the library committee wrote to the most renowned authors of their day to request their autographs on a piece of muslin of a specific size. Autograph quilts were very popular at the time, so the authors would have known what to do. The quilters collected the muslin pieces through the mail and sewed each one into an Album block. Next they sewed the blocks together, assembled the top, and quilted it at a special Quilting Bee Dance, where the finished masterpiece was raffled off."

"I've heard about the raffle," said Courtney. "I don't know who won the quilt, but someone eventually donated the Authors' Album quilt to the library. It was displayed on the wall behind the circulation desk until the 1950s—"

"When a new, larger, modern library was built a few blocks away," Krolich broke in smoothly. "University Realty was responsible for the demolition of the old library and the construction of the new. As the leading real estate developer in the Elm Creek Valley, we've been the most sought-after firm for projects of this scope and scale since our founding decades ago."

"Of course," said Pat, but Summer merely nodded. She had no doubt that University Realty had also been responsible for the construction of the condos that now stood on the site of the original library, a prime lot on the town square on the edge of the historic district. The current library was very nice, if no longer as modern as Krolich implied, but if location was everything in real estate, the original site was far more desirable, and thus far more valuable, than the current lot. University Realty must have made a fortune on the deal.

"We assume the quilt had been entrusted to University Realty for safekeeping during the demolition, with the intention of returning it to the new library when it was complete." Krolich shrugged and winced, comically chagrined. "Unfortunately, it must have been tucked away a bit *too* safely, because it remained in the vault until we discovered it during our relocation—very safe, to be sure, but forgotten."

"Not entirely forgotten," said Courtney evenly. "After the new library opened, the director wrote to your predecessor to arrange for the quilt's return. A few months later, she wrote again to request a thorough search of your offices for the quilt and for any information regarding chain of custody. We still have the carbon copies of those letters in our archives."

"After all this time? You librarians really do archive everything." Krolich grinned, a flash of whitened teeth. "If we'd had a few librarians on our staff back in the day, the quilt never would have been misplaced."

"At least Authors' Album was found at last, undamaged and whole," said Courtney, her thin smile telling Summer that she was unmoved by Krolich's flattery. "We were all immeasurably relieved and delighted when we received your email last week telling us so."

"But—"Just in time, Summer caught herself. Last week? University Realty had moved into the former site of Grandma's Attic more than a year before. Why hadn't they returned Authors' Album long ago? "But you must be even happier now to have the quilt restored to you at last," she said instead. "Are you planning to display it behind the circulation desk, like they did in the original library?"

Courtney seemed about to reply, but Krolich spoke first. "Actually, our board of directors has liaised with the library's board, and we've agreed to donate the quilt to the Waterford Historical Society."

"Surely you don't mean that," Pat exclaimed. "I'd be delighted to accept, but as Courtney said, this quilt is priceless. If the library doesn't have room to display it, you could sell it and use the proceeds to fund all sorts of essential projects."

"Our board did consider that," Courtney acknowledged, giving Krolich a slow, sidelong glance, "but Gregory and his colleagues made a very persuasive case for entrusting it to the historical society, to ensure that it remains in the Elm Creek Valley and is available to the public via your exhibit. Now that I've seen this lovely gallery and I've met you and your curator"—she offered Summer a nod of mutual understanding—"I wholeheartedly support this decision. I'm confident that Authors' Album will be in good hands."

"You have my word on that," said Pat sincerely.

"And mine." Yet it seemed to Summer as if Courtney still had misgivings, as if she had agreed to the donation only reluctantly. Inspired, she quickly added, "However, we should put all this in writing and not rely upon our good word alone. Courtney, if you agree, we can include a clause in the contract prohibiting the historical society from ever selling the quilt, and immediately transferring ownership to the Waterford Public Library if the historical society ever determines that it can no longer properly care for it."

Courtney mulled that over, nodding. "Yes, that's an excellent idea. I'm sure the library board of directors would approve."

"Hold on," said Krolich, frowning. "If the historical society ever decides to give away the quilt, University Realty might want it back."

"But the quilt never actually belonged to University Realty," Summer pointed out. "It was in your vault, but you were never the legal owners."

"One of our volunteers is an expert on property law," Pat mused. "I'm sure we can trust him to work out the legal details."

"You should have University Realty's legal team look over the agreement too, Gregory," Courtney told him, "just to make sure we're all on the same page."

Krolich grimaced, but he nodded, looking extremely displeased.

"Now then," said Courtney, turning away from Krolich, "how about that tour?"

Summer readily agreed, but first she and Pat carried Authors'

Album to the long table along the near wall, which Summer used as a workstation. They covered the surface with a clean sheet and gently draped the quilt over it, preparing it for inspection later. Next Summer led their visitors on a tour of the quilts and other artifacts already on display, noting the spaces she had reserved for the other quilts they had acquired but were still cleaning and restoring. When Summer paused in front of the wall where she thought Authors' Album could be shown to its best advantage, Krolich wandered on ahead, peering closely at the object label for the Loyal Union Sampler.

Summer made her best guess about what had captured his attention. "We'll credit both the Waterford Public Library and University Realty for the donation of the Authors' Album," she assured him, glancing for confirmation to Courtney, who inclined her head graciously.

Without looking their way, Krolich nodded curtly in response, but he moved on to the next quilt before the women could catch up to him. Evidently he wanted his space, so Summer let him be, focusing her attention on Courtney, glancing his way every now and then in case he needed anything. She didn't like Krolich, or trust him, but he was a gallery visitor as well as a contributor of sorts, and she was a professional.

She couldn't help noticing, though, that his frown deepened as he moved from one display to the next, his expression turning increasingly displeased as he read the object labels.

Eventually, the group reunited in the hallway just outside the doorway. Krolich had slung his now-empty duffel bag over his shoulder again, his manner agitated. "Why would you include all those miscellaneous objects in the exhibit?" he demanded, jerking his thumb toward the doorway. "Aren't you concerned about aesthetics?"

"Do you mean the photos and documents?" Summer asked. "I assure you, they aren't miscellaneous, but very thoughtfully curated, and displayed in an aesthetically pleasing manner. Their purpose is to pay homage to quilts that were inspired by or played a role in our shared local history, but couldn't be acquired for our exhibit. I hope eventually to locate these lost quilts, but until we do, the artifacts will tell their story."

"That's an inspired idea," said Courtney. Krolich scowled.

By then their meeting had run over the allotted time, so Pat and Summer escorted their guests downstairs to the foyer, where they thanked them again for Authors' Album and invited them to the grand opening gala in August.

"I wouldn't miss it," said Courtney graciously.

"I'll have to check my calendar," said Krolich. He yanked open the left door and strode outside, his duffel bag smacking the doorframe as he passed. Courtney offered Pat and Summer a faint smile and a bemused shrug, and she waited a moment before she too departed, as if to emphasize that they were not together.

"What was his problem?" Summer asked Pat after the door closed with a solid, reassuring click.

"Don't even get me started," said Pat. "He was so dreadful to all of us when he was trying to seize Union Hall. He really has some nerve, strolling in here like some sort of community benefactor, commenting on renovations to a building he hoped would be a pile of rubble in a landfill by now."

"I'm sorry he didn't offer you the financial donation you were expecting."

"I wasn't really expecting it," Pat admitted, "merely hoping against hope for it. But Authors' Album is a wonderful addition to our collection. I'm rather surprised he donated it rather than offering to sell it to us."

"He didn't donate it," Summer reminded her. "Courtney Langdon and the Waterford Public Library board did."

"Yes, of course," Pat conceded. "Still, I had the distinct impression that it was his idea, and that Courtney was only reluctantly going along with it."

"I thought so too, but only at first," said Summer as together they headed back upstairs to the gallery. "By the time they left, Courtney seemed reassured and very approving. Krolich, though . . ." Summer shook her head. "Something was off. I don't think he liked what he saw in the gallery. I think he regrets returning the quilt, but thought it was too late to take it back."

Pat laughed lightly. "He couldn't, even if he wanted to. The library has been the rightful owner all along. If their board of directors wants us to have Authors' Album, it's entirely up to them. Krolich doesn't get a veto."

Summer nodded, but she couldn't shake her suspicion that Krolich had more influence over the library's decision than either he or Courtney had revealed. If he had pressured the library to donate the quilt, Summer was absolutely sure that it wasn't a sincere expression of remorse for his attempts to destroy Union Hall. More likely, it was a calculated public relations measure, a gesture of goodwill to bolster University Realty's reputation in the court of public opinion—or to forestall potential legal action that might drag him and his company into an altogether different court. Hadn't he committed fraud? Who else would have made Abel Wright's memoirs disappear from the Rare Books Room just when the historical society needed them? What about the questionable methods he had used to convince the zoning commission and the city council to dismiss the historical society's request for a hearing? Summer wasn't a lawyer, but it sure sounded like Krolich ought to be very nervous, and very eager to win over his former rivals.

Summer was thrilled to have Authors' Album in the exhibit, but Krolich's sudden, unexpected generosity couldn't convince her to trust him.

**Authors' Album.** 76" x 76". Cotton top and backing with cotton batting. Pieced, embroidered, and quilted by Dorothea Granger (Nelson), Violet Pearson Engle, et al., Creek's Crossing, PA, 1850.

*Authors' Album* is a splendid example of a quilt that combines two popular themes seen elsewhere in this exhibit: a signature quilt, which incorporates autographed fabrics into a pieced block, and an opportunity quilt, a collaborative project raffled off to raise funds for a worthy cause. The 61 eight-inch blocks were pieced from a variety of cotton prints in hues of Turkey red, Prussian blue, dark green, "double pinks," brown, and light beige. The Album block, a traditional pattern also known as Chimney Sweep, was a popular choice for signature quilts throughout the nineteenth century.

In 1850, Dorothea Granger (later Dorothea Nelson) led a campaign to build the first public library in the Elm Creek Valley. She and the other members of the library committee wrote to the most renowned authors, artists, and politicians of the era and asked each to contribute a 2" x 4.5" rectangle of unbleached muslin autographed in black ink. Sixty-one "distinguished personages" responded, including President Zachary Taylor, abolitionist and author Frederick Douglass, women's suffrage pioneer Elizabeth Cady Stanton, author Henry David Thoreau, and celebrated poet Elizabeth Barrett Browning. Only two residents of the Elm Creek Valley signed patches: Hiram Engle, the mayor of Creek's Crossing, and his wife, Violet Pearson Engle. Since the number of autographs received would determine the number of blocks in the quilt, it is possible that Mr. and Mrs. Engle were invited to contribute the autographs not only to honor them as prominent members of the community, but also to make up the numbers necessary for this on-point layout, which presents the autographs in an aesthetically pleasing, horizontal orientation.

According to letters in the Nelson-Granger family papers, after the quilt top was assembled, women of the community quilted and bound the pieced top at a special Quilting Bee Dance at the Creek's Crossing schoolhouse. The finished quilt was raffled off that same evening. According to an account of the event that appeared in the *Creek's Crossing Informer* two days later, raffle ticket sales, fees to sponsor engraved bronze plates to adorn the future library's bookshelves, and proceeds from the dance raised more than $500 for the founding of the new library.

The winner of the raffle was Cyrus Pearson, son of the library board president and stepson of the mayor. "In an unexpected display of generosity," the *Informer* noted, "Mr. Pearson presented the quilt to his dear mother, who in turn donated the extraordinary quilt, so beautifully fashioned by herself and other ladies of Creek's Crossing, to the library board. When the much-anticipated addition to the Town Square is complete, this masterpiece of fabric and thread shall be displayed therein for all to enjoy." The following month, however, the *Grangerville Herald* reported that Violet Pearson Engle's generosity had been exaggerated. "According to an eyewitness, not an hour after Mr. Pearson won the quilt and presented it to his mother, Mr. Thomas Nelson, the Creek's Crossing schoolmaster, purchased it from Mrs. Engle for five dollars," the reporter wrote. "Immediately thereafter, Mr. Nelson quietly offered it to Mrs. [Charles] Claverton, a member of the library board. Why the mayor's wife undeservedly accepted the applause and admiration of the assembly, and why Mr. Nelson has not claimed rightful credit for the deed, remains a mystery this reporter cannot explain to his complete satisfaction."

Longtime residents of the Elm Creek Valley will recall seeing the *Authors' Album* given pride of place above the circulation desk in the original Waterford Public Library on the town square. During the transition from the older building to the new library in the 1950s, the quilt was entrusted to University Realty and placed in storage for safekeeping. Regrettably, the quilt's location was unknown for more than fifty years, until it was discovered a year ago in University Realty's vault when the company was moving to its current location on Main Street.

Authors' Album was generously donated to the Waterford Historical Society by the Waterford Public Library and University Realty. We are grateful for the gift, as well as for the encouraging reminder that even after decades, a quilt believed lost forever may yet be found.

# 12

Summer's search for newspaper articles about Authors' Album and the Quilting Bee Dance brought her to the Rare Books Room three times during the first week of August. The former assistant archivist had departed for his new job weeks before, leaving Audrey with only part-time student support at the reference desk while the search for his replacement continued.

"I don't understand why you haven't had dozens of qualified applicants begging for interviews," Summer told Audrey when she returned her latest batch of microfilm. If Summer weren't so unbelievably busy herself, she'd be tempted to volunteer until they hired someone new, just to ease Audrey's burden. "What about an incoming MLIS student? Classes don't start for another month, but maybe someone would be willing to come early."

Audrey sighed and shook her head. "I emailed a job announcement to all of our current and incoming MLIS students the same day Bradley gave his two-week notice. Unfortunately, the timing was all wrong. Assistantships are offered in the spring as part of an admitted student's financial aid package, so everyone has already been sorted."

"Maybe someone will ask to switch departments after they get to know the library."

"One can only hope, although it's considered bad form to poach another department's graduate assistants." Audrey managed a wry smile. "It takes a certain type of scholar to prefer our old books and fragile manuscripts to the exciting, brave new world of digitized materials and collaborative databases."

"You can count me among the former," said Summer. "Handwritten manuscripts and antique texts are so infused with history and meaning—from the author, yes, but also from everyone who has studied them since the ink was put to paper."

Audrey raised her eyebrows, amused. "This, from the young woman who carries her mobile and laptop everywhere?"

"Not everywhere," Summer protested, smiling. "I appreciate the best qualities of both, old and new. I love original sources, and I love technology that makes my life easier, especially if it can save me massive amounts of time searching for obscure details. A few weeks ago, a library assistant in main reference mentioned a new resource in the works, something about searchable newspaper archives—"

"You must mean Enrique," said Audrey, nodding. "He's quite the advocate for these online databases. He assures me that eventually we'll be able to search digitized archives from virtually any library in the world through the World Wide Web."

Unexpectedly, Summer felt heat rise in her cheeks. "Enrique? I think that was his name. If I recall correctly." Of course she remembered his name. Every time she entered the Waterford College Library and headed upstairs to the Rare Books Room, she craned her neck in the direction of the reference department, hoping to catch a glimpse of him. Only two days before, she had invented an excuse to look up statistics about property values on the town square, but to her disappointment, someone else was working the reference desk when she arrived. "I would've saved myself countless hours this summer if I'd had access to a digitized newspaper database."

"You may have a few more years to wait. At the last ALA conference, I heard that the Library of Congress is developing something called the National Digital Library Program, but it's still in the early stages. You should speak with Enrique if you're curious. His master's capstone project is about emerging technologies and library accessibility, which makes him our resident expert."

"Maybe I'll do that," said Summer, aiming for nonchalance but probably falling far short. She was moving back to Chicago in a month, she reminded herself firmly. There was absolutely no point in striking up a friendship or whatever with someone she would have to say goodbye to just as she was getting to know him.

"I offered Enrique our assistant archivist position as soon as Bradley gave notice," Audrey remarked as she processed Summer's microfilm rolls and set them on the returns cart for her student page to shelve. "He earned his BA in history from Carnegie Mellon."

"He's a historian?"

"Yes, that's why I thought he would be a good fit for the job. I pleaded my case, but he's committed to the public library track. He's very passionate about making resources and services available to everyone, regardless of education or income, especially to children living in underserved communities."

"Really?" Just what she needed, another reason to admire him. She didn't want to appear overly interested, but she couldn't help adding, "It's great that he's focusing on people who need libraries most."

"I agree." Audrey's brow furrowed slightly. "There was a moment not long ago when I thought his preferences had changed. He would stop by the Rare Books Room nearly every day before or after his shift, but never on any official library business. He would look around and chat with me for a bit, but leave without ever explaining what had brought him to our wing. I hope he wasn't evaluating the Rare Books Room as a potential workplace only to find it wanting."

"I can't believe that. Maybe he was looking for another MLIS student, or—" Or for her, Summer hoped, although that was unlikely. "Or signs of trouble, because of the thefts."

Audrey's expression darkened. "Maybe so. We've all been

extra-vigilant over the past year. Fortunately, our new security measures seem to be working."

Or, Summer thought, Gregory Krolich hadn't tested them because his current schemes didn't require the theft of library books.

Bidding Audrey goodbye and good luck, Summer packed up her
things and left the Rare Books Room. As she headed downstairs, she
briefly considered inventing another excuse to wander through the
main reference department, but she managed to resist temptation,
heading straight for the exit without allowing herself even a glance
in the wrong direction. She barely had enough time to grab a quick
takeout lunch before she was expected at Union Hall. No distractions,
she reminded herself firmly. She couldn't afford them.

She was halfway across the quad when her cell phone rang. As she
dug her phone from her pocket, for one entirely irrational moment,
she thought it might be Enrique. One glance at the caller ID gave
her a different reason to smile. "Hey, Julianne," she answered, shifting
her backpack as she held the phone to her ear. "So good to hear from
you. How are you?"

"Hey, Summer. I'm good. How are things in the countryside?"

"Oh, I'm living the dream. Fresh air, sunshine, farmers markets—"

"Quilting, libraries—"

"You know me so well."

"After nearly two years as your roommate, I would hope so. But
I might forget most of the details if you don't come back soon and
remind me. Are you still determined to stick out this rural exile until
you finish that thesis?"

"Absolutely. Believe it or not, my crazy scheme is working. I'm
actually making progress."

"So you've had a breakthrough?"

"I suppose you could call it that." Summer passed through the
main campus gates and waited for the light to change before crossing
Main Street. "The words are coming and the pages are accumulating."

"That's great!"

"It must be all the stimulating fresh country air." Although she spoke lightly, Summer felt her expression hardening as her gaze lit upon the steel gray–and-blue University Realty sign hanging above the entrance to what had once been Bonnie's beloved quilt shop. No gift of a marvelous, long-lost antique quilt would ever compensate for the anguish and ruin Krolich had inflicted upon Summer's friend, if that's what he was trying to do.

"That's wonderful, Summer. I'm so happy for you. Maricela will be too when I tell her." Julianne hesitated. "So, you're going to renew your lease?"

"Sure, eventually."

"It's just that it's already August, and our leases are up at the end of the month. Maricela and I have already renewed ours. No pressure, but we wanted to make sure that you're definitely coming back, and that you want to keep your room, because if you aren't or you don't we'll need to find someone else pretty quickly or—"

"Let me stop you there," Summer broke in, laughing. "My lease runs through the end of December. I took over Shane's at winter quarter, remember? I spent the fall on the futon in the living room until he graduated and moved out so I could take over his room."

"Oh, of course. How could we have forgotten that?"

"Well, it was two years ago. It was memorable but not in a good way. All those months with an extra person in the apartment, my stuff piled up in the corner of the living room—"

"That never bothered us! We were just grateful that you were willing to move in under those conditions. That lumpy futon, Shane's inability to clean up after himself in the kitchen—"

"Yeah, in hindsight it was pretty bad. Maybe you're blocking the memory out of guilt."

"That's probably it." Julianne hesitated. "So you're definitely coming back?"

"Of course," said Summer, surprised. "What else would I do? Where else would I go?"

"Actually, you seem very happy where you are. Happier than you've been for months."

"You know the university has residency requirements." Summer shifted the phone to her other ear, willing the light to change. "If I don't come back to Chicago, I don't get my doctorate."

"That wouldn't be the worst thing in the world, though, would it?"

Summer inhaled deeply, disconcerted. First Sarah, now Julianne. "No, I suppose in the whole scheme of all the troubles afflicting humanity, not earning a doctorate doesn't even make the top hundred." The light changed. "Listen, I've got to go," Summer said as she hurried across the street. "Don't worry about me. Really. I'm fine. If my plans change, I'll let you know." She said a hasty goodbye and hung up.

*If her plans change?*

Why had she said that? Her plans weren't changing.

She felt her throat constricting as she hurried up the hill, past shops and restaurants and student apartments. Julianne's tentative questions echoed Sarah's and, if she was perfectly honest, her own: Of course she *could* finish her thesis, earn her master's, and move on to her doctorate, but *should* she?

Maybe not, she realized so suddenly that she stopped short on the sidewalk, clutching the straps of her backpack as she caught her breath and blinked back tears of frustration. Her friends valued her happiness and well-being more than her achievements. They weren't trying to discourage her. They simply saw how unhappy and conflicted she was, and they wanted to help. They just weren't sure how.

But how could Summer assure her friends that continuing on her present course was best for her when she couldn't even convince herself? And realistically, *would* she be able to earn her doctorate and get tenure at a university if she was miserable every step of the way? Did she even want to?

This was exactly the sort of distressing conundrum she always talked through with her mom, but Gwen was the last person Summer could confide in about this particular issue. But it was already August, and she was running out of time. Maybe she should risk disappointing her mom, just to get some clarity.

She inhaled deeply and continued on her way, stopping briefly at the Daily Grind to pick up an Italian roast and a blueberry scone. She had been shut up indoors most of the morning, and the day was too beautiful to miss, so she found an unoccupied bench on the grassy town square and enjoyed her lunch in the shade of an oak tree.

Summer allowed herself one sip and one bite before opening her backpack and taking out her notes for the conclusion of her thesis. Without the enticing distraction of the Granger-Nelson papers, she hoped to squeeze in some thesis work during her lunch break, a task that was proving increasingly difficult back at the manor, since every discovery compelled her to seek more.

Recently she had found a few brief descriptions of the quilt she had come to think of as the Sugar Camp Quilt in letters and journal entries, as well as several pen-and-ink sketches. Summer assumed Dorothea had drawn the blocks and layout while planning the project with her uncle, but contextual clues in the letters strongly suggested that she had made the illustrations from memory many years after the quilt went missing. A small envelope holding one of the sketches included something else truly unexpected and astonishing—ten precious fabric swatches, the colors as bright and vibrant as they must have been when Dorothea had trimmed them ages ago. Summer thought it very likely that the swatches had not been exposed to sunlight for more than a century.

Summer thrilled to each new discovery, although none so far revealed the location of the Sugar Camp Quilt. As far as the historical record was concerned, the quilt had simply vanished one day, never to be seen again. Summer's prevailing theory was that a fugitive slave fleeing north along the Underground Railroad in midwinter had taken the

Sugar Camp Quilt from the Grangers' station out of a desperate need to fend off the bitter cold. Runaways were meant to memorize the clues and leave the quilt behind to guide other fugitives, but perhaps someone hadn't known this. Or perhaps on the night in question the cold had been too brutal, the need for warmth and comfort too great, and the runaway's survival had depended upon bringing the quilt along.

Summer might never find the answers, but even so, the search for clues captivated her imagination. No wonder it was nearly impossible to tear herself away from the Granger-Nelson papers and focus on work that didn't inspire her. That was why she had deliberately left Kathleen's file at Elm Creek Manor that morning. She was determined that nothing would distract her attention away from her thesis notes, at least not for the half hour she could spare for lunch.

"So this is where you prefer to work now." A man's voice interrupted her reverie, just as she took a large sip of coffee. "Is it because I mistook you for an MLIS student? I honestly didn't mean to imply that you spend too much time at the library."

Startled, she glanced up from her notebook, cup still raised to her lips, to discover Enrique smiling down at her. "Hi," she said, clearing her throat, quickly touching the back of her hand to her lips to blot away any stray drops of coffee. "Please don't worry about it. It was an honest mistake."

He smiled, skeptical. "You sure?"

"Absolutely. For what it's worth, I happen to believe it's impossible to spend too much time in a library."

"How could anyone blame me for thinking you're an MLIS student when you say things like that?" He lifted his chin to indicate the cup in her hand. "Was the Daily Grind just on your way to the library? Italian roast with steamed almond milk, right?"

"Good memory," said Summer, impressed. "But I've just *come from* the library, actually." She inclined her head toward Union Hall, on the far end of the town square. "That's where I'm headed next. I'm working on a research project for the Waterford Historical Society."

He gestured to the papers and notebooks she had spread across the entire bench. "Are you writing a research paper for them? A grant application?"

"Oh, this? No, this is for another project." Summer gathered the scattered papers into a neat pile on her lap. A frisson of delight swept through her when Enrique sat down as soon as there was enough room on the bench. "This is for my master's thesis—my three-months-overdue master's thesis, to be precise."

"Ouch."

"I know, right?" She managed a wry smile as she tucked the stack of papers into her backpack. "My adviser gave me an extension until the end of August, but if I don't make it—" She shook her head. "To be honest, I don't have a backup plan."

"You won't need one. You'll finish."

She raised her eyebrows at him. "You're very confident for some-one who doesn't even know me."

"I have a good feeling about your chances. Probably because you've been spending so much time in the library."

"So much for your theory. I haven't been spending all these weeks in the Rare Books Room working on my thesis. That's been for the historical society project."

Enrique nodded thoughtfully, took a deep drink of his coffee, and leaned back against the bench. "Can you tell me about it?"

"Which one?"

"Whichever one you'd rather talk about."

She pretended to consider. "Hmm. Tough choice. Complain about my thesis or rave about the quilt exhibit?"

"Quilt exhibit?"

"You heard me." If he yawned from sheer boredom or cracked a grandmother-in-a-rocking-chair joke, at least she would no longer find him attractive.

But of course he did neither. He listened with apparently genuine interest as she told him about the quilt exhibit, even though she left out all the most exciting parts about Gregory Krolich concealing evidence, stealing memoirs from the Rare Books Room, and allegedly bribing city council members. It occurred to her that as an aspiring librarian, Enrique would probably find the stolen books connection intriguing. If he wasn't put off by her quilt-hunting talk and dared risk a second conversation someday, she would fill him in on the rest.

"So you're a museum curator," he said, when she had finished the condensed version of the tale. "I wasn't off by much when I thought you were a librarian."

"How do you figure?"

"Isn't a librarian a book curator? Same thing."

Summer smiled. "It's not quite the same thing, and anyway, I'm only a museum curator until September. Then it's back to Chicago and full-time academics. Fortunately, there will still be libraries involved."

"Chicago?" His eyebrows rose. "You're from Chicago?"

"No, I'm from here—well, not originally. I was born in Kentucky. I lived in New York state for a while and moved to Waterford when I was ten. But yeah, I'm a grad student in history at the University of Chicago."

"Oh, okay." His disappointment was unmistakable. "I thought you were in grad school at Waterford College."

For a moment, she fervently wished that she were. "No, I'm just home for the summer. I thought I'd mentioned that."

He shook his head. "No, I would've remembered."

"Do you have something against the University of Chicago, or is it the city itself you dislike?" she teased. "Did they offend you in some way? Is it their pizza? Personally, I object to their hot dogs, but I'm a vegetarian."

He managed a grin. "I'm fine with Chicago and the university. I love the pizza. It's just—" He held her gaze for a moment. "Chicago is kind of far away, you know?"

"I know," she said, looking away, taking a sip of her coffee to conceal her sudden dismay. She had the strangest sensation of reaching out for a falling object only to watch it tumble past her fingertips. "But I still have a month left—to finish my thesis, I mean—before I have to go back."

"Then I should let you get back to work." He rose, but just when she thought he was going to say goodbye and walk away, he said, "I'd really like to see your exhibit. When is that grand opening gala?"

"It's Saturday, August twenty-eighth, but you don't have to wait until then. The gallery is open to visitors now. I'd be happy to give you a tour."

"Would you? I'd like that."

"Of course." Summer rose, slipped her backpack over her shoulders, and collected her coffee cup and the paper bag that now held only a napkin and blueberry scone crumbs. "When would be good for you? My mornings are usually packed, but I could do a Friday or Saturday afternoon."

"I'm off Friday afternoons. How about one o'clock this Friday?"

"Sounds great," Summer replied, trying to contain the grin she felt spreading over her face. Enrique was smiling too, though not as cheerfully as before she told him she was leaving town at the end of the month. Unless she was seriously misreading him, there was a mutual, tangible note of regret in their parting despite their smiles, a wordless acknowledgment that they liked each other, but they knew it couldn't go anywhere.

Later, back at the manor, when Summer told the other Elm Creek Quilters she had to skip the evening program that night so she could get straight to work on her thesis, they were far more interested in why she might miss dinner on Friday.

"You have a date," Agnes exclaimed, eyes shining, clasping her hands together.

"He sounds very nice," said Gretchen. "I hope you have a lovely time."

"It's not a date," Summer said emphatically. "It's one historian showing another historian around an exhibit about local history."

"I thought he was a librarian," said Diane, bemused.

"He's that too."

"A historian librarian who likes quilts," mused Gwen, grinning. "He sounds perfect for you, kiddo."

Summer shot her a look. "Except that I'm going back to Chicago in a month," she said pointedly.

Her mother shrugged. "If you want."

"If I *want*?" Summer said, pitch rising with each word. "What does *that* mean?"

Her mother shrugged again, beaded necklaces clinking softly. "I'm just saying that's not your only option."

Summer was so astounded it left her light-headed. "What other options are there?"

"Well, just off the top of my head, you could finish your master's degree, put in for a leave of absence, and take a year off to figure out what you want to do next."

Summer gaped at her. "*That* was just off the top of your head?"

"I believe this has turned into a private family discussion," Sylvia broke in smoothly, gesturing for the other Elm Creek Quilters to follow the last few campers from the banquet hall. "Let's give Gwen and Summer the room, shall we?"

"Not now, not just when it's getting good," Diane protested, but Sylvia placed a hand on her back and firmly guided her toward the doorway. The others left more willingly, but not without a few parting glances of concern for the mother and daughter.

As soon as they were alone, Summer pulled out a chair at the nearest table and sank into it. "How long have you known I'm not sure I want to continue?" she asked. "Did Sarah tell you?"

"Whatever you confided to Sarah, she didn't breathe a word of it to me." Her mother pulled out another chair and sat down facing her, leaning to the side to rest an arm on the table. "Kiddo, ever since you showed up unexpectedly in June and confessed that you hadn't really earned your degree, I knew you were dealing with a much bigger obstacle than writer's block."

"I do have writer's block."

"Maybe. Maybe not. You've always been an excellent writer, and to paraphrase Diane, you could have pounded out a few more pages, typed 'The End,' and called it a thesis." Gwen sighed, her expression full of love and understanding. "As a wizened old professor, I've learned that sometimes when a student can't quite seem to complete an important chapter in her life, it's often because she doesn't really want to move on to the next."

Summer covered her eyes with her hands, took a steadying breath, and rubbed her forehead. "Maybe that's my problem," she said, letting her hands fall to her lap. "I mean, seriously, how many papers have I written in my life? Thousands, probably, many of them far more difficult than this one. There's no reason why I shouldn't be able to complete this thesis."

"And you will."

"I know. Really, I do. If you locked me in a room with nothing but coffee and blueberry scones and refused to let me out until it was finished, I'd have it done in a day."

"I would never do that."

"But you get my point."

"Yes, kiddo, I do. But please don't try it."

Summer studied her. "Be honest. Brutally honest. Wouldn't you be disappointed in me if I didn't get my doctorate?"

"Not in the least."

"Really?"

"Yes, really. And for the record, I'd be devastated if you didn't want to return to graduate school but you did it anyway, because you thought that's what *I* wanted."

"I don't know what I want." Summer swallowed hard, fighting back tears. "Actually, I do. I want bits of studying history and pieces of teaching at quilt camp and I want to stitch them all together into the perfect career. I want to teach Modern Quilting at Elm Creek Manor and study antique documents and manuscripts in a glorious old library." She forced a shaky laugh. "Where do I apply for *that* job?"

"If I knew, I might fill out an application myself." Her mom took her hand and clasped it in both of her own. "Kiddo, a doctoral program is a huge commitment. Don't you think you owe it to yourself to take some time to think it over?"

"You mean take a leave of absence from the university."

Her mother nodded.

Summer inhaled deeply. She couldn't pretend the idea wasn't tempting. "What about my fellowship? If I lose my funding now, I can't take on massive debt to pay for school later."

"I'm sure the history department would put your fellowship on hold for a year. They must have policies in place for such contingencies. Waterford College does."

Summer closed her eyes and sank back in her chair. It would be such a relief to have time to consider other options before plunging into a doctoral program. She hadn't really thought about what she would do if she didn't become a professor like her mom. That expectation was always there in the back of her mind, even when she turned down Penn in order to help launch Elm Creek Quilts.

Time to think—what a gift that would be.

Sitting up, she leaned over to rest her hands on her mom's shoulders and kissed her on the cheek. "Thanks, Mom. I should have talked this over with you months ago."

"I think you needed to figure a few things out on your own first."

Summer fell silent, thinking, scarcely noticing the faint clattering of dishes and silverware all around them as the kitchen staff bused the tables. "I'm going to consider taking a leave of absence," she finally said. "I'll check the university website and find out how to apply, what the deadlines are, and all that."

"If you need to talk anything over, I'm always here for you."

"I know," said Summer, and kissed her again.

She felt drained as she climbed the stairs to her third-floor bedroom, yet also tremendously relieved. She should have known her mom would understand. Gwen's own life had followed an unpredictable winding way from the time she had left her parents' home until she settled down as a respectable college professor. Of course she would empathize with Summer's shifting goals and changes of mind and heart.

Alone in her room, Summer set up her laptop and spent an hour searching around the University of Chicago website, bookmarking pages, taking notes, weighing the choices and consequences. When she had learned all she could without actually speaking with an adviser, she moved on to her thesis. By then, her mind was so weary that she skipped past the conclusion to the endnotes and bibliography, straightforward compilation and editing work that didn't require too much analysis or creativity. When she grew too tired for even that, she went to bed—two hours earlier than usual but not a moment too soon.

The next morning, she woke feeling lighter, freer, as if a world of possibilities had suddenly opened up before her.

Sunrise Yoga on the verandah was a joy. Anna's breakfast was sublimely delicious. Conversation and laughter in the banquet hall lifted her spirits. Somehow the thought that she might not have to leave Elm Creek Manor in a month after all inspired her to delight in the simplest, most familiar pleasures as if they were entirely new.

Even later that morning, when she examined all the details she had assembled about the Sugar Camp Quilt and realized that she had not even the faintest hint of a trail to follow and would almost certainly never acquire the quilt, she accepted the loss with good grace. She made clear photocopies of Dorothea's sketches and passages from her letters and journals that mentioned the quilt, and framed them with care. Next she mounted the fabric swatches on acid-free paper and framed those as well. She took another day to write the object label, and on Thursday, she arranged the artifacts in the gallery on the wall opposite the entrance. She knew it was very unlikely that a visitor would see the display, immediately recognize the long-lost quilt, and tell Summer how to acquire it, but that didn't keep her from hoping.

Every day, such impossible hopes became a bit more likely. Over the past few weeks, as word of the Museum of Lost Quilts had spread, enthusiastic quilt lovers and history buffs had traveled from hundreds of miles around to view the growing collection—and to admire the ongoing renovations to Union Hall and donate generously to the venture. Summer's project was not yet complete, but Agnes, Pat, Sylvia, and the other Elm Creek Quilters assured her it was already a success.

On Friday, after Sunrise Yoga and her Modern Quilting class, Summer had a quick lunch in the kitchen—Greek yogurt with apple confit left over from the previous night's dinner—before changing into her favorite sage-green jersey knit cotton dress and brushing her auburn hair until it shone. She tried to slip out the back door discreetly, but Maggie and two campers spotted her in the west wing hallway.

"Have fun," Maggie called to her in passing, adding for the campers' benefit, "Summer has a date."

"Oh, how exciting," one of the campers exclaimed. "Good luck, dear."

"Don't do anything we wouldn't do," the other called, and the three women burst out laughing. Summer paused to shake her head at them in feigned exasperation before hurrying on her way.

She was waiting in the foyer of Union Hall when Enrique arrived a few minutes before one o'clock, dressed in khakis and a light blue button-down with the sleeves rolled up partway, revealing strong forearms he probably didn't get from hefting books. Summer basked in his admiring smile as she welcomed him and gave him a brief tour of the main floor before leading him upstairs to the gallery.

About two dozen visitors were exploring the exhibit when they arrived. When they paused just inside the doorway to take in the scene, Summer was pleased to see that Enrique seemed visibly impressed. "I don't know the first thing about how to make a quilt," he admitted, "but this looks amazing."

"Let me show you around," she said, playfully offering him her hand. Without hesitation, he smiled and took it.

There was no one single correct way to view the exhibit, but Summer had arranged the quilts so they could be viewed in her own favorite order, chronologically. They began with the Sugar Camp Quilt artifacts, followed immediately by the Authors' Album, and on from there, reaching the object labels for the victory quilts near the midpoint and ending with those for In Honor of Linda's Retirement. If she didn't have her tour guide routine so well practiced, she would have been more nervous, but when it was clear Enrique was sincerely interested in Union Hall's transformation from notorious neighborhood eyesore to a jewel of the historic district, she relaxed and simply enjoyed his company. She found herself unexpectedly pleased that while he admired the artistry of the quilts, his attention lingered longest on the artifacts and the object labels she had written.

"It's like telling the story of a community through quilting," he remarked as they admired the Loyal Union Sampler. "I never would have guessed that quilts could have played such a significant role in a town's history. This was an inspired idea, Summer."

"I wish I could say I thought of it," Summer admitted. "Agnes Emberly, a member of the Waterford Historical Society and a very dear friend of mine from Elm Creek Quilts, deserves all the credit for the idea. I just acquired the quilts, set up the exhibit, and wrote the object labels."

"You say that like it's not a huge deal, but it is." His brow furrowed. "Wait. Elm Creek Quilts?"

"You really haven't been in town long, have you?" she teased. "Elm Creek Quilts is another very important part of my life, but that's a long story, too long to squeeze into this tour."

"I'd love to hear it," he said, smiling. "Would you be free to tell me over dinner tomorrow night?"

Before Summer could reply, a sudden commotion drew her attention, and she glanced past Enrique's shoulder to find a cluster of men and women in dark business attire blocking the gallery doorway. Her breath caught in her throat at the sight of Gregory Krolich front and center, jaw set, scanning the room through narrowed eyes. Instinctively she took a step backward so Enrique's shoulders and the end of a partition wall mostly blocked her from the real estate developer's view. Instead Krolich's gaze fixed upon the nearest docent, a white-haired, retired pharmacist who was minding the gallery from his post near the donation box. Krolich strode over to him, and as Summer watched, aghast, a heated exchange broke out, sharp words and firm replies flying back and forth ever louder.

"Excuse me a moment," Summer murmured to Enrique, hurrying over to intervene. "Good afternoon, Mr. Krolich," she greeted him smoothly. She nodded to the docent. "Thank you, Dr. Horne. I'll take this."

"I'll be right over there in case you need me," Dr. Horne said, with a hard look for Krolich in parting.

Summer took a quick, steadying breath. "Is there something I can do for you, Mr. Krolich?" she asked, gesturing toward Authors' Album. "I hope you noticed how beautifully Authors' Album complements the exhibit."

He gestured sharply, dismissing her pleasantries, which his companions apparently interpreted as a signal to hurry over. "It's the most important quilt here, obviously, and the most valuable," he said as the three men and two women gathered behind him, their expressions resolute and indignant. "If I had known you intended to put a skewed political slant on this exhibit, I never would have encouraged the library to donate that quilt to you."

"Excuse me?" said Summer, baffled.

"What do you mean by 'skewed political slant'?" asked Enrique. Summer hadn't realized he had followed her, but she found his presence reassuring, as if she had backup. She hoped she wouldn't need it.

"I'm referring to the offensive, biased interpretations of our community's history tacked on to these quilt descriptions." Krolich jabbed his finger toward the three nearest object labels. "In addition to the specific, calculated, malicious attacks on my own company, you've worked anti-business spin into nearly every display. I speak on behalf of a committee of concerned citizens who demand the immediate removal of the offensive material."

While Summer was absorbing that, Krolich introduced his companions, too swiftly for her to catch all the names. She did gather that three of them were presidents of the Waterford, Grangerville, and Woodfall chambers of commerce, one was the deputy mayor of Waterford, and another was the director of something rather alarmingly called the Coalition to Save American Children.

"Why must your exhibit labels include irrelevant critical commentary instead of a simple, factual, impartial description of the item on display?" one of the women queried, mouth pinched in a frown. "Mr. Krolich says you portray the people of Waterford as racists!"

"Mr. Krolich says?" Summer echoed, puzzled. "So you haven't read the object labels yourself?"

"I don't need to read them," the woman huffed. "Why should I read lies and slander?"

"I wrote those object labels," said Summer, "and I assure you, while I'm not infallible, I definitely didn't include any lies or slander."

"What exactly do you hope to accomplish by dredging up unpleasant incidents from the past?" another man asked, aggrieved. "Do you want to drive away tourist dollars and business investment?"

"Of course not."

"Then why emphasize insignificant, unproven, possibly untrue details that reflect badly upon prominent citizens from our venerable history?" Krolich countered.

"Yes, especially when that includes honored founding citizens, many of whose descendants still live in the Elm Creek Valley?" the other woman chimed in. "Why couldn't you be more positive and focus on our founders' accomplishments instead?"

As several of the indignant representatives all spoke at once, other gallery visitors paused what they were doing to observe the confrontation, their expressions curious and wary.

Enrique raised his hands for calm. "I'm not from Waterford," he said, "but I've read every one of the object labels in this exhibit, and it's evident that both historical accomplishments and failures are mentioned. As an objective observer, I feel that I've seen a fair and equitable depiction of the Elm Creek Valley's history."

"Objective observer, indeed," the first woman snapped. "I saw you holding hands with the curator!"

"No one cares about your *opinions*, young lady," the eldest of the men scolded, wagging his finger at Summer. "Stick to the facts instead of stirring up trouble."

"That's unnecessary, sir," said Enrique firmly. "Let's calm down and discuss this rationally."

Summer touched his arm and offered him a quick look to say that she had this. Turning back to Krolich's posse, she met their accusing glares with a calm, level gaze. "I assure you, these object labels include carefully researched facts, each verified by the historical record." Her heart was pounding, but she kept her voice steady. "I've provided narrative description and analysis, free of judgment. If you've found factual errors, I will, of course, correct them immediately. If, however, a historical fact you learn from this exhibit simply challenges your assumptions or makes you uncomfortable, I'd encourage you to—"

"Quilts are meant to be cozy and beautiful," the first woman interrupted, raising her voice and glancing around the gallery, clearly hoping to win over the exhibit visitors. "These quilts are lovely on their own, but you had to spoil everything with your radical agenda."

"I for one won't allow it," the eldest man declared, breaking away from the pack. Storming over to the Loyal Union Sampler, he snatched the object label from its frame. As he continued down the row, removing one sheet of card stock after another, his companions joined him, sweeping through the gallery, seizing the object labels, sometimes while visitors were still reading them. Summer, Enrique, and Dr. Horne tried to intervene without escalating the tumult or endangering the quilts, but Krolich and his companions managed to seize every page. One man had tried to remove the artifacts from the Cleopatra's Fan display, but Summer had put herself between him and the wall, pushing his arms aside whenever he tried to reach past her.

"You do realize this is theft, don't you?" said Enrique, fixing Krolich with a steely gaze. "Theft, vandalism—"

"It's just paper," Krolich retorted, although he took a step back. "Relax."

"Yes, it's just paper," said the second woman gleefully. To demonstrate, she tore the object label for Gerda's Log Cabin into halves, quarters, and eighths and tossed them into the air.

"No, I have a better idea," said Krolich, fixing Summer with an imperious glare as the scraps drifted to the floor like confetti. "We'll take these with us and edit them to remove the offensive material. If you display our approved, revised versions instead, we'll have no further objections."

"And if I don't?" asked Summer, incredulous.

"Miss Sullivan, I think you seriously underestimate our influence in this community." Krolich gestured to indicate himself and his companions, who nodded emphatically or lifted their chins, trying to assume an air of dignity. "If you refuse to cooperate, we'll do everything in our considerable power to shut down this exhibit permanently." He glanced around the room appraisingly. "What a pity it would be if you ended up losing Union Hall anyway, after all your audacious, expensive attempts to preserve it."

Summer could only watch, dumbfounded, as Krolich and his crew strode from the gallery, leaving startled and bemused visitors staring after them, murmuring incredulously to one another.

Dr. Horne stooped to pick up the scattered pieces of paper from the floor. "Some people are born ignorant," he declared, shaking his head. "Others have ignorance thrust upon them."

A laugh burst from her throat, but it sounded like a sob.

"Summer?" Enrique asked, placing a hand on her shoulder. "Are you okay?"

"I'm fine," she said, inhaling deeply to calm her temper, which was roiling. "Do you have time to see another part of Union Hall I haven't shown you yet?"

"Sure," he said, puzzled. "Where, and—if you don't mind the question—why?"

"The historical society president's office is where," she said, taking his hand and leading him to the doorway. "Why? To print out new object labels, of course. Did Krolich really think we wouldn't have them backed up on a hard drive somewhere?"

But she knew replacing the stolen object labels was a temporary fix at best. Soon Krolich would be back with his revised versions. She already knew she'd loathe them, that they'd be full of redactions and revisionist history. She'd never consent to using them, and he'd never permit anything else.

Krolich didn't care about the object labels and the unpleasant historical truths they revealed. Well, maybe he did find them objectionable, since they revealed some rather sordid aspects of Waterford's past, but he wasn't waging a cultural war.

This was all about bringing the Waterford Historical Society's capital campaign to an abrupt halt. This was his last, desperate attempt to seize Union Hall.

And one thing history had proved time and again was that Krolich didn't care what harm he caused or laws he broke if it meant getting what he wanted.

**Sugar Camp Quilt.** 84" x 84" (estimated). Cotton top and backing with wool batting. Designed by Jacob Kuehner. Pieced, appliquéd, and quilted by Dorothea Granger (Nelson), Creek's Crossing, PA, 1849.

An early resident of the Elm Creek Valley, Jacob Kuehner ran a prosperous farm on the northern outskirts of Creek's Crossing from 1823–1850. Although he is best remembered in the present day for his generous bequests of land and funds for the establishment of Waterford College, in his time, he was most renowned for his sugar camp, which was famous for producing the best maple sugar in the county. He was also well known for his stern, taciturn demeanor, which concealed deep religious convictions and a commitment to social justice. Even his own family did not suspect that he was a stationmaster on the Underground Railroad.

When Jacob Kuehner asked his niece Dorothea Granger to make him a quilt including both traditional blocks and five unusual patterns of his own design, she agreed, enduring his demands and his criticism as she painstakingly followed his precise instructions. When she completed the quilt and gave it to him as a Christmas gift, she was astonished and offended when he seemed to reject it, ostensibly abandoning it in the rough shelter at his sugar camp. Only after Kuehner's untimely death in early 1850 did Dorothea discover that the shelter was a station on the Underground Railroad, and the quilt contained hidden clues to guide runaway slaves north to freedom.

In sketches Dorothea made from memory later in life, thirty-six Delectable Mountains blocks are arranged in three concentric squares around a Compass Star, a variation with one elongated point angled toward the upper left. Thirty-five of the Delectable Mountains blocks have four half-square triangles on the two adjacent legs of the largest right triangle, but the block in the upper left corner has five peaks on one side and three on the other, a symbolic representation of the Four Brothers Mountains.

When taken together, these two clues indicated that a runaway departing Kuehner's sugar camp should head northwest toward the distinctive mountain range. The four remaining clues, running on the diagonal from the central Compass Star to the upper left corner, are more difficult to interpret. One block with blue curved pieces might indicate a ford across Elm Creek or a tributary of the Juniata, while another composed of brown fabrics could instruct the fugitive to follow the line of a particular fence. The last landmark clue, a variation of the Spider Web block, resembles a water wheel on an axle. An excerpt from one of Dorothea's last letters, displayed here, speaks fondly of Aaron and Ursula Braun, who for several decades ran a mill in the town of Woodfall, northwest of Creek's Crossing. Since contemporary newspaper and journal sources confirm that the Brauns were staunch abolitionists, it is very likely that their mill was the next station on the route north to freedom.

The current location of the *Sugar Camp Quilt* is unknown. It is entirely possible that, like many mid-nineteenth-century fabric items, it has not withstood the effects of time and wear. The quilt went missing from Jacob Kuehner's sugar camp in early 1850, perhaps taken by a runaway who urgently needed protection from the dangerous cold of a Pennsylvania winter's night. Letters Dorothea wrote late in life indicate that she tried to find the quilt, but her search was unsuccessful.

The sketches, letters, and fabric swatches displayed here may be all that remains of Jacob Kuehner and Dorothea Granger's *Sugar Camp Quilt*, which helped an untold number of enslaved persons find freedom in Canada. These artifacts from the Granger-Nelson family papers appear in this exhibit courtesy of Kathleen Barrett, great-great-granddaughter of Dorothea Granger Nelson.

# 13

Pat wasn't in her office when Summer and Enrique knocked on the door, but it was unlocked, so Summer hurried to the computer and opened the files she had previously sent Pat for review. While the printer churned out two copies of each, one copy on card stock for the exhibit and another on standard paper for herself, Summer called Pat's cell phone. When it went straight to voicemail, Summer briefly described the gallery incident and asked Pat to call her back as soon as possible. "Would you mind taking another look at the object labels first?" she asked before she hung up. "The files I shared are still on your office computer, and I have the originals on my laptop."

It was a good thing too, Summer thought as she slipped the paper printouts into her backpack. Krolich might have stolen some card stock pages but he couldn't delete their backup files, just as he couldn't erase facts he disliked from the historical record.

Summer and Enrique took the card stock pages upstairs to the gallery, where they divided the pile in half and began restoring the object labels to their proper frames. Dr. Horne approached Summer as she was placing her last card next to the victory quilt artifacts. "Are you all right?" he asked, brow furrowing. "You held your ground, but it must have been upsetting."

"I'm fine, thanks," she replied, glancing across the gallery to Enrique, who carefully compared the Loyal Union Sampler to the description on the object label he held before placing the page into the frame. This would certainly be a first date to remember. "I'm just a bit stunned. And angry."

"I should have intervened before things got out of control," Dr. Horne said, shaking his head. "Truth is, I never saw that confrontation coming. That developer's commercials are all over the TV and the radio, and he was just here a few days ago with you and Pat."

"None of this was your fault," Summer assured him, slipping the straps of her backpack over her shoulders. "How could you have guessed they'd make a scene? They looked like perfectly rational adults when they walked in. Keep your eyes open, though. They might be back."

"Oh, I'll be watching for them. You can be sure of that. I'll warn the other docents too."

Summer thanked him and hurried to join Enrique, whose back was turned to her as he spoke with a mother and young daughter who had witnessed the incident. "Who *were* those people?" the mother asked, indignant. "How dare they ruin your exhibit?"

"You're not supposed to take other people's papers and tear them up and litter," the daughter piped up, tugging her mother's hand in her excitement. "They weren't setting a good example."

"No, they weren't," Enrique replied solemnly. "We're going to do everything we can to make sure nothing like this happens again."

As the pair walked off, satisfied, Summer drew closer to Enrique and murmured, "'We'? Did you register as a volunteer when I was busy with the printer?"

He quickly turned and smiled. "Hope I didn't overstep. I must have looked official, carrying those object labels around."

"I suppose I did draft you, didn't I?" Her cell phone rang. She took it from her dress pocket and drew in a quick breath at the sight of the familiar number. "Enrique, I'm sorry. It's Pat. I could call her back—"

"No, that's okay. Take it. I can find my own way out." He smiled encouragingly as he turned toward the door. "Good luck. Let me know what I can do to help."

She thanked him and took the call. "Hi, Pat," she said, quickly leaving the gallery rather than disrupt the exhibit yet again. She headed left, away from the staircase, but she glanced back over her shoulder just in time to glimpse Enrique quickly descending the stairs. He didn't look up. "Did you get my message?"

"I did, and I can't decide if I'm more furious or astonished. Summer, I honestly can't recall any offensive content in your object labels. If I had, I would have said something when I reviewed them."

"That's what I thought, but now I'm second-guessing myself. I admit I don't like Krolich, but I never intended to offend him, or anyone else."

"I'm sure you didn't. My inclination is to ignore him."

"But he threatened to shut down the exhibit."

"Let him try. What exactly does he think he can do? He already tried to have Union Hall condemned and taken away from us, and he failed. University Realty clearly isn't going to contribute to our capital campaign, so we're not indebted to him in any way."

"Would you mind taking a second look at the object labels just in case?"

"Of course, but I'm sure they're fine. I'm less confident that I'll approve of Krolich's revised versions."

"I can't wait to read them," said Summer, forcing a laugh, though her stomach wrenched at the thought.

They hung up. Still anxious, Summer walked through the gallery one last time just to make sure no new disruptions were brewing before heading home to the manor. She didn't see her mom or any of the other Elm Creek Quilters as she went up to her room, where she dutifully turned on her computer and opened her thesis. She managed to get a paragraph out before she gave up, too distracted and indignant to continue.

Later, when she appeared at the banquet hall just in time for dinner, her friends' surprised glances told her that they hadn't expected to see her there. "How was the date?" Sarah asked tentatively as they joined the buffet line together.

"It was great, up to a point." Summer lowered her voice and drew closer. "I'll explain later, when we have more time and fewer campers around. It's been a day."

Sarah's eyebrows rose. "That bad, huh?"

"Worse than you think. Krolich showed up."

"You can't be serious. Krolich crashed your date?"

"To be fair, he didn't know I was on a date. He thought he was just ruining a regular workday."

"Unbelievable. Why can't he just admit defeat and go away?" Sarah paused. "But you *are* now saying it was a date?"

Summer sighed, suddenly weary. "Meet me in the kitchen after the evening program and I'll give you the whole story. I could use an objective opinion."

"I'll see you there. I can't promise I'll be objective, but I'm sure I'll have an opinion."

The evening's entertainment—a performance by the Waterford College Ballroom Dance Team followed by music from the Quilterettes, a five-woman a cappella group of campers from Neenah, Wisconsin—distracted Summer from her concerns for a good ninety minutes, but they returned in full strength as their guests dispersed to their rooms. Summer helped the staff tidy up, and when she went to the kitchen to meet Sarah afterward, she was not surprised to discover the other Elm Creek Quilters waiting there too.

Summer had barely sat down when her mom set a steaming cup of her favorite ginger-lemon tea on the refectory table in front of her. Anna quickly followed up with several plates of lemon shortbread, enough for everyone. "Spill it, kiddo," her mom said kindly, settling onto the bench opposite her. "What happened?"

So Summer sipped the comforting tea and told them about the

incident at the gallery. She skipped over a few details—how she and Enrique had held hands throughout the tour, how attractive she found him, how his interest in her work flattered her—not because her friends wouldn't be interested, but because they would be *too* interested.

"Pat and I both read and approved the text of every object label as you completed it," Agnes declared indignantly after Summer finished. "We found absolutely nothing inappropriate. You've done nothing wrong, dear."

"Thanks, Agnes. I hope you'll still feel that way after a second look, but if not, I'll revise the labels. I'm not willing to jeopardize the Waterford Historical Society's fundraising just to spare my pride." Summer took the printouts from her backpack and distributed them around the table, two or three to each Elm Creek Quilter. "Would you please read them carefully and note anything even remotely objectionable?"

Her friends agreed, and after a quick search through purses and tote bags for pens and pencils, they got to work. Rather than peer over their shoulders, Summer carried her mug of tea to one of the booths where a window looked out upon the rear parking lot, the towering elms, the creek and the bridge over it. As night descended, the darkening view was replaced by her own reflection in the glass. Now and then she stole a few glances at her friends, wincing at the sound of a pen scratching on paper because it probably meant someone had found a problem, smiling slightly when someone heaved a sigh, because she knew their exasperation was meant for Gregory Krolich, not herself.

"We're done," Maggie finally said.

Leaving her empty mug in the kitchen sink, Summer returned to her place at the refectory table, where her friends had arranged the printouts in a neat pile. She leafed through them and saw a few smiley faces and the occasional exclamation point or star where someone had responded to a particularly fascinating detail, but no one had underlined anything they considered inappropriate. She did find four question marks in the margins of the Authors' Album label where University Realty was linked to the quilt's fifty-year misplacement, and six on the label for In Honor of Linda's Retirement where Summer had described College Realty's razing of the original Waterford Public Library.

Summer set the two object labels side by side on the table before her, then glanced around the table at her friends. "It looks like there's a consensus?"

"Yes," said Gwen firmly. "We agree that you've done nothing wrong."

"But we do understand why Krolich wouldn't like what he read here and here," said Diane, reaching out to tap each of the two marked-up pages. "Some of these details don't exactly put his company in the best light."

"I can see that," Summer admitted.

"But we're not suggesting you should change a single word," Sarah hastened to add. "Everything you wrote is true. These things happened, and you have evidence from the historical record to prove it."

"You struck the proper tone too," said Gretchen. "A straightforward presentation of the facts, free of accusations or mockery."

"You were more diplomatic than I would have been," said Sarah. "If University Realty didn't want to develop a notorious reputation as a merciless destroyer of historic buildings, then they shouldn't have mercilessly destroyed so many historic buildings. I bet Krolich has a wrecking ball tattooed on his—"

"Sarah," Sylvia admonished.

"Arm. I was going to say arm."

"What I don't understand," said Maggie, frowning in puzzlement, "is why he didn't simply bring his concerns to you and Pat directly. That's how reasonable adults handle conflict. He could have called, or emailed, or arranged another meeting. Why bring in a delegation of outraged civic leaders to make a scene at Union Hall?"

"That bothers me too," said Anna, leaning back against the

kitchen counter. "You might have worked out a compromise over coffee at the Daily Grind, but he didn't even try. It's almost as if his point wasn't really to get the object labels changed."

"You think?" asked Diane archly.

"Wherever Gregory Krolich is concerned," said Sylvia, "it's not unreasonable to assume an ulterior motive."

"I think the point was to intimidate us. I think he wants to shut down the exhibit and the historical society's capital campaign with it." When Summer glanced around the table, her friends responded with apprehensive nods and murmured assent. "So here's what I need to decide: Should I change the object labels to appease him? Not because I agree with his complaints, but to thwart whatever borderline-illegal scheme he's plotting this time?"

A chorus of objections rose from around the table.

"I hate to see a bully win," said Sarah.

"And I'd hate to see you compromise your integrity, Summer," said Agnes. "None of us at the Waterford Historical Society would ever ask you to do such a thing."

"Not even to save Union Hall?"

"Union Hall isn't in any immediate danger, even if Mr. Krolich hopes we think so, but no, not even then," said Agnes. "Please don't change a word of your quilt descriptions. Sometimes the truth makes us uncomfortable. That never justifies a lie."

"The historian's task is not only to uncover historical facts but to interpret them, to construct a full, unbiased narrative that will help others understand how the past informs the present," said Gwen. "That's precisely what you've done for each of the quilts and artifacts you've studied. I'm proud of the work you've done, and I wouldn't have you suppress it, not for the world."

"I'm with Gwen," Sarah declared. "I have your back, Summer, come what may."

Summer felt a surge of relief and affection as her friends chimed in their agreement.

Then, looking pained, Diane tentatively raised a hand. "Krolich isn't entirely wrong. Hear me out," she said, raising her voice as her friends responded with gasps and groans. "I agree with the—whatever Maggie called them—"

"The delegation of outraged civic leaders," Maggie supplied helpfully.

"Right. I agree with them on one point and one point only. Some parts of history are better off forgotten." Diane looked around the table, seeking affirmation, rolling her eyes when she didn't get it. "Dredging up conflicts and problems from decades in the past just divides us as a community, and as a country. We're not responsible for our ancestors' behavior. Can't we just move on?"

"I'm sorry, Diane," said Sylvia, peering at her over the rims of her glasses, "but that's rather disrespectful to all the people whose daily lives are still affected by the consequences of past wrongdoing."

"We can't move on from a problem if it hasn't been properly re-solved," said Gwen, a trifle sharply. "And a problem can't be resolved if some people won't even acknowledge it exists."

Diane held up her hands. "I'm just offering my opinion. I'm sure I'm not the only person who feels this way. The only person at this table, maybe, but not the only person in Waterford."

"That's certainly true," said Summer. "I met six like-minded peo-ple earlier this afternoon. So, Diane, how would you suggest I revise the object labels to make them more acceptable without distorting historical reality?"

Diane regarded her in sheer astonishment. "Are you kidding? You shouldn't change a word."

Gwen guffawed, but for a moment Summer could only blink at Diane, bewildered. "I shouldn't?"

"Controversy sells tickets," Diane explained, shrugging as if it were obvious. "Once word spreads that a quilt exhibit offended a bunch of businessmen so much that they threatened to shut it down, everyone will want to see for themselves what all the fuss is about.

Krolich and company will probably regret giving the exhibit so much free publicity."

"I agree with Diane," said Gwen, as if she couldn't quite believe it herself. "Krolich may be able to intimidate his fellow business tycoons and local politicians who are beholden to him, but he's forgetting the thousands of Waterford College students and faculty who also live in this town."

"And all the quilters and history buffs," Agnes chimed in.

"That's right," said Gwen, nodding. "If Krolich insists that we shouldn't talk about racism or the dangers of unbridled capitalism, he's going to hear from a lot of neighbors who strongly disagree. And if he tries to shut down the quilt exhibit, most folks around here would see that as a corporate bully trying to squash the little guy."

"Exactly," said Diane. "Krolich is just going to draw more attention to the stories he wants to bury, and the Waterford Historical Society will reap the rewards."

"*If* the exhibit can go on without interference," said Summer, "*and* if these hypothetical, vast crowds of curious spectators drop some cash in the donation box as they pass by."

And yet she felt a glimmer of hope. She'd prefer for the exhibit to go on as she had originally envisioned it, free of controversy and conflict, but if Krolich made that impossible, she'd seize whatever silver lining she could find. And maybe things weren't as bad as she thought. Maybe Krolich's revisions would be fairly minor. Maybe all he would ask would be to have the name of his company removed.

"Thank you, everyone," she said, much relieved, looking around the table at the wise, kind, loving faces of her mom and their friends. "Whatever happens next, I feel ready for it, thanks to you."

"We're always here for you, dear," said Agnes.

"Everything will be all right, kiddo," her mom said, rising from the bench to wrap her in a hug. Summer clung to her for a moment, blinking back tears, but when she pulled away, she was smiling.

Their guests had long since retired to their rooms, or to their friends' rooms, to stay up late quietly chatting and sewing, savoring every last moment of the last night of quilt camp. Gwen, Anna, Diane, and Agnes left for their homes, sharing rides as usual, while Sylvia, Sarah, and Gretchen joined their husbands, and Maggie and Summer went off to their solitary rooms. Summer checked her email before she climbed into bed, but Pat had not written, not that Summer had expected Krolich to submit his revisions so soon. She resigned herself to an indefinite wait, one that might not end well for Union Hall.

All through the next day, she was grateful for the routine of camp, which kept her both busy and grounded—Sunrise Yoga on the verandah, a delicious Farewell Breakfast, a particularly hilarious show-and-tell on the cornerstone patio, nostalgic farewells as their campers departed, room inspections and preparations for the cleaning crew, a relaxed lunch in the kitchen to celebrate another successful week. Afterward, as the faculty dispersed to enjoy their afternoon off, Summer strolled through the orchard to find restful calm in the scenery, the sweet fragrances, and the hum of honeybees as she picked some newly ripened Ginger Gold apples to enjoy for dessert later. Then she collected her laptop, notes, and research books, settled into an Adirondack chair on the verandah with a glass of iced tea by her side, and began the conclusion to her thesis.

She had a solid outline in place by dinnertime. As usual for a Saturday, that meant leftovers in the kitchen, with everyone's mealtimes overlapping a little or a lot, conversations ebbing and flowing with arrivals and departures, laughter and fond reminiscences shared in abundance. Summer volunteered to tidy up for everyone, and after she finished, she put on the kettle, fixed herself a cup of tea, and settled in at her favorite booth to write the first two paragraphs of her conclusion.

Evening descended. She took a break to walk outside in the moonlight, lingering on the bridge to listen to Elm Creek flowing, soothing and musical and reassuringly constant. Returning indoors, she found Sylvia and Andrew in the kitchen, smiling over photos of

Andrew's grandchildren that had arrived in the mail earlier that day. Summer joined them, admiring the pictures as she enjoyed a crisp, slightly tart Ginger Gold, but eventually she bade the older couple good night, loaded her things into her backpack, and climbed the two flights to her room.

It was only after she had climbed into bed and lay listening to the wind stir the curtains in the darkness that she remembered the last moments of the gallery tour the previous afternoon. Enrique had asked her out to dinner for that evening, but Krolich and his delegation had interrupted, and she had never given Enrique her answer. He had not repeated the question, and in the ensuing disruption, she had forgotten about it, until now. They hadn't exchanged phone numbers or emails, though they surely would have, if their date had not ended so abruptly.

Waterford was a small college town and he knew where she worked and hung out, she thought drowsily as she drifted off to sleep. If he wanted to get in touch with her, he would find a way.

The next morning began quietly, with yoga alone on the verandah and breakfast in the kitchen with the manor's permanent residents, but the day picked up speed when the other Elm Creek Quilters arrived to prepare for a new week of quilt camp. They were setting up for registration when a thunderstorm rolled in. With the rain still pouring down as the campers were soon to arrive, Sarah enlisted the Elm Creek Husbands and all the kitchen staff Anna could spare to the front entrance, to escort guests under the cover of large black umbrellas from the cars and taxis pulling into the circular drive and up the front stairs to shelter beneath the verandah roof. Inside, Gwen had set the storm mats in place to reduce the water and mud tracked in on the black marble floor, and Summer and Maggie had arranged stacks of soft, fluffy towels for anyone who needed to dry off.

As the day passed, the ongoing storm made additional work for all the Elm Creek Quilters, but Summer still found time to pull her silenced phone from her pocket to look for voicemails, and, less frequently, to race upstairs to her bedroom to check her email. Summer received a voicemail from Julianne, an incredulous, indignant reply to Summer's email describing the gallery incident, as well as two automated emails from the University of Chicago about registration and payment schedules. Pat did not get in touch, and neither did Enrique.

The rain continued throughout the afternoon and well into the evening, so at the last minute, the Candlelight ceremony was moved from the cornerstone patio to the main foyer. With the lights dimmed, the foyer's tall ceiling and the quilts displayed from the balustrades created a different, grander yet still intimate ambience. Afterward, as the quilters retired for the night, Summer was relieved to see that no one seemed disappointed by the change of venue. With any luck, Saturday morning would be sunny and clear, and their guests could enjoy the cornerstone patio at the Farewell Breakfast.

Monday morning dawned humid and overcast, but Sunrise Yoga was well attended, and Summer's Modern Quilting class was full of lively, eager quilters who kept her on her toes with their questions and jokes. She didn't mind the enforced break from her phone and computer during the morning, but at lunch, she surreptitiously took her phone from her pocket so frequently that Agnes, seated one place over, couldn't help noticing her distraction. "No news from Pat?" she inquired sympathetically when their table companions returned to the buffet for seconds, leaving them briefly alone.

Agnes didn't mean it as a rebuke, but Summer felt chagrined anyway. "No, not yet," she said, putting her phone away and resolving to keep it out of sight until lunch was finished.

"No news is good news, I suppose," said Agnes, smiling kindly. "Will you be seeing Pat at Union Hall this afternoon?"

"I'm all caught up on my work in the gallery, so I thought I'd stay here and work on my thesis instead."

"Does this mean you've finished setting up the exhibit?"

"Not quite. We still have an empty space perfect for one large quilt or two smaller ones, but until someone offers us a suitable quilt or I find a new lead to pursue, there's not a lot for me to do."

"Well, Pat asked me to lead the planning committee for the grand opening gala, so if you have spare time—" Agnes broke off as their lunch companions returned to the table with their dessert plates.

"When my thesis is done," Summer promised her in an undertone, and Agnes nodded, understanding that there was no such thing as spare time for a graduate student with an overdue thesis.

After lunch, Summer withdrew to her room to get writing. Despite everything, she had to smile at the irony. Until recently, her work at Union Hall had offered her a welcome distraction from the misery of her thesis, and now, she hoped that working on her thesis would keep her too busy to brood over the incident at Union Hall. Paragraph after paragraph filled the pages, not easily, but steadily and well. By the time she started getting hungry for supper, she was nearly halfway through the conclusion.

She was just about to head down to the banquet hall when her cell phone rang. She snatched it up from the desk and flipped it open, not bothering to check the caller ID. "Hello," she said, a bit breathless, bolting from her chair.

"Summer?"

"Yes, it's me. Hi, Pat." She was relieved and suddenly apprehensive and slightly disappointed that it wasn't Enrique, all at the same time. "Any news? Good or bad?"

"A bit of one and a bit of the other. Are you sitting down?"

"No, I'm pacing."

"That'll work too. First, exhibit attendance held steady over the weekend, and donations kept pace."

"That's great." Yet Summer didn't let her hopes rise. It was early days. Krolich might still be scheming, moving the pieces into place and awaiting the perfect moment to strike.

"Unfortunately, there was an incident this morning—another woman removing object labels from their frames."

"Are you kidding?"

"I wish. She was quiet and crafty, not like that gang on Friday. She kept a wall between herself and the docent at all times, but the docent heard a suspicious noise, came around the corner quickly, and caught her in the act. Well, not *literally* caught her. Spotted her. The docent tried to grab the thief, but—well, it was June Reinhart, and she's eighty-five years old and maybe one hundred pounds after a big meal."

"Oh, no." Summer could totally see June trying to tackle a troublemaker, heedless of her own safety. "I hope she wasn't hurt."

"June's fine, but furious. She gave the police an excellent description, but the woman got away with five object labels. I've already replaced them. Unfortunately, since it's just paper and easily reprinted, the police aren't taking it very seriously. One officer suggested that maybe the woman thought they were free handouts."

"Then why did she run away?"

"I had the same question. The officer just shrugged. I filed a report all the same."

"Good. We have to treat it like the crime it is."

"I also assigned two additional docents to the gallery, so there aren't any blind spots anymore. All of our usual volunteers have asked for shifts, and they've recruited friends. Even some of the contractors have offered to serve as security guards."

"I'd take them up on it."

"I would, but I don't want to take them away from the remodeling work. That's essential too. As are our long-awaited security cameras, which were finally installed about an hour ago."

"At long last," said Summer, relieved. "We can't really complain about the wait, though, considering that they're an in-kind donation and cost us nothing."

"Oh, believe me, the installers heard only heartfelt thanks from the moment they arrived until the last test was run." Pat sighed. "Unfortunately, that wasn't enough for one of our quilt donors. She heard about Friday's incident from a friend, and she asked for her quilt back."

"Oh, no." Summer braced herself. "Which one?"

"The alphabet quilt that the Woodfall Elementary students made in the 1960s."

"Oh, okay. That's too bad." Summer was sorry to lose anything from the exhibit, but this particular quilt was a minor work, included more for its sentimental value than its actual historical relevance or artistic merit. What troubled her most was that the donor no longer trusted them to protect her quilt. "Any more news?"

"Only this. About twenty minutes ago, we received Krolich's revised object labels via certified mail."

"Wow. Very official. Is he establishing a paper trail so we can't claim we never received them?"

"Probably. It's his money to waste. Maybe he couldn't spare the ten minutes it would've taken him to walk the file over from his office."

Summer immediately pictured the much-loathed steel gray–and-blue sign swinging above the University Realty door, and just as quickly shoved the image away. "You're forgetting he'd have to walk back again."

"Fine. Twenty minutes round-trip. He could've sent an intern."

Summer felt an unexpected surge of sympathy for anyone unfortunate enough to work as Krolich's intern. No doubt Krolich made some poor, hopeful Waterford College student pay *him* for the privilege of making his coffee. "So, how bad is it?"

"About what you'd expect from him. Can you come in tomorrow to discuss?"

"I'm dreading it, but yes, I'll come. One o'clock?"

"Sure. I'll bring the coffee."

"I'll bring—I don't know what. A positive attitude? A willingness to compromise?"

"Couldn't hurt," Pat said, and hung up.

Summer ended up bringing a few of Anna's fabulous cranberry-almond scones, fortuitously left over from breakfast. Pat greeted her with a grim smile and a steaming cup of French roast, then seized a scone so fiercely that Summer knew she was angrier than she let on.

Summer soon understood why. Pat had already read Krolich's proposed new object labels several times over, and to her credit, she had not filled the margins with expletives and exclamation points. Summer took a bracing drink of coffee and settled into her chair, eyeing the crisp white sheets of University Realty letterhead in disbelief. "He doesn't seriously expect us to use these actual pages, and imply that his company is sponsoring the exhibit, does he?"

"I'm sure he'd be delighted if we did." Pat gestured, turning her wrist wearily as if unspooling a sheaf of bad news. "You might as well get it over with."

Summer forced herself to read them all through without pausing to vent.

As she had expected, Krolich had expunged any mention of College Realty or University Realty from the pages, except for the line thanking University Realty for donating the Authors' Album, credit he didn't actually deserve. On the Creek's Crossing Album label, Krolich had crossed out the lines describing how the Wrights had been away protesting at a KKK rally on the town square when their home was ransacked and set ablaze, as well as Summer's theory that the quilt had remained in the thief's possession in Creek's Crossing for many years before it was donated to the historical society. He also changed Summer's phrase for the culprits, "unidentified person or group," to "migrant itinerants," which told her he wanted to blame outsiders for the crimes, despite the evidence that at least one local person had been involved.

And that was only the first page.

On the object label for the victory quilts, he deleted the entire last paragraph, removing any suggestion that the quilt guilds in

Waterford and Grangerville were defined by anything other than their city limits. He cut more than half of the text for In Honor of Linda's Retirement, concluding with, "In 1976, the First Bank of Waterford building was razed to make way for the construction of a College Realty apartment building, Hill Street Commons." He permitted nothing about the ensuing controversy, the accusations of bribery, or the establishment of the historic district. Page after page of revisions and deletions followed, sanitizing the history of the Elm Creek Valley until it resembled a suburb from a 1950s sitcom more than an actual place where real people had lived.

"I can't use these," Summer said, shaking her head as she set the stack of papers on Pat's desk. "But I understand why you might feel that you have to. I'm willing to resign if—"

"Don't even finish that thought," Pat broke in. "This is the Waterford Historical Society. It's contrary to our mission to sacrifice historical accuracy to appease one belligerent man. We won't do it."

Summer nodded, grateful that she and Pat agreed. "Are you going to respond, or can we just keep the original object labels in place and hope he doesn't notice?"

"He'd notice eventually, he or one of his cronies." Pat reached for the phone, clearly reluctant to place the call. "Silence would only delay the inevitable. I'll respond to him as a courtesy and tell him we're not changing a thing."

Summer wished her good luck and left her to it, though she suspected courtesy would be wasted on him.

After spending an hour in the gallery conferring with the three docents on duty, answering visitors' questions, and studying the two empty spaces on the gallery walls, wondering how to fill them, Summer went home to Elm Creek Manor. She stopped by the kitchen for a cup of iced tea and a brief chat with Anna, then headed upstairs to her desk and her laptop, where she silenced her phone, closed her email app, and fixed her thesis with a look of such concentrated determination that she had to laugh. Was she trying to intimidate her thesis into submission? "Whatever it takes," she murmured aloud.

She placed her hands on the keyboard and got to work.

For the rest of the afternoon, she drove herself onward, taking brief breaks to stretch or sip her iced tea, but always returning promptly to her thesis. She let nothing break her focus, not the occasional laughter and conversation of passersby in the hallway outside her room, the faint aromas of the delectable dishes Anna was preparing for dinner, not the industrious hum of a sewing machine in a nearby room, not the nagging worry that Enrique's silence meant that he had lost interest entirely. Perhaps he even considered himself lucky that Krolich's interruption had prevented her from accepting his invitation to dinner. Whenever distracting thoughts crept in, she resolutely pushed them away.

When at last she left her room and descended the grand oak staircase to join the other faculty and campers in the banquet hall, she was forty-five minutes late for supper, but she had a complete first draft of her thesis saved on her laptop and backed up on a flash drive. She wasn't taking any chances of losing it now.

Summer spotted an empty chair at her mom's table, so she quickly helped herself at the buffet and seated herself there, pausing along the way to whisper her good news to Sarah, who sat at an adjacent table, and to her mom, who beamed proudly and whispered congratulations. Despite Summer's attempt at discretion, the news spread quickly among the Elm Creek Quilters. Maggie must have shared it with her entire table, because midway through dessert, she and her nine campers suddenly burst into applause. There was no keeping it quiet after that, and as campers finished eating and left the banquet hall, many stopped by Summer's table to congratulate her. They were undeterred by her demurrals that she hadn't earned her degree yet— she still had to revise her thesis, submit it, and receive her adviser's approval—so Summer accepted their praise graciously and with good humor. She had been struggling so long to finish that draft that perhaps this was the real achievement. Receiving her diploma would just make it official.

"Sylvia called a faculty meeting in the library at seven o'clock," Gwen told her as she finished her chocolate biscotti and cappuccino.

"I'll be there," Summer promised. "Any idea what it's about?"

"Not a clue," her mom replied. "I assume it's to discuss whatever she and Agnes have been whispering about for the past few days."

Summer nodded, although she had been so preoccupied with her own concerns that she hadn't noticed any whispering. She hoped it was good news, or at least something entirely routine, like sewing machine maintenance reminders or changes to the next week's course schedule.

At the appointed time, Summer reported to the library only to find she was the last to arrive, except for Anna, who hurried in a moment later, still in her apron and toque. From the glances Summer's friends exchanged, she quickly surmised that no one knew why the last-minute meeting had been called, except for Sylvia and Agnes, who stood between the oak desk and the central chairs and sofas waiting for them to get settled, Sylvia's expression serene, Agnes's full of barely suppressed delight.

"Let's begin with a round of applause for our youngest Elm Creek Quilter, who successfully completed the first draft of her master's thesis today," said Sylvia, gesturing gracefully to Summer.

Everyone cheerfully obliged, except for Summer, who buried her face in her hands for a moment, grinning. As the cheers continued, Sylvia raised her hands for order. "Ever since she returned home, Summer has been working very hard to put together the quilt exhibit at Union Hall, and the grand opening gala is coming up soon."

"As you may recall, Summer mentioned that there is still space in the gallery for one more quilt," said Agnes.

"Two, actually," said Summer ruefully. "One contributor withdrew her quilt out of concern for security."

"Oh, dear. What a shame," said Gretchen, shaking her head. "I hope she changes her mind."

"Not me," Diane declared. "I say, good riddance. Security in the gallery has never been better. This fair-weather friend is probably Krolich's employee or something."

"Or one of his tenants," said Sarah. "Someone he has leverage over."

Again Sylvia raised her hands for attention. "It's more likely that she is simply concerned about the safety of her irreplaceable antique. If we didn't have so many trusted friends at the Waterford Historical Society, we might feel exactly the same in her place." She turned to Summer, smiling fondly. "I stand corrected. *Two* empty spaces remain in the gallery. As a sign of our support for you, dear, and of our belief in the mission of the exhibit, Agnes and I propose that an Elm Creek Quilter fill one of those spaces with a quilt that is very special to all of us."

A murmur of surprise and curiosity went up from the group.

"You've already loaned us Gerda's Log Cabin," said Summer, puzzled. "I'd gladly accept another of your quilts, but I don't need a contribution as a sign of your support. I already know I have it."

"*You* know, but other people might require a reminder," said Agnes earnestly. "Everyone who sees this quilt and reads the brilliant object label you'll write for it will understand that the Museum of Lost Quilts has received the official endorsement of Elm Creek Quilts."

"I understand that our endorsement carries weight in certain circles," Sylvia remarked.

"In quilting circles, few endorsements are more impressive," said Sarah, smiling. "Which quilt did you have in mind, Sylvia? Elm Creek Medallion? Christmas Memories?"

"I wasn't thinking of one of my quilts, Sarah, but one of yours."

"One of mine? But I moved to Waterford only eight years ago—well, eight and a half. None of my quilts ever played a role in local history."

"That's not entirely true." Sylvia regarded Sarah over the rims of her glasses, amused. "You're thinking of the distant past, as if that's the only local history that matters."

"You lost me," said Diane.

"Agnes and I believe that Sarah should loan her first sampler to the exhibit," said Sylvia. "A loan, not a donation. We understand that Sarah made the quilt for Matt as an anniversary gift."

"Still lost," said Diane, shaking her head and shrugging. "What does Sarah's sampler have to do with local history?"

"Quite a lot, actually," said Gwen, nodding thoughtfully. "That's the quilt Sarah made when Sylvia taught her to quilt."

"I know *that*," said Diane, rolling her eyes. "All of the original Elm Creek Quilters, including me, helped quilt and bind the top right here at the manor, in that antique standing frame all the Bergstrom women used. That was the same day Sarah proposed that Sylvia turn the manor into a quilt camp." Diane paused. "Oh. I think I see where you're going with this."

"Without those quilting lessons, Sarah wouldn't have befriended Sylvia, and she wouldn't have intervened when Krolich tried to buy Elm Creek Manor," said Gwen. "If Sylvia had sold her family estate and returned to Sewickley, a tremendous amount of local history would have been destroyed, some of it before it was ever discovered."

"Don't forget the influence Elm Creek Quilts has had on the region through the years," Anna added. "The contributions to the artistic community, the tourism industry, the local economy, and all the other ways we can't measure. Just as one example, would Union Hall have been saved if Elm Creek Manor had been razed a few years before?"

"I don't see how," said Agnes. "Sylvia and I never would have reunited. Summer and Sylvia likely never would have met, except briefly as customer and clerk at Grandma's Attic. Gerda Bergstrom's long-lost memoir and quilts wouldn't have been discovered, and all those marvelous stories would have been lost forever."

"Sarah's quilting lessons with Sylvia were the impetus for so much good in the Elm Creek Valley," said Gretchen. "It all began with that sampler."

"It all began with our *friendship*," Sarah corrected. "First mine and Sylvia's, and then mine with the wonderful quilters I met at Grandma's Attic, and then all of us together."

"Fair point, but we can't hang our friendship on a gallery wall," Diane reminded her. "We *can* display a symbol of that friendship—your sampler."

"Hear! Hear!" cried Summer as cheers and applause went up from the circle of friends. "Brava, Sarah!"

Sarah's cheeks flushed pink with embarrassment. "I appreciate this, I really do, but I'd be mortified to have the public see my first quilt, with all its beginner's mistakes, displayed in a museum alongside true works of art. Why don't we contribute our round robin quilt instead?"

"Nope," said Gwen, shaking her head decisively. "That quilt is very important to us, personally, but it didn't affect local history."

"What do you say, Sarah?" asked Summer. "I can't imagine a better addition to the exhibit than your sampler, imperfect stitches and all."

"And why shouldn't the quilt be imperfect?" asked Agnes. "We all know that history has never been perfect. It's in the imperfections where the true story emerges."

"Put that in the object label, kiddo," said Gwen.

"I will," said Summer with a laugh, "if Sarah agrees?"

Sarah hesitated, thinking it over. "All right," she said tentatively, but looking pleased and flattered too. "If you all insist my sampler belongs in this exhibit, I'll trust your judgment. But it can only be a loan. Matt and I use that quilt on our bed. I'll need it back when the weather turns colder."

"Absolutely," Summer assured her. "Upon the first frost warning in the weather forecast, I'll take the sampler down and return it to you right away."

If she was there to do it, Summer reminded herself, startled that she had momentarily forgotten. She was supposed to be in Chicago by then.

But when she thought ahead to autumn, and the first frost that would inevitably follow, she had imagined herself at Elm Creek Manor, watching the leaves turn, enjoying the last of the orchard's harvest, helping Matt and Sarah prepare the estate for winter, reading a book in the library while a fire blazed on the hearth.

She had much to think about and many decisions to make—as well as a thesis to revise, a quilt exhibit to complete, and a grand opening gala to prepare for, all while an unscrupulous foe watched and schemed, eager to bring it all crashing down around them.

Summer was heartened by her friends' love and support, but she knew it was only a matter of time before Gregory Krolich struck back.

**Sarah's Sampler.** 80" x 96". Cotton top and backing with cotton batting. Pieced and appliquéd by Sarah McClure, quilted by the Elm Creek Quilters, Waterford, PA, 1996.

This charming quilt, the most recently made object in this exhibit, is an excellent example of the traditional sampler, a beginner's project intended to provide the maker with the opportunity to learn or to practice particular skills and techniques essential to the quilting arts. Sarah McClure, a resident of Waterford since 1996, designed and sewed the sampler during her lessons with master quilter Sylvia Bergstrom Compson, an acclaimed, award-winning quilter whose family has deep roots in the Elm Creek Valley. McClure credits the project, and her instructor, with teaching her how to sew a running stitch by hand, sew a straight seam by machine, set in pieces (i.e., attach a third piece within the angle created by two other pieces), sew curves, do needle-turned appliqué, layer the top with batting and backing, baste the three layers, quilt by hand, make and attach a hanging sleeve, and bind the quilt.

Although each of the twelve 12" sampler blocks was chosen to help McClure master a particular quilting skill, careful thought was given to a selection that also created a balanced, attractive overall design. The sampler blocks are, from left to right: Top Row: Ohio Star, Bachelor's Puzzle, Double Nine-Patch, LeMoyne Star. Center Row: Posies Round the Square, Little Red Schoolhouse, Lancaster Rose, Hands All Around. Bottom Row: Sawtooth Star, Chimneys and Cornerstones, Contrary Wife, Sister's Choice. The blocks are arranged in a Garden Maze setting with a Twisted Ribbon outermost border.

After completing *Sarah's Sampler* and the quilting lessons that were the impetus for it, McClure proposed to Compson that they launch a new business, Elm Creek Quilts, and transform the Bergstrom estate into a quilt camp, an artists' retreat for both experienced and aspiring quilters. Since its inception, Elm Creek Quilts has contributed millions of dollars to the local economy, boosted tourism, strengthened the local artistic community, encouraged the preservation and study of local history, and inspired countless thousands to learn to quilt and to cherish the heirloom quilts within their own families.

*Sarah's Sampler* appears in this exhibit on loan from the private collection of Sarah and Matthew McClure.

# 14

When Summer and Sarah delivered Sarah's Sampler to Union Hall, they found the gallery nearly empty of visitors, with only three women wandering the aisles admiring the displays. As they were hanging the quilt next to the display for Linda McLoughlin's lost Cleopatra's Fan, Dr. Horne came over to assist. "Attendance has been down for the past two days," he remarked, holding the ladder steady while Summer attached the brackets to the wall. "I trust it's because most folks are waiting for the grand opening gala."

Summer and Sarah exchanged a wary look. Attendance had been rising every week until now.

"Do you suppose Krolich organized a boycott?" Sarah asked Summer in an undertone after Dr. Horne resumed his patrol of the gallery.

"That would make it the quietest boycott in history," said Summer, adjusting the drape of the sampler, so colorful and charming on the gallery wall. How well she remembered helping Sarah quilt and bind it that warm August day eight years before, never knowing that the quilting bee weekend at Elm Creek Manor was only the first of many wonderful quilting adventures they would share. "Wouldn't it be more like him to kick off a boycott with a dramatic public announcement?"

"You'd think so," said Sarah. "Let him do his worst. Like Diane said, controversy will only draw more attention to the exhibit, which means bigger crowds and more money for the capital campaign."

At that moment, one of the visitors approached them, eyes shining. "This was lovely," she gushed, gesturing broadly to indicate the entire exhibit. "It's so much better than the reviews say. I almost didn't come, but I'm so I glad did." She glanced at her watch and quickly hurried off again, pausing at the donation box to deposit a few bills on her way out the door.

"That was odd," Sarah said, gazing after her. Summer nodded, a sudden knot of apprehension tightening in her stomach until she reminded herself that their exhibit hadn't even officially opened yet. Reviews, if any were forthcoming, wouldn't be published until later in August. The visitor must have misunderstood an article she had read about some other quilt exhibit.

Summer's worries had receded to the back of her mind by the time she and Sarah left the gallery, in a bit of a rush since they were expected back at the manor soon. When they stepped outside into the shade of the portico, Summer stopped short at the sight of Enrique walking up the cobblestone path, a takeout cup from the Daily Grind in each hand.

Sarah halted too, just as Enrique caught sight of them and smiled. "Hey, Summer," he called, pausing at the foot of the limestone stairs. He nodded to Sarah. "Hi, Summer's friend."

Summer laughed. "Hi, Summer's coffee delivery guy."

"Call me Enrique." He climbed the stairs and handed Summer one of the cups. "Italian roast with steamed almond milk." He regarded Sarah inquisitively and extended the other cup, which he obviously had purchased for himself. "Can I interest you in a house roast with cream and sugar?"

"No, thanks," Sarah replied, grinning, as she quickly hurried past him and descended the stairs. "No time. I have to—make a call. I'll meet you at the van, Summer," she called over her shoulder.

Enrique turned back to Summer, eyebrows rising.

"That was my friend Sarah," she said, smiling. "I'll introduce you next time."

"She's in a hurry."

"So she says." Summer took a sip of her coffee and found it perfect. "Thanks for this. How did you know I'd be here?"

He shrugged. "I took a chance. Hey, Summer, I don't want to make things awkward, but did you get any of my messages?"

Her heart thumped. "No," she said. "You left messages? Where?"

"Here." He lifted his chin to indicate Union Hall. "Once on voicemail, once with a woman who firmly told me to leave you alone and not to call here again because she was reporting all harassing calls to the police."

"Oh, no." Summer clasped a hand to her forehead, chagrined. "I'm so sorry, Enrique. The historical society has been getting some pretty obnoxious emails and phone calls ever since Krolich and crew visited. She must have thought you were with them."

"I get it. She's just looking out for you." He smiled so endearingly that she had to remind herself to pay attention to what he was saying rather than the distracting warmth rising in her chest. "Anyway, I took only half of her advice. I stopped calling, but I'm clearly not leaving you alone."

"Clearly not."

"But if *you* tell me to leave you alone—"

"I haven't," she said quickly. "I won't. Yes."

"Yes what?"

"I didn't get a chance to answer when you asked me out to dinner the other day. The answer is yes. But not this Saturday. I have to finish my thesis so I can get on with my life."

"Great," he replied, looking both pleased and a bit surprised. And no wonder—she was acting giddy.

They exchanged cell phone numbers, but then Summer had to run. She was grinning so broadly as she approached the Elm Creek Quilts minivan that Sarah broke out laughing. "So that's the librarian histo-rian?" she teased, climbing behind the wheel as Summer took the front passenger seat. "Or is it historian librarian? Either way, he's gorgeous."

"Really?" Craning her neck, Summer peered through the window, trying to catch one last glimpse of him. "I hadn't noticed."

The two friends laughed together.

Later that evening, while the campers were racing through the manor and around the estate on a quilter's scavenger hunt, Summer was up in her room, doing her best to focus on her thesis. She read through it carefully, line by line, rewriting and deleting and elaborat-ing where needed. She had taken Jeremy up on his offer to proofread her first draft, and when Anna had come in to work that morning, she had brought her husband's marked-up copy complete with a page of helpful notes. Reviewing her work and responding to Jeremy's comments would take Summer several days of intense revising, but knowing she was nearly finished motivated her to push on.

Enrique didn't call her that evening, but he did the next afternoon. They chatted about her studies and his, the quilt exhibit and workplace drama at the Waterford College Library. Audrey still had not found someone to replace Bradley in the Rare Books Room, and there were rumors that operating hours would be reduced. "I might take some extra shifts up there just to keep the doors open," said Enrique.

"I'm sure Audrey would be grateful," said Summer. "She and countless numbers of students, faculty, and alumni, including myself, who rely on those archives."

"Speaking of second jobs, what is this other place you work at? Elm Street Quilts?"

"Elm *Creek* Quilts," Summer corrected. It was a surprisingly common mistake. Sarah and Diane found it extremely irksome, but Summer didn't let it bother her. "Would you believe I helped launch the most popular quilt camp in the country?"

"Quilt camp?"

"I can't believe you've never heard of it," she teased. "But as I said before, it's a long story, and unfortunately I have only a few minutes. I need to get through two more pages of revisions today."

"Then we need to have that dinner," he said. "I've got to hear this story before you leave for Chicago."

"Actually . . ." She hesitated before deciding to tell him. "I might not be going back as soon as I thought. I'm considering a leave of absence."

"Wait, really?"

"Yes, but that's something else we can talk about at dinner—after I finish my thesis."

If she needed more motivation to focus and finish, anticipation of a date with Enrique would certainly provide it.

Summer was more than halfway through her revisions by Friday, but she had misgivings about neglecting the gallery, even though her work on the exhibit was essentially finished. At lunchtime, Agnes assured her that she, Pat, and their able volunteers were taking care of all the arrangements for the grand opening gala so Summer could focus on her thesis.

"How are things at the gallery otherwise?" Summer asked.

"Attendance is still down, but no one has stolen any more object labels." Then Agnes hesitated. "There have been a few unpleasant emails and harassing phone calls, but Pat has it under control."

"Maybe too much control."

"Beg pardon?"

"Nothing. Never mind. So Krolich hasn't made any more trouble?"

"Not yet," said Agnes, but her expression told Summer she didn't expect that to last.

Summer didn't either. She and her friends waited apprehensively for Krolich to call a press conference or take out a full-page ad in the *Waterford Register* denouncing the exhibit, but the days passed, and the dreaded confrontation didn't come.

"If he's going to retaliate, I wish he'd just get it over with," Diane groused one evening after a faculty meeting.

"Careful what you wish for," Gwen warned.

"Maybe the stress of waiting is Krolich's revenge," ventured Maggie, hopeful. "Maybe he thinks making us worry needlessly is punishment enough."

None of them believed that, Summer least of all. When she had accepted the curator's role, she never imagined she'd stir up any controversy or conflict. Now she felt torn between curiosity and caution, her irresistible need to understand her hometown's often troubled past versus her concerns that the truths she uncovered might embarrass or hurt others—or cost the Waterford Historical Society their last chance to save Union Hall. Yet as the grand opening gala approached, she was ever mindful that the collective memories that had been deliberately lost were usually those most in need of unflinching scrutiny.

She also couldn't abide a bully.

If she conceded to Krolich's demands, it wasn't as if he'd walk away from this victory sated. Even if he got everything he wanted, it wouldn't be enough. In a few weeks or a few months, he would push another nonprofit around, make unreasonable demands of another competitor, use his money and influence to bend lawmakers to his will, as he always had and probably always would, until he was finally held accountable. Krolich hated losing, and it absolutely infuriated him when someone he considered his inferior stood up to him. Sarah had done so when she had saved Elm Creek Manor, and Agnes had when she uncovered his plot to cheat Bonnie out of her condo and business.

No wonder he nursed a particularly bitter grudge against quilters. So why did he seem to be lying low this time?

Lying low in order to ambush them, maybe?

One morning, Summer was wrapping up her Modern Quilting class when it suddenly occurred to her that Krolich might be waiting for the grand opening gala to make his move. Her heart plummeted as she envisioned angry demonstrators waving signs and chanting ugly slogans on the sidewalk outside Union Hall.

As soon as she straightened up her classroom, she raced outside to the verandah, called Pat, and tersely shared her newest worry. "We had the same thought," Pat told her. "I've hired security and alerted the police. It'll be fine."

"Good. That's good." Summer clasped a hand to her forehead and inhaled deeply. "It's so unfair that we have to worry about this."

"*You* don't," Pat told her firmly. "You did your part by setting up the exhibit. We can take it from here."

Summer knew that, but the exhibit's success was so important to her that it was difficult to tear herself away, even though she had other work demanding her attention.

Late Saturday evening she finished revising her thesis, and on Sunday morning before the new campers arrived, she emailed the document to Dr. Alvarez. She had expected to feel exultant, as if she were breaking the tape at an imaginary finish line, but she was too preoccupied for anything more than a fleeting sense of joy and relief. She would celebrate properly at the gala.

The next morning, her cell phone rang just as she was entering the ballroom to set up for her Modern Quilting class. It was Dr. Alvarez calling to let her know that she had finished reading the thesis. "I'm very pleased with your mastery of the subject, and your writing, as ever, is excellent," she said, evidently on her way to campus, judging by the familiar background noises of a typical Hyde Park street during the morning rush. "I know the circumstances posed an unforeseen challenge, but you saw it through. I've submitted your grade to the registrar, so within forty-eight hours, you will have officially earned your master's. Congratulations."

Summer drew in a shaky breath, overcome with relief. "Thank you so much, Dr. Alvarez. This is wonderful news. I'm so grateful for your guidance, and for your infinite patience."

"I had every confidence in you," she said kindly. "Welcome to the doctoral program. Now that you're permitted to register, I'll email you a list of classes I strongly encourage all my first-year doctoral students to take. I look forward to seeing you back on campus again soon."

"Actually, Professor . . ." Summer closed her eyes and plunged ahead. "I've decided to apply for a leave of absence from the university."

"A leave of absence? Is something wrong?"

"No, not exactly. It's just that it's been a difficult few months, and I'd like to take a year off to reflect and decide what I want to do next."

"I see." Dr. Alvarez's concern and disappointment were unmistakable. "Of course you must do what you feel is best. I should caution you, however, that often when students take that much time off, they find it very difficult to resume their studies later. Most never do. Have you considered taking a quarter off, instead of an entire year?"

Summer hesitated. "I hadn't considered that, but I will." Why not? The application process was the same, and a quarter ought to be long enough for her to figure things out.

Dr. Alvarez wished her well and encouraged her to call or email if she wanted to discuss her plans as they evolved. Summer thanked her, and when they hung up, she took a moment to collect her thoughts before hurrying off to class. Her footsteps seemed lighter, her pace swifter, as if she had left a heavy burden on the ground behind her.

After class, she settled comfortably in an Adirondack chair on the verandah with her laptop, her heart thudding from nervous excitement as she filled out the online form to apply for a leave of absence. Telling Dr. Alvarez had been the hard part. Waiting for confirmation from the registrar would be a bit easier. Deciding how she would spend her unexpectedly free autumn quarter—well, that would be a joy. She would finish out the season of quilt camp, of course, but what might come after that, she had no idea. It was a bit terrifying, but also thrilling, to be on the cusp of a new, unknown, and possibly wonderful path.

She was nearly finished with the application when an email from Kathleen Barrett landed in her inbox. "I'm so sorry to hear about the exhibit," Kathleen had written. "I know you had such high hopes for it. If circumstances change and you decide to make another go at it, I'd be happy to loan you Dorothea's Dove in the Window again. When would it be convenient for me to pick up the quilt from you?"

Bewildered, Summer read the email again more carefully. Kathleen must have heard about Krolich's scene in the gallery, and possibly about his demands for revisions to the object labels, but what did she mean by "make *another* go"? The historical society was still very much invested in the first one. Did Kathleen assume they would close the exhibit rather than defy Krolich?

Summer set her laptop aside and walked to the far end of the verandah, where she looked out upon the trees encircling the north gardens and considered how to respond. After a long moment, she returned to her computer. "I assume you're referring to the recent criticism of the object labels," she typed, aiming for a reassuring tone. "Pat and I have carefully reviewed each one and found no historical errors or distortions. The quilt exhibit is going on as scheduled, and we'd very much appreciate including Dove in the Window according to the terms of our original agreement. Please let me know if you have any questions or concerns. I hope to see you at the grand opening gala on Saturday, August 28."

She sent the message on its way and continued working on her application for leave, but a vague, nagging worry settled in the back of her mind. She felt only somewhat reassured later that afternoon when Kathleen emailed again to say, "Very glad to hear it. I must have misread the ad. Looking forward to seeing you on August 28!"

"What ad?" Summer asked aloud, uneasy. She quickly emailed Kathleen back with the same question, but Kathleen must have stepped away from her computer because she didn't immediately reply.

Summer was in her room changing for dinner when her computer pinged to announce a new email. She thought it might be a response from Kathleen, or a message from the U of C registrar regarding her application, but she was pleasantly surprised to see Denisha Williams's name in the header. The subject line, however, made her heart plummet: "Quilt Exhibit & Strange Rumors."

Summer sank into her chair, eyes fixed on the screen. "I was so sorry to hear that the quilt exhibit at Union Hall was canceled," Denisha had written. "Several of us from the Grangerville Quilt Guild were planning to attend the opening night gala together. As a historian myself, I loved your concept for the exhibit. I'm surprised you found only three suitable quilts to display. I wish I'd been able to help you find our guild's victory quilt, if that would have made a difference." She closed by asking Summer to keep in touch.

"Only three quilts?" Summer murmured, bewildered. There were nearly two dozen lovely quilts adorning the gallery walls. And why did Denisha too assume the quilt exhibit had been canceled?

Summer immediately replied to correct the misunderstanding, and to encourage Denisha and her guild friends to attend the grand opening gala. She also asked why Denisha thought there were only three quilts and where she had heard that the exhibit was canceled. The similarities between Kathleen's comments and Denisha's were too specific to be coincidental.

She was just about to head downstairs to the banquet hall when Denisha responded. "I'm happy to hear that the show will go on, but something is definitely wrong. I saw the cancellation notice in the Community Events section of the *Waterford Register* this morning. As to the rest, I assumed you knew. The reviews on local quilting boards haven't been kind, and unfortunately they're making the rounds of all the local quilt guild email lists. So sorry to be the bearer of bad news. Please let me know if there's anything I can do to help." She ended with a brief list of URLs, the first of which included the domain for the *Register*.

Summer braced herself before opening the link, but that wasn't enough to prepare her for the shock of what she found.

There in the list of upcoming community events—concerts, guided arboretum walks, children's library programs—was an announcement stating, "The historical quilt exhibit at Union Hall, currently under reconstruction, has been canceled due to unforeseen circumstances" and that there were no plans to reschedule. Contact information was included, but Pat's predecessor was incorrectly listed as the historical society president, the email domain was misspelled, and the phone number had an extra digit. Most readers would note the cancellation and skim right past the errors without noticing them, but whoever had placed the ad didn't actually mean for anyone to contact the historical society.

The rest of the links were even worse. One took Summer to the local chapter of a large online quilting guild, where someone calling herself "MaryQuilter" had posted a one-star review of the exhibit. "I really wanted to like this show," she began, "but the descriptions of the quilts were so contrived that I couldn't get into it. Also, it's frustrating that I drove all that way and paid for parking and $25 admission to see only three quilts. They weren't even that interesting or pretty. Save your money and your time. Wish I had. If I could give this exhibit zero stars I would."

Ten comments followed. Nine of them thanked MaryQuilter for the warning and vowed to stay away. One asked her if she was sure she had gone to the right building, or if she had wandered in while the quilts were still being hung, because there were at least two dozen quilts there now, all perfectly lovely. "I'm also confused why you would say there was a $25 admission," the commenter added. "They're accepting donations, but there's no admission fee. Tickets for the grand opening gala are $25, but that's a special event, with food and entertainment. Is that what you bought?"

"MaryQuilter" had not replied.

The lone relatively positive comment was little consolation to

Summer as she clicked on the other links. "MaryQuilter" had copied and pasted the same wildly inaccurate criticism on at least six websites, sometimes verbatim, sometimes altering an adjective or the various fees she had been forced to pay. On the last site, someone had commented, "Guys it doesn't matter. Just saw in the paper that its canclled prolly due 2 neg reviews." To that someone replied, "*It's* not *its*—but I agree that's probably why. Quality matters. Do better, Waterford Historical Society."

Summer closed her eyes and pushed back her chair, sick to her stomach, sick at heart. The fraudulent ad, the glaring lies, the phony reviews—surely this explained the sharp decline in attendance and donations, and the perplexing reaction of the gallery visitor who had been astounded by how much better the exhibit was than the reviews claimed.

Krolich was behind it, obviously. He was so much better than the Elm Creek Quilters at being evil and conniving that they never could have anticipated an attack like this. It was, Summer was forced to admit, brilliantly malicious. Why spark publicity and intrigue for an exhibit by denouncing it when he could steer people away by labeling it boring, expensive, and inconvenient—and, in the end, canceled altogether?

The grand opening gala was in five days. Krolich had left them little time to respond to his disinformation campaign, but it might be enough. It would have to be.

Summer's appetite had fled, but she hurried downstairs to the banquet hall and swiftly made the rounds of the tables, quietly asking the Elm Creek Quilters to join her for an emergency meeting in the library before the evening program. She was able to speak with everyone except Anna, who was in the kitchen, caught up in one of the busiest times of her workday. "It's about the exhibit" was all Summer would tell her friends while in earshot of so many curious campers. "Krolich struck back, and I missed the early warning signs."

While the other Elm Creek Quilters finished dining with the

campers, Summer hurried past the butler's pantry and out the back door, phoning Pat as soon as she stepped outside. The historical society president listened in stunned silence as Summer explained what she had learned. "But we gave the *Waterford Register* our own press release weeks ago," Pat said, incredulous. "I personally submitted our event listing to the community page."

"Krolich or one of his minions must have contacted the paper after you did," said Summer, sinking down upon the bottom step and resting her elbows on her knees. "They must have pretended to be from the historical society and passed off their phony announcement as a correction."

"I'll contact them again and ask them to run a retraction," said Pat, a tremor of fury in her voice. "We missed the Sunday paper, which has the largest readership, and we're probably too late for tomorrow's edition, but they can run it beginning Wednesday."

"And they can update their website immediately," said Summer. "Maybe we should send an updated press release to all of the regional papers just in case."

"Consider it done."

Summer thought quickly. "A friend of mine is a producer at the public radio affiliate on campus. I'll email her the press release and ask her to mention the exhibit and the gala in as many station breaks as they can."

"Good, good." Pat heaved a sigh. "This will help, but it may not be enough, especially with those fake negative reviews being shared online."

"I'm just getting started," Summer assured her. "Krolich isn't going to win this one. I promise you that."

They hung up. Summer hurried back inside, fervently hoping she'd be able to keep that promise.

There was still a half hour remaining in the dinner service when the other Elm Creek Quilters joined her in the library. Only Anna was absent; she sent word via Gretchen that she and staff would keep watch over the banquet hall and set up for the evening program after dinner. Quickly, pacing a bit to work off her smoldering anger, Summer told her friends what Krolich and his cronies had done.

"That man is an absolute menace," Agnes declared, her blue eyes furious behind her dainty pink glasses. "He lies with impunity, and he carries on with all manner of wrongdoing and always gets away with it."

"We won't let him get away with it this time," said Sylvia, her expression resolute. "Thoughts, everyone? We have much to repair and not a lot of time."

Ideas flew swiftly back and forth; suggestions were made and considered. They quickly agreed that they should focus on refuting the misinformation and promoting the grand opening gala. It was Sylvia who reminded them that their greatest resource was their strong ties to the quilting community. "Rally the quilters, and everything else will fall into place," she declared, and after that, the way forward became clear. The Elm Creek Quilters quickly divided up the necessary tasks, each eager and determined to do her bit.

Summer would update the website with a dedicated page describing the quilt exhibit and linking to the Waterford Historical Society's page, where tickets to the gala could be purchased.

Sarah would email the same information directly to all the campers and fans who subscribed to their newsletter, encouraging them to tour the exhibit and noting that Anna would be catering the grand opening gala. "Anyone within driving distance will come to the gala just to savor the yummy food they usually can get only at quilt camp," Sarah said, tapping her pencil on her pad for emphasis.

Maggie would send Sarah's newsletter to her own mailing list, a database of all the quilt shops in Pennsylvania she had visited through the years to promote her pattern book. "I have lists for other states too, if we need them," she said, "but let's start local."

Diane would focus on businesses and public services, borrowing images from Sarah's newsletter to design posters announcing the exhibit and the gala. "If I submit the file to the print shop by eight o'clock, the posters will be ready by noon," she said. "By twelve-thirty, I'll be posting them in shop windows and on library bulletin boards throughout Waterford. By Friday afternoon, I'll have the entire Elm Creek Valley covered—if those of you with free periods in the afternoon can substitute teach my classes." Summer, Maggie, and Gretchen promptly volunteered.

Gretchen, working from the sign-up sheets for the shuttle from Elm Creek Manor to Union Hall, would identify guests who had visited the exhibit during their week at camp. After Sarah sent her email newsletter, Gretchen would write to those quilters directly and encourage them to post online reviews if they had enjoyed the visit. "I'll send links to the same sites where this 'MaryQuilter' person posted, plus a few more," Gretchen said. "Before long, I'm sure the authentic positive reviews will overwhelm the phony bad ones."

Sylvia would phone the presidents of all quilt guilds within fifty miles and invite them to attend private tours of the exhibit in the days leading up to the gala. If they liked what they saw, and surely they would, Sylvia would encourage them to spread the word to their members.

Agnes had the most inspired idea of all. She proposed to invite local dignitaries to attend a VIP gathering an hour before the grand opening, where Summer would offer tours before the anticipated crowds arrived. Afterward, for a donation of $100, each VIP guest could purchase a muslin rectangle to autograph. The Elm Creek Quilters would sew them into a modern replica of the Authors' Album, which would be displayed in the gallery among the most significant quilts in the region's history for decades to come.

"What local celebrity could resist such an honor?" Agnes asked, beaming. "We'll raise a nice sum for the capital campaign, and Summer will fill the last empty space on the gallery walls."

It was an optimistic note on which to end the meeting.

As everyone hurried off to finish preparations for the evening program, Summer drew her mother aside. "I wanted to let you know that I officially applied for a leave of absence for the fall quarter," she said, quickly adding, "Dr. Alvarez recommended a quarter instead of an entire year."

"No surprise there. She doesn't want to lose her prize pupil. But in the end, you have to do what's in *your* best interest, not hers." Her mom pulled her in for a hug. "I'm proud of you, kiddo."

Summer had to laugh. "You're proud of me for quitting?"

"You aren't quitting," her mother said firmly, holding her at arm's length and looking her squarely in the eye. "You just earned your master's degree from one of the most prestigious universities in the country. Now you're embracing a whole new adventure. That's not quitting. That's daring."

"I like the sound of that," said Summer, already feeling immensely better.

As soon as the evening program ended, Summer hurried upstairs to the library to get started on updating the website only to find Sarah already seated at the oak desk, swiftly composing the special edition of the Elm Creek Quilts newsletter. Phone calls would have to wait until morning, but anything that could be done despite the late hour *must* be done right away. Krolich had a massive head start, and they couldn't waste a moment if they were to catch up and eventually pass him.

The next day, while keeping Elm Creek Quilt Camp running smoothly and pleasantly for their guests, Summer and her friends raced to rally support among their friends and allies, to staunch the flow of Krolich's lies, and to spread the word about the grand opening gala. When they weren't leading camp activities, they were working on their computers and telephones, updating one another on their progress whenever they crossed paths. In swift, quiet exchanges in the halls, Summer learned that Sylvia had already scheduled several back-to-back quilt guild tours on Wednesday and Thursday afternoons, and Agnes had received ten confirmations for the VIP reception and was expecting at least twice more of that number.

Summer was on her way from the kitchen to the banquet hall when Diane rushed past on her way to the back door. "Thanks for filling in for me at Quick Piecing," she called, waving with one hand and clutching her purse to her side with the other.

"Happy to," Summer called after her, but the door had already banged shut behind her. Summer was actually taking over Beginning Quilting, and Maggie was doing Quick Piecing, but as long as both classes were covered, it didn't matter.

Later, at another brief faculty meeting in the library between supper and the evening program, Diane reported that she and two friends from her book club had distributed posters throughout the downtown and the strip mall on the northwest side of the city. Tomorrow they planned to hit Grangerville and the smaller villages to the east. Thursday they would tackle Summit Pass and environs, and Friday they would visit Woodfall and the unincorporated areas to the north.

"Here's something I should have anticipated but didn't," said Diane, her voice taking on an edge. "Most places were happy to display our posters, but occasionally, managers would look them over and decline, babbling apologies and excuses as they herded us out the door. Eventually we figured out what all these places had in common."

"University Realty is their landlord," Sarah guessed, bouncing James gently on her knee as he made a grab for the pen tucked behind her ear.

"Exactly," said Diane.

"It's terrible that people live in perpetual dread of that man," said Gretchen. "Did he warn them not to help the historical society? Threaten them?"

"He holds their leases," Diane said. "We all know what he did to Bonnie. She lost her condo and her business to University Realty, and it was all perfectly legal."

"Well, it shouldn't be," said Gretchen, pushing her bifocals up the bridge of her nose and folding her thin arms over her chest.

As Summer exchanged glances with her mother and Sarah, she knew that they shared the same thought: By now, Krolich would have realized that they were fighting back.

On Wednesday, Summer hurried to the kitchen before Sunrise Yoga and found Joe and Andrew seated at a booth together, drinking coffee, eating bacon and eggs with buttered toast, and sharing the newspaper, Andrew starting with the front-page news, Joe the sports section. "I bet you're looking for this," Andrew remarked, his eyes kind as he held out the local-news section to her. It was already folded open to the Community Events columns, which told her that she was not the first to rush downstairs to look for the retraction.

"Second column, near the bottom," Joe supplied helpfully.

Summer scanned the page, and there it was—an announcement of the exhibit and the grand opening gala, correct in every detail. She breathed a sigh of relief. "Thank you, gentlemen," she said, returning the paper with a grin and hurrying off to meet her yoga students on the verandah.

After her Modern Quilting class, Summer found time to stop by the library for a quick chat with Sarah, who had heartening news. Already their campers were responding with great enthusiasm to the newsletter and website updates. Gretchen's friendly appeals for real reviews had resulted in honest, factual, and overwhelmingly positive posts, significantly outnumbering Krolich's phony ones and revealing the ridiculous claims for the falsehoods they were. Agnes had filled nearly all the available spots for the VIP event, and on their way to the manor that morning, she and Diane had twice heard the public radio station announce the gala during station breaks.

Their conversation was cut short by Caroline, stacking blocks in the play corner, her unhappy wail announcing that she needed a diaper change. Summer had to hurry off to Union Hall anyway; she had scarcely enough time to get to the gallery before her tour with the Woodfall Sew-and-Sews would begin, the first of several that day.

Thursday proved to be just as busy, with all of the Elm Creek

Quilters scrambling to promote the exhibit and counter Krolich's misinformation while keeping quilt camp humming along and their guests happily occupied. Summer was in the gallery catching her breath during a brief respite between tours when she was approached by a man in his forties with artfully tousled hair and three days' growth of beard. He carried a pad and pen as well as a pocket recorder, which announced his profession even before he introduced himself as Steve Lathrop, a reporter with the *Waterford Register*. "I understand you're the curator," he said, holding up the recorder. "Mind if I ask you a few questions?"

"Why don't we talk while I show you around the exhibit?" said Summer, gesturing to the Creek's Crossing Album, her favorite place to begin.

Mindful of the time, she focused on the highlights, emphasizing the theme of the exhibit and the historical society's fundraising goals. She lingered before her favorite quilts and described them in more detail, and she explained why she had included documents and photos in tribute to the lost quilts. Steve asked her several rather insightful questions, taking notes as well as recording their conversation, but whenever he queried her about "the controversy," she offered him diplomatic responses and redirected the conversation to the quilts and the fascinating stories they told.

Afterward, Steve seemed well satisfied with the interview. "It's unusual for my editor to ask for a full-page feature article, especially on such short notice," he remarked as she escorted him downstairs to the exit.

She quickly hid her astonishment. "I didn't realize you were writing a feature. I thought it would be a paragraph or two for the Community Events column. I hope I've given you enough information."

"I have everything I need." He smiled slightly as he switched off the recorder and tucked it into his pocket. "Our publisher doesn't like being played for a fool, especially when his credibility is on the line. He's determined to find out who placed that phony announcement.

In the meantime, he figures that promoting your exhibit will make that person, whoever he is, very unhappy."

"That would certainly foil his evil plans," said Summer lightly, smiling. "If it all wasn't just an unfortunate misunderstanding."

"Sure. That's likely," said Steve, sardonic. He tapped his pad with his pen. "My story will run tomorrow, barring mechanical failure at the printing press or a sudden case of writer's block on my part."

She shuddered. "Don't even get me started on the horrors of writer's block."

He smiled, a quizzical light in his eye, but when her gaze shifted to a group of four women who had just entered the foyer, very likely her next tour, he merely thanked her for the interview and departed.

Summer had every reason to hope for a glowing article in the morning paper. Support from the quilting community was strong, enthusiastic, and still growing. It was heartening, and she was grateful for it—and yet she feared that it would all be for nothing, that they were too late, that the damage had been done. The grand opening gala would be only sparsely attended, the capital campaign would languish, the exhibit would close, and Union Hall would be lost. Summer would fail, and in doing so, she would let down everyone who had counted on her.

It could happen that way, but it hadn't yet. In two days' time, she would know who had won and what had been lost.

# 15

On the afternoon of Saturday, August 28, a perfectly warm, clear, sunny day, Summer slipped into one of her favorite professional yet festive dresses. The powder-blue, sleeveless chambray frock boasted a jewel neckline, a natural waist, a fitted bodice with embroidered floral motifs, a full A-line skirt, and a sash that tied in a bow in the back—a bit retro in style, flattering and perfect for the gala. She brushed her hair until it shone, the auburn waves now long enough to touch her shoulders, then pinned back one side with a vintage pearl hairpin Sylvia had given her years before, an heirloom they had discovered while searching through trunks in the attic for an old treadle sewing machine manual. Scrutinizing herself in the mirror, Summer decided that she looked the part of a confident, expert museum curator, even though her stomach quaked nervously. She and her friends had done their utmost to prepare for and to promote the event. Now all that remained was to throw open the doors and discover whether they would meet with enthusiastic guests, angry protestors, or absolute indifference.

When she descended the grand oak staircase, Summer found the manor's permanent residents waiting for her in the front foyer, all smartly attired and smiling up at her with pride and affection. Sarah and Matt had even hired a babysitter for the occasion so they could give the exhibit their undivided attention. Summer knew that Anna and Jeremy were already at Union Hall, setting up the catering in the lobby, while Agnes, Diane, and Pat were adding last-minute touches to the gallery—vases of fresh flowers, comfortable chairs, and two tables with attractive displays of information about the exhibit, the history of Union Hall, the mission of the Waterford Historical Society, and the capital campaign.

"You've done such a marvelous job organizing this exhibit, dear," said Sylvia when Summer joined them, taking her hand and squeezing it warmly. "We can't wait to celebrate the grand opening."

"We're all so proud of you," Gretchen chimed in, smiling.

"Now that all the hard work is behind you, you can relax and enjoy your triumph," said Sarah, giving her a quick hug. In a whisper she added, "You look fabulous."

"Thanks," Summer murmured back. "You do too." What she didn't say was that she wouldn't be able to enjoy her triumph until much later that night, when she was absolutely sure it *was* one.

Anna and her sous chef had taken the Elm Creek Quilts minivan to Union Hall a few hours before, the back loaded with equipment and delicacies, so while Joe, Gretchen, Sylvia, Andrew, and Maggie climbed into the Hartleys' car, Summer squeezed into the cab of the McClures' pickup, Matt at the wheel and Sarah in the middle. Summer and Sarah had many details to discuss as they rode along, but as they entered Waterford's historic district, they abruptly fell silent, stunned by a scene unfolding on the opposite side of the street from Union Hall.

Five men and women, several of whom Summer vaguely recognized, milled about on the sidewalk in front of the old city hall, glowering angrily as they paced back and forth with picket signs. "Leave the Past in the Past," said one sign. "Stop Dividing Our Community," demanded another. "WHS=Waterford Hatred Society," declared a third. A fourth was turned mostly away from them, but Summer glimpsed something about protecting the children.

"You've got to be kidding me," said Sarah flatly.

For a moment Summer could only shake her head, dumbfounded. "I don't see Krolich," she said as Matt drove past the protestors and halted in a parking spot half a block away. "But I'm sure that's the delegation of outraged civic leaders who were with him that day in the gallery."

"Krolich probably promised he'd march on Union Hall alongside them, but then he failed to show," said Matt, turning off the engine and setting the parking brake. "He always did prefer to have someone else do his dirty work for him."

"Let's hope this is as dirty as it gets," said Summer as she climbed down from the cab and smoothed her dress. As she and the McClures approached Union Hall on the opposite side of the street, she expected the delegation to shout slogans and curses at them, but they merely brandished their signs, lengthened their strides, and threw withering glares. From the way the eldest man kept glancing in the direction of University Realty and frowning, the delegation probably wondered where Krolich was too.

At that moment Summer saw Pat coming down the cobblestone walk to greet them at the gate. "Ignore the *un*welcoming committee," Pat said wryly, opening the gate and propping it open for the guests they all hoped would be arriving soon. "They started out on the sidewalk in front of Union Hall, but the police asked them to move to the other side of the street so they wouldn't impede traffic." Pat inclined her head to indicate the police car parked farther down the block.

"I admit I'm surprised they resorted to a protest," said Summer. "Krolich wouldn't risk drawing attention to the exhibit unless his original scheme wasn't—"

She would have said more, but at that moment, one of the double doors opened and Enrique stepped outside onto the covered porch, looking very fine and perfectly at ease in tan chinos, a white shirt unbuttoned at the top, and a navy sports coat.

Catching sight of her, he smiled and hurried down the limestone stairs to meet her. "Hey, Summer," he said, taking her hand and kissing her on the cheek. He made it seem like a friendly, casual gesture, but as he turned to say hello to the others, the warmth of his lips lingered on her skin, rendering her momentarily breathless.

"What are you doing here?" she murmured as they fell in step behind Sarah and Matt, with Pat leading the way up the cobblestone walk.

He feigned bewilderment. "You invited me."

"I know that," she said, amused. "But I wasn't expecting you so early."

"I thought the crew might need help setting up."

Summer gave him a sidelong look as they climbed the front stairs. "You thought there might be trouble."

"That too." Enrique glanced over his shoulder at the increasingly disgruntled-looking protestors across the street. "If that's the worst they can do, I'm not worried."

Summer knew that was *not* the worst Krolich could do, but she was determined not to worry.

She entered the foyer, where Anna and her assistants had arranged the appetizers, beverages, and sweets enticingly, their delicious aromas filling the light, airy space. The same Waterford College jazz quintet that performed frequently at quilt camp was setting up along the wall near Pat's office. Next Summer went upstairs to inspect the gallery, where she found everything in perfect order, the docents at their posts, the quilts and artifacts beautifully displayed. All the while, Enrique remained by her side, a gallant escort, ready to assist if she should need him.

Soon thereafter, the VIPs arrived—the mayors of Waterford, Grangerville, Woodfall, and other Elm Creek Valley towns; the provost of Waterford College; their state senator and assemblyperson; business leaders, with the notable absence of Gregory Krolich; local philanthropists; prominent artists, writers, and scholars; and others. After welcoming their guests with Anna's marvelous refreshments, Summer,

Agnes, and Pat led three separate groups on tours of the exhibit, beginning at the information table and concluding at Authors' Album. After describing the antique masterpiece in detail, the guides invited the special guests to purchase a muslin patch for a new autograph quilt, which was expected to be completed and displayed in the exhibit within a year. All were intrigued and flattered to be asked to contribute, and each bought and signed a patch. Afterward, the VIPs mingled in the gallery, returned to the foyer for more delicious food and drink, or accompanied Pat and other Waterford Historical Society officers to view the ongoing renovations elsewhere in Union Hall.

Everywhere Summer went, she overheard guests marveling over the once neglected building's astonishing transformation and the fascinating stories behind the extraordinary quilts in the gallery. The glowing reviews from their special guests were everything Summer could have hoped for, but as the hour approached for the main event to begin, her heart pounded with a dizzying mixture of apprehension and excitement. Krolich might have another stealth attack ready to deploy. The Elm Creek Quilters' efforts to rally support might prove to be too little, too late to counteract the phony, negative reviews online. The capital campaign could end that night in failure.

With ten minutes to go before the front doors would be thrown open in welcome, Summer turned to Enrique, gave his hand a quick squeeze, and said, "Do you mind if I have a moment alone?"

"Of course not," he said, squeezing back. "This is your night. Take all the time you need. I'll be around."

She smiled her thanks, then left the gallery and hurried down the second-floor hallway to a vacant office that faced the front of the building. Easing the door open, she groped along the wall for the light switch, but apparently the rewiring was not yet complete, for the room remained dark, with scattered tools, sawhorses, drop cloths, and containers of plaster and paint barely visible in the shadows. Opening the door fully to allow light from the hallway to spill inside, Summer gathered her skirt close, picked her way carefully through the clutter to a window on the opposite wall, took a steadying breath, and gazed outside.

The protestors across the street had vanished. Summer wondered whether they had given up, disappointed and disgruntled, when their ringleader didn't show up to march with them. Perhaps they had slunk away in confusion and shame when they finally realized that their bullying tactics wouldn't work against decent, ordinary people united in support of a just cause. For all their bluster, their empty threats had never possessed more power than their listeners granted them.

No one seemed to be listening now. They had better things to do.

The sidewalk in front of Union Hall and the cobblestone walkway leading to the entrance were packed with people dressed in their summer finery, smiling and chatting with one another, fanning themselves with their tickets, admiring the improvements to the exterior of the grand old building and the gardens surrounding it.

Summer moved away from the window and pressed a hand to her mouth to muffle a cry of joy. Friends, neighbors, quilters, history buffs, art lovers—they had all turned out to support the historical society, and in numbers that exceeded Summer's wildest hopes.

Heart overflowing with gratitude, she hurried downstairs to the foyer to welcome them.

Enrique was waiting for her at the bottom of the staircase, and together they reached the entrance just as Agnes and Pat opened the double doors. Assuming her assigned place just inside the entrance, Summer greeted guests and collected tickets, but it quickly became evident that the flow of the crowd was too much for one person. When Summer threw Enrique an entreating look, he stepped up to the opposite side of the doorway and began accepting tickets as the line passed between them.

And what a line it was. Quilt campers with whom Summer had shared breakfast on the cornerstone patio earlier that morning entered, waving their tickets and teasing her about how surprised she was to see them again so soon. Friends from high school greeted her with fond hugs and congratulations and promises to get together. Neighbors who had known Summer since she and her mom had moved to Waterford explained that they had read the glowing review in the *Register* the previous day and immediately bought their tickets. "We're all so proud of you," enthused her mom's next-door neighbor, while her husband nodded heartily beside her.

Occasionally Summer and Enrique would both glance up from swiftly collecting tickets and welcoming visitors, their eyes would meet, and they would smile, and each time Summer felt warmth and happiness bubbling up inside her.

Nearly a half hour passed before the steady flow of arrivals slowed, but before it ended entirely, Summer glimpsed an elderly woman with a familiar cloud of white hair farther down the line, and beside her, a tall, slender, elegant figure in a glamorous gown and oversized dark sunglasses. "Vinnie?" Summer exclaimed, astonished, as the pair drew closer. "Julia?"

"Surprise," Vinnie sang, pulling Summer into an embrace. "Didn't we tell you back in June that we'd come if we could?"

"You did," Summer replied, smiling. "I'm so happy you made it."

"Not all of us Cross-Country Quilters could, unfortunately. Our friends had other commitments, work and family and things. But since Megan couldn't drive me this time, Julia sent a limo!" Beaming, Vinnie patted Julia on the forearm. "A limo, all for me, all the way from Cincinnati! What an extravagance!"

"It was really no trouble," said Julia indulgently, sharing a fond look with Summer over Vinnie's head. "A little birthday gift from me to you, a trifle."

"Nonsense. It's quite a big deal." Drawing closer to Summer, Vinnie added confidentially, "It's so exciting to have a famous Hollywood star as a close personal friend. I highly recommend it."

"Congratulations on your premiere, Summer," said Julia, giving the crowds filling the foyer an approving nod. "Fabulous turnout.

Impressive architecture. I give you two thumbs-up and five out of five stars."

"Wait until you see the quilts," said Summer, gesturing to the staircase. "It's an extraordinary collection and I'm sure you'll love it. And while we're on the subject of things you'll love, did you know Anna is doing the catering?"

Vinnie gasped and clasped her hands together. "How wonderful! But now I don't know where to begin, refreshments or quilts? What do you think, Julia?"

"I think we're holding up the line," Julia replied, amused. She put a hand on Vinnie's arm and guided her forward. "We'll catch up with you later, Summer."

Vinnie smiled and waved goodbye over her shoulder as she and Julia moved on into the foyer.

As twilight descended, the line slowed enough that Summer could occasionally pause to observe the guests enjoying the refreshments, climbing the elegant staircase to the second floor, and passing in and out of the gallery. Everyone seemed to be in excellent spirits, and Summer could only hope that their goodwill would manifest as strong support for the capital campaign.

With so few new guests arriving, Pat asked a docent to mind the door so that she, Agnes, and Summer could mingle, answering guests' questions and leading tours upon request.

"Something to eat first?" Enrique asked, extending his hand.

"Yes," said Summer emphatically, interlacing her fingers through his. "I'm famished. But then it's back to work."

Together they browsed the buffet, filling small plates with Anna's delicacies, taking two glasses of white wine from the bar, and retreating to a quiet corner where they could chat and observe the crowd. They agreed that everyone seemed to be having a wonderful time, and they both wondered what Krolich might be doing at that moment. Crying into a beer at a dive bar near his office, they speculated, or lurking outside Union Hall, nose pressed against a windowpane, glaring bitterly at the revelers, cursing his rotten luck for letting the historic building and the valuable plot of land it stood upon slip from his grasp.

The thought of Krolich watching them, maliciously plotting even now, made Summer shiver.

"Forget about him," said Enrique, slipping an arm over her shoulders. "There's nothing he can do to ruin this night."

Summer leaned against him, somewhat comforted, though she knew Krolich might be down but he was definitely not out. Unless he was exposed and held accountable one day, he would continue his shady dealings and greedy schemes as long as they remained profitable.

But tonight was not his night. Tonight belonged to the historical society and all the friends and supporters who had rallied around them to put their capital campaign over the top.

"Summer," someone called out.

Summer turned to see Pat beckoning her from the bottom of the staircase, where she was conversing with a man and a woman clad in well-tailored suits. As they all regarded her expectantly, Summer smiled and held up a finger to indicate that she would be over in a minute. "Enrique," she said, turning back to him, apologetic. "I'm sorry to keep abandoning you, but—"

"Go on," he said, smiling, as he took her plate. "Work the crowd. Raise money. If Krolich shows up, I'll ask him very nicely to leave."

She thanked him and hurried off to join Pat, who introduced her to her companions, the mayor and the chair of the zoning commission. Summer had noticed them earlier among the VIPs, but neither had been in her tour group. Both had taken office earlier that spring, she remembered, the mayor through a special election and the zoning commission chair by appointment.

The mayor complimented her on the exhibit, but then his expression turned serious. "The historical society has expressed concerns that when University Realty first proposed acquiring Union Hall, the zoning commission condemned the property without due process," he said, while the head of the zoning commission nodded gravely. "They have questions about whether the city council dismissed their request for a hearing due to inappropriate influence from a University Realty executive."

Summer wished he would just go ahead and use the words "Krolich" and "bribery," but she understood why he might need to be more circumspect. "With respect, Mayor," she said, "I believe these questions and concerns are shared by others in the community, not only the Waterford Historical Society."

"I know that for a fact," the chair of the zoning commission said, frowning. "I have the angry emails to prove it."

"We're fully cooperating with police investigators," the mayor said, lowering his voice. "If any laws were broken, all legal options will be on the table, and measures will be taken to make sure this never happens again."

"I'm pleased to hear that," said Summer. She was tempted to suggest that the investigation begin with his own deputy mayor, who earlier that evening had been protesting the very event the mayor had attended as a special guest.

"Your display for the Cleopatra's Fan quilt was enlightening, to say the least," said the chair of the zoning commission. "Collusion between members of the city council and University Realty may go back decades. We'll certainly pass that along to the police investigators. In the meantime, I'm going to propose a thorough evaluation of our historic district ordinances. I believe we should expand them to include more properties. If nothing else, we should institute a six-month moratorium between an official declaration that a property is neglected and the date it can be condemned, sold, or razed."

"That would be wonderful," said Summer. "Pat and her colleagues have sacrificed so much to save Union Hall over the past year. A moratorium would have spared them that ordeal."

"I'd do it all again," said Pat, "but I'm glad to know that maybe no one else will ever have to."

The mayor gave Summer his card, and he and the zoning commission chair departed with assurances that they would be in touch. A moment later, Pat was called away to chat with a potential benefactor.

Alone again, Summer looked around for Enrique but didn't see him. She headed upstairs to the gallery, where she passed Agnes on her way out, clutching an otherwise ordinary tote bag to her side with a white-knuckle grip. "We have to keep emptying the donation box," she confided in an undertone, breathless, her blue eyes bright with excitement. "The checks keep piling up almost as fast as we can collect them and deposit them in the safe. I'm not complaining, but if I'd known I'd be sprinting up and down stairs all evening, I would have worn my sneakers."

"They'd look cute with your dress," Summer remarked. "Do you need me to help?"

"No, no, dear. You have plenty to do already." Agnes chuckled a bit as she bustled off with the tote bag full of donations.

Summer continued into the gallery, where she immediately spotted Vinnie and Julia at the center of a rather large gathering of eager guests. Summer watched a moment longer, bemused, until she realized that Julia had started an impromptu fundraiser of her own. "A fan asked to take a photo with her," Vinnie explained in an undertone, examining the camera one of Julia's starry-eyed admirers handed her before approaching the star. "Julia said, 'I'll do you one better. I'll pose for a photo *and* autograph your exhibit program if you drop ten dollars into that donation box.' She's been at it ever since."

"How generous of her," said Summer, pleased. "And what an inspired idea. I wish I'd thought of it."

"Vinnie, we're ready," Julia prompted, her arm resting lightly on her fan's shoulders.

Vinnie gave a start. "Sorry, Summer, I'm on the clock," she said, and hurried off to snap the photo.

Summer continued making the rounds of the gallery, greeting friends and nodding cordially to guests she hadn't met, pausing to answer questions or to graciously accept compliments. Quite a few guests lingered before Authors' Album, reading the autographs and excitedly pointing out favorite authors to their companions. Spotting Courtney from the Waterford Public Library on the fringes, Summer approached and greeted her. "I have a confession to make," said Courtney as they admired the quilt. "When Gregory Krolich first notified us that they'd found Authors' Album at long last, we were thrilled, and we couldn't wait to display the quilt behind the circulation desk again. It was Krolich who insisted we donate the quilt to the Waterford Historical Society."

Summer's heart dipped, but she kept her smile in place. "I thought I sensed some tension between you two. If you want us to return the quilt to you—"

"Oh, no," said Courtney, placing a hand on Summer's arm. "Everyone on the library board is impressed with your gallery, and we all want the quilt to stay in the exhibit. I just thought you ought to know the circumstances." She inhaled deeply as if steeling herself. "University Realty holds the leases for several of our board members or their relatives. As unbelievable as this may seem, Krolich strongly insinuated that they could face rent hikes or eviction if the vote to donate the quilt didn't go the way he wanted."

"Actually, that's *entirely* believable," said Summer. "We've dealt with Krolich before. We're all too familiar with his rather sketchy way of doing business."

Courtney pursed her lips and gave her head a tiny shake. "As for me, I hope that's my first and last time doing any business with him. In fact, I'm going to insist on it."

They parted company as they continued their separate tours of the gallery. Before long Summer came to the display for the Sugar Camp Quilt, where she found her mom engrossed in conversation with Kathleen Barrett. Both women glanced up at Summer's approach.

"There she is," said Kathleen, smiling, "the woman of the hour."

"This exhibit is truly extraordinary, kiddo," said Gwen proudly, pulling her into an embrace. "I've been hearing rave reviews all night.

Naturally I've been claiming credit for teaching you everything you know."

"I'd expect nothing less," Summer teased right back, kissing her on the cheek.

"It really is wonderful, Summer," Kathleen said. "My only regret is that I couldn't offer you the Sugar Camp Quilt itself, but only descriptions, sketches, and swatches."

"And I've been trying to convince her how invaluable those artifacts truly are," said Gwen, nudging Kathleen playfully. "I think I'm making some headway."

"Oh, you're very persuasive," Kathleen assured her, amused. To Summer she added, "Did I mention that I have most of the Granger-Nelson family papers, but a few other boxes belong to my cousins?"

Summer nodded. "Yes, you did. I wish I'd been able to examine the rest of the collection."

"Consider your wish granted—or at least it soon will be."

"What do you mean?"

"Recently my cousins and I had a long-overdue talk," said Kathleen. "We've decided to gather all of the papers together in a single archive and donate it to a library or museum. I haven't forgotten your praise for the Waterford College Library Rare Books Room. May I take you up on your offer for a tour and an introduction to your librarian friend?"

"Absolutely," said Summer, delighted. "I'll get in touch with Audrey Pfenning, the head archivist, and we'll set up a meeting and a tour as soon as possible."

And as soon as the archive was cataloged and available to the university community, Summer would be first in line to study it. If there was even a slight chance that the papers Kathleen's cousins held contained clues to the whereabouts of the Sugar Camp Quilt, Summer was willing to search every page.

As Gwen and Kathleen moved on to explore the exhibit together, Summer wandered in the other direction, hoping to find Enrique.

As she passed the display for the two victory quilts, she paused at the sight of a woman with a familiar cascade of long, glossy braids, gathered in a gold-and-bronze batik scarf at the nape of her neck.

"Denisha?" said Summer. Denisha turned, and so too did the woman beside her, whom Summer also recognized—Nancy Cardellini, president of the Waterford Quilting Guild. "And Nancy. How lovely to see you both."

"I wouldn't have missed this for anything," said Nancy. "I think half the guild is here tonight, and the rest are going to be so envious when we tell them what they missed."

"It truly is a wonderful exhibit, Summer," said Denisha. "And to think that my friends and I thought it was canceled. Those phony on-line reviews were so vile, and whoever wrote them was deplorable—but let's not spoil the evening saying another word about *that*."

"Let's not," Summer agreed, smiling. "So how do you two know each other? I assume there's a quilting connection, but I know you're not in the same guild."

Denisha and Nancy exchanged a glance. "We actually met only recently," said Denisha. "Your research into our separate victory quilts raised some troubling questions about our shared history."

"Denisha reached out to me," Nancy explained, "to see if together we could uncover more information about the two quilts—documents from our files, personal reflections from our more senior members, anything, really."

"I hope you'll share your discoveries with me," said Summer. "I'd love to add them to the exhibit."

"We did find a few photos you might appreciate," said Nancy. "I'll have copies made for you."

"We discovered something else even more valuable," said Denisha. "Your exhibit has made us much more aware of the past discord between our two guilds. We agreed that it's long past time for reconciliation."

"Beginning in September, the officers from both guilds are planning to meet once a month to discuss opportunities for collaboration," said Nancy. "We could cooperate on charitable projects, for example, or our two guilds could put on the annual Waterford Summer Quilt Festival together."

"So many quilters from Grangerville submit their quilts to the juried exhibition," said Denisha. "Why shouldn't we share in the planning and all the other work too?"

"We owe it all to you, Summer," said Nancy, giving her arm a fond squeeze. "You were brave enough to ask the questions that got us thinking."

"And talking," Denisha added. "And perhaps more importantly, listening to one another."

Summer was so happy that for a moment she couldn't speak. "I can't wait to see what masterpieces your two guilds will create together," she said warmly.

She bade them goodbye and continued on her way, marveling at all she had heard. How astonishing and gratifying it was to learn how her exhibit had already made a difference in her community, and in the lives of people who had been touched by the stories the quilts told.

No matter what else happened that night, no matter what befell Union Hall in the future, the Museum of Lost Quilts was a triumph.

Leaving the gallery, Summer walked to the balcony overlooking the foyer, where a happy throng mingled amid music and laughter below. Her heart was full. She would never forget how her dearest friends had rallied to help her, not only to put together that fabulous gala, but to encourage her through her struggles to finish her thesis.

A motion caught her eye, and she glanced down to discover Enrique waving to her from the bottom of the staircase. She felt warmth rise into her cheeks as she smiled back at him, and she quickly made her way down the hall to the landing, only to find him already halfway up the stairs, accompanied by someone she knew well— Audrey Pfenning.

"I was just talking about you, Audrey," Summer called as she quickly descended to meet them. "Do you have a moment to talk somewhere a bit quieter?"

Audrey and Enrique exchanged a furtive, hopeful look. "I was just about to ask you the same question," said Audrey.

Summer considered the options. At the moment, the foyer and gallery were no place for a quiet chat. Most of Union Hall was full of remodeling hazards. Pat's office was much too crowded and cramped, and Agnes would likely be in and out, making deposits in the safe.

Then it came to her.

"I know a place," she said, beckoning Audrey and Enrique to follow as she descended the stairs. She led them to the theater, which was still far from finished, but at least the clutter had been cleared away. A few guests were strolling near the stage, admiring the renovations, but Summer spotted a few folding chairs some distance away, below the box seats, house right. "That should do nicely," she said, leading them inside.

But Enrique paused in the doorway. "I'll leave you to it," he said, nodding to each of them. When his eyes met Summer's, he winced, sheepish. "I just want to apologize in advance if I wasn't supposed to say anything."

"Say anything about what?" Summer replied, but he merely nodded and turned to go.

Summer turned to Audrey, eyebrows raised, putting aside for the moment her own reasons for wanting to chat. "What's going on?"

"Shall we sit?" Audrey suggested, gesturing to the chairs.

Mystified, Summer led her across the room, where they sat down in folding chairs facing each other. "Don't keep me in suspense," Summer said, laughing a bit at their enigmatic behavior.

"First of all, Enrique didn't mean to divulge your secret," Audrey began, clasping her hands together in her lap. "We were discussing the library and it just slipped out."

"My secret? What secret?"

"Enrique told me that you're taking a leave of absence from the University of Chicago."

"Oh. That." Summer muffled a sigh and relaxed into her chair. "That's not really a secret. I would have told you, but it's a very recent decision, and I haven't seen you in a while."

"Enrique will be relieved to hear that. He was absolutely mortified that he had betrayed your confidence." Audrey fixed her with a speculative gaze, a slight smile turning the corners of her mouth. "May I assume that you're having second thoughts about your career plans?"

"More than second thoughts. I took a leave of absence to give myself time to think, but I've already made up my mind that I won't be pursuing my doctorate in history at the University of Chicago." Summer paused, and almost to herself, added, "I haven't told my roommates yet. I probably should soon. That won't be a fun conversation."

"If they're your friends, they'll want what's best for you." Audrey too paused. "While you're considering your options, may I suggest one?"

"Sure."

"It's obvious you adore the Rare Books and Special Collections Department at the Waterford College Library as much as I do myself. Why not come work for us?"

For a moment Summer could only blink at her. "Do you mean as a library page?"

"I had something more challenging in mind. I'd like you to become the new assistant archivist."

"But—" Summer gave her head a quick shake. "That would be amazing, but I don't think I'm qualified. I have a master's degree, but not the right kind."

"Perhaps not, but you're closer to it than you might think." Audrey leaned forward, her eyes bright with anticipation. "The archivist program at Waterford College involves simultaneously earning a master's degree in history *and* in library and information sciences. Since you've already earned the history master's, you can complete the MLIS coursework and practicum in one academic year."

Summer felt sparks of hope and astonishment. "I could?"

"Oh, yes. You wouldn't be the first to come through the program that way. The department would offer you the assistant archivist job for your tuition waiver, and—if you find the work fulfilling, and if you don't regret giving up the excitement of the city for a small college town—in a few years, when I retire, you could take over as head archivist."

Summer drew in a breath. Of all the revelations of that momentous day, this one truly overwhelmed her. "It sounds perfect," she said—and then she discovered the flaw in the plan. "But it must be months too late to enroll for this fall. My applications would've been due last December. I'll have to wait an entire year."

Audrey waved that off, smiling. "No, you wouldn't. If the program were full, it would be a different story, but we do have space available, you're a Waterford College alumna, and I'm the chair of the MLIS admissions committee. Apply by Monday afternoon and I'm absolutely certain you'll be admitted."

Monday. That didn't give her much time to weigh other options, but really, what else could possibly come along that would be more perfect than this? "You'll have my application Monday," she promised, smiling. "With all my recent experience racing to meet important deadlines, I know exactly how to get it done."

Audrey's face fell slightly. "That reminds me. There is one other matter I should mention."

Summer braced herself. "Yes?"

"I know how much you disliked writing your thesis. You should be aware that the archivist program will require you to complete a capstone project."

"Another thesis?"

"It *could* be a thesis, if you prefer and your adviser agrees, but most students prepare an artifact or archive for Special Collections. From what I've seen of the research you've conducted over the past few months, and of this remarkable exhibit, I'm absolutely certain you'll complete the capstone with top marks." Audrey paused to consider. "The biggest challenge might be finding a suitable subject."

But Summer had already found one.

If she accepted Audrey's proposal, she could spend the next year studying and working in her beloved Rare Books Room. She could move home to save money and be closer to campus, and visit Elm Creek Manor frequently to see friends and teach the occasional quilt class. She could explore the Granger-Nelson family papers until she knew every page and every precious artifact, uncovering all the stories that otherwise would have been lost and sharing them so they would never be forgotten again.

"As it happens, I might have just the archive," Summer said, rising. "There's someone here I'd like you to meet—Kathleen Barrett, a descendant of Dorothea Granger Nelson. She's interested in donating the Granger-Nelson family papers to Waterford College."

Audrey's eyes widened in astonishment as she too rose. "You haven't even submitted your application yet and you've already acquired an archive for us? I wish I'd proposed this months ago."

But Summer knew she wouldn't have been ready to accept such an offer months ago. She had needed time to reflect, to learn, and to remember what mattered most, what truly made her happy.

What better time than now—on this joyful occasion in this extraordinary place?

For too long she had worried that she had lost her way, when all along, her choices had led her exactly where she needed to be. Her path had been circuitous but true, yet it was only visible when she glanced back over her shoulder and saw how far she had come.

She couldn't wait to follow its winding way ever forward.

**Elm Creek Valley Album.** 76" x 76". Cotton top and backing with cotton batting. Pieced by Sylvia Bergstrom Compson, Agnes Emberly, and Gretchen Hartley, and quilted by Maggie Flynn, Waterford, PA, 2005.

Inspired by *Authors' Album* (left), *Elm Creek Valley Album* is also a signature quilt based upon the traditional Album block. Both quilts were created to raise funds for local worthy causes, but the fundraising methods used were quite different. Whereas *Authors' Album* generated income from raffle ticket sales, the quilters behind the *Elm Creek Valley Album* accepted donations from local dignitaries in exchange for the privilege to sign a patch for the quilt. Most of the 61 autographs were collected on Saturday, August 28, 2004 at a festive gala celebrating the grand opening of the quilt gallery at Union Hall, but others, such as the signatures from Pennsylvania's governor and U.S. senators, were obtained through the mail after the event.

The *Elm Creek Valley Album* fundraiser was only one part of an exceptionally successful capital campaign conducted by the Waterford Historical Society from 2003–2005. The income generated from the campaign not only enabled the historical society to complete extensive renovations to the more than 140-year-old Union Hall, but also allowed them to establish a substantial endowment that will fund Waterford Historical Society programs, including the maintenance of Union Hall and ongoing preservation efforts, well into the future.

For more information about the dignitaries featured in both signature quilts, including supplementary materials for elementary and middle school teachers, please contact Summer Sullivan, Assistant Archivist, Rare Books and Special Collections Department, Waterford College Library.

# AUTHOR'S NOTE

Perceptive Elm Creek Quilts fans with excellent memories may have noticed a few chronological discrepancies between *The Museum of Lost Quilts* and *The Wedding Quilt*. It wasn't your imagination. I had to tweak the timeline a bit in order to continue writing the series.

When I wrote *The Wedding Quilt*, I thought it would be the last Elm Creek Quilts novel. (I should have known better; I'd thought the same thing about *Round Robin* and *The Master Quilter* and I was wrong both times.) With *The Wedding Quilt*, though, I was certain I'd reached the end, and it was important to me to wrap up unresolved storylines before the final chapter. In order to reveal how my readers' beloved characters finally found their happy endings (or otherwise, in the case of the villains), I needed to flash forward into what was, at the time, the "distant future" of the mid to late 2020s.

But *The Wedding Quilt* wasn't the last Elm Creek Quilts novel after all.

When I decided to continue the series, I faced two rather significant obstacles. The first was that the "distant future" had become the present day, or nearly so, and things had not turned out as I had envisioned in *The Wedding Quilt*. In a scene set in 2028, for example, Sarah reflects upon how innovation and sacrifice enabled the world to solve the climate crisis—but as I write this, it's clear that my estimated date was wildly optimistic. We're making progress, but we're still going to be working on solutions for the climate crisis well past 2028.

As if my inability to flawlessly predict the future wasn't bad enough, my diligence in wrapping up all those unresolved storylines left me little room to continue the series. Instead of the satisfying conclusion to the beloved series I had intended, *The Wedding Quilt* had become an anthology of spoilers. I knew I wouldn't find writing a new Elm Creek Quilts novel creatively fulfilling if all the plot and character developments were constrained by flash-forwards I had written more than a decade before. I was also concerned that readers wouldn't enjoy the stories as much, since they already knew how everything would turn out in the end.

I might have let those obstacles discourage me, if not for the countless requests I've received through the years for more Elm Creek Quilts novels. My loyal readers have made it clear how much they long to return to Elm Creek Manor and reunite with the Elm Creek Quilters, characters they've come to think of as friends.

If you've attended any of my author events, either in person or online, you know how grateful I am for my readers, whether they've been enjoying my novels since *The Quilter's Apprentice* came out in 1999 or if they discovered me last month when their book club read *Canary Girls*. Rather than disappoint Elm Creek Quilts fans by not continuing the series, I resolved to find a way.

Eventually I realized that I should just embrace the inevitable continuity errors, pick up the story at a pivotal moment, and carry on with a new narrative, disregarding anything in *The Wedding Quilt* beyond 2002.

Moving forward, some of the events depicted in *The Wedding Quilt* may yet unfold as written, but not all of them will, and nothing about the characters' futures is predetermined. I encourage readers to consider *The Wedding Quilt* to be a dream sequence or a scene from an alternative universe. That's what I'm going to do.

Thanks for reading, and welcome home to Elm Creek Manor.

*Warm Regards,*
*Jennifer Chiaverini*

# ACKNOWLEDGMENTS

Many thanks to Maria Massie, Rachel Kahan, Emily Fisher, Ariana Sinclair, Elsie Lyons, and everyone at William Morrow who contributed to *The Museum of Lost Quilts*. Geraldine Neidenbach, Marty Chiaverini, Michael Chiaverini, and Heather Neidenbach were my first readers, and their insightful comments and questions were very much appreciated. Nic Neidenbach is always there for me whenever I need help with technology gone awry. I'm deeply grateful to each and every one of you.

Most of all, I thank my husband, Marty, and my sons, Nick and Michael, for their enduring love, steadfast support, and constant encouragement. I couldn't have completed this book without you, and I'll be forever grateful for your courage, optimism, resilience, and humor in challenging times. All my love, always.

# ABOUT THE AUTHOR

Jennifer Chiaverini is the *New York Times* bestselling author of thirty-four novels, including critically acclaimed historical fiction and the beloved Elm Creek Quilts series. Her works of nonfiction include seven collections of quilt patterns and original designs featured in *Country Woman, Quiltmaker, Quilt,* and other magazines. In 2020, she was awarded an Outstanding Achievement Award from the Wisconsin Library Association for her novel *Resistance Women.* A graduate of the University of Notre Dame and the University of Chicago, she lives with her husband and two sons in Madison, Wisconsin.